The Author

ALICE MUNRO was born in Wingham, Ontario, in 1931. After high school she attended the University of Western Ontario for two years, then married and moved to Vancouver and Victoria, where she became the mother of three daughters. In 1972 she returned to southwestern Ontario where she lives now with her second husband.

From her first collection of short stories, *Dance of the Happy Shades* (1968), through her most recent collection, *Hateship, Friendship, Courtship, Loveship, Marriage* (2001), Munro fashions extraordinary stories out of ordinary human situations. Universally acknowledged as one of the finest short fiction writers in English, she roots her fiction in her Ontario world, venturing at various times throughout Canada and beyond, to explore the many variegated dimensions of the human condition.

Her many honours include the Giller Prize, three Governor General's Awards for Fiction, the W.H. Smith Prize in the United Kingdom, and the National Book Circle Critics Award, the top fiction prize in the United States.

Alice Munro resides in southwestern Ontario.

THE NEW CANADIAN LIBRARY

Alice Munro

NO LOVE LOST

Selected and with an Afterword by Jane Urquhart

McCLELLAND & STEWART

Original New Canadian Library edition 2003

Library and Archives Canada Cataloguing in Publication

Munro, Alice, 1931-
No love lost / Alice Munro ; selected and with
an afterword by Jane Urquhart.

(New Canadian library)
Includes bibliographical references.
ISBN 0-7710-3481-4

I. Urquhart, Jane, 1949- II. Title. III. Series.

PS8576.U57N6 2003 C813'.54 C2002-905663-2
PR9199.3.M8N6 2003

We acknowledge the financial support of the Government of Canada through the Book Publishing Industry Development Program and that of the Government of Ontario through the Ontario Media Development Corporation's Ontario Book Initiative. We further acknowledge the support of the Canada Council for the Arts and the Ontario Arts Council for our publishing program.

Typesetting by M&S, Toronto
Printed and bound in the United States of America

McClelland & Stewart Ltd.
75 Sherbourne Street
Toronto, Ontario
M5A 2P9
www.mcclelland.com

3 4 5 6 7 14 13 12 11 10

Contents

Bardon Bus	1
Carried Away	23
Mischief	70
The Love of a Good Woman	112
Simon's Luck	185
Hateship, Friendship, Courtship, Loveship, Marriage	211
The Bear Came Over the Mountain	263
The Albanian Virgin	312
Meneseteung	359
The Children Stay	384
Afterword	416

No Love Lost

Bardon Bus

I THINK OF being an old maid, in another generation. There were plenty of old maids in my family. I come of straitened people, madly secretive, tenacious, economical. Like them, I could make a little go a long way. A piece of Chinese silk folded in a drawer, worn by the touch of fingers in the dark. Or the one letter, hidden under maidenly garments, never needing to be opened or read because every word is known by heart, and a touch communicates the whole. Perhaps nothing so tangible, nothing but the memory of an ambiguous word, an intimate, casual tone of voice, a hard, helpless look. That could do. With no more than that I could manage, year after year as I scoured the milk pails, spit on the iron, followed the cows along the rough path among the alder and the black-eyed Susans, spread the clean wet overalls to dry on the fence, and the tea towels on the bushes. Who would the man be? He could be anybody. A soldier killed at the Somme or a farmer down the road with a rough-tongued wife and a crowd of children; a boy who went to Saskatchewan and promised to send for me, but never did, or the preacher who rouses me every Sunday with lashings of fear and promises of torment. No matter. I could fasten on any of them, in secret. A lifelong secret, lifelong dream-life. I could go round singing in the kitchen, polishing the stove, wiping the lamp chimneys, dipping water for the tea from the drinking-pail. The faintly sour smell of the scrubbed tin, the worn scrub-cloths. Upstairs my bed with the high headboard, the crocheted spread, and the rough, friendly-smelling flannelette sheets, the hot-water bottle to ease my cramps or be clenched between my legs. There I come back again and again to the center of my fantasy, to the moment when you give yourself up, give yourself over, to the assault which is guaranteed to finish off everything you've been before. A stubborn virgin's belief, this belief in perfect mastery; any broken-down wife could tell you there is no such thing.

Dipping the dipper in the pail, lapped in my harmless craziness, I'd sing hymns, and nobody would wonder.

> *"He's the Lily of the Valley,*
> *The Bright and Morning Star.*
> *He's the Fairest of Ten Thousand to my Soul."*

2

This summer I'm living in Toronto, in my friend Kay's apartment, finishing a book of family history which some rich people are paying me to write. Last spring, in connection with this book, I had to spend some time in Australia. There I met an anthropologist whom I had known slightly, years before, in Vancouver. He was then married to his first wife (he is now married to his third) and I was married to my first husband (I am now divorced). We both lived in Fort Camp, which was the married students' quarters, at the university.

The anthropologist had been investigating language groups in northern Queensland. He was going to spend a few weeks in the city, at a university, before joining his wife in India. She was there on a grant, studying Indian music. She is the new sort of wife with serious interests of her own. His first wife had been a girl with a job, who would help him get through the university, then stay home and have children.

We met at lunch on Saturday, and on Sunday we went up the river on an excursion boat, full of noisy families, to an animal preserve. There we looked at wombats curled up like blood puddings, and disgruntled, shoddy emus, and walked under an arbor of brilliant unfamiliar flowers and had our pictures taken with koala bears. We brought each other up-to-date on our lives, with jokes, sombre passages, buoyant sympathy. On the way back we drank gin from the bar on the boat, and kissed, and made a mild spectacle of ourselves. It was almost impossible to talk because of the noise of the engines, the crying babies, the children shrieking and chasing each other, but he said, "Please come and see my house. I've got a borrowed house. You'll like it. Please, I can't wait to ask you, please come and live with me in my house."

"Should I?"

"I'll get down on my knees," he said, and did.

"Get up, behave!" I said. "We're in a foreign country."

"That means we can do anything we like."

Some of the children had stopped their game to stare at us. They looked shocked and solemn.

3

I call him X, as if he were a character in an old-fashioned novel, that pretends to be true. X is a letter in his name, but I chose it also because it seems to suit him. The letter X seems to me expansive and secretive. And using just the letter, not needing a name, is in line with a system I often employ these days. I say to myself, "Bardon Bus, No. 144," and I see a whole succession of scenes. I see them in detail; streets and houses. LaTrobe Terrace, Paddington. Schools like large, pleasant bungalows, betting shops, frangipani trees dropping their waxy, easily bruised, and highly scented flowers. It was on this bus that we rode downtown, four or five times in all, carrying our string bags, to shop for groceries at Woolworths, meat at Coles, licorice and chocolate ginger at the candy store. Much of the city is built on ridges between gullies, so there was a sense of coming down through populous but half-wild hill villages into the central part of town, with its muddy river and pleasant colonial shabbiness. In such a short time everything seemed remarkably familiar and yet not to be confused with anything we had known in the past. We felt we knew the lives of the housewives in sun-hats riding with us on the bus, we knew the insides of the shuttered, sun-blistered houses set up on wooden posts over the gullies, we knew the streets we couldn't see. This familiarity was not oppressive but delightful, and there was a slight strangeness to it, as if we had come by it in a way we didn't understand. We moved through a leisurely domesticity with a feeling of perfect security – a security we hadn't felt, or so we told each other, in any of our legal domestic arrangements, or in any of the places where we more properly belonged. We had a holiday of lightness of spirit without the holiday feeling of being at loose ends. Every day X went off to the university and I went downtown to the research library, to look at old newspapers on the microfilm reader.

One day I went to the Toowong Cemetery to look for some graves. The cemetery was more magnificent and ill-kempt than cemeteries are in Canada. The inscriptions on some of the splendid white stones had a surprising informality. "Our Wonderful Mum," and "A Fine Fellow." I wondered what this meant, about Australians, and then I thought how we are always wondering what things mean, in another country, and how I would talk this over with X.

The sexton came out of his little house, to help me. He was a young man in shorts, with a full-blown sailing ship tattooed on his chest. *Australia Felix* was its name. A harem girl on the underside of one arm, a painted warrior on top. The other arm decorated with dragons and banners. A map of Australia on the back of one hand; the Southern Cross on the back of the other. I didn't like to peer at his legs, but had an impression of complicated scenes like a vertical comic strip, and a chain of medallions wreathed in flowers, perhaps containing girls' names. I took care to get all these things straight, because of the pleasure of going home and telling X.

He too would bring things home: conversations on the bus; word derivations; connections he had found.

We were not afraid to use the word love. We lived without responsibility, without a future, in freedom, with generosity, in constant but not wearying celebration. We had no doubt that our happiness would last out the little time required. The only thing we reproached ourselves for was laziness. We wondered if we would later regret not going to the Botanical Gardens to see the lotus in bloom, not having seen one movie together; we were sure we would think of more things we wished we had told each other.

4

I dreamed that X wrote me a letter. It was all done in clumsy block printing and I thought, that's to disguise his handwriting, that's clever. But I had great trouble reading it. He said he wanted us to go on a trip to Cuba. He said the trip had been offered to him by a clergyman he met in a bar. I wondered if the clergyman might be a spy. He said we could go skiing in Vermont. He said he did not want to interfere with my life but he did want to shelter me. I loved that word. But the complications of the dream multiplied. The letter had been delayed. I tried to phone him and I couldn't get the telephone dial to work. Also it seemed I had the responsibility of a baby, asleep in a dresser drawer. Things got more and more tangled and dreary, until I woke. The word shelter was still in my head. I had to feel it shrivel. I was lying on a mattress on the floor of Kay's apartment at the corner of Queen and Bathurst streets at eight o'clock in the morning. The windows were open in the summer heat, the streets full of people going to work, the streetcars stopping and starting and creaking on the turn.

This is a cheap, pleasant apartment with high windows, white walls, unbleached cotton curtains, floorboards painted in a glossy gray. It has been a cheap temporary place for so long that nobody ever got around to changing it, so the wainscoting is still there, and the old-fashioned perforated screens over the radiators. Kay has some beautiful faded rugs, and the usual cushions and spreads, to make the mattresses on the floor look more like divans and less like mattresses. A worn-out set of bedsprings is leaning against the wall, covered with shawls and scarves and pinned-up charcoal sketches by Kay's former lover, the artist. Nobody can figure a way to get the springs out of here, or imagine how they got up here in the first place.

Kay makes her living as a botanical illustrator, doing meticulous drawings of plants for textbooks and government handbooks. She lives on a farm, in a household of adults and children who come and go and one day are gone for good. She keeps this place in Toronto, and comes down for a day or so every couple of weeks. She likes this stretch of Queen Street, with its taverns and secondhand stores and quiet derelicts. She doesn't stand much chance here of running into people who went to Branksome Hall with her, or danced at her wedding. When Kay married, her bridegroom wore a kilt, and his brother officers made an arch of swords. Her father was a brigadier-general; she made her debut at Government House. I often think that's why she never tires of a life of risk and improvisation, and isn't frightened by the sound of brawls late at night under these windows, or the drunks in the doorway downstairs. She doesn't feel the threat that I would feel, she never sees herself slipping under.

Kay doesn't own a kettle. She boils water in a saucepan. She is ten years younger than I am. Her hips are narrow, her hair long and straight and dark and streaked with gray. She usually wears a beret and charming, raggedy clothes from the second-hand stores. I have known her six or seven years and during that time she has often been in love. Her loves are daring, sometimes grotesque.

On the boat from Centre Island she met a paroled prisoner, a swarthy tall fellow with an embroidered headband, long gray-black hair blowing in the wind. He had been sent to jail for wrecking his ex-wife's house, or her lover's house; some crime of passion Kay boggled at, then forgave. He said he was part Indian and when he had cleared up some business in Toronto he would take her to his native island off the coast of British Columbia, where they would ride horses along the beach. She began to take riding lessons.

During her break-up with him she was afraid for her life. She found threatening, amorous notes pinned to her nightgowns and underwear. She changed her locks, she went to the police, but she didn't give up on love. Soon she was in love with the artist, who had never wrecked a house but was ruled by signs from the spirit world. He had gotten a message about her before they met, knew what she was going to say before she said it, and often saw an ominous blue fire around her neck, a yoke or a ring. One day he disappeared, leaving those sketches, and a lavish horrible book on anatomy which showed real sliced cadavers, with innards, skin, and body hair in their natural colors, injected dyes of red or blue illuminating a jungle of blood vessels. On Kay's shelves you can read a history of her love affairs: books on prison riots, autobiographies of prisoners, from the period of the parolee; this book on anatomy and others on occult phenomena, from the period of the artist; books on caves, books by Albert Speer, from the time of the wealthy German importer who taught her the word *spelunker*; books on revolution which date from the West Indian.

She takes up a man and his story wholeheartedly. She learns his language, figuratively or literally. At first she may try to disguise her condition, pretending to be prudent or ironic. "Last week I met a peculiar character –" or, "I had a funny conversation with a man at a party, did I tell you?" Soon a tremor, a sly flutter, an apologetic but stubborn smile. "Actually I'm afraid I've fallen for him, isn't that terrible?" Next time you see her she'll be in deep, going to fortune-tellers, slipping his name into every other sentence; with this mention of the name there will be a mushy sound to her voice, a casting down of the eyes, an air of cherished helplessness, appalling to behold. Then comes the onset of gloom, the doubts and anguish, the struggle either to free herself or to keep him from freeing himself; the messages left with answering services. Once she disguised herself as an old woman, with a gray wig and a tattered fur coat; she walked up and down, in the cold, outside the house of the woman she thought to be her supplanter. She will talk coldly, sensibly, wittily, about her mistake, and tell discreditable things she has gleaned about her lover, then make desperate phone calls. She will get drunk, and sign up for rolfing, swim therapy, gymnastics.

In none of this is she so exceptional. She does what women do. Perhaps she does it more often, more openly, just a bit more ill-advisedly, and more fervently. Her powers of recovery, her faith, are never exhausted. I joke about her, everybody does, but I defend her too, saying that she is not condemned to living with reservations and withdrawals, long-drawn-out dissatisfactions, inarticulate wavering miseries. Her trust is total, her miseries are sharp, and she survives without visible damage. She doesn't allow for drift or stagnation and the spectacle of her life is not discouraging to me.

She is getting over someone now; the husband, the estranged husband, of another woman at the farm. His name is Roy; he too is an anthropologist.

"It's really a low ebb falling in love with somebody who's

lived at the farm," she says. "Really low. Somebody you know all about."

I tell her I'm getting over somebody I met in Australia, and that I plan to be over him just about when I get the book done, and then I'll go and look for another job, a place to live.

"No rush, take it easy," she says.

I think about the words "getting over." They have an encouraging, crisp, everyday sound. They are in tune with Kay's present mood. When love is fresh and on the rise she grows mystical, tentative; in the time of love's decline, and past the worst of it, she is brisk and entertaining, straightforward, analytical.

"It's nothing but the desire to see yourself reflected," she says. "Love always comes back to self-love. The idiocy. You don't want them, you want what you can get from them. Obsession and self-delusion. Did you ever read those journals of Victor Hugo's daughter, I think that's who it was?"

"No."

"I never did either, but I read about them. The part I remember, the part I remember reading about, that struck me so, was where she goes out into the street after years and years of loving this man, obsessively loving him, and she meets him. She passes him in the street and she either doesn't recognize him or she does but she can't connect the real man any more with the person she loves, in her head. She can't connect him at all."

5

When I knew X in Vancouver he was a different person. A serious graduate student, still a Lutheran, stocky and resolute, rather a prig in some people's opinion. His wife was more scatterbrained; a physiotherapist named Mary, who liked sports and dancing. Of the two, you would have said she might be the one to run off. She had blonde hair, big teeth; her gums showed. I watched her play baseball at a picnic. I had to go off and sit in the bushes, to nurse my baby. I was twenty-one, a simple-looking girl, a nursing mother. Fat and pink on the outside; dark judgments and strenuous ambitions within. Sex had not begun for me, at all.

X came around the bushes and gave me a bottle of beer.

"What are you doing back here?"

"I'm feeding the baby."

"Why do you have to do it here? Nobody would care."

"My husband would have a fit."

"Oh. Well, drink up. Beer's supposed to be good for your milk, isn't it?"

That was the only time I talked to him, so far as I can remember. There was something about the direct approach, the slightly clumsy but determined courtesy, my own unexpected, lightened feeling of gratitude, that did connect with his attentions to women later, and his effect on them. I am sure he was always patient, unalarming; successful, appreciative, sincere.

6

I met Dennis in the Toronto Reference Library and he asked me out to dinner.

Dennis is a friend of X's, who came to visit us in Australia. He is a tall, slight, stiff, and brightly smiling young man – not so young either, he must be thirty-five – who has an elaborately courteous and didactic style.

I go to meet him thinking he may have a message for me. Isn't it odd, otherwise, that he would want to have dinner with an older woman he has met only once before? I think he may tell me whether X is back in Canada. X told me that they would probably come back in July. Then he was going to spend a year writing his book. They might live in Nova Scotia during that year. They might live in Ontario.

When Dennis came to see us in Australia, I made a curry. I was pleased with the idea of having a guest and glad that he arrived in time to see the brief evening light on the gully. Our house like the others was built out on posts, and from the window where we ate we looked out over a gully like an oval bowl, ringed with small houses and filled with jacaranda, poinciana, frangipani, cypress, and palm trees. Leaves like fans, whips, feathers, plates; every bright, light, dark, dusty, glossy shade of green. Guinea fowl lived down there, and flocks of rackety kookaburras took to the sky at dusk. We had to scramble down a steep dirt bank under the house to get to the wash-hut, and peg the clothes on a revolving clothesline. There we encountered spider-webs draped like tent-tops, matched like lids and basins with one above and one below. We had to watch out for the one little spider that weaves a conical web and has a poison for which there is no antidote.

We showed Dennis the gully and told him this was a typical old Queensland house with the high tongue-and-groove walls and the ventilation panels over the doors filled with graceful carved vines. He did not look at anything with much interest, but talked about China, where he had just been. X said afterwards that Dennis always talked about the last place he'd been and the last people he'd seen, and never seemed to notice anything, but that he would probably be talking about us, and describing this place, to the next people he had dinner with, in the next city. He said that Dennis spent most of his life travelling, and talking about it, and that he knew a lot of people just well enough that when he showed up somewhere he had to be asked to dinner.

Dennis told us that he had seen the recently excavated Army Camp at Sian, in China. He described the rows of life-sized soldiers, each of them so realistic and unique, some still bearing traces of the paint which had once covered them and individualized them still further. Away at their backs, he said, was a wall of earth. The terra-cotta soldiers looked as if they were marching out of the earth.

He said it reminded him of X's women. Row on row and always a new one appearing at the end of the line.

"The Army marches on," he said.

"Dennis, for God's sake," said X.

"But do they really come out of the earth like that?" I said to Dennis. "Are they intact?"

"Are which intact?" said Dennis with his harsh smile. "The soldiers or the women? The women aren't intact. Or not for long."

"Could we get off the subject?" said X.

"Certainly. Now to answer your question," said Dennis, turning to me. "They are very seldom found as whole figures. Or so I understand. Their legs and torsos and heads have to be matched up, usually. They have to be put together and stood on their feet."

"It's a lot of work, I can tell you," said X, with a large sigh.

"But it's not that way with the women," I said to Dennis. I spoke with a special, social charm, almost flirtatiously, as I often do when I detect malice. "I think the comparison's a bit off. Nobody has to dig the women out and stand them on their feet. Nobody put them there. They came along and joined up of their own free will and some day they'll leave. They're not a standing army. Most of them are probably on their way to someplace else anyway."

"Bravo," said X.

When we were washing the dishes, late at night, he said, "You didn't mind Dennis saying that, did you? You didn't mind if I went along with him a little bit? He has to have his legends."

I laid my head against his back, between the shoulder blades.

"Does he? No. I thought it was funny."

"I bet you didn't know that soap was first described by Pliny and was used by the Gauls. I bet you didn't know they boiled goat's tallow with the lye from the wood ashes."

"No. I didn't know that."

7

Dennis hasn't said a word about X, or about Australia. I wouldn't have thought his asking me to dinner strange, if I had remembered him better. He asked me so he would have somebody to talk to. Since Australia he has been to Iceland, and the Faeroe Islands. I ask him questions. I am interested, and surprised, even shocked, when necessary. I took trouble with my makeup and washed my hair. I hope that if he does see X, he will say that I was charming.

Besides his travels Dennis has his theories. He develops theories about art and literature, history, life.

"I have a new theory about the life of women. I used to feel it was so unfair the way things happened to them."

"What things?"

"The way they have to live, compared to men. Specifically with aging. Look at you. Think of the way your life would be, if you were a man. The choices you would have. I mean sexual choices. You could start all over. Men do. It's in all the novels and it's in life too. Men fall in love with younger women. Men want younger women. Men can get younger women. The new marriage, new babies, new families."

I wonder if he is going to tell me something about X's wife; perhaps that she is going to have a baby.

"It's such a coup for them, isn't it?" he says in his malicious, sympathetic way. "The fresh young wife, the new baby when other men their age are starting on grandchildren. All those men envying them and trying to figure out how to do the same. It's the style, isn't it? It must be hard to resist starting over and having that nice young mirror to look in, if you get the opportunity."

"I think I might resist it," I say cheerfully, not insistently. "I don't really think I'd want to have a baby, now."

"That's it, that's just it, though, you don't get the opportunity! You're a woman and life only goes in one direction for a woman. All this business about younger lovers, that's just froth, isn't it? Do you want a younger lover?"

"I guess not," I say, and pick my dessert from a tray. I pick a creamy pudding with pureed chestnuts at the bottom of it and fresh raspberries on top. I purposely ate a light dinner, leaving plenty of room for dessert. I did that so I could have something to look forward to, while listening to Dennis.

"A woman your age can't compete," says Dennis urgently. "You can't compete with younger women. I used to think that was so rottenly unfair."

"It's probably biologically correct for men to go after younger women. There's no use whining about it."

"So the men have this way of renewing themselves, they get this refill of vitality, while the women are you might say removed from life. I used to think that was terrible. But now my thinking has undergone a complete reversal. Do you know what I think now? I think women are the lucky ones! Do you know why?"

"Why?"

"Because they are forced to live in the world of loss and death! Oh, I know, there's face-lifting, but how does that really help? The uterus dries up. The vagina dries up."

I feel him watching me. I continue eating my pudding.

"I've seen so many parts of the world and so many strange things and so much suffering. It's my conclusion now that you won't get any happiness by playing tricks on life, it's only by natural renunciation and by accepting deprivation, that we prepare for death and therefore that we get any happiness. Maybe my ideas seem strange to you?"

I can't think of anything to say.

8

Often I have a few lines of a poem going through my head, and I won't know what started it. It can be a poem or rhyme that I didn't even know I knew, and it needn't be anything that conforms to what I think is my taste. Sometimes I don't pay any attention to it, but if I do, I can usually see that the poem, or the bit of it I've got hold of, has some relation to what is going on in my life. And that may not be what seems to be going on.

For instance last spring, last autumn in Australia, when I was happy, the line that would go through my head, at a merry clip, was this:

"Even such is time, that takes in trust –"

I could not go on, though I knew trust rhymed with dust, and that there was something further along about "and in the dark and silent grave, shuts up the story of our days." I knew the poem was written by Sir Walter Raleigh on the eve of his execution. My mood did not accord with such a poem and I said it, in my head, as if it was something pretty and light-hearted. I did not stop to wonder what it was doing in my head in the first place.

And now that I'm trying to look at things soberly I should remember what we said when our bags were packed and we were waiting for the taxi. Inside the bags our clothes that had shared drawers and closet space, tumbled together in the wash, and been pegged together on the clothesline where the kookaburras sat, were all sorted and separated and would not rub together any more.

"In a way I'm glad it's over and nothing spoiled it. Things are so often spoiled."

"I know."

"As it is, it's been perfect."

I said that. And that was a lie. I had cried once, thought I was ugly, thought he was bored.

But he said, "Perfect."

On the plane the words of the poem were going through my head again, and I was still happy. I went to sleep thinking the bulk of X was still beside me and when I woke I filled the space quickly with memories of his voice, looks, warmth, our scenes together.

I was swimming in memories, at first. Those detailed, repetitive scenes were what buoyed me up. I didn't try to escape them, didn't wish to. Later I did wish to. They had become a plague. All they did was stir up desire, and longing, and hopelessness, a trio of miserable caged wildcats that had been installed in me without my permission, or at least without my understanding how long they would live and how vicious they would be. The images, the language, of pornography and romance are alike; monotonous and mechanically seductive, quickly leading to despair. That was what my mind dealt in; that is what it still can deal in. I have tried vigilance and reading serious books but I can still slide deep into some scene before I know where I am.

On the bed a woman lies in a yellow nightgown which has not been torn but has been pulled off her shoulders and twisted up around her waist so that it covers no more of her than a crumpled scarf would. A man bends over her, naked, offering a drink of water. The woman, who has almost lost consciousness, whose legs are open, arms flung out, head twisted to the side as if she has been struck down in the course of some natural disaster – this woman rouses herself and tries to hold the glass in her shaky hands. She slops water over her breast, drinks, shudders, falls back. The man's hands are trembling, too. He drinks out of the same glass, looks at her, and laughs. His laugh is rueful, apologetic, and kind, but it is also amazed, and his amazement is not far from horror. How are we capable of all this? his laugh says, what is the meaning of it?

He says, "We almost finished each other off."

The room seems still full of echoes of the recent commotion, the cries, pleas, brutal promises, the climactic sharp announcements and the long subsiding spasms.

The room is brimming with gratitude and pleasure, a rich broth of love, a golden twilight of love. Yes, yes, you can drink the air.

You see the sort of thing I mean, that is my torment.

9

This is the time of year when women are tired of sundresses, prints, sandals. It is already fall in the stores. Thick sweaters and skirts are pinned up against black or plum-colored velvet. The young salesgirls are made up like courtesans. I've become feverishly preoccupied with clothes. All the conversations in the stores make sense to me.

"The neckline doesn't work. It's too stark. I need a flutter. Do you know what I mean?"

"Yes. I know what you mean."

"I want something very classy and very provocative. Do you know what I mean?"

"Yes. I know exactly what you mean."

For years I've been wearing bleached-out colors which I suddenly can't bear. I buy a deep-red satin blouse, a purple shawl, a dark-blue skirt. I get my hair cut and pluck my eyebrows and try a lilac lipstick, a brownish rouge. I'm appalled to think of the way I went around in Australia, in a faded wraparound cotton skirt and T-shirt, my legs bare because of the heat, my face bare too and sweating under a cotton hat.

My legs with the lumps of veins showing. I'm half convinced that a more artful getup would have made a more powerful impression, more dramatic clothes might have made me less discardable. I have fancies of meeting X unexpectedly at a party or on a Toronto street, and giving him a shock, devastating him with my altered looks and late-blooming splendor. But I do think you have to watch out, even in these garish times; you have to watch out for the point at which the splendor collapses into absurdity. Maybe they are all watching out, all the old women I see on Queen Street: the fat woman with pink hair; the eighty-year-old with painted-on black eyebrows; they may all be thinking they haven't gone too far yet, not quite yet. Even the buttercup woman I saw a few days ago on the streetcar, the little, stout, sixtyish woman in a frilly yellow dress well above the knees, a straw hat with yellow ribbons, yellow pumps dyed-to-match on her little fat feet – even she doesn't aim for comedy. She sees a flower in the mirror: the generous petals, the lovely buttery light.

I go looking for earrings. All day looking for earrings which I can see so clearly in my mind. I want little filigree balls of silver, of diminishing size, dangling. I want old and slightly tarnished silver. It's a style I well remember; you'd think the secondhand stores would be sure to have them. But I can't find them, I can't find anything resembling them, and they seem more and more necessary. I go into a little shop on a side street near College and Spadina. The shop is all done up in black paper with cheap, spooky effects – for instance a bald, naked mannequin sitting on a stepladder, dangling some beads. A dress such as I wore in the fifties, a dance dress of pink net and sequins, terribly scratchy under the arms, is displayed against the black paper in a way that makes it look sinister, and desirable.

I look around for the tray of jewelry. The salesgirls are busy dressing a customer hidden from me by a three-way mirror. One salesgirl is fat and gypsyish with a face warmly colored as an apricot. The other is spiky and has a crest of white hair surrounded by black hair, like a skunk. They are shrieking with pleasure as they bring hats and beads for the customer to try. Finally everybody is satisfied and a beautiful young lady, who is not a young lady at all but a pretty boy dressed up as a lady, emerges from the shelter of the mirror. He is wearing a black velvet dress with long sleeves and a black lace yoke; black pumps and gloves; a little black hat with a dotted veil. He is daintily and discreetly made up; he has a fringe of brown curls; he is the prettiest and most ladylike person I have seen all day. His smiling face is tense and tremulous. I remember how when I was ten or eleven years old I used to dress up as a bride in old curtains, or as a lady in rouge and a feathered hat. After all the effort and contriving and my own enchantment with the finished product there was a considerable letdown. What are you supposed to do now? Parade up and down on the sidewalk? There is a great fear and daring and disappointment in this kind of display.

He has a boyish, cracking voice. He is brash and timid.

"How do I look, momma?"

"You look very nice."

10

I am at a low point. I can recognize it. That must mean I will get past it.

I am at a low point, certainly. I cannot deal with all that assails me unless I get help and there is only one person I want help from and that is X. I can't continue to move my body along the streets unless I exist in his mind and in his eyes. People have this problem frequently, and we know it is their own fault and they have to change their way of thinking, that's all. It is not an honorable problem. Love is not serious though it may be fatal. I read that somewhere and I believe it. Thank God I don't know where he is. I can't telephone him, write letters to him, waylay him on the street.

A man I had broken with used to follow me. Finally he persuaded me to go into a café and have a cup of tea with him.

"I know what a spectacle I am," he said. "I know if you did have any love left for me this would destroy it."

I said nothing.

He beat the spoon against the sugar bowl.

"What do you think of, when you're with me?"

I meant to say, "I don't know," but instead I said, "I think of how much I want to get away."

He reared up trembling and dropped the spoon on the floor.

"You're free of me," he said in a choking voice.

This is the scene both comic and horrible, stagy and real. He was in desperate need, as I am now, and I didn't pity him, and I'm not sorry I didn't.

11

I have had a pleasant dream that seems far away from my waking state. X and I and some other people I didn't know or can't remember were wearing innocent athletic underwear outfits, which changed at some point into gauzy bright white clothes, and these turned out to be not just clothes but our substances, our flesh and bones and in a sense our souls. Embraces took place which started out with the usual urgency but were transformed, by the lightness and sweetness of our substance, into a rare state of content. I can't describe it very well, it sounds like a movie-dream of heaven, all banality and innocence. So I suppose it was. I can't apologize for the banality of my dreams.

12

I go along the street to Rooneem's Bakery and sit at one of their little tables with a cup of coffee. Rooneem's is an Estonian bakery where you can usually find a Mediterranean housewife in a black dress, a child looking at the cakes, and a man talking to himself.

I sit where I can watch the street. I have a feeling X is somewhere in the vicinity. Within a thousand miles, say, within a hundred miles, within this city. He doesn't know my address but he knows I am in Toronto. It would not be so difficult to find me.

At the same time I'm thinking that I have to let go. What you have to decide, really, is whether to be crazy or not, and I haven't the stamina, the pure, seething will, for prolonged craziness.

There is a limit to the amount of misery and disarray you will put up with, for love, just as there is a limit to the amount of mess you can stand around a house. You can't know the limit beforehand, but you will know when you've reached it. I believe this.

When you start really letting go this is what it's like. A lick of pain, furtive, darting up where you don't expect it. Then a lightness. The lightness is something to think about. It isn't just relief. There's a queer kind of pleasure in it, not a self-wounding or malicious pleasure, nothing personal at all. It's an uncalled-for pleasure in seeing how the design wouldn't fit and the structure wouldn't stand, a pleasure in taking into account, all over again, everything that is contradictory and persistent and unaccommodating about life. I think so. I think there's something in us wanting to be reassured about all that, right alongside – and at war with – whatever there is that wants permanent vistas and a lot of fine talk.

I think about my white dream and how it seemed misplaced. It strikes me that misplacement is the clue, in love, the heart of the problem, but like somebody drunk or high I can't quite get a grasp on what I see.

What I need is a rest. A deliberate sort of rest, with new definitions of luck. Not the sort of luck Dennis was talking about. You're lucky to be sitting in Rooneem's drinking coffee, with people coming and going, eating and drinking, buying cakes, speaking Spanish, Portuguese, Chinese, and other languages that you can try to identify.

13

Kay is back from the country. She too has a new outfit, a dark-green schoolgirl's tunic worn without a blouse or brassiere. She has dark-green knee socks and saddle oxfords.

"Does it look kinky?"

"Yes it does."

"Does it make my arms look dusky? Remember in some old poem a woman had dusky arms?"

Her arms do look soft and brown.

"I meant to get down on Sunday but Roy came over with a friend and we all had a corn roast. It was lovely. You should come out there. You should."

"Some day I will."

"The kids ran around like beautiful demons and we drank up the mead. Roy knows how to make fertility dolls. Roy's friend is Alex Walther, the anthropologist. I felt I should have known about him but I didn't. He didn't mind. He's a nice man. Do you know what he did? After dark when we were sitting around the fire he came over to me and just sighed, and laid his head on my lap. I thought it was such a nice simple thing to do. Like a St. Bernard. I've never had anybody do that before."

Carried Away

LETTERS

IN THE dining room of the Commercial Hotel, Louisa opened the letter that had arrived that day from overseas. She ate steak and potatoes, her usual meal, and drank a glass of wine. There were a few travellers in the room, and the dentist who ate there every night because he was a widower. He had shown an interest in her in the beginning but had told her he had never before seen a woman touch wine or spirits.

"It is for my health," said Louisa gravely.

The white tablecloths were changed every week and in the meantime were protected by oilcloth mats. In winter, the dining room smelled of these mats wiped by a kitchen rag, and of coal fumes from the furnace, and beef gravy and dried potatoes and onions – a smell not unpleasant to anybody coming in hungry from the cold. On each table was a little cruet stand with the bottle of brown sauce, the bottle of tomato sauce, and the pot of horseradish.

The letter was addressed to "The Librarian, Carstairs Public Library, Carstairs, Ontario." It was dated six weeks before – January 4, 1917.

Perhaps you will be surprised to hear from a person you don't know and that doesn't remember your name. I hope you are still the same Librarian though enough time has gone by that you could have moved on.

What has landed me here in Hospital is not too serious. I see worse all around me and get my mind off of all that by picturing things and wondering for instance if you are still there in the Library. If you are the one I mean, you are about of medium size or perhaps not quite, with light brownish hair. You came a few months before it was time for me to go in the Army following on Miss Tamblyn who had been there since I first became a user aged nine or ten. In her time the books were pretty much every which way, and it was as much as your life was worth to ask her for the least help or anything since she was quite a dragon. Then when you came what a change, it was all put into sections of Fiction and Non-Fiction and History and Travel and you got the magazines arranged in order and put out as soon as they arrived, not left to molder away till everything in them was stale. I felt gratitude but did not know how to say so. Also I wondered what brought you there, you were an educated person.

My name is Jack Agnew and my card is in the drawer. The last book I took out was very good – H.G. Wells, Mankind in the Making. *My education was to Second Form in High School, then I went into Douds as many did. I didn't join up right away when I was eighteen so you will not see me as a Brave Man. I am a person tending to have my own ideas always. My only relative in Carstairs, or anyplace, is my father Patrick Agnew. He works for Douds not at the factory but at the house doing the gardening. He is a lone wolf even more than me and goes out to the country fishing every chance he gets. I write him a letter sometimes but I doubt if he reads it.*

After supper Louisa went up to the Ladies' Parlor on the second floor, and sat down at the desk to write her reply.

I am very glad to hear you appreciated what I did in the Library though it was just the normal organization, nothing special.

I am sure you would like to hear news of home, but I am a poor person for the job, being an outsider here. I do talk to people in the Library and in the hotel. The travellers in the hotel mostly talk about how business is (it is brisk if you can get the goods) and a little about sickness, and a lot about the War. There are rumors on rumors and opinions galore, which I'm sure would make you laugh if they didn't make you angry. I will not bother to write them down because I am sure there is a Censor reading this who would cut my letter to ribbons.

You ask how I came here. There is no interesting story. My parents are both dead. My father worked for Eaton's in Toronto in the Furniture Department, and after his death my mother worked there too in Linens. And I also worked there for a while in Books. Perhaps you could say Eaton's was our Douds. I graduated from Jarvis Collegiate. I had some sickness which put me in hospital for a long time, but I am quite well now. I had a great deal of time to read and my favorite authors are Thomas Hardy, who is accused of being gloomy but I think is very true to life – and Willa Cather. I just happened to be in this town when I heard the Librarian had died and I thought, perhaps that is the job for me.

A good thing your letter reached me today as I am about to be discharged from here and don't know if it would have been sent on to where I am going. I am glad you did not think my letter was too foolish.

If you run into my father or anybody you do not need to say anything about the fact we are writing to each other. It is nobody's business and I know there are plenty of people would laugh at me writing to the Librarian as they did at me going to the Library even, why give them the satisfaction?

I am glad to be getting out of here. So much luckier than some I see that will never walk or have their sight and will have to hide themselves away from the world.

You asked where did I live in Carstairs. Well, it was not anyplace to be proud of. If you know where Vinegar Hill is and you turned off on Flowers Road it is the last house on the right, yellow paint once upon a time. My father grows potatoes, or did. I used to take them around town with my wagon, and every load I sold got a nickel to keep.

You mention favorite authors. At one time I was fond of Zane Grey, but I drifted away from reading fiction stories to reading History or Travel. I sometimes read books away over my head, I know, but I do get something out of them. H.G. Wells I mentioned is one and Robert Ingersoll who writes about religion. They have given me a lot to think about. If you are very religious I hope I have not offended you.

One day when I got to the Library it was a Saturday afternoon and you had just unlocked the door and were putting the lights on as it was dark and raining out. You had been caught out with no hat or umbrella and your hair had got wet. You took the pins out of it and let it come down. Is it too personal a thing to ask if you have it long still or have you cut it? You went over and stood by the radiator and shook your hair on it and the water sizzled like grease in the frying pan. I was sitting reading in the London Illustrated News *about the War. We exchanged a smile. (I didn't mean to say your hair was greasy when I wrote that!)*

I have not cut my hair though I often think about it. I do not know if it is vanity or laziness that prevents me.

I am not very religious.

I walked up Vinegar Hill and found your house. The potatoes are looking healthy. A police dog disputed with me, is he yours?

The weather is getting quite warm. We have had the flood on the river, which I gather is an annual Spring event. The water got into the hotel basement and somehow contaminated our drinking supply so that we were given free beer or ginger ale. But only if we lived or were staying there. You can imagine there were plenty of jokes.

I should ask if there is anything that I could send you.

I am not in need of anything particular. I get the tobacco and other bits of things the ladies in Carstairs do up for us. I would like to read some books by the authors you have mentioned but I doubt whether I would get the chance here.

The other day there was a man died of a heart attack. It was the News of all time. Did you hear about the man who died of a heart attack? That was all you heard about day and night here. Then everybody would laugh which seems hard-hearted but it just seemed so strange. It was not even a hot time so you couldn't say maybe he was scared. (As a matter of fact he was writing a letter at the time so I had better look out.) Before and after him others have died being shot up or blown up but he is the famous one, to die of a heart attack. Everybody is saying what a long way to come and a lot of expense for the Army to go to, for that.

The summer has been so dry the watering tank has been doing the streets every day, trying to lay the dust. The children would dance along behind it. There was also a new thing in town – a cart with a little bell that went along selling ice cream, and the children were pretty attentive to this as well. It was pushed by the man who had an accident at the factory – you know who I mean, though I can't recall his name. He lost his arm to the elbow. My room at the hotel, being on the third floor, it was like an oven, and I often walked about till after midnight. So did many other people, sometimes in pajamas. It was like a dream. There was still a little water in the river, enough to go out in a rowboat, and the Methodist minister did that on a Sunday in August. He was praying for rain in a public service. But there was a small leak in the boat and the water came in and wet his feet and eventually the boat sank and left him standing in the water, which did not nearly reach his waist. Was it an accident or a malicious trick? The talk was all that his prayers were answered but from the wrong direction.

I often pass the Douds' place on my walks. Your father keeps the lawns and hedges looking beautiful. I like the house, so original and airy-looking. But it may not have been cool even there, because I heard the voice of the mother and baby daughter late at night as if they were out on the lawn.

Though I told you there is nothing I need, there is one thing I would like. That is a photograph of you. I hope you will not think I am overstepping the bounds to ask for it. Maybe you are engaged to somebody or have a sweetheart over here you are writing to as well as me. You are a cut above the ordinary and it would not surprise me if some Officer had spoken for you. But now that I have asked I cannot take it back and will just leave it up to you to think what you like of me.

Louisa was twenty-five years old and had been in love once, with a doctor she had known in the sanitorium. Her love was returned, eventually, costing the doctor his job. There was some harsh doubt in her mind about whether he had been told to leave the sanitorium or had left of his own accord, being weary of the entanglement. He was married, he had children. Letters had played a part that time, too. After he left, they were still writing to one another. And once or twice after she was released. Then she asked him not to write anymore and he didn't. But the failure of his letters to arrive drove her out of Toronto and made her take the travelling job. Then there would be only the one disappointment in the week, when she got back on Friday or Saturday night. Her last letter had been firm and stoical, and some consciousness of herself as a heroine of love's tragedy went with her around the country as she hauled her display cases up and down the stairs of small hotels and talked about Paris styles and said that her sample hats were bewitching, and drank her solitary glass of wine. If she'd had anybody to tell, though, she would have laughed at just that notion. She would have said love was all hocus-pocus, a deception, and she believed that. But at the prospect she still felt a hush, a flutter along the nerves, a bowing down of sense, a flagrant prostration.

She had a picture taken. She knew how she wanted it to be. She would have liked to wear a simple white blouse, a peasant girl's smock with the string open at the neck. She did not own a blouse of that description and in fact had only seen them in pictures. And she would have liked to let her hair down. Or if it had to be up, she would have liked it piled very loosely and bound with strings of pearls.

Instead she wore her blue silk shirt-waist and bound her hair as usual. She thought the picture made her look rather pale, hollow-eyed. Her expression was sterner and more foreboding than she had intended. She sent it anyway.

I am not engaged, and do not have a sweetheart. I was in love once and it had to be broken off. I was upset at the time but I knew I must bear it, and now I believe that it was all for the best.

She had wracked her brains, of course, to remember him. She could not remember shaking out her hair, as he said she had done, or smiling at any young man when the raindrops fell on the radiator. He might as well have dreamed all that, and perhaps he had.

She had begun to follow the war in a more detailed way than she had done previously. She did not try to ignore it anymore. She went along the street with a sense that her head was filled with the same exciting and troubling information as everybody else's. Saint-Quentin, Arras, Montdidier, Amiens, and then there was a battle going on at the Somme River, where surely there had been one before? She laid open on her desk the maps of the war that appeared as double-page spreads in the magazines. She saw in colored lines the German drive to the Maine, the first thrust of the Americans at Château-Thierry. She looked at the artist's brown pictures of a horse rearing up during an air attack, of some soldiers in East Africa drinking out of coconuts, and of a line of German prisoners with bandaged heads or limbs and bleak, sullen expressions. Now she felt what everybody else did – a constant fear and misgiving and at the same time this addictive excitement. You could look up from your life of the moment and feel the world crackling beyond the walls.

I am glad to hear you do not have a sweetheart though I know that is selfish of me. I do not think you and I will ever meet again. I don't say that because I've had a dream about what will happen or am a gloomy person always looking for the worst. It just seems to me it is the most probable thing to happen, though I don't dwell on it and go along every day doing the best I can to stay alive. I am not trying to worry you or get your sympathy either but just explain how the idea I won't ever see Carstairs again makes me think I can say anything I want. I guess it's like being sick with a fever. So I will say I love you. I think of you up on a stool at the Library reaching to put a book away and I come up and put my hands on your waist and lift you down, and you turning around inside my arms as if we agreed about everything.

Every Tuesday afternoon the ladies and girls of the Red Cross met in the Council Chambers, which was just down the hall from the Library. When the Library was empty for a few moments, Louisa went down the hall and entered the room full of women. She had decided to knit a scarf. At the sanitorium she had learned how to knit a basic stitch, but she had never learned or had forgotten how to cast on or off.

The older women were all busy packing boxes or cutting up and folding bandages from sheets of heavy cotton that were spread on the tables. But a lot of girls near the door were eating buns and drinking tea. One was holding a skein of wool on her arms for another to wind.

Louisa told them what she needed to know.

"So what do you want to knit, then?" said one of the girls with some bun still in her mouth.

Louisa said, a muffler. For a soldier.

"Oh, you'll want the regulation wool," another said, more politely, and jumped off the table. She came back with some balls of brown wool, and fished a spare pair of needles out of her bag, telling Louisa they could be hers.

"I'll just get you started," she said. "It's a regulation width, too."

Other girls gathered around and teased this girl, whose name was Corrie. They told her she was doing it all wrong.

"Oh, I am, am I?" said Corrie. "How would you like a knitting needle in your eye? Is it for a friend?" she said solicitously to Louisa. "A friend overseas?"

"Yes," said Louisa. Of course they would think of her as an old maid, they would laugh at her or feel sorry for her, according to whatever show they put on, of being kind or brazen.

"So knit up good and tight," said the one who'd finished her bun. "Knit up good and tight to keep him warm!"

One of the girls in this group was Grace Horne. She was a shy but resolute-looking girl, nineteen years old, with a broad face, thin lips often pressed together, brown hair cut in a straight bang, and an attractively mature body. She had become engaged to Jack Agnew before he went overseas, but they had agreed not to say anything about it.

SPANISH FLU

Louisa had made friends with some of the travellers who stayed regularly at the hotel. One of these was Jim Frarey, who sold typewriters and office equipment and books and all sorts of stationery supplies. He was a fair-haired, rather round-shouldered but strongly built man in his middle forties. You would think by the look of him that he sold something heavier and more important in the masculine world, like farm implements.

Jim Frarey kept travelling all through the Spanish flu epidemic, though you never knew then if stores would be open for business or not. Occasionally the hotels, too, would be closed, like the schools and movie houses and even – Jim Frarey thought this a scandal – the churches.

"They ought to be ashamed of themselves, the cowards," he said to Louisa. "What good does it do anybody to lurk around home and wait for it to strike? Now you never closed the Library, did you?"

Louisa said only when she herself was sick. A mild case, hardly lasting a week, but of course she had to go to the hospital. They wouldn't let her stay in the hotel.

"Cowards," he said. "If you're going to be taken, you'll be taken. Don't you agree?"

They discussed the crush in the hospitals, the deaths of doctors and nurses, the unceasing drear spectacle of the funerals. Jim Frarey lived down the street from an undertaking establishment in Toronto. He said they still got out the black horses, the black carriage, the works, to bury such personages as warranted a fuss.

"Day and night they went on," he said. "Day and night." He raised his glass and said, "Here's to health, then. You look well yourself."

He thought that in fact Louisa was looking better than she used to. Maybe she had started putting on rouge. She had a pale-olive skin, and it seemed to him that her cheeks used to be without color. She dressed with more dash, too, and took more trouble to be friendly. She used to be very on-again, off-again, just as she chose. She was drinking whisky, now, too, though she would not try it without drowning it in water. It used to be only a glass of wine. He wondered if it was a boyfriend that had made the difference. But a boyfriend might perk up her looks without increasing her interest in all and sundry, which was what he was pretty sure had happened. It was more likely time running out and the husband prospects thinned out so dreadfully by the war. That could set a woman stirring. She was smarter and better company and better-looking, too, than most of the married ones. What happened with a woman like that? Sometimes just bad luck. Or bad judgment at a time when it mattered. A little too sharp and self-assured, in the old days, making the men uneasy?

"Life can't be brought to a standstill all the same," he said. "You did the right thing, keeping the Library open."

This was in the early winter of 1919, when there had been a fresh outbreak of flu after the danger was supposed to be past. They seemed to be all alone in the hotel. It was only about nine o'clock but the hotelkeeper had gone to bed. His wife was in the hospital with the flu. Jim Frarey had brought the bottle of whisky from the bar, which was closed for fear of contagion – and they sat at a table beside the window, in the dining room. A winter fog had collected outside and was pressing against the window. You could barely see the streetlights or the few cars that trundled cautiously over the bridge.

"Oh, it was not a matter of principle," Louisa said. "That I kept the Library open. It was a more personal reason than you think."

Then she laughed and promised him a peculiar story. "Oh, the whisky must have loosened my tongue," she said.

"I am not a gossip," said Jim Frarey.

She gave him a hard laughing look and said that when a person announced they weren't a gossip, they almost invariably were. The same when they promised never to tell a soul.

"You can tell this where and when you like just as long as you leave out the real names and don't tell it around here," she said. "That I hope I can trust you not to do. Though at the moment I don't feel as if I cared. I'll probably feel otherwise when the drink wears off. It's a lesson, this story. It's a lesson in what fools women can make of themselves. So, you say, what's new about that, you can learn it every day!"

She began to tell him about a soldier who had started writing letters to her from overseas. The soldier remembered her from when he used to go into the Library. But she didn't remember him. However, she replied in a friendly way to his first letter and a correspondence sprang up between them. He told her where he had lived in the town and she walked past the house so that she could tell him how things looked there. He told her what books he'd read and she gave some of the same kind of information. In short, they both revealed something of themselves and feelings warmed up on either side. On his side first, as far as any declarations went. She was not one to rush in like a fool. At first, she thought she was simply being kind. Even later, she didn't want to reject and embarrass him. He asked for a picture. She had one taken, it was not to her liking, but she sent it. He asked if she had a sweetheart and she replied truthfully that she did not. He did not send any picture of himself nor did she ask for one, though of course she was curious as to what he looked like. It would be no easy matter for him to have a picture taken in the middle of a war. Furthermore, she did not want to seem like the sort of woman who would withdraw kindness if looks did not come up to scratch.

He wrote that he did not expect to come home. He said he was not so afraid of dying as he was of ending up like some of the men he had seen when he was in the hospital, wounded. He did not elaborate, but she supposed he meant the cases they were just getting to know about now – the stumps of men, the blinded, the ones made monstrous with burns. He was not whining about his fate, she did not mean to imply that. It was just that he expected to die and picked death over some other options and he thought about her and wrote to her as men do to a sweetheart in such a situation.

When the war ended, it was a while since she had heard from him. She went on expecting a letter every day and nothing came. Nothing came. She was afraid that he might have been one of those unluckiest of soldiers in the whole war – one of those killed in the last week, or on the last day, or even in the last hour. She searched the local paper every week, and the names of new casualties were still being printed there till after New Year's but his was not among them. Now the paper began to list as well the names of those returning home, often printing a photo with the name, and a little account of rejoicing. When the soldiers were returning thick and fast there was less room for these additions. And then she saw his name, another name on the list. He had not been killed, he had not been wounded – he was coming home to Carstairs, perhaps was already there.

It was then that she decided to keep the Library open, though the flu was raging. Every day she was sure he would come, every day she was prepared for him. Sundays were a torment. When she entered the Town Hall she always felt he might be there before her, leaning up against the wall awaiting her arrival. Sometimes she felt it so strongly she saw a shadow that she mistook for a man. She understood now how people believed they had seen ghosts. Whenever the door opened she expected to look up into his face. Sometimes she made a pact with herself not to look up till she had counted to ten. Few people came in, because of the flu. She set herself jobs of rearranging things, else she would have gone mad. She never locked up until five or ten minutes after closing time. And then she fancied that he might be across the street on the Post Office steps, watching her, being too shy to make a move. She worried of course that he might be ill, she always sought in conversation for news of the latest cases. No one spoke his name.

It was at this time that she entirely gave up on reading. The covers of books looked like coffins to her, either shabby or ornate, and what was inside them might as well have been dust.

She had to be forgiven, didn't she, she had to be forgiven for thinking, after such letters, that the one thing that could never happen was that he wouldn't approach her, wouldn't get in touch with her at all? Never cross her threshold, after such avowals? Funerals passed by her window and she gave no thought to them, as long as they were not his. Even when she was sick in the hospital her only thought was that she must get back, she must get out of bed, the door must not stay locked against him. She staggered to her feet and back to work. On a hot afternoon she was arranging fresh newspapers on the racks and his name jumped out at her like something in her feverish dreams.

She read a short notice of his marriage to a Miss Grace Horne. Not a girl she knew. Not a Library user.

The bride wore fawn silk crêpe with brown-and-cream piping, and a beige straw hat with brown velvet streamers.

There was no picture. Brown-and-cream piping. Such was the end, and had to be, to her romance.

But on her desk at the Library, a matter of a few weeks ago, on a Saturday night after everybody had gone and she had locked the door and was turning out the lights, she discovered a scrap of paper. A few words written on it. *I was engaged before I went overseas.* No name, not his or hers. And there was her photograph, partly shoved under the blotter.

He had been in the Library that very evening. It had been a busy time, she had often left the desk to find a book for somebody or to straighten up the papers or to put some books on the shelves. He had been in the same room with her, watched her, and taken his chance. But never made himself known.

I was engaged before I went overseas.

"Do you think it was all a joke on me?" Louisa said. "Do you think a man could be so diabolical?"

"In my experience, tricks like that are far more often indulged in by the women. No, no. Don't you think such a thing. Far more likely he was sincere. He got a little carried away. It's all just the way it looks on the surface. He was engaged before he went overseas, he never expected to get back in one piece but he did. And when he did, there is the fiancée waiting – what else could he do?"

"What indeed?" said Louisa.

"He bit off more than he could chew."

"Ah, that's so, that's so!" Louisa said. "And what was it in my case but vanity, which deserves to get slapped down!" Her eyes were glassy and her expression roguish. "You don't think he'd had a good look at me any one time and thought the original was even worse than that poor picture, so he backed off?"

"I do not!" said Jim Frarey. "And don't you so belittle yourself."

"I don't want you to think I am stupid," she said. "I am not so stupid and inexperienced as that story makes me sound."

"Indeed I don't think you are stupid at all."

"But perhaps you think I am inexperienced?"

This was it, he thought – the usual. Women after they have told one story on themselves cannot stop from telling another. Drink upsets them in a radical way, prudence is out the window.

She had confided in him once before that she had been a patient in a sanitorium. Now she told about being in love with a doctor there. The sanitorium was on beautiful grounds up on Hamilton Mountain, and they used to meet there along the hedged walks. Shelves of limestone formed the steps and in sheltered spots there were such plants as you do not commonly see in Ontario – azaleas, rhododendrons, magnolias. The doctor knew something about botany and he told her this was the Carolinian vegetation. Very different from here, lusher, and there were little bits of woodland, too, wonderful trees, paths worn under the trees. Tulip trees.

"Tulips!" said Jim Frarey. "Tulips on the trees!"

"No, no, it is the shape of their leaves!"

She laughed at him challengingly, then bit her lip. He saw fit to continue the dialogue, saying, "Tulips on the trees!" while she said no, it is the leaves that are shaped like tulips, no, I never said that, stop! So they passed into a state of gingerly evaluation – which he knew well and could only hope she did – full of small pleasant surprises, half-sardonic signals, a welling-up of impudent hopes, and a fateful sort of kindness.

"All to ourselves," Jim Frarey said. "Never happened before, did it? Maybe it never will again."

She let him take her hands, half lift her from her chair. He turned out the dining-room lights as they went out. Up the stairs they went, that they had so often climbed separately. Past the picture of the dog on his master's grave, and Highland Mary singing in the field, and the old King with his bulgy eyes, his look of indulgence and repletion.

"It's a foggy, foggy night, and my heart is in a fright," Jim Frarey was half singing, half humming as they climbed. He kept an assured hand on Louisa's back. "All's well, all's well," he said as he steered her round the turn of the stairs. And when they took the narrow flight of steps to the third floor he said, "Never climbed so close to Heaven in this place before!"

But later in the night Jim Frarey gave a concluding groan and roused himself to deliver a sleepy scolding. "Louisa, Louisa, why didn't you tell me that was the way it was?"

"I told you everything," said Louisa in a faint and drifting voice.

"I got a wrong impression, then," he said. "I never intended for this to make a difference to you."

She said that it hadn't. Now without him pinning her down and steadying her, she felt herself whirling around in an irresistible way, as if the mattress had turned into a child's top and was carrying her off. She tried to explain that the traces of blood on the sheets could be credited to her period, but her words came out with a luxurious nonchalance and could not be fitted together.

ACCIDENTS

When Arthur came home from the factory a little before noon he shouted, "Stay out of my way till I wash! There's been an accident over at the works!" Nobody answered. Mrs. Feare, the housekeeper, was talking on the kitchen telephone so loudly that she could not hear him, and his daughter was of course at school. He washed, and stuffed everything he had been wearing into the hamper, and scrubbed up the bathroom, like a murderer. He started out clean, with even his hair slicked and patted, to drive to the man's house. He had had to ask where it was. He thought it was up Vinegar Hill but they said no, that was the father – the young fellow and his wife live on the other side of town, past where the Apple Evaporator used to be, before the war.

He found the two brick cottages side by side, and picked the left-hand one, as he'd been told. It wouldn't have been hard to pick which house, anyway. News had come before him. The door to the house was open, and children too young to be in school yet hung about in the yard. A small girl sat on a kiddie car, not going anywhere, just blocking his path. He stepped around her. As he did so an older girl spoke to him in a formal way – a warning.

"Her dad's dead. Hers!"

A woman came out of the front room carrying an armload of curtains, which she gave to another woman standing in the hall. The woman who received the curtains was gray-haired, with a pleading face. She had no upper teeth. She probably took her plate out, for comfort, at home. The woman who passed the curtains to her was stout but young, with fresh skin.

"You tell her not to get up on that stepladder," the gray-haired woman said to Arthur. "She's going to break her neck taking down curtains. She thinks we need to get everything washed. Are you the undertaker? Oh, no, excuse me! You're Mr. Doud. Grace, come out here! Grace! It's Mr. Doud!"

"Don't trouble her," Arthur said.

"She thinks she's going to get the curtains all down and washed and up again by tomorrow, because he's going to have to go in the front room. She's my daughter. I can't tell her anything."

"She'll quiet down presently," said a sombre but comfortable-looking man in a clerical collar, coming through from the back of the house. Their minister. But not from one of the churches Arthur knew. Baptist? Pentecostal? Plymouth Brethren? He was drinking tea.

Some other woman came and briskly removed the curtains.

"We got the machine filled and going," she said. "A day like this, they'll dry like nobody's business. Just keep the kids out of here."

The minister had to stand aside and lift his teacup high, to avoid her and her bundle. He said, "Aren't any of you ladies going to offer Mr. Doud a cup of tea?"

Arthur said, "No, no, don't trouble."

"The funeral expenses," he said to the gray-haired woman. "If you could let her know –"

"Lillian wet her pants!" said a triumphant child at the door. "Mrs. Agnew! Lillian peed her pants!"

"Yes. Yes," said the minister. "They will be very grateful."

"The plot and the stone, everything," Arthur said. "You'll make sure they understand that. Whatever they want on the stone."

The gray-haired woman had gone out into the yard. She came back with a squalling child in her arms. "Poor lamb," she said. "They told her she wasn't supposed to come in the house so where could she go? What could she do but have an accident!"

The young woman came out of the front room dragging a rug.

"I want this put on the line and beat," she said.

"Grace, here is Mr. Doud come to offer his condolences," the minister said.

"And to ask if there is anything I can do," said Arthur.

The gray-haired woman started upstairs with the wet child in her arms and a couple of others following.

Grace spotted them.

"Oh, no, you don't! You get back outside!"

"My mom's in here."

"Yes and your mom's good and busy, she don't need to be bothered with you. She's here helping me out. Don't you know Lillian's dad's dead?"

"Is there anything I can do for you?" Arthur said, meaning to clear out.

Grace stared at him with her mouth open. Sounds of the washing machine filled the house.

"Yes, there is," she said. "You wait here."

"She's overwhelmed," the minister said. "It's not that she means to be rude."

Grace came back with a load of books.

"These here," she said. "He had them out of the Library. I don't want to have to pay fines on them. He went every Saturday night so I guess they are due back tomorrow. I don't want to get in trouble about them."

"I'll look after them," Arthur said. "I'd be glad to."

"I just don't want to get in any trouble about them."

"Mr. Doud was saying about taking care of the funeral," the minister said to her, gently admonishing. "Everything including the stone. Whatever you want on the stone."

"Oh, I don't want anything fancy," Grace said.

On Friday morning last there occurred in the sawmill operation of Douds Factory a particularly ghastly and tragic accident. Mr. Jack Agnew, in reaching under the main shaft, had the misfortune to have his sleeve caught by a setscrew in an adjoining flunge, so that his arm and shoulder were drawn under the shaft. His head in consequence was brought in contact with the circular saw, that saw being about one foot in diameter. In an instant the unfortunate young man's head was separated from his body, being severed at an angle below the left ear and through the neck. His death is believed to have been instantaneous. He never spoke or uttered a cry so it was not any sound of his but by the spurt and shower of his blood that his fellow-workers were horribly alerted to the disaster.

This account was reprinted in the paper a week later for those who might have missed it or who wished to have an extra copy to send to friends or relations out of town (particularly to people who used to live in Carstairs and did not anymore). The misspelling of "flange" was corrected. There was a note apologizing for the mistake. There was also a description of a very large funeral, attended even by people from neighboring towns and as far away as Walley. They came by car and train, and some by horse and buggy. They had not known Jack Agnew when he was alive, but, as the paper said, they wished to pay tribute to the sensational and tragic manner of his death. All the stores in Carstairs were closed for two hours that afternoon. The hotel did not close its doors but that was because all the visitors needed somewhere to eat and drink.

The survivors were a wife, Grace, and a four-year-old daughter, Lillian. The victim had fought bravely in the Great War and had only been wounded once, not seriously. Many had commented on this irony.

The paper's failure to mention a surviving father was not deliberate. The editor of the paper was not a native of Carstairs, and people forgot to tell him about the father until it was too late.

The father himself did not complain about the omission. On the day of the funeral, which was very fine, he headed out of town as he would have done ordinarily on a day he had decided not to spend at Douds. He was wearing a felt hat and a long coat that would do for a rug if he wanted to take a nap. His overshoes were neatly held on his feet with the rubber rings from sealing jars. He was going out to fish for suckers. The season hadn't opened yet, but he always managed to be a bit ahead of it. He fished through the spring and early summer and cooked and ate what he caught. He had a frying pan and a pot hidden out on the riverbank. The pot was for boiling corn that he snatched out of the fields later in the year, when he was also eating the fruit of wild apple trees and grapevines. He was quite sane but abhorred conversation. He could not altogether avoid it in the weeks following his son's death, but he had a way of cutting it short.

"Should've watched out what he was doing."

Walking in the country that day, he met another person who was not at the funeral. A woman. She did not try to start any conversation and in fact seemed as fierce in her solitude as himself, whipping the air past her with long fervent strides.

The piano factory, which had started out making pump organs, stretched along the west side of town, like a medieval town wall. There were two long buildings like the inner and outer ramparts, with a closed-in bridge between them where the main offices were. And reaching up into the town and the streets of workers' houses you had the kilns and the sawmill and the lumberyard and storage sheds. The factory whistle dictated the time for many to get up, blowing at six o'clock in the morning. It blew again for work to start at seven and at twelve for dinnertime and at one in the afternoon for work to recommence, and then at five-thirty for the men to lay down their tools and go home.

Rules were posted beside the time clock, under glass. The first two rules were:

> ONE MINUTE LATE IS FIFTEEN MINUTES PAY. BE PROMPT. DON'T TAKE SAFETY FOR GRANTED. WATCH OUT FOR YOURSELF AND THE NEXT MAN.

There had been accidents in the factory and in fact a man had been killed when a load of lumber fell on him. That had happened before Arthur's time. And once, during the war, a man had lost an arm, or part of an arm. On the day that happened, Arthur was away in Toronto. So he had never seen an accident – nothing serious, anyway. But it was often at the back of his mind now that something might happen.

Perhaps he did not feel so sure that trouble wouldn't come near him, as he had felt before his wife died. She had died in 1919, in the last flurry of the Spanish flu, when everyone had got over being frightened. Even she had not been frightened. That was nearly five years ago and it still seemed to Arthur like the end of a carefree time in his life. But to other people he had always seemed very responsible and serious – nobody had noticed much difference in him.

In his dreams of an accident there was a spreading silence, everything was shut down. Every machine in the place stopped making its customary noise and every man's voice was removed, and when Arthur looked out of the office window he understood that doom had fallen. He never could remember any particular thing he saw that told him this. It was just the space, the dust in the factory yard, that said to him *now*.

The books stayed on the floor of his car for a week or so. His daughter Bea said, "What are those books doing here?" and then he remembered.

Bea read out the titles and the authors. *Sir John Franklin and the Romance of the Northwest Passage*, by G.B. Smith. *What's Wrong with the World?*, G.K. Chesterton. *The Taking of Quebec*, Archibald Hendry. *Bolshevism: Practice and Theory*, by Lord Bertrand Russell.

"Bol-*shev*-ism," Bea said, and Arthur told her how to pronounce it correctly. She asked what it was, and he said, "It's something they've got in Russia that I don't understand so well myself. But from what I hear of it, it's a disgrace."

Bea was thirteen at this time. She had heard about the Russian Ballet and also about dervishes. She believed for the next couple of years that Bolshevism was some sort of diabolical and maybe indecent dance. At least this was the story she told when she was grown up.

She did not mention that the books were connected with the man who had had the accident. That would have made the story less amusing. Perhaps she had really forgotten.

The Librarian was perturbed. The books still had their cards in them, which meant they had never been checked out, just removed from the shelves and taken away.

"The one by Lord Russell has been missing a long time."

Arthur was not used to such reproofs, but he said mildly, "I am returning them on behalf of somebody else. The chap who was killed. In the accident at the factory."

The Librarian had the Franklin book open. She was looking at the picture of the boat trapped in the ice.

"His wife asked me to," Arthur said.

She picked up each book separately, and shook it as if she expected something to fall out. She ran her fingers in between the pages. The bottom part of her face was working in an unsightly way, as if she was chewing at the inside of her cheeks.

"I guess he just took them home as he felt like it," Arthur said.

"I'm sorry?" she said in a minute. "What did you say? I'm sorry."

It was the accident, he thought. The idea that the man who had died in such a way had been the last person to open these books, turn these pages. The thought that he might have left a bit of his life in them, a scrap of paper or a pipe cleaner as a marker, or even a few shreds of tobacco. That unhinged her.

"No matter," he said. "I just dropped by to bring them back."

He turned away from her desk but did not immediately leave the Library. He had not been in it for years. There was his father's picture between the two front windows, where it would always be.

A.V. Doud, founder of the Doud Organ Factory and Patron of this Library. A Believer in Progress, Culture, and Education. A True Friend of the Town of Carstairs and of the Working Man.

The Librarian's desk was in the archway between the front and back rooms. The books were on shelves set in rows in the back room. Green-shaded lamps, with long pull cords, dangled down in the aisles between. Arthur remembered years ago some matter brought up at the Council Meeting about buying sixty-watt bulbs instead of forty. This Librarian was the one who had requested that, and they had done it.

In the front room, there were newspapers and magazines on wooden racks, and some round heavy tables, with chairs, so that people could sit and read, and rows of thick dark books behind glass. Dictionaries, probably, and atlases and encyclopedias. Two handsome high windows looking out on the main street, with Arthur's father hanging between them. Other pictures around the room hung too high, and were too dim and crowded with figures for the person down below to interpret them easily. (Later, when Arthur had spent many hours in the Library and had discussed these pictures with the Librarian, he knew that one of them represented the Battle of Flodden Field, with the King of Scotland charging down the hill into a pall of smoke, one the funeral of the Boy King of Rome, and one the Quarrel of Oberon and Titania, from *A Midsummer Night's Dream*.)

He sat down at one of the reading tables, where he could look out the window. He picked up an old copy of the *National Geographic*, which was lying there. He had his back to the Librarian. He thought this the tactful thing to do, since she seemed somewhat wrought-up. Other people came in, and he heard her speak to them. Her voice sounded normal enough now. He kept thinking he would leave, but did not.

He liked the high bare window full of the light of the spring evening, and he liked the dignity and order of these rooms. He was pleasantly mystified by the thought of grown people coming and going here, steadily reading books. Week after week, one book after another, a whole life long. He himself read a book once in a while, when somebody recommended it, and usually he enjoyed it, and then he read magazines, to keep up with things, and never thought about reading a book until another one came along, in this almost accidental way.

There would be little spells when nobody was in the Library but himself and the Librarian.

During one of these, she came over and stood near him, replacing some newspapers on the rack. When she finished this, she spoke to him, with a controlled urgency.

"The account of the accident that was printed in the paper – I take it that was more or less accurate?"

Arthur said that it was possibly too accurate.

"Why? Why do you say that?"

He mentioned the public's endless appetite for horrific details. Ought the paper to pander to that?

"Oh, I think it's natural," the Librarian said. "I think it's natural to want to know the worst. People do want to picture it. I do myself. I am very ignorant of machinery. It's hard for me to imagine what happened. Even with the paper's help. Did the machine do something unexpected?"

"No," Arthur said. "It wasn't the machine grabbing him and pulling him in, like an animal. He made a wrong move or at any rate a careless move. Then he was done for."

She said nothing, but did not move away.

"You have to keep your wits about you," Arthur said. "Never let up for a second. A machine is your servant and it is an excellent servant, but it makes an imbecile master."

He wondered if he had read that somewhere, or had thought it up himself.

"And I suppose there are no ways of protecting people?" the Librarian said. "But you must know all about that."

She left him then. Somebody had come in.

The accident was followed by a rush of warm weather. The length of the evenings and the heat of the balmy days seemed sudden and surprising, as if this were not the way winter finally ended in that part of the country, almost every year. The sheets of floodwater shrank magically back into the bogs, and the leaves shot out of the reddened branches, and barnyard smells drifted into town and were wrapped in the smell of lilacs.

Instead of wanting to be outdoors on such evenings, Arthur found himself thinking of the Library, and he would often end up there, sitting in the spot he had chosen on his first visit. He would sit for half an hour, or an hour. He looked at the London *Illustrated News*, or the *National Geographic* or *Saturday Night* or *Collier's*. All of these magazines arrived at his own house and he could have been sitting there, in the den, looking out at his hedged lawns, which old Agnew kept in tolerable condition, and the flower beds now full of tulips of every vivid color and combination. It seemed that he preferred the view of the main street, where the occasional brisk-looking new Ford went by, or some stuttering older-model car with a dusty cloth top. He preferred the Post Office, with its clock tower telling four different times in four different directions – and, as people liked to say, all wrong. Also the passing and loitering on the sidewalk. People trying to get the drinking fountain to work, although it wasn't turned on till the First of July.

It was not that he felt the need of sociability. He was not there for chat, though he would greet people if he knew them by name, and he did know most. And he might exchange a few words with the Librarian, though often it was only "Good evening" when he came in, and "Good night" when he went out. He made no demands on anybody. He felt his presence to be genial, reassuring, and, above all, natural. By sitting here, reading and reflecting, here instead of at home, he seemed to himself to be providing something. People could count on it.

There was an expression he liked. *Public servant.* His father, who looked out at him here with tinted baby-pink cheeks and glassy blue eyes and an old man's petulant mouth, had never thought of himself so. He had thought of himself more as a public character and benefactor. He had operated by whims and decrees, and he had got away with it. He would go around the factory when business was slow, and say to one man and another, "Go home. Go on home now. Go home and stay there till I can use you again." And they would go. They would work in their gardens or go out shooting rabbits and run up bills for whatever they had to buy, and accept that it couldn't be otherwise. It was still a joke with them, to imitate his bark. *Go on home!* He was their hero more than Arthur could ever be, but they were not prepared to take the same treatment today. During the war, they had got used to the good wages and to being always in demand. They never thought of the glut of labor the soldiers had created when they came home, never thought about how a business like this was kept going by luck and ingenuity from one year to the next, even from one season to the next. They didn't like changes – they were not happy about the switch now to player pianos, which Arthur believed were the hope of the future. But Arthur would do what he had to, though his way of proceeding was quite the opposite of his father's. Think everything over and then think it over again. Stay in the background except when necessary. Keep your dignity. Try always to be fair.

They expected all to be provided. The whole town expected it. Work would be provided just as the sun would rise in the mornings. And the taxes on the factory raised at the same time rates were charged for the water that used to come free. Maintenance of the access roads was now the factory's responsibility instead of the town's. The Methodist Church was requesting a hefty sum to build the new Sunday school. The town hockey team needed new uniforms. Stone gateposts were being erected for the War Memorial Park. And every year the smartest boy in the senior class was sent to university, courtesy of Douds.

Ask and ye shall receive.

Expectations at home were not lacking either. Bea was agitating to go away to private school and Mrs. Feare had her eye on some new mixing apparatus for the kitchen, also a new washing machine. All the trim on the house was due to be painted this year. All that wedding-cake decoration that consumed paint by the gallon. And in the midst of this what had Arthur done but order himself a new car – a Chrysler sedan.

It was necessary – he had to drive a new car. He had to drive a new car, Bea had to go away to school, Mrs. Feare had to have the latest, and the trim had to be as fresh as Christmas snow. Else they would lose respect, they would lose confidence, they would start to wonder if things were going downhill. And it could be managed, with luck it could all be managed.

For years after his father's death, he had felt like an impostor. Not steadily, but from time to time he had felt that. And now the feeling was gone. He could sit here and feel that it was gone.

He had been in the office when the accident happened, consulting with a veneer salesman. Some change in noise registered with him, but it was more of an increase than a hush. It was nothing that alerted him – just an irritation. Because it happened in the sawmill, nobody would know about the accident immediately in the shops or in the kilns or in the yard, and work in some places continued for several minutes. In fact Arthur, bending over the veneer samples on his desk, might have been one of the last people to understand that there had been an intervention. He asked the salesman a question, and the salesman did not answer. Arthur looked up and saw the man's mouth open, his face frightened, his salesman's assurance wiped away.

Then he heard his own name being called – both "Mr. Doud!" as was customary and "Arthur, Arthur!" by such of the older men as had known him as a boy. Also he heard "saw" and "head" and "Jesus, Jesus, Jesus!"

Arthur could have wished for the silence, the sounds and objects drawing back in that dreadful but releasing way, to give him room. It was nothing like that. Yelling and questioning and running around, himself in the midst being propelled to the sawmill. One man had fainted, falling in such a way that if they had not got the saw turned off a moment before, it would have got him, too. It was his body, fallen but entire, that Arthur briefly mistook for the body of the victim. Oh, no, no. They pushed him on. The sawdust was scarlet. It was drenched, brilliant. The pile of lumber here was all merrily spattered, and the blades. A pile of work clothes soaked in blood lay in the sawdust and Arthur realized that it was the body, the trunk with limbs attached. So much blood had flowed as to make its shape not plain at first – to soften it, like a pudding.

The first thing he thought of was to cover that. He took off his jacket and did so. He had to step up close, his shoes squished in it. The reason no one else had done this would be simply that no one else was wearing a jacket.

"Have they gone a-get the doctor?" somebody was yelling. "Gone a-get the doctor!" a man quite close to Arthur said. "Can't sew his head back on – doctor. Can he?"

But Arthur gave the order to get the doctor; he imagined it was necessary. You can't have a death without a doctor. That set the rest in motion. Doctor, undertaker, coffin, flowers, preacher. Get started on all that, give them something to do. Shovel up the sawdust, clean up the saw. Send the men who had been close by to wash themselves. Carry the man who had fainted to the lunchroom. Is he all right? Tell the office girl to make tea.

Brandy was what was needed, or whisky. But he had a rule against it, on the premises.

Something still lacking. Where was it? There, they said. Over there. Arthur heard the sound of vomiting, not far away. All right. Either pick it up or tell somebody to pick it up. The sound of vomiting saved him, steadied him, gave him an almost lighthearted determination. He picked it up. He carried it delicately and securely as you might carry an awkward but valuable jug. Pressing the face out of sight, as if comforting it, against his chest. Blood seeped through his shirt and stuck the material to his skin. Warm. He felt like a wounded man. He was aware of them watching him and he was aware of himself as an actor must be, or a priest. What to do with it, now that he had it against his chest? The answer to that came, too. Set it down, put it back where it belongs, not of course fitted with exactness, not as if a seam could be closed. Just more or less in place, and lift the jacket and tug it into a new position.

He couldn't now ask the man's name. He would have to get it in some other way. After the intimacy of his services here, such ignorance would be an offense.

But he found he did know it – it came to him. As he edged the corner of his jacket over the ear that had lain and still lay upward, and so looked quite fresh and usable, he received a name. Son of the fellow who came and did the garden, who was not always reliable. A young man taken on again when he came back from the war. Married? He thought so. He would have to go and see her. As soon as possible. Clean clothes.

The Librarian often wore a dark-red blouse. Her lips were reddened to match, and her hair was bobbed. She was not a young woman anymore, but she maintained an eye-catching style. He remembered that years ago when they had hired her, he had thought that she got herself up very soberly. Her hair was not bobbed in those days – it was wound around her head, in the old style. It was still the same color – a warm and pleasant color, like leaves – oak leaves, say, in the fall. He tried to think how much she was paid. Not much, certainly. She kept herself looking well on it. And where did she live? In one of the boarding houses – the one with the schoolteachers? No, not there. She lived in the Commercial Hotel.

And now something else was coming to mind. No definite story that he could remember. You could not say with any assurance that she had a bad reputation. But it was not quite a spotless reputation, either. She was said to take a drink with the travellers. Perhaps she had a boyfriend among them. A boyfriend or two.

Well, she was old enough to do as she liked. It wasn't quite the same as the way it was with a teacher – hired partly to set an example. As long as she did her job well, and anybody could see that she did. She had her life to live, like everyone else. Wouldn't you rather have a nice-looking woman in here than a crabby old affair like Mary Tamblyn? Strangers might drop in, they judge a town by what they see, you want a nice-looking woman with a nice manner.

Stop that. Who said you didn't? He was arguing in his head on her behalf just as if somebody had come along who wanted her chucked out, and he had no intimation at all that that was the case.

What about her question, on the first evening, regarding the machines? What did she mean by that? Was it a sly way of bringing blame?

He had talked to her about the pictures and the lighting and even told her how his father had sent his own workmen over here, paid them to build the Library shelves, but he had never spoken of the man who had taken the books out without letting her know. One at a time, probably. Under his coat? Brought back the same way. He must have brought them back, or else he'd have had a houseful, and his wife would never stand for that. Not stealing, except temporarily. Harmless behavior, but peculiar. Was there any connection? Between thinking you could do things a little differently that way and thinking you could get away with a careless move that might catch your sleeve and bring the saw down on your neck?

There might be, there might be some connection. A matter of attitude.

"That chap – you know the one – the accident –" he said to the Librarian. "The way he took off with the books he wanted. Why do you think he did that?"

"People do things," the Librarian said. "They tear out pages. On account of something they don't like or something they do. They just do things. I don't know."

"Did he ever tear out some pages? Did you ever give him a lecture? Ever make him scared to face you?"

He meant to tease her a little, implying that she would not be likely to scare anybody, but she did not take it that way.

"How could I when I never spoke to him?" she said. "I never saw him. I never saw him, to know who he was."

She moved away, putting an end to the conversation. So she did not like to be teased. Was she one of those people full of mended cracks that you could only see close up? Some old misery troubling her, some secret? Maybe a sweetheart had been lost in the war.

On a later evening, a Saturday evening in the summer, she brought the subject up herself, that he would never have mentioned again.

"Do you remember our talking once about the man who had the accident?"

Arthur said he did.

"I have something to ask you and you may think it strange."

He nodded.

"And my asking it – I want you to – it is confidential."

"Yes, indeed," he said.

"What did he look like?"

Look like? Arthur was puzzled. He was puzzled by her making such a fuss and secret about it – surely it was natural to be interested in what a man might look like, who had been coming in and making off with her books without her knowing about it – and because he could not help her, he shook his head. He could not bring any picture of Jack Agnew to mind.

"Tall," he said. "I believe he was on the tall side. Otherwise I cannot tell you. I am really not such a good person to ask. I can recognize a man easily but I can't ever give much of a physical description, even when it's someone I see on a daily basis."

"But I thought you were the one – I heard you were the one –" she said. "Who picked him up. His head."

Arthur said stiffly, "I didn't think that you could just leave it lying there." He felt disappointed in the woman, uneasy and ashamed for her. But he tried to speak matter-of-factly, keeping reproach out of his voice.

"I could not even tell you the color of his hair. It was all – all pretty much obliterated, by that time."

She said nothing for a moment or two and he did not look at her. Then she said, "It must seem as if I am one of those people – one of those people who are fascinated by these sorts of things."

Arthur made a protesting noise, but it did, of course, seem to him that she must be like that.

"I should not have asked you," she said. "I should not have mentioned it. I can never explain to you why I did. I would like just to ask you, if you can help it, never to think that that is the kind of person I am."

Arthur heard the word "never." She could never explain to him. He was never to think. In the midst of his disappointment he picked up this suggestion, that their conversations were to continue, and perhaps on a less haphazard basis. He heard a humility in her voice, but it was a humility that was based on some kind of assurance. Surely that was sexual.

Or did he only think so, because this was the evening it was? It was the Saturday evening in the month when he usually went to Walley. He was going there tonight, he had only dropped in here on his way, he had not meant to stay as long as he had done. It was the night when he went to visit a woman whose name was Jane MacFarlane. Jane MacFarlane lived apart from her husband, but she was not thinking of getting a divorce. She had no children. She earned her living as a dressmaker. Arthur had first met her when she came to his house to make clothes for his wife. Nothing had gone on at that time, and neither of them had thought of it. In some ways Jane MacFarlane was a woman like the Librarian – good-looking, though not so young, plucky and stylish and good at her work. In other ways, not so like. He could not imagine Jane ever presenting a man with a mystery, and following that up with the information that it would never be solved. Jane was a woman to give a man peace. The submerged dialogue he had with her – sensual, limited, kind – was very like the one he had had with his wife.

The Librarian went to the switch by the door, and turned out the main light. She locked the door. She disappeared among the shelves, turning out the lights there, too, in a leisurely way. The town clock was striking nine. She must think that it was right. His own watch said three minutes to.

It was time to get up, time for him to leave, time to go to Walley.

When she had finished dealing with the lights, she came and sat down at the table beside him.

He said, "I would never think of you in any way that would make you unhappy."

Turning out the lights shouldn't have made it so dark. They were in the middle of summer. But it seemed that heavy rain clouds had moved in. When Arthur had last paid attention to the street, he had seen plenty of daylight left: country people shopping, boys squirting each other at the drinking fountain, and young girls walking up and down in their soft, cheap, flowery summer dresses, letting the young men watch them from wherever the young men congregated – the Post Office steps, the front of the feed store. And now that he looked again he saw the street in an uproar from the loud wind that already carried a few drops of rain. The girls were shrieking and laughing and holding their purses over their heads as they ran to shelter, store clerks were rolling up awnings and hauling in the baskets of fruit, the racks of summer shoes, the garden implements that had been displayed on the sidewalks. The doors of the Town Hall banged as the farm women ran inside, grabbing on to packages and children, to cram themselves into the Ladies' Rest Room. Somebody tried the Library door. The Librarian looked over at it but did not move. And soon the rain was sweeping like curtains across the street, and the wind battered the Town Hall roof, and tore at the treetops. That roaring and danger lasted a few minutes, while the power of the wind went by. Then the sound left was the sound of the rain, which was now falling vertically and so heavily they might have been under a waterfall.

If the same thing was happening at Walley, he thought, Jane would know enough not to expect him. This was the last thought he had of her for a long while.

"Mrs. Feare wouldn't wash my clothes," he said, to his own surprise. "She was afraid to touch them."

The Librarian said, in a peculiarly quivering, shamed, and determined voice, "I think what you did – I think that was a remarkable thing to do."

The rain made such a constant noise that he was released from answering. He found it easy then to turn and look at her. Her profile was dimly lit by the wash of rain down the windows. Her expression was calm and reckless. Or so it seemed to him. He realized that he knew hardly anything about her – what kind of person she really was or what kind of secrets she could have. He could not even estimate his own value to her. He only knew that he had some, and it wasn't the usual.

He could no more describe the feeling he got from her than you can describe a smell. It's like the scorch of electricity. It's like burnt kernels of wheat. No, it's like a bitter orange. I give up.

He had never imagined that he would find himself in a situation like this, visited by such a clear compulsion. But it seemed he was not unprepared. Without thinking over twice or even once what he was letting himself in for, he said, "I wish –"

He had spoken too quietly, she did not hear him.

He raised his voice. He said, "I wish we could get married."

Then she looked at him. She laughed but controlled herself.

"I'm sorry," she said. "I'm sorry. It's just what went through my mind."

"What was that?" he said.

"I thought – that's the last I'll see of him."

Arthur said, "You're mistaken."

TOLPUDDLE MARTYRS

The passenger train from Carstairs to London had stopped running during the Second World War and even the rails were taken up. People said it was for the War Effort. When Louisa went to London to see the heart specialist, in the mid-fifties, she had to take the bus. She was not supposed to drive anymore.

The doctor, the heart specialist, said that her heart was a little wonky and her pulse inclined to be jumpy. She thought that made her heart sound like a comedian and her pulse like a puppy on a lead. She had not come fifty-seven miles to be treated with such playfulness but she let it pass, because she was already distracted by something she had been reading in the doctor's waiting room. Perhaps it was what she had been reading that had made her pulse jumpy.

On an inside page of the local paper she had seen the headline LOCAL MARTYRS HONORED, and simply to put in the time she had read further. She read that there was to be some sort of ceremony that afternoon at Victoria Park. It was a ceremony to honor the Tolpuddle Martyrs. The paper said that few people had heard of the Tolpuddle Martyrs, and certainly Louisa had not. They were men who had been tried and found guilty for administering illegal oaths. This peculiar offense, committed over a hundred years ago in Dorset, England, had got them transported to Canada and some of them had ended up here in London, where they lived out the rest of their days and were buried without any special notice or commemoration. They were considered now to be among the earliest founders of the Trade Union movement, and the Trade Unions Council, along with representatives of the Canadian Federation of Labor and the ministers of some local churches, had organized a ceremony taking place today on the occasion of the hundred-and-twentieth anniversary of their arrest.

Martyrs is laying it on somewhat, thought Louisa. They were not executed, after all.

The ceremony was to take place at three o'clock and the chief speakers were to be one of the local ministers, and Mr. John (Jack) Agnew, a union spokesman from Toronto.

It was a quarter after two when Louisa came out of the doctor's office. The bus to Carstairs did not leave until six o'clock. She had thought she would go and have tea and something to eat on the top floor of Simpsons, then shop for a wedding present, or if the time fitted go to an afternoon movie. Victoria Park lay between the doctor's office and Simpsons, and she decided to cut across it. The day was hot and the shade of the trees pleasant. She could not avoid seeing where the chairs had been set up, and a small speakers' platform draped in yellow cloth, with a Canadian flag on the one side and what she supposed must be a Labor Union flag on the other. A group of people had collected and she found herself changing course in order to get a look at them. Some were old people, very plainly but decently dressed, the women with kerchiefs around their heads on the hot day, Europeans. Others were factory workers, men in clean short-sleeved shirts and women in fresh blouses and slacks, let out early. A few women must have come from home, because they were wearing summer dresses and sandals and trying to keep track of small children. Louisa thought that they would not care at all for the way she was dressed – fashionably, as always, in beige shantung with a crimson silk tam – but she noticed, just then, a woman more elegantly got up than she was, in green silk with her dark hair drawn tightly back, tied with a green-and-gold scarf. She might have been forty – her face was worn, but beautiful. She came over to Louisa at once, smiling, showed her a chair and gave her a mimeographed paper. Louisa could not read the purple printing. She tried to get a look at some men who were talking beside the platform. Were the speakers among them?

The coincidence of the name was hardly even interesting. Neither the first name nor the last was all that unusual.

She did not know why she had sat down, or why she had come over here in the first place. She was beginning to feel a faintly sickening, familiar agitation. She could feel that over nothing. But once it got going, telling herself that it was over nothing did no good. The only thing to do was to get up and get away from here before any more people sat down and hemmed her in.

The green woman intercepted her, asked if she was all right.

"I have to catch a bus," said Louisa in a croaky voice. She cleared her throat. "An out-of-town bus," she said with better control, and marched away, not in the right direction for Simpsons. She thought in fact that she wouldn't go there, she wouldn't go to Birks for the wedding present or to a movie either. She would just go and sit in the bus depot until it was time for her to go home.

Within half a block of the bus depot she remembered that the bus had not taken her there that morning. The depot was being torn down and rebuilt – there was a temporary depot several blocks away. She had not paid quite enough attention to which street it was on – York Street, east of the real depot, or King? At any rate, she had to detour, because both of these streets were being torn up, and she had almost decided she was lost when she realized she had been lucky enough to come upon the temporary depot by the back way. It was an old house – one of those tall yellow-gray brick houses dating from the time when this was a residential district. This was probably the last use it would be put to before being torn down. Houses all around it must have been torn down to make the large gravelled lot where the buses pulled in. There were still some trees at the edge of the lot and under them a few rows of chairs that she had not noticed when she got off the bus before noon. Two men were sitting on what used to be the veranda of the house, on old car seats. They wore brown shirts with the bus company's insignia but they seemed to be halfhearted about their work, not getting up when she asked if the bus to Carstairs was leaving at six o'clock as scheduled and where could she get a soft drink?

Six o'clock, far as they knew.

Coffee shop down the street.

Cooler inside but only Coke and orange left.

She got herself a Coca-Cola out of the cooler in a dirty little indoor waiting room that smelled of a bad toilet. Moving the depot to this dilapidated house must have thrown everyone into a state of indolence and fecklessness. There was a fan in the room they used as an office, and she saw, as she went by, some papers blow off the desk. "Oh, shit," said the office girl, and stamped her heel on them.

The chairs set up in the shade of the dusty city trees were straight-backed old wooden chairs originally painted different colors – they looked as if they had come from various kitchens. Strips of old carpet and rubber bathroom mats were laid down in front of them, to keep your feet off the gravel. Behind the first row of chairs she thought she saw a sheep lying on the ground, but it turned into a dirty-white dog, which trotted over and looked at her for a moment in a grave semi-official way – gave a brief sniff at her shoes, and trotted away. She had not noticed if there were any drinking straws and did not feel like going back to look. She drank Coke from the bottle, tilting back her head and closing her eyes.

When she opened them, a man was sitting one chair away, and was speaking to her.

"I got here as soon as I could," he said. "Nancy said you were going to catch a bus. As soon as I finished with the speech, I took off. But the bus depot is all torn up."

"Temporarily," she said.

"I knew you right away," he said. "In spite of – well, many years. When I saw you, I was talking to somebody. Then I looked again and you'd disappeared."

"I don't recognize you," said Louisa.

"Well, no," he said. "I guess not. of course. You wouldn't."

He was wearing tan slacks, a pale-yellow short-sleeved shirt, a cream-and-yellow ascot scarf. A bit of a dandy, for a union man. His hair was white but thick and wavy, the sort of springy hair that goes in ripples, up and back from the forehead, his skin was flushed and his face was deeply wrinkled from the efforts of speechmaking – and from talking to people privately, she supposed, with much of the fervor and persuasiveness of his public speeches. He wore tinted glasses, which he took off now, as if willing that she should see him better. His eyes were a light blue, slightly bloodshot and apprehensive. A good-looking man, still trim except for a little authoritative bulge over the belt, but she did not find these serviceable good looks – the careful sporty clothes, the display of ripply hair, the effective expressions – very attractive. She preferred the kind of looks Arthur had. The restraint, the dark-suited dignity that some people could call pompous, that seemed to her admirable and innocent.

"I always meant to break the ice," he said. "I meant to speak to you. I should have gone in and said goodbye at least. The opportunity to leave came up so suddenly."

Louisa did not have any idea what to say to this. He sighed. He said, "You must have been mad at me. Are you still?"

"No," she said, and fell back, ridiculously, on the usual courtesies. "How is Grace? How is your daughter? Lillian?"

"Grace is not so well. She had some arthritis. Her weight doesn't help it. Lillian is all right. She's married but she still teaches high school. Mathematics. Not too usual for a woman."

How could Louisa begin to correct him? Could she say, No, your wife Grace got married again during the war, she married a farmer, a widower. Before that she used to come in and clean our house once a week. Mrs. Feare had got too old. And Lillian never finished high school, how could she be a high-school teacher? She married young, she had some children, she works in the drugstore. She had your height and your hair, dyed blond. I often looked at her and thought she must be like you. When she was growing up, I used to give her my stepdaughter's outgrown clothes.

Instead of this, she said, "Then the woman in the green dress – that was not Lillian?"

"Nancy? Oh, no! Nancy is my guardian angel. She keeps track of where I'm going, and when, and have I got my speech, and what I drink and eat and have I taken my pills. I tend toward high blood pressure. Nothing too serious. But my way of life's no good. I'm on the go constantly. Tonight I've got to fly out of here to Ottawa, tomorrow I've got a tough meeting, tomorrow night I've got some fool banquet."

Louisa felt it necessary to say, "You knew that I got married? I married Arthur Doud."

She thought he showed some surprise. But he said, "Yes, I heard that. Yes."

"We worked hard, too," said Louisa sturdily. "Arthur died six years ago. We kept the factory going all through the thirties even though at times we were down to three men. We had no money for repairs and I remember cutting up the office awnings so that Arthur could carry them up on a ladder and patch the roof. We tried making everything we could think of. Even outdoor bowling alleys for those amusement places.

Then the war came and we couldn't keep up. We could sell all the pianos we could make but also we were making radar cases for the Navy. I stayed in the office all through."

"It must have been a change," he said, in what seemed a tactful voice. "A change from the Library."

"Work is work," she said. "I still work. My stepdaughter Bea is divorced, she keeps house for me after a fashion. My son has finally finished university – he is supposed to be learning about the business, but he has some excuse to go off in the middle of every afternoon. When I come home at suppertime, I am so tired I could drop, and I hear the ice tinkling in their glasses and them laughing behind the hedge. Oh, Mud, they say when they see me, Oh, poor Mud, sit down here, get her a drink! They call me Mud because that was my son's name for me when he was a baby. But they are neither of them babies now. The house is cool when I come home – it's a lovely house if you remember, built in three tiers like a wedding cake. Mosaic tiles in the entrance hall. But I am always thinking about the factory, that is what fills my mind. What should we do to stay afloat? There are only five factories in Canada making pianos now, and three of them are in Quebec with the low cost of labor. No doubt you know all about that. When I talk to Arthur in my head, it is always about the same thing. I am very close to him still but it is hardly in a mystical way. You would think as you get older your mind would fill up with what they call the spiritual side of things, but mine just seems to get more and more practical, trying to get something settled. What a thing to talk to a dead man about."

She stopped, she was embarrassed. But she was not sure that he had listened to all of this, and in fact she was not sure that she had said all of it.

"What started me off–" he said. "What got me going in the first place, with whatever I have managed to do, was the Library. So I owe you a great deal."

He put his hands on his knees, let his head fall.

"Ah, rubbish," he said.

He groaned, and ended up with a laugh.

"My father," he said, "You wouldn't remember my father?"

"Oh, yes."

"Well. Sometimes I think he had the right idea."

Then he lifted his head, gave it a shake, and made a pronouncement.

"Love never dies."

She felt impatient to the point of taking offense. This is what all the speechmaking turns you into, she thought, a person who can say things like that. Love dies all the time, or at any rate it becomes distracted, overlaid – it might as well be dead.

"Arthur used to come and sit in the Library," she said. "In the beginning I was very provoked with him. I used to look at the back of his neck and think, Ha, what if something should hit you there! None of that would make sense to you. It wouldn't make sense. And it turned out to be something else I wanted entirely. I wanted to marry him and get into a normal life.

"A normal life," she repeated – and a giddiness seemed to be taking over, a widespread forgiveness of folly, alerting the skin of her spotty hand, her dry thick fingers that lay not far from his, on the seat of the chair between them. An amorous flare-up of the cells, of old intentions. *Oh, never dies.*

Across the gravelled yard came a group of oddly dressed folk. They moved all together, a clump of black. The women did not show their hair – they had black shawls or bonnets covering their heads. The men wore broad hats and black braces. The children were dressed just like their elders, even to the bonnets and hats. How hot they all looked in those clothes – how hot and dusty and wary and shy.

"The Tolpuddle Martyrs," he said, in a faintly joking, resigned, and compassionate voice. "Ah, I guess I'd better go over. I'd better go over there and have a word with them."

That edge of a joke, the uneasy kindness, made her think

of somebody else. Who was it? When she saw the breadth of his shoulders from behind, and the broad flat buttocks, she knew who.

Jim Frarey.

Oh, what kind of a trick was being played on her, or what kind of trick was she playing on herself! She would not have it. She pulled herself up tightly, she saw all those black clothes melt into a puddle. She was dizzy and humiliated. She would not have it.

But not all black, now that they were getting closer. She could see dark blue, those were the men's shirts, and dark blue and purple in some of the women's dresses. She could see faces – the men's behind beards, the women's in their deep-brimmed bonnets. And now she knew who they were. They were Mennonites.

Mennonites were living in this part of the country, where they never used to be. There were some of them around Bondi, a village north of Carstairs. They would be going home on the same bus as she was.

He was not with them, or anywhere in sight.

A traitor, helplessly. A traveller.

Once she knew that they were Mennonites and not some lost unidentifiable strangers, these people did not look so shy or dejected. In fact they seemed quite cheerful, passing around a bag of candy, adults eating candy with the children. They settled on the chairs all around her.

No wonder she was feeling clammy. She had gone under a wave, which nobody else had noticed. You could say anything you liked about what had happened – but what it amounted to was going under a wave. She had gone under and through it and was left with a cold sheen on her skin, a beating in her ears, a cavity in her chest, and revolt in her stomach. It was anarchy she was up against – a devouring muddle. Sudden holes and impromptu tricks and radiant vanishing consolations.

But these Mennonite settlings are a blessing. The plop of behinds on chairs, the crackling of the candy bag, the meditative sucking and soft conversations. Without looking at Louisa, a little girl holds out the bag, and Louisa accepts a butterscotch mint. She is surprised to be able to hold it in her hand, to have her lips shape thank-you, then to discover in her mouth just the taste that she expected. She sucks on it as they do on theirs, not in any hurry, and allows that taste to promise her some reasonable continuance.

Lights have come on, though it isn't yet evening. In the trees above the wooden chairs someone has strung lines of little colored bulbs that she did not notice until now. They make her think of festivities. Carnivals. Boats of singers on the lake.

"What place is this?" she said to the woman beside her.

On the day of Miss Tamblyn's death it happened that Louisa was staying in the Commercial Hotel. She was a traveller then for a company that sold hats, ribbons, handkerchiefs and trimmings, and ladies' underwear to retail stores. She heard the talk in the hotel, and it occurred to her that the town would soon need a new Librarian. She was getting very tired of lugging her sample cases on and off trains, and showing her wares in hotels, packing and unpacking. She went at once and talked to the people in charge of the Library. A Mr. Doud and a Mr. Macleod. They sounded like a vaudeville team but did not look it. The pay was poor, but she had not been doing so well on commission, either. She told them that she had finished high school, in Toronto, and had worked in Eaton's Book Department before she switched to travelling. She did not think it necessary to tell them that she had only worked there five months when she was discovered to have t.b., and that she had then spent four years in a sanitorium. The t.b. was cured, anyway, her spots were dry.

The hotel moved her to one of the rooms for permanent guests, on the third floor. She could see the snow-covered hills over the rooftops. The town of Carstairs was in a river valley. It had three or four thousand people and a long main street that ran downhill, over the river, and uphill again. There was a piano and organ factory.

The houses were built for lifetimes and the yards were wide and the streets were lined with mature elm and maple trees. She had never been here when the leaves were on the trees. It must make a great difference. So much that lay open now would be concealed.

She was glad of a fresh start, her spirits were hushed and grateful. She had made fresh starts before and things had not turned out as she had hoped, but she believed in the swift decision, the unforeseen intervention, the uniqueness of her fate.

The town was full of the smell of horses. As evening came on, big blinkered horses with feathered hooves pulled the sleighs across the bridge, past the hotel, beyond the streetlights, down the dark side roads. Somewhere out in the country they would lose the sound of each other's bells.

Mischief

ROSE FELL in love with Clifford at a party which Clifford and Jocelyn gave and Patrick and Rose attended. They had been married about three years at this time, Clifford and Jocelyn a year or so longer.

Clifford and Jocelyn lived out past West Vancouver, in one of those summer cottages, haphazardly winterized, that used to line the short curving streets between the lower highway and the sea. The party was in March, on a rainy night. Rose was nervous about going to it. She felt almost sick as they drove through West Vancouver, watched the neon lights weeping in the puddles on the road, listened to the condemning tick of the windshield wipers. She would often afterwards look back and see herself sitting beside Patrick, in her low-cut black blouse and black velvet skirt which she hoped would turn out to be the right thing to wear; she was wishing they were just going to the movies. She had no idea that her life was going to be altered.

Patrick was nervous too, although he would not have admitted it. Social life was a puzzling, often disagreeable business for them both. They had arrived in Vancouver knowing nobody. They followed leads. Rose was not sure whether they really longed for friends, or simply believed they ought to have them. They dressed up and went out to visit people, or tidied up the living room and waited for the people who had been invited to visit them. In some cases they established steady visiting patterns. They had some drinks, during those evenings, and around eleven or eleven-thirty – which hardly ever came soon enough – Rose went out to the kitchen and made coffee and something to eat. The things she made to eat were usually squares of toast, with a slice of tomato on top, then a square of cheese, then a bit of bacon, the whole thing broiled and held together with a toothpick. She could not manage to think of anything else.

It was easier for them to become friends with people Patrick liked than with people Rose liked because Rose was very adaptable, in fact deceitful, and Patrick was hardly adaptable at all. But in this case, the case of Jocelyn and Clifford, the friends were Rose's. Or Jocelyn was. Jocelyn and Rose had known enough not to try to establish couple-visiting. Patrick disliked Clifford without knowing him because Clifford was a violinist; no doubt Clifford disliked Patrick because Patrick worked in a branch of his family's department store. In those days the barriers between people were still strong and reliable; between arty people and business people; between men and women.

Rose did not know any of Jocelyn's friends, but understood they were musicians and journalists and lecturers at the University and even a woman writer who had had a play performed on the radio. She expected them to be intelligent, witty, and easily contemptuous. It seemed to her that all the time she and Patrick were sitting in the living rooms, visiting or being visited, really clever and funny people, who had a right to despise them, were conducting irregular lives and parties elsewhere. Now came the chance to be with those people, but her stomach rejected it, her hands were sweating.

Jocelyn and Rose had met in the maternity ward of the North Vancouver General Hospital. The first thing Rose saw, on being taken back to the ward after having Anna, was Jocelyn sitting up in bed reading the Journals of André Gide. Rose knew the book by its colors, having noticed it on the drugstore stands. Gide was on the list of writers she meant to work through. At that time she read only great writers.

The immediately startling and comforting thing to Rose, about Jocelyn, was how much Jocelyn looked like a student, how little she had let herself be affected by the maternity ward. Jocelyn had long black braids, a heavy pale face, thick glasses, no trace of prettiness, and an air of comfortable concentration.

A woman in the bed beside Jocelyn was describing the arrangement of her kitchen cupboards. She would forget to tell where she kept something – rice, say, or brown sugar – and then she would have to start all over again, making sure her audience was with her by saying "Remember on the right hand highest shelf next the stove, that's where I keep the packages of soup but not the canned soup, I keep the canned soup underneath the counter in with the canned goods, well, right next to that –"

Other women tried to interrupt, to tell how they kept things, but they were not successful, or not for long. Jocelyn sat reading, and twiddling the end of a braid between her fingers, as if she was in a library, at college, as if she was researching for a paper, and this world of other women had never closed down on her at all. Rose wished she could manage as well.

She was still dazed from the birth. Whenever she closed her eyes she saw an eclipse, a big black ball with a ring of fire. That was the baby's head, ringed with pain, the instant before she pushed it out. Across this image, in disturbing waves, went the talking woman's kitchen shelves, dipping under their glaring weight of cans and packages. But she could open her eyes and see Jocelyn, black and white, braids falling over her hospital nightgown. Jocelyn was the only person she saw who looked calm and serious enough to match the occasion.

Soon Jocelyn got out of bed, showing long white unshaved legs and a stomach still stretched by pregnancy. She put on a striped bathrobe. Instead of a cord, she tied a man's necktie around her waist. She slapped across the hospital linoleum in her bare feet. A nurse came running, warned her to put on slippers.

"I don't own any slippers."

"Do you own shoes?" said the nurse rather nastily.

"Oh, yes. I own shoes."

Jocelyn went back to the little metal cabinet beside her bed and took out a pair of large, dirty, run-over moccasins. She went off making as sloppy and insolent a noise as before.

Rose was longing to know her.

The next day Rose had her own book out to read. It was *The Last Puritan*, by George Santayana, but unfortunately it was a library copy; the title on the cover was rubbed and dim, so it was impossible that Jocelyn should admire Rose's reading material as Rose had admired hers. Rose didn't know how she could get to talk to her.

The woman who had explained about her cupboards was talking about how she used her vacuum cleaner. She said it was very important to use all the attachments because they each had a purpose and after all you had paid for them. Many people didn't use them. She described how she vacuumed her living-room drapes. Another woman said she had tried to do that but the material kept getting bunched up. The authoritative woman said that was because she hadn't been doing it properly.

Rose caught Jocelyn's eye around the corner of her book.

"I hope you polish your stove knobs," she said quietly.

"I certainly do," said Jocelyn.

"Do you polish them every day?"

"I used to polish them twice a day but now that I have the new baby I just don't know if I'll get around to it."

"Do you use that special stove-knob polish?"

"I certainly do. And I use the special stove-knob cloths that come in that special package."

"That's good. Some people don't."

"Some people will use anything."

"Old dishrags."

"Old snotrags."

"Old snot."

After this their friendship bloomed in a hurry. It was one of those luxuriant intimacies that spring up in institutions; in schools, at camp, in prison. They walked in the halls, disobeying the nurses. They annoyed and mystified the other women. They became hysterical as schoolgirls, from the things they read aloud to each other. They did not read Gide or Santayana but the copies of *True Love* and *Personal Romances* which they had found in the waiting room.

"It says here you can buy false calves," Rose read. "I don't see how you'd hide them, though. I guess you strap them on your legs. Or maybe they just sit here inside your stockings but wouldn't you think they'd show?"

"On your legs?" said Jocelyn. "You strap them on your legs? Oh, false calves! False calves! I thought you were talking about false *calves*! False baby cows!"

Anything like that could set them off.

"False baby cows!"

"False tits, false bums, false baby cows!"

"What will they think of next!"

The vacuum-cleaning woman said they were always butting in and spoiling other people's conversations and she didn't see what was so funny about dirty language. She said if they didn't stop the way they carried on they would sour their milk.

"I've been wondering if maybe mine *is* sour," Jocelyn said. "It's an awfully disgusting color."

"What color?" Rose asked.

"Well. Sort of blue."

"Good God, maybe it's ink!"

The vacuum-cleaning woman said she was going to tell the

nurse they were swearing. She said she was no prude, but. She asked if they were fit to be mothers. How was Jocelyn going to manage to wash diapers, when anybody could see she never washed her dressing gown?

Jocelyn said she planned to use moss, she was an Indian.

"I can believe it," the woman said.

After this Jocelyn and Rose prefaced many remarks with: *I'm no prude, but.*

"I'm no prude but would you look at this pudding!"

"I'm no prude but it feels like this kid has a full set of teeth."

The nurse said, wasn't it time for them to grow up?

Walking in the halls, Jocelyn told Rose that she was twenty-five, that her baby was to be called Adam, that she had a two-year-old boy at home, named Jerome, that her husband's name was Clifford and that he played the violin for a living. He played in the Vancouver Symphony. They were poor. Jocelyn came from Massachusetts and had gone to Wellesley College. Her father was a psychiatrist and her mother was a pediatrician. Rose told Jocelyn that she came from a small town in Ontario and that Patrick came from Vancouver Island and that his parents did not approve of the marriage.

"In the town I come from," Rose said, exaggerating, "everybody says yez. What'll yez have? How're yez doin."

"Yez?"

"Youse. It's the plural of you."

"Oh. Like Brooklyn. And James Joyce. Who does Patrick work for?"

"His family's store. His family has a department store."

"So aren't you rich now? Aren't you too rich to be in the ward?"

"We just spent all our money on a house Patrick wanted."

"Didn't you want it?"

"Not so much as he did."

That was something Rose had never said before.

They plunged into more random revelations.

Jocelyn hated her mother. Her mother had made her sleep in a room with white organdy curtains and had encouraged her to collect ducks. By the time she was thirteen Jocelyn had probably the largest collection in the world of rubber ducks, ceramic ducks, wooden ducks, pictures of ducks, embroidered ducks. She had also written what she described as a hideously precocious story called "The Marvelous Great Adventures of Oliver the Grand Duck," which her mother actually got printed and distributed to friends and relatives at Christmas time.

"She is the sort of person who just covers everything with a kind of rotten smarminess. She sort of oozes over everything. She never talks in a normal voice, never. She's coy. She's just so filthy coy. Naturally she's a great success as a pediatrician. She has these rotten coy little names for all the parts of your body."

Rose, who would have been delighted with organdy curtains, perceived the fine lines, the ways of giving offence, that existed in Jocelyn's world. It seemed a much less crude and provisional world than her own. She doubted if she could tell Jocelyn about Hanratty but she began to try. She delivered Flo and the store in broad strokes. She played up the poverty. She didn't really have to. The true facts of her childhood were exotic enough to Jocelyn, and of all things, enviable.

"It seems more real," Jocelyn said. "I know that's a romantic notion."

They talked of their youthful ambitions. (They really believed their youth to be past.) Rose said she had wanted to be an actress though she was too much of a coward ever to walk on a stage. Jocelyn had wanted to be a writer but was shamed out of it by memories of the Grand Duck.

"Then I met Clifford," she said. "When I saw what real talent was, I knew that I would probably just be fooling around, trying to write, and I'd be better off nurturing him, or whatever the hell it is I do for him. He is really gifted.

Sometimes he's a squalid sort of person. He gets away with it because he is really gifted."

"I think *that* is a romantic notion," Rose said firmly and jealously. "That gifted people ought to get away with things."

"Do you? But great artists always have."

"Not women."

"But women usually aren't great artists, not in the same way."

These were the ideas of most well-educated, thoughtful, even unconventional or politically radical young women of the time. One of the reasons Rose did not share them was that she had not been well educated. Jocelyn said to her, much later in their friendship, that one of the reasons she found it so interesting to talk to Rose, from the start, was that Rose had ideas but was uneducated. Rose was surprised at this, and mentioned the college she had attended in Western Ontario. Then she saw by an embarrassed withdrawal or regret, a sudden lack of frankness in Jocelyn's face – very unusual with her – that that was exactly what Jocelyn had meant.

After the difference of opinion about artists, and about men and women artists, Rose took a good look at Clifford when he came visiting in the evening. She thought him wan, self-indulgent, and neurotic-looking. Further discoveries concerning the tact, the effort, the sheer physical energy Jocelyn expended on this marriage (it was she who fixed the leaky taps and dug up the clogged drains) made Rose certain that Jocelyn was wasting herself, she was mistaken. She had a feeling that Jocelyn did not see much point in marriage with Patrick, either.

At first the party was easier than Rose had expected. She had been afraid that she would be too dressed-up; she would have liked to wear her toreador pants but Patrick would never have stood for it. But only a few of the girls were in slacks. The rest wore stockings, earrings, outfits much like her own. As at any gathering of young women at that time, three or four were noticeably pregnant. And most of the men were in suits and shirts and ties, like Patrick. Rose was relieved. Not only did she want Patrick to fit into the party; she wanted him to accept the people there, to be convinced they were not all freaks. When Patrick was a student he had taken her to concerts and plays and did not seem overly suspicious of the people who participated in them; indeed he rather favored these things, because they were detested by his family, and at that time – the time he chose Rose – he was having a brief rebellion against his family. Once he and Rose had gone to Toronto and sat in the Chinese temple room at the Museum, looking at the frescoes. Patrick told her how they were brought in small pieces from Shansi province; he seemed quite proud of his knowledge, and at the same time disarmingly, uncharacteristically humble, admitting he had got it all on a tour. It was since he had gone to work that he had developed harsh opinions and delivered wholesale condemnations. Modern Art was a Hoax. Avant-garde plays were filthy. Patrick had a special, mincing, spitting way of saying avant-garde, making the words seem disgustingly pretentious. And so they were, Rose thought. In a way, she could see what he meant. She could see too many sides of things; Patrick had not that problem.

Except for some great periodic fights she was very docile with Patrick, she tried to keep in favor. It was not easy to do so. Even before they were married he had a habit of delivering reproving lectures, in response to a simple question or observation. Sometimes in those days she would ask him a question in the hope that he would show off some superior knowledge that she could admire him for, but she was usually sorry she had asked, the answer was so long and had such a scolding tone, and the knowledge wouldn't be so superior, either. She did want to admire him, and respect him; it seemed that was a leap she was always on the edge of taking.

Later she thought that she did respect Patrick, but not in the way he wanted to be respected, and she did love him, not in the way he wanted to be loved. She didn't know it then. She thought she knew something about him, she thought she knew that he didn't really want to be whatever he was zealously making himself into. That arrogance might be called respect; that highhandedness, love. It didn't do anything to make him happy.

A few men wore jeans and turtlenecks or sweatshirts. Clifford was one of them, all in black. It was the time of the beatniks in San Francisco. Jocelyn had called Rose up on the phone and read her *Howl*. Clifford's skin looked very tanned, against the black, his hair was long for the time and almost as light a color as unbleached cotton; his eyes too were very light in color, a bright gray-blue. He looked small and cat-like to Rose, rather effeminate; she hoped Patrick wouldn't be too put off by him.

There was beer to drink, and a wine punch. Jocelyn, who was a splendid cook, was stirring a pot of jambalaya. Rose made a trip to the bathroom to remove herself from Patrick, who seemed to want to stick close to her (she thought he was being a watchdog; she forgot that he might be shy). When she came out he had moved on. She drank three cups of punch in quick succession and was introduced to the woman who had written the play. To Rose's surprise this woman was one of the drabbest, least confident-looking people in the room.

"I liked your play," Rose told her. As a matter of fact she had found it mystifying, and Patrick had thought it was revolting. It seemed to be about a woman who ate her own children. Rose knew that was symbolic, but couldn't quite figure out what it was symbolic of.

"Oh, but the production was terrible!" the woman said. In her embarrassment, her excitement and eagerness to talk about her play, she sprayed Rose with punch. "They made it so literal. I was afraid it would just come across as gruesome and I meant it to be quite delicate, I meant it to be so different from the way they made it." She started telling Rose everything that had gone wrong, the miscasting, the chopping of the most important – the *crucial* – lines. Rose felt flattered, listening to these details, and tried inconspicuously to wipe away the spray.

"But you did see what I meant?" the woman said.

"Oh, yes!"

Clifford poured Rose another cup of punch and smiled at her.

"Rose, you look delicious."

Delicious seemed an odd word for Clifford to use. Perhaps he was drunk. Or perhaps, hating parties altogether as Jocelyn said he did, he had taken on a role; he was the sort of man who told a girl she looked delicious. He might be adept at disguises, as Rose thought she herself was getting to be. She went on talking to the writer and a man who taught English Literature of the Seventeenth Century. She too might have been poor and clever, radical and irreverent, for all anybody could tell.

A man and a girl were embracing passionately in the narrow hall. Whenever anybody wanted to get through, this couple had to separate, but they continued looking at each other, and did not even close their mouths. The sight of those wet open mouths made Rose shiver. She had never been embraced like that in her life, never had her mouth opened like that. Patrick thought French-kissing was disgusting.

A little bald man named Cyril had stationed himself outside the bathroom door, and was kissing any girl who came out, saying, "Welcome, sweetheart, so glad you could come, so glad you went."

"Cyril is awful," the woman writer said. "Cyril thinks he has to try to act like a poet. He can't think of anything to do but hang around the john and upset people. He thinks he's outrageous."

"Is he a poet?" Rose said.

The lecturer in English Literature said, "He told me he had burned all his poems."

"How flamboyant of him," Rose said. She was delighted with herself for saying this, and with them for laughing.

The lecturer began to think of Tom Swifties.

"I can never think of any of those things," said the writer mournfully, "I care too much about language."

Loud voices were coming from the living room. Rose recognized Patrick's voice, soaring over and subduing everyone else's. She opened her mouth to say something, anything, to cover him up – she knew some disaster was on the way – but just then a tall, curly-haired, elated-looking man came through the hall, pushing the passionate couple unceremoniously apart, holding up his hands for attention.

"Listen to this," he said to the whole kitchen. "There's this guy in the living room you wouldn't believe him. Listen."

There must have been a conversation about Indians going on in the living room. Now Patrick had taken it over.

"Take them away," said Patrick. "Take them away from their parents as soon as they're born and put them in a civilized environment and educate them and they will turn out just as good as whites any day." No doubt he thought he was expressing liberal views. If they thought this was amazing, they should have got him on the execution of the Rosenbergs or the trial of Alger Hiss or the necessity for nuclear testing.

Some girl said mildly, "Well, you know, there is their own culture."

"Their culture is done for," said Patrick. "Kaput." This was a word he was using a good deal right now. He could use some words, clichés, editorial phrases – *massive reappraisal* was one of them – with such relish and numbing authority that you would think he was their originator, or at least that the very fact of his using them gave them weight and luster.

"They want to be civilized," he said. "The smarter ones do."

"Well, perhaps they don't consider they're exactly uncivilized," said the girl with an icy demureness that was lost on Patrick.

"Some people need a push."

The self-congratulatory tones, the ripe admonishment, caused the man in the kitchen to throw up his hands, and wag his head in delight and disbelief. "This has got to be a Socred politician."

As a matter of fact Patrick did vote Social Credit.

"Yes, well, like it or not," he was saying, "they have to be dragged kicking and screaming into the twentieth century."

"Kicking and screaming?" someone repeated.

"Kicking and screaming into the twentieth century," said Patrick, who never minded saying anything again.

"What an interesting expression. So humane as well."

Wouldn't he understand now, that he was being cornered, being baited and laughed at? But Patrick, being cornered, could only grow more thunderous. Rose could not listen any longer. She headed for the back passage, which was full of all the boots, coats, bottles, tubs, toys, that Jocelyn and Clifford had pitched out of the way for the party. Thank God it was empty of people. She went out of the back door and stood burning and shivering in the cool wet night. Her feelings were as confused as anybody's can get. She was humiliated, she was ashamed of Patrick. But she knew that it was his style that most humiliated her, and that made her suspect something corrupt and frivolous in herself. She was angry at those other people who were cleverer, or at least far quicker, than he was. She wanted to think badly of them. What did they care about Indians, really? Given a chance to behave decently to an Indian, Patrick might just come out ahead of them. This was a long shot, but she had to believe it. Patrick was a good person. His opinions were not good, but he was. The core of

Patrick, Rose believed, was simple, pure and trustworthy. But how was she to get at it, to reassure herself, much less reveal it to others?

She heard the back door close and was afraid that Jocelyn had come out looking for her. Jocelyn was not someone who could believe in Patrick's core. She thought him stiff-necked, thick-skulled, and essentially silly.

It was not Jocelyn. It was Clifford. Rose didn't want to have to say anything to him. Slightly drunk as she was, woebegone, wet-faced from the rain, she looked at him without welcome. But he put his arms around her and rocked her.

"Oh Rose. Rose baby. Never mind. Rose."

So this was Clifford.

For five minutes or so they were kissing, murmuring, shivering, pressing, touching. They returned to the party by the front door. Cyril was there. He said, "Hey, wow, where have you two been?"

"Walking in the rain," said Clifford coolly. The same light possibly hostile voice in which he had told Rose she looked delicious. The Patrick-baiting had stopped. Conversation had become looser, drunker, more irresponsible. Jocelyn was serving jambalaya. She went to the bathroom to dry her hair and put lipstick on her rubbed-bare mouth. She was transformed, invulnerable. The first person she met coming out was Patrick. She had a wish to make him happy. She didn't care now what he had said, or would say.

"I don't think we've met, sir," she said, in a tiny flirtatious voice she used with him sometimes, when they were feeling easy together. "But you may kiss my hand."

"For crying out loud," said Patrick heartily, and he did squeeze her and kiss her, with a loud smacking noise, on the cheek. He always smacked when he kissed. And his elbows always managed to dig in somewhere and hurt her.

"Enjoying yourself?" Rose said.

"Not bad, not bad."

During the rest of the evening, of course, she was playing the game of watching Clifford while pretending not to watch him, and it seemed to her he was doing the same, and their eyes met, a few times, without expressions sending a perfectly clear message that rocked her on her feet. She saw him quite differently now. His body that had seemed small and tame now appeared to her light and slippery and full of energy; he was like a lynx or a bobcat. He had his tan from skiing. He went up Seymour Mountain and skied. An expensive hobby, but one which Jocelyn felt could not be denied him, because of the problems he had with his image. His masculine image, as a violinist, in this society. So Jocelyn said. Jocelyn had told Rose all about Clifford's background: the arthritic father, the small grocery store in a town in upstate New York, the poor tough neighborhood. She had talked about his problems as a child; the inappropriate talent, the grudging parents, the jeering schoolmates. His childhood left him bitter, Jocelyn said. But Rose no longer believed that Jocelyn had the last word on Clifford.

The party was on a Friday night. The phone rang the next morning, when Patrick and Anna were at the table eating eggs.

"How are you?" said Clifford.

"Fine."

"I wanted to phone you. I thought you might think I was just drunk or something. I wasn't."

"Oh, no."

"I've thought about you all night. I thought about you before, too."

"Yes." The kitchen was dazzling. The whole scene in front of her, of Patrick and Anna at the table, the coffee pot with dribbles down the side, the jar of marmalade, was exploding with joy and possibility and danger. Rose's mouth was so dry she could hardly talk.

"It's a lovely day," she said. "Patrick and Anna and I might go up the mountain."

"Patrick's home?"

"Yes."

"Oh God. That was dumb of me. I forgot nobody else works Saturdays. I'm over here at a rehearsal."

"Yes."

"Can you pretend it's somebody else? Pretend it's Jocelyn."

"Sure."

"I love you, Rose," said Clifford, and hung up.

"Who was that?" said Patrick.

"Jocelyn."

"Does she have to call when I'm home?"

"She forgot. Clifford's at a rehearsal so she forgot other people aren't working." Rose delighted in saying Clifford's name. Deceitfulness, concealment, seemed to come marvelously easy to her; that might almost be a pleasure in itself.

"I didn't realize they'd have to work Saturdays," she said, to keep on the subject. "They must work terribly long hours."

"They don't work any longer hours than normal people, it's just strung out differently. He doesn't look capable of much work."

"He's supposed to be quite good. As a violinist."

"He looks like a jerk."

"Do you think so?"

"Don't you?"

"I guess I never considered him, really."

Jocelyn phoned on Monday and said she didn't know why she gave parties, she was still wading through the mess.

"Didn't Clifford help clean it up?"

"You are joking. I hardly saw him all weekend. He rehearsed Saturday and played yesterday. He says parties are my idea, I can deal with the aftermath. It's true. I get these fits of gregariousness, a party is the only cure. Patrick was interesting."

"Very."

"He's quite a stunning type, really, isn't he?"

"There are lots and lots like him. You just don't get to meet them."

"Woe is me."

This was just like any other conversation with Jocelyn. Their conversations, their friendship, could go on in the same way. Rose did not feel bound by any loyalty to Jocelyn because she had divided Clifford. There was the Clifford Jocelyn knew, the same one she had always presented to Rose; there was also the Clifford Rose knew, now. She thought Jocelyn could be mistaken about him. For instance, when she said his childhood had left him bitter. What Jocelyn called bitterness seemed to Rose something more complex and more ordinary; just the weariness, suppleness, deviousness, meanness, common to a class. Common to Clifford's class, and Rose's. Jocelyn had been insulated in some ways, left stern and innocent. In some ways she was like Patrick.

From now on Rose did see Clifford and herself as being one sort of people, and Jocelyn and Patrick, though they seemed so different, and so disliked each other, as being another sort. They were whole and predictable. They took the lives they were leading absolutely seriously. Compared to them, both Clifford and Rose were shifty pieces of business.

If Jocelyn fell in love with a married man, what would she do? Before she even touched his hand, she would probably call a conference. Clifford would be invited, and the man himself, and the man's wife, and very likely Jocelyn's psychiatrist. (In spite of her rejection of her family Jocelyn believed that going to a psychiatrist was something everybody should do at developing or adjusting stages of life and she went herself, once a week.) Jocelyn would consider the implications; she would look things in the face. Never try to sneak her pleasure. She had never learned to sneak things. That was why it was unlikely that she would ever fall in love with another man. She was not greedy. And Patrick was not greedy either now, at least not for love.

If loving Patrick was recognizing something good, and guileless, at the bottom of him, being in love with Clifford was something else altogether. Rose did not have to believe that Clifford was good, and certainly she knew he was not guileless. No revelation of his duplicity or heartlessness, towards people other than herself, could have mattered to her. What was she in love with, then, what did she want of him? She wanted tricks, a glittering secret, tender celebrations of lust, a regular conflagration of adultery. All this after five minutes in the rain.

Six months or so after that party Rose lay awake all night. Patrick slept beside her in their stone and cedar house in a suburb called Capilano Heights, on the side of Grouse Mountain. The next night it was arranged that Clifford would sleep beside her, in Powell River, where he was playing with the touring orchestra. She could not believe that this would really happen. That is, she placed all her faith in the event, but could not fit it into the order of things that she knew.

During all these months Clifford and Rose had never gone to bed together. They had not made love anywhere else, either. This was the situation: Jocelyn and Clifford did not own a car. Patrick and Rose owned a car, but Rose did not drive it. Clifford's work did have the advantage of irregular hours, but how was he to get to see Rose? Could he ride the bus across the Lions Gate Bridge, then walk up her suburban street in broad daylight, past the neighbors' picture windows? Could Rose hire a baby sitter, pretend she was going to see the dentist, take the bus over to town, meet Clifford in a restaurant, go with him to a hotel room? But they didn't know which hotel to go to; they were afraid that without luggage they would be turned out on the street, or reported to the Vice Squad, made to sit in the Police Station while Jocelyn and

Patrick were summoned to come and get them. Also, they didn't have enough money.

Rose had gone over to Vancouver, though, using the dentist excuse, and they had sat in a café, side by side in a black booth, kissing and fondling, right out in public in a place frequented by Clifford's students and fellow musicians; what a risk to take. On the bus going home Rose looked down her dress at the sweat blooming between her breasts and could have fainted at the splendor of herself, as well as at the thought of the risk undertaken. Another time, a very hot August afternoon, she waited in an alley behind the theater where Clifford was rehearsing, lurked in the shadows then grappled with him deliriously, unsatisfactorily. They saw a door open, and slipped inside. There were boxes stacked all around. They were looking for some nesting spot when a man spoke to them.

"Can I do anything for you?"

They had entered the back storeroom of a shoe store. The man's voice was icy, terrifying. The Vice Squad. The Police Station. Rose's dress was undone to the waist.

Once they met in a park, where Rose often took Anna, and pushed her on the swings. They held hands on a bench, under cover of Rose's wide cotton skirt. They laced their fingers together and squeezed painfully. Then Anna surprised them, coming up behind the bench and shouting, "Boo! I caught you!" Clifford turned disastrously pale. On the way home Rose said to Anna, "That was funny when you jumped out behind the bench. I thought you were still on the swing."

"I know," said Anna.

"What did you mean, you'd caught us?"

"I *caught* you," said Anna, and giggled, in what seemed to Rose a disturbingly pert and knowledgeable way.

"Would you like a fudgsicle? I would!" Rose said gaily, with thoughts of blackmail and bargains, Anna dredging this up for *her* psychiatrist in twenty years' time. The episode made her feel shaky and sick and she wondered if it had given Clifford a distaste for her. It had, but only temporarily.

As soon as it was light she got out of bed and went to look at the day, to see if it would be good for flying. The sky was clear; no sign of the fog that often grounded planes at this time of year. Nobody but Clifford knew she was going to Powell River. They had been planning this for six weeks, ever since they knew he was going on tour. Patrick thought she was going to Victoria, where she had a friend whom she had known at college. She had pretended, during the past few weeks, to have been in touch with this friend again. She had said she would be back tomorrow night. Today was Saturday. Patrick was at home to look after Anna.

She went into the dining room to check the money she had saved from Family Allowance checks. It was in the bottom of the silver muffin dish. Thirteen dollars. She meant to add that to what Patrick gave her to get to Victoria. Patrick always gave her money when she asked, but he wanted to know how much and what for. Once when they were out walking she wanted to go into a drugstore; she asked him for money and he said, with no more than customary sternness, "What for?" and Rose began to cry, because she had been going to buy vaginal jelly. She might just as well have laughed, and would have, now. Since she had fallen in love with Clifford, she never quarreled with Patrick.

She figured out again the money she would need. The plane ticket, the money for the airport bus, from Vancouver, and for the bus or maybe it would have to be a taxi into Powell River, something left over for food and coffee. Clifford would pay for the hotel. The thought filled her with sexual comfort, submissiveness, though she knew Jerome needed new glasses, Adam needed rubber boots. She thought of that neutral, smooth, generous bed, which already existed, was waiting for them. Long ago when she was a young girl (she was now twenty-three) she had often thought of bland rented beds and locked doors, with such luxuriant hopes, and now she did again, though for a time in between, before and after she was married, the thought of anything connected with sex irritated her, rather in the way Modern Art irritated Patrick.

She walked around the house softly, planning her day as a series of actions. Take a bath, oil and powder herself, put her diaphragm and jelly in her purse. Remember the money. Mascara, face cream, lipstick. She stood at the top of the two steps leading down into the living room. The walls of the living room were moss green, the fireplace was white, the curtains and slipcovers had a silky pattern of gray and green and yellow leaves on a white background. On the mantel were two Wedgwood vases, white with a circlet of green leaves. Patrick was very fond of these vases. Sometimes when he came home from work he went straight into the living room and shifted them around a bit on the mantel, thinking their symmetrical position had been disturbed.

"Has anybody been fooling around with these vases?"

"Well of course. As soon as you leave for work I rush in and juggle them around."

"I meant Anna. You don't let her touch them, do you?"

Patrick didn't like to hear her refer to the vases in any joking way. He thought she didn't appreciate the house. He didn't know, but maybe could guess what she had said to Jocelyn, the first time Jocelyn came here, and they were standing where Rose stood now, looking down at the living room.

"The department store heir's dream of elegance."

At this treachery even Jocelyn looked abashed. It was not exactly true. Patrick dreamed of getting much more elegant. And it was not true in the implication that it had all been Patrick's choice, and that Rose had always held aloof from it. It had been Patrick's choice, but there were a lot of things she had liked at one time. She used to climb up and polish the glass drops of the dining-room chandelier, using a cloth dipped in water and baking soda. She liked the chandelier; its drops had a blue or lilac cast. But people she admired would not have chandeliers in their dining rooms. It was unlikely that they would have dining rooms. If they did, they would have thin white candles stuck into the branches of a black metal candleholder, made in Scandinavia. Or else they would have heavy candles in wine bottles, loaded with drippings of colored wax. The people she admired were inevitably poorer than she was. It seemed a bad joke on her, after being poor all her life in a place where poverty was never anything to be proud of, that now she had to feel apologetic and embarrassed about the opposite condition – with someone like Jocelyn, for instance, who could say *middle-class prosperity* so viciously and despisingly.

But if she hadn't been exposed to other people, if she hadn't learned from Jocelyn, would she still have liked the house? No. She must have been souring on it, anyway. When people came to visit for the first time Patrick always took them on a tour, pointing out the chandelier, the powder room with concealed lighting, by the front door, the walk-in closets and the louvered doors opening on to the patio. He was as proud of this house, as eager to call attention to its small distinctions, as if he, not Rose, had grown up poor. Rose had been uneasy about these tours from the start, and tagged along in silence, or made deprecating remarks which Patrick did not like. After a while she stayed in the kitchen, but she could still hear Patrick's voice and she knew beforehand everything he would say. She knew that he would pull the dining-room curtains and point to the small illuminated fountain – Neptune with a fig-leaf – he had put in the garden, and then he would say,

"Now there is our answer to the suburban swimming-pool mania!"

After she bathed she reached for a bottle of what she thought was baby oil, to pour over her body. The clear liquid ran down over her breasts and belly, stinging and burning. She looked at the label and saw that this was not baby oil at all, it was nail polish remover. She scrubbed it off, splashed herself with cold water, towelled desperately, thinking of ruined skin, the hospital; grafts, scars, punishment.

Anna was scratching sleepily but urgently at the bathroom door. Rose had locked it, for this preparation, though she didn't usually lock it when she took a bath. She let Anna in.

"Your front is all red," Anna said, as she hoisted herself on to the toilet. Rose found the baby oil and tried to cool herself with it. She used too much, and got oily spots on her new brassiere.

She had thought Clifford might write to her while he was touring, but he did not. He called her from Prince George, and was businesslike.

"When do you get into Powell River?"

"Four o'clock."

"Okay, take the bus or whatever they have into town. Have you ever been there?"

"No."

"Neither have I. I only know the name of our hotel. You can't wait there."

"How about the bus depot? Every town has a bus depot."

"Okay, the bus depot. I'll pick you up there probably about five o'clock, and we can get you into some other hotel. I hope to God there's more than one. Okay then."

He was pretending to the other members of the orchestra that he was spending the night with friends in Powell River.

"I could go and hear you play," Rose said. "Couldn't I?"

"Well. Sure."

"I'd be very inconspicuous. I'd sit at the back. I'll disguise myself as an old lady. I love to hear you play."

"Okay."

"You don't mind?"

"No."

"Clifford?"

"Yes?"

"You still want me to come?"

"Oh, Rose."

"I know. It's just the way you sound."

"I'm in the hotel lobby. They're waiting for me. I'm supposed to be talking to Jocelyn."

"Okay. I know. I'll come."

"Powell River. The bus depot. Five o'clock."

This was different from their usual telephone conversations. Usually they were plaintive and silly; or else they worked each other up so that they could not talk at all.

"Heavy breathing there."

"I know."

"We'll have to talk about something else."

"What else is there?"

"Is it foggy where you are?"

"Yes. Is it foggy where you are too?"

"Yes. Can you hear the foghorn?"

"Yes."

"Isn't it a horrible sound?"

"I don't mind it, really. I sort of like it."

"Jocelyn doesn't. You know how she describes it? She says it's the sound of a cosmic boredom."

They had at first avoided speaking of Jocelyn and Patrick at all. Then they spoke of them in a crisp practical way, as if they were adults, parents, to be outwitted. Now they could mention them almost tenderly, admiringly, as if they were their children.

There was no bus depot in Powell River. Rose got into the airport limousine with four other passengers, all men, and told the driver she wanted to go to the bus depot.

"You know where that is?"

"No," she said. Already she felt them all watching her.

"Did you want to catch a bus?"

"No."

"Just wanted to go to the bus depot?"

"I planned to meet somebody there."

"I didn't even know there was a bus depot here," said one of the passengers.

"There isn't, that I know of," said the driver. "Now there is a bus, it goes down to Vancouver in the morning and it comes back at night, and it stops at the old men's home. The old loggers' home. That's where it stops. All I can do is take you there. Is that all right?"

Rose said it would be fine. Then she felt she had to go on explaining.

"My friend and I just arranged to meet there because we couldn't think where else. We don't know Powell River at all and we just thought, every town has a bus depot!"

She was thinking that she shouldn't have said *my friend*, she should have said *my husband*. They were going to ask her what she and her friend were doing here if neither of them knew the town.

"My friend is playing in the orchestra that's giving a concert here tonight. She plays the violin."

All looked away from her, as if that was what a lie deserved. She was trying to remember if there was a female violinist. What if they should ask her name?

The driver let her off in front of a long two-story wooden building with peeling paint.

"I guess you could go in the sunporch, there at the end. That's where the bus picks them up, anyway."

In the sunporch there was a pool table. Nobody was playing. Some old men were playing checkers; others watched. Rose thought of explaining herself to them but decided not to; they seemed mercifully uninterested. She was worn out by her explanations in the limousine.

It was ten past four by the sunporch clock. She thought she could put in the time till five by walking around the town.

As soon as she went outside she noticed a bad smell, and became worried, thinking it might come from herself. She got out the stick cologne she had bought in the Vancouver airport – spending money she could not afford – and rubbed it on her wrists and neck. The smell persisted, and at last she realized it came from the pulp mills. The town was difficult to walk around in because the streets were so steep, and in many places there was no sidewalk. There was no place to loiter. She thought people stared at her, recognizing a stranger. Some men in a car yelled at her. She saw her own reflection in store windows and understood that she looked as if she wanted to be stared at and yelled at. She was wearing black velvet toreador pants, a tight-fitting high-necked black sweater and a beige jacket which she slung over her shoulder, though there was a chilly wind. She who had once chosen full skirts and soft colors, babyish angora sweaters, scalloped necklines, had now taken to wearing dramatic sexually advertising clothes. The new underwear she had on at this moment was black lace and pink nylon. In the waiting room at the Vancouver airport she had done her eyes with heavy mascara, black eyeliner, and silver eyeshadow; her lipstick was almost white. All this was a fashion of those years and so looked less ghastly than it would seem later, but it was alarming enough. The assurance with which she carried such a disguise fluctuated considerably. She would not have dared parade it in front of Patrick or Jocelyn. When she went to see Jocelyn she always wore her baggiest slacks and sweaters. Nevertheless when she opened the door Jocelyn would say, "Hello, Sexy," in a tone of friendly scorn. Jocelyn herself had become spectacularly unkempt. She dressed exclusively in old clothes of Clifford's. Old pants that didn't quite zip up on her because her stomach had never flattened out after Adam, and frayed white shirts Clifford had once worn for performances. Apparently Jocelyn thought the whole business of keeping your figure and wearing makeup and trying to look in any way seductive was sourly amusing, beneath contempt; it was like vacuuming the curtains. She said that Clifford felt the same way. Clifford, reported Jocelyn, was attracted by the very absence of female artifice and trappings; he liked unshaved legs and hairy armpits and natural smells. Rose wondered if Clifford had really said this, and why. Out of pity, or comradeliness; or as a joke?

Rose found a public library and went in and looked at the titles of the books, but she could not pay attention. There was a fairly incapacitating though not unpleasant buzzing throughout her head and body. At twenty to five she was back in the sunporch, waiting.

She was still waiting at ten past six. She had counted the money in her purse. A dollar and sixty-three cents. She could not go to a hotel. She did not think they would let her stay in the sunporch all night. There was nothing at all that she could do except pray that Clifford might still arrive. She did not believe he would. The schedule had been changed; he had been summoned home because one of the children was sick; he had broken his wrist and couldn't play the violin; Powell River was not a real place at all but a bad-smelling mirage where guilty travelers were trapped for punishment. She wasn't really surprised. She had made the jump that wasn't to be made, and this was how she had landed.

Before the old men went in to supper she asked them if they knew of a concert being given that night in the high school auditorium. They answered grudgingly, no.

"Never heard of them giving no concerts here."

She said that her husband was playing in the orchestra, it was on tour from Vancouver, she had flown up to meet him; she was supposed to meet him here.

Here?

"Maybe got lost," said one of the old men in what seemed to her a spiteful, knowing way. "Maybe your husband got lost, heh? Husbands always getting lost!"

It was nearly dark out. This was October, and further north than Vancouver. She tried to think what to do. The only thing that occurred to her was to pretend to pass out, then claim loss of memory. Would Patrick ever believe that? She would have to say she had no idea what she was doing in Powell River. She would have to say she didn't remember anything she had said in the limousine, didn't know anything about the orchestra. She would have to convince policemen and doctors, be written about in the newspapers. Oh, where was Clifford, why had he abandoned her, could there have been an accident on the road? She thought she should destroy the piece of paper in her purse, on which she had written his instructions. She thought that she had better get rid of her diaphragm as well.

She was going through her purse when a van parked outside. She thought it must be a police van; she thought the old men must have phoned up and reported her as a suspicious character.

Clifford got out and came running up the sunporch steps. It took her a moment to recognize him.

They had beer and hamburgers in one of the hotels, a different hotel from the one where the orchestra was staying. Rose's hands were shaking so that she slopped the beer. There had been a rehearsal he hadn't counted on, Clifford said. Then he had been about half an hour looking for the bus depot.

"I guess it wasn't such a bright idea, the bus depot."

Her hand was lying on the table. He wiped the beer off with a napkin, then put his own hand over hers. She thought of this often, afterwards.

"We better get you checked in here."

"Don't we check in together?"

"Better if it's just you."

"Ever since I got here," Rose said, "it has been so peculiar. It has been so sinister. I felt everybody knew." She started telling him, in what she hoped was an entertaining way, about the limousine driver, the other passengers, the old men in the Loggers' Home. "It was such a relief when you showed up, such a terrible relief. That's why I'm shaking." She told him about her plan to fake amnesia and the realization that she had better throw her diaphragm away. He laughed, but without delight, she thought. It seemed to her that when she spoke of the diaphragm his lips tightened, in reproof or distaste.

"But it's lovely now," she said hastily. This was the longest conversation they had ever had, face to face.

"It was just your guilt-feelings," he said. "Which are natural."

He stroked her hand. She tried to rub her finger on his pulse, as they used to do. He let go.

Half an hour later, she was saying, "Is it all right if I still go to the concert?"

"Do you still want to?"

"What else is there to do?"

She shrugged as she said this. Her eyelids were lowered, her lips full and brooding. She was doing some sort of imitation, of Barbara Stanwyck perhaps, in similar circumstances. She didn't intend to do an imitation, of course. She was trying to find some way to be so enticing, so aloof and enticing, that she would make him change his mind.

"The thing is, I have to get the van back. I have to pick up the other guys."

"I can walk. Tell me where it is."

"Uphill from here, I'm afraid."

"That won't hurt me."

"Rose. It's much better this way, Rose. It really is."

"If you say so." She couldn't manage another shrug. She still thought there must be some way to turn things around and start again. Start again; set right whatever she had said or done wrong; make none of this true. She had already made the mistake of asking what she had said or done wrong and he had said, nothing. Nothing. She had nothing to do with it, he said. It was being away from home for a month that had made him see everything differently. Jocelyn. The children. The damage.

"It's only mischief," he said.

He had got his hair cut shorter than she had ever seen it. His tan had faded. Indeed, indeed, he looked as if he had shed a skin, and it was the skin that had hankered after hers. He was again the pale, and rather irritable, but dutiful, young husband she had observed paying visits to Jocelyn in the maternity ward.

"What is?"

"What we're doing. It's not some big necessary thing. It's ordinary mischief."

"You called me from Prince George." Barbara Stanwyck had vanished, Rose heard herself begin to whine.

"I know I did." He spoke like a nagged husband.

"Did you feel like this then?"

"Yes and no. We'd made all the plans. Wouldn't it have been worse if I'd told you on the phone?"

"What do you mean, mischief?"

"Oh, Rose."

"What do you mean?"

"You know what I mean. If we went ahead with this, what good do you think it would do anybody? Rose? Really?"

"Us," Rose said. "It would do us good."

"No it wouldn't. It would end up in one big mess."

"Just once."

"No."

"You said just once. You said we would have a memory instead of a dream."

"Jesus. I said a lot of puke."

He had said her tongue was like a little warm-blooded snake, a pretty snake, and her nipples like berries. He would not care to be reminded.

Overture to Ruslan and Ludmilla: Glinka
Serenade for Strings: Tchaikovsky
Beethoven's Sixth Symphony, the Pastoral: First Movement
The Moldau: Smetana
William Tell Overture: Rossini

She could not hear any of this music for a long time without a specific attack of shame, that was like a whole wall crumbling in on her, rubble choking her.

Just before Clifford left on tour, Jocelyn had phoned Rose and said that her baby sitter could not come. It was the day she went to see her psychiatrist. Rose offered to come and look after Adam and Jerome. She had done this before. She made the long trip on three buses, taking Anna with her.

Jocelyn's house was heated by an oil stove in the kitchen, and an enormous stone fireplace in the small living room. The oil stove was covered with spill-marks; orange peel and coffee grounds and charred wood and ashes tumbled out of the fireplace. There was no basement and no clothes dryer. The weather was rainy, and the ceiling-racks and stand-up racks were draped with damp graying sheets and diapers, hardening towels. There was no washing machine either. Jocelyn had washed those sheets in the bathtub.

"No washer or dryer but she's going to a psychiatrist," said Patrick, to whom Rose sometimes disloyally reported what she knew he would like to hear.

"She must be crazy," Rose said. She made him laugh.

But Patrick didn't like her going to baby-sit.

"You're certainly at her beck and call," he said. "It's a wonder you don't go and scrub her floors for her."

As a matter of fact, Rose did.

When Jocelyn was there, the disorder of the house had a certain willed and impressive quality. When she was gone, it became unbearable. Rose would go to work with a knife, scraping at ancient crusts of Pablum on the kitchen chairs, scouring the coffee pot, wiping the floor. She did spare some time for investigation. She went into the bedroom – she had to watch out for Jerome, a precocious and irritating child – and looked at Clifford's socks and underwear, all crumpled in with Jocelyn's old nursing brassieres and torn garter belts. She looked to see if he had a record on the turntable, wondering if it would be something that would make him think of her.

Telemann. Not likely. But she played it, to hear what he had been hearing. She drank coffee from what she believed to be his dirty breakfast cup. She covered the casserole of Spanish rice from which he had taken his supper the night before. She sought out traces of his presence (he didn't use an electric razor, he used old-fashioned shaving soap in a wooden bowl), but she believed that his life in that house, Jocelyn's house, was all pretense, and waiting, like her own life in Patrick's house.

When Jocelyn came home Rose felt she ought to apologize for the cleaning she had done, and Jocelyn, really wanting to talk about her fight with the psychiatrist who reminded her of her mother, agreed that it certainly was a cowardly mania, this thing Rose had about housecleaning, and she had better go to a psych herself, if she ever wanted to get rid of it. She was joking; but going home on the bus, with Anna cranky and no preparations made for Patrick's supper, Rose did wonder why she always seemed to be on the wrong end of things, disapproved of by her own neighbors because she didn't pay enough attention to housework, and reproved by Jocelyn for being insufficiently tolerant of the natural chaos and refuse of life. She thought of love, to reconcile herself. She was loved, not in a dutiful, husbandly way but crazily, adulterously, as Jocelyn and her neighbors were not. She used that to reconcile herself to all sorts of things: to Patrick, for instance, turning over in bed with an indulgent little clucking noise that meant she was absolved of all her failings for the moment, they were to make love.

The sane and decent things Clifford had said cut no ice with Rose at all. She saw that he had betrayed her. Sanity and decency were never what she had asked of him. She watched him, in the auditorium of the Powell River High School. She watched him playing his violin, with a somber and attentive expression she had once seen directed towards herself. She did not see how she could do without.

In the middle of the night she phoned him, from her hotel to his.

"Please talk to me."

"That's okay," said Clifford, after a moment's silence. "That's okay, Joss."

He must have a roommate, whom the phone might have wakened. He was pretending to talk to Jocelyn. Or else he was so sleepy he really thought she was Jocelyn.

"Clifford, it's me."

"That's okay," Clifford said. "Take it easy. Go to sleep."

He hung up the phone.

Jocelyn and Clifford are living in Toronto. They are not poor any more. Clifford is successful. His name is seen on record jackets, heard on the radio. His face and more frequently his hands have appeared on television as he labors at his violin. Jocelyn has dieted and become slender, has had her hair cut and styled; it is parted in the middle and curves away from her face, with a wing of pure white rising from each temple.

They live in a large brick house on the edge of a ravine. There are bird-feeders in the back yard. They have installed a sauna. Clifford spends a good deal of time sitting there. He thinks that will keep him from becoming arthritic, like his father. Arthritis is his greatest fear.

Rose used to go to see them sometimes. She was living in the country, by herself. She taught at a community college and liked to have a place to stay overnight when she came in to Toronto. They seemed glad to have her. They said she was their oldest friend.

One time when Rose was visiting them Jocelyn told a story about Adam. Adam had an apartment in the basement of the house. Jerome lived downtown, with his girlfriend. Adam brought his girls here.

"I was reading in the den," said Jocelyn, "when Clifford was out. I heard this girl, down in Adam's apartment, saying *no, no!* The noise from his apartment comes straight up into the den. We warned him about that, we thought he'd be embarrassed –"

"I didn't think he'd be embarrassed," said Clifford.

"But he just said, we should put on the record player. So, I kept hearing the poor unknown girl bleating and protesting, and I didn't know what to do. I thought these situations are really new, there are no precedents, are you supposed to stop your son from raping some girl if that's what he's doing, right under your nose or at least under your feet? I went downstairs eventually and I started getting all the family skis out of the closet that backs on his bedroom, I stayed there slamming those skis around, thinking I'd say I was going to polish them. It was July. Adam never said anything to me. I wish he'd move out."

Rose told about how much money Patrick had and how he had married a sensible woman even richer than he was, who had made a dazzling living room with mirrors and pale velvet and a wire sculpture like blasted bird cages. Patrick did not mind Modern Art any more.

"Of course it isn't the same," said Rose to Jocelyn, "it isn't the same house. I wonder what she has done with the Wedgwood vases."

"Maybe she has a campy laundry room. She keeps the bleach in one and the detergent in the other."

"They sit perfectly symmetrically on the shelf."

But Rose had her old, old, twinge of guilt.

"Just the same, I like Patrick."

Jocelyn said, "Why?"

"He's nicer than most people."

"Silly rot," said Jocelyn. "And I bet he doesn't like you."

"That's right," Rose said. She started to tell them about her trip down on the bus. It was one of the times when she was not driving her car, because too many things were wrong with it and she could not afford to get it fixed.

"The man in the seat across from me was telling me about how he used to drive big trucks. He said we never seen trucks in this country like they got in the States." She put on her country accent. "In the Yewnited States they got these special roads what they call turnpikes, and only trucks is allowed to go on them. They get serviced on these roads from one end of the country to the other and so most people never sees them at all. They're so big the cab is half the size of a bus and they got a driver in there and an assistant driver and another driver and another assistant driver havin a sleep. Toilet and kitchen and beds and all. They go eighty, ninety miles an hour, because there is never no speed limit on them turnpikes."

"You are getting very weird," said Clifford. "Living up there."

"Never mind the trucks," Jocelyn said. "Never mind the old mythology. Clifford wants to leave me again."

They settled down to drinking and talking about what Clifford and Jocelyn should do. This was not an unfamiliar conversation. What does Clifford really want? Does he really want not to be married to Jocelyn or does he want something unattainable? Is he going through a middle-age crisis?

"Don't be so banal," Clifford said to Rose. She was the one who said middle-age crisis. "I've been going through this ever since I was twenty-five. I've wanted out ever since I got in."

"That is new, for Clifford to say that," said Jocelyn. She went out to the kitchen to get some cheese and grapes. "For him to actually come out and say that," she yelled from the kitchen. Rose avoided looking at Clifford, not because they had any secrets but because it seemed a courtesy to Jocelyn not to look at each other while she was out of the room.

"What is happening now," said Jocelyn, coming back with a platter of cheese and grapes in one hand and a bottle of gin in the other, "is that Clifford is wide open. He used to bitch and stew and some other bilge would come out that had nothing to do with the real problem. Now he just comes out with it. The great blazing truth. It's a total illumination."

Rose had a bit of difficulty catching the tone. She felt as if living in the country had made her slow. Was Jocelyn's talk a parody, was she being sarcastic? No. She was not.

"But then I go and deflate the truth for you," said Clifford. grinning. He was drinking beer from the bottle. He thought beer was better for him than gin. "It's absolutely true I've wanted out ever since I got in. And it's also true that I wanted in, and I wanted to stay in. I wanted to be married to you and I want to be married to you and I couldn't stand being married to you and I can't stand being married to you. It's a static contradiction."

"It sounds like hell," Rose said.

"I didn't say that. I am just making the point that it is no middle-age crisis."

"Well, maybe that was oversimplifying," said Rose. Nevertheless, she said firmly, in the sensible, down-to-earth, countrified style she was adopting for the moment, all they were hearing about was Clifford. What did Clifford really want, what did Clifford need? Did he need a studio, did he need a holiday, did he need to go to Europe by himself? What made him think, she said, that Jocelyn could be endlessly concerned about his welfare? Jocelyn was not his mother.

"And it's your fault," she said to Jocelyn, "for not telling him to put up or shut up. Never mind what he really wants. Get out or shut up. That's all you need to say to him. Shut up or get out," she said to Clifford with mock gruffness. "Excuse me for being so unsubtle. Or frankly hostile."

She didn't run any risk at all by sounding hostile, and she knew it. She would run a risk by being genteel and indifferent. The way she was talking now was a proof that she was their true friend and took them seriously. And so she did, up to a point.

"She's right, you fucking son-of-a-bitch," said Jocelyn experimentally. "Shut up or get out."

When Jocelyn called Rose on the phone, years ago, to read her the poem *Howl*, she was not able, in spite of her usual boldness of speech, to say the word *fuck*. She tried to force herself, then she said, "Oh, it's stupid, but I can't say it. I'm going to have to say eff. You'll know what I mean when I say eff?"

"But she said it's your fault," said Clifford. "You want to be the mother. You want to be the grownup. You want to be long-suffering."

"Balls," said Jocelyn. "Oh, maybe. Maybe, yes. Maybe I do."

"I bet at school you were always latching on to those kids with the problems," said Clifford with his tender grin. "Those poor kids, the ones with acne or awful clothes or speech impediments. I bet you just persecuted those poor kids with friendliness."

Jocelyn picked up the cheese knife and waved it at him.

"You be careful. You haven't got acne or a speech impediment. You are sickeningly good-looking. And talented. And lucky."

"I have nearly insuperable problems coming to terms with the adult male role," said Clifford priggishly. "The psych says so."

"I don't believe you. Psychs never say anything like nearly insuperable. And they don't use that jargon. And they don't make those judgments. I don't believe you, Clifford."

"Well, I don't really go to the psych at all. I go to the dirty movies down on Yonge."

Clifford went off to sit in the sauna.

Rose watched him leave the room. He was wearing jeans, and a T-shirt that said *Just passin thru*. His waist and hips were narrow as a twelve-year-old's. His gray hair was cut in a very short brush cut, showing his skull. Was this the way musicians wore their hair nowadays, when politicians and accountants were bushy and bearded, or was it Clifford's own perversity? His tan looked like pancake makeup, though it was probably all real. There was something theatrical about him altogether, tight and glittery and taunting. Something obscene about his skinniness and sweet, hard smile.

"Is he well?" she said to Jocelyn. "He's terribly thin."

"He wants to look like that. He eats yogurt and black bread."

"You can never split up," Rose said, "because your house is too beautiful." She stretched out on the hooked rug. The living room had white walls, thick white curtains, old pine furniture, large bright paintings, hooked rugs. On a low round table at her elbow was a bowl of polished stones for people to pick up and hold and run through their fingers. The stones came from Vancouver beaches, from Sandy Cove and English Bay and Kitsilano and Ambleside and Dundarave. Jerome and Adam had collected them a long time ago.

Jocelyn and Clifford left British Columbia soon after Clifford returned from his provincial tour. They went to Montreal, then to Halifax, then to Toronto. They seemed hardly to remember Vancouver. Once they tried to think of the name of the street where they had lived and it was Rose who had to supply it for them. When Rose lived in Capilano Heights she used to spend a lot of time remembering the parts of Ontario where she had lived, being faithful, in a way, to that earlier landscape. Now that she was living in Ontario she put the same sort of effort into remembering things about Vancouver, puzzling to get details straight, that were in themselves quite ordinary. For instance, she tried to remember just where you waited for the Pacific Stage bus, when you were going from North Vancouver to West Vancouver. She pictured herself getting on that old green bus around one o'clock, say, on a spring day. Going to baby-sit for Jocelyn. Anna with her, in her yellow slicker and rainhat. Cold rain. The long, swampy stretch of land as you went into West Vancouver. Where the shopping-centers and high-rises are now. She could see the streets, the houses, the old Safeway, St. Mawes Hotel, the thick closing-in of the woods, the place where you got off the bus at the little store. Black Cat cigarettes sign. Cedar dampness as you walked in through the woods to Jocelyn's house. Deadness of early afternoon. Nap time. Young women drinking coffee looking out of rainy windows. Retired couples walking dogs. Pad of feet on the thick mold. Crocuses, early daffodils, the cold bulbs blooming. That profound difference of the air close to the sea, the inescapable dripping vegetation, the stillness. Anna pulling on her hand, Jocelyn's brown wooden cottage ahead. Such a rich weight of apprehension, complications descending as she neared that house.

Other things she was not so keen on remembering.

She had wept on the plane, behind her sunglasses, all the way from Powell River. She wept, sitting in the waiting room at the Vancouver airport. She was not able to stop weeping and go home to Patrick. A plainclothes policeman sat down beside her, opened his jacket to show her his badge, asked if there was anything he could do for her. Someone must have summoned him. Terrified at being so conspicuous, she fled to the Ladies'. She didn't think to comfort herself with a drink, didn't think of looking for the bar. She never went to bars then. She didn't take a tranquilizer, didn't have any, didn't know about them. Maybe there weren't such things.

The suffering. What was it? It was all a waste, it reflected no credit. An entirely dishonorable grief. All mashed pride and ridiculed fantasy. It was as if she had taken a hammer and deliberately smashed her big toe. That's what she thinks sometimes. At other times she thinks it was necessary, it was the start of wrecks and changes, the start of being where she is now instead of in Patrick's house. Life making a gigantic fuss, as usual, for a small effect.

Patrick could not speak when she told him. He had no lecture prepared. He didn't speak for a long time but followed her around the house while she kept justifying herself, complaining. It was as if he wanted her to go on talking, though he couldn't credit what she was saying, because it would be much worse if she stopped.

She didn't tell him the whole truth. She said that she had "had an affair" with Clifford, and by the telling gave herself a dim secondhand sort of comfort, which was pierced, presently, but not really destroyed, by Patrick's look and silence. It seemed ill-timed, unfair of him, to show such a bare face, such an inappropriate undigestible chunk of grief.

Then the phone rang, and she thought it would be Clifford, experiencing a change of heart. It was not Clifford, it was a man she had met at Jocelyn's party. He said he was directing a radio play, and he needed a country girl. He remembered her accent.

Not Clifford.

She would rather not think of any of this. She prefers to see through metal window-frames of dripping cedars and salmonberry bushes and the proliferating mortal greenery of the rain forest some small views of lost daily life. Anna's yellow slicker. The smoke from Jocelyn's foul fire.

"Do you want to see the junk I've been buying?" said Jocelyn, and took Rose upstairs. She showed her an embroidered skirt and a deep-red satin blouse. A daffodil-colored silk pajama suit. A long shapeless rough-woven dress from Ireland.

"I'm spending a fortune. What I would once have thought

was a fortune. It took me so long. It took us both so long, just to be able to spend money. We could not bring ourselves to do it. We despised people who had color television. And you know something – color television is great! We sit around now and say, what would we like? Maybe one of those little toaster-ovens for the cottage? Maybe I'd like a hair blower? All those things everybody else has known about for years but we thought we were too good for. You know what we are, we say to each other? We're Consumers! And it's Okay!

"And not just paintings and records and books. We always knew they were okay. Color TV! Hair dryers! Waffle irons!"

"Remote-control birdcages!" Rose cried cheerfully.

"That's the idea."

"Heated towels."

"Heated towel racks, dummy! They're lovely."

"Electric carving knives, electric toothbrushes, electric toothpicks."

"Some of those things are not as bad as they sound. Really they're not."

Another time when Rose came down Jocelyn and Clifford had a party. When everyone had gone home the three of them, Jocelyn and Clifford and Rose, sat around on the living-room floor, all fairly drunk, and very comfortable. The party had gone well. Rose was feeling a remote and wistful lust; a memory of lust, maybe. Jocelyn said she didn't want to go to bed.

"What can we do?" said Rose. "We shouldn't drink any more."

"We could make love," Clifford said.

Jocelyn and Rose said, "Really?" at exactly the same time. Then they linked their little fingers and said, "Smoke goes up the chimney."

Following which, Clifford removed their clothes. They

didn't shiver, it was warm in front of the fire. Clifford kept switching his attention nicely from one to the other. He got out of his own clothes as well. Rose felt curious, disbelieving, hardly willing, slightly aroused and, at some level she was too sluggish to reach for, appalled and sad. Though Clifford paid preliminary homage to them both, she was the one he finally made love to, rather quickly on the nubbly hooked rug. Jocelyn seemed to hover above them making comforting noises of assent.

The next morning Rose had to go out before Jocelyn and Clifford were awake. She had to go downtown on the subway. She found she was looking at men with that speculative hunger, that cold and hurtful need, which for a while she had been free of. She began to get very angry. She was angry at Clifford and Jocelyn. She felt that they had made a fool of her, cheated her, shown her a glaring lack, that otherwise she would not have been aware of. She resolved never to see them again and to write them a letter in which she would comment on their selfishness, obtuseness, and moral degeneracy. By the time she had the letter written to her own satisfaction, in her head, she was back in the country again and had calmed down. She decided not to write it. Sometime later she decided to go on being friends with Clifford and Jocelyn, because she needed such friends occasionally, at that stage of her life.

The Love of a Good Woman

FOR THE last couple of decades, there has been a museum in Walley, dedicated to preserving photos and butter churns and horse harnesses and an old dentist's chair and a cumbersome apple peeler and such curiosities as the pretty little porcelain-and-glass insulators that were used on telegraph poles.

Also there is a red box, which has the letters D.M. WILLENS, OPTOMETRIST printed on it, and a note beside it, saying, "This box of optometrist's instruments though not very old has considerable local significance, since it belonged to Mr. D.M. Willens, who drowned in the Peregrine River, 1951. It escaped the catastrophe and was found, presumably by the anonymous donor, who dispatched it to be a feature of our collection."

The ophthalmoscope could make you think of a snowman. The top part, that is – the part that's fastened onto the hollow handle. A large disk, with a smaller disk on top. In the large disk a hole to look through, as the various lenses are moved. The handle is heavy because the batteries are still inside. If you took the batteries out and put in the rod that is provided, with a disk on either end, you could plug in an electric cord. But it might have been necessary to use the instrument in places where there wasn't any electricity.

The retinoscope looks more complicated. Underneath the

round forehead clamp is something like an elf's head, with a round flat face and a pointed metal cap. This is tilted at a forty-five-degree angle to a slim column, and out of the top of the column a tiny light is supposed to shine. The flat face is made of glass and is a dark sort of mirror.

Everything is black, but that is only paint. In some places where the optometrist's hand must have rubbed most often, the paint has disappeared and you can see a patch of shiny silver metal.

I. JUTLAND

This place was called Jutland. There had been a mill once, and some kind of small settlement, but that had all gone by the end of the last century, and the place had never amounted to much at any time. Many people believed that it had been named in honor of the famous sea battle fought during the First World War, but actually everything had been in ruins years before that battle ever took place.

The three boys who came out here on a Saturday morning early in the spring of 1951 believed, as most children did, that the name came from the old wooden planks that jutted out of the earth of the riverbank and from the other straight thick boards that stood up in the nearby water, making an uneven palisade. (These were in fact the remains of a dam, built before the days of cement.) The planks and a heap of foundation stones and a lilac bush and some huge apple trees deformed by black knot and the shallow ditch of the millrace that filled up with nettles every summer were the only other signs of what had been here before.

There was a road, or a track, coming back from the township road, but it had never been gravelled, and appeared on the maps only as a dotted line, a road allowance. It was used quite a bit in the summer by people driving to the river to swim or at night by couples looking for a place to park. The turnaround spot came before you got to the ditch, but the whole area was so overrun by nettles, and cow parsnip, and woody wild hemlock in a wet year, that cars would sometimes have to back out all the way to the proper road.

The car tracks to the water's edge on that spring morning were easy to spot but were not taken notice of by these boys, who were thinking only about swimming. At least, they would call it swimming; they would go back to town and say that they had been swimming at Jutland before the snow was off the ground.

It was colder here upstream than on the river flats close to the town. There was not a leaf out yet on the riverbank trees – the only green you saw was from patches of leeks on the ground and marsh marigolds fresh as spinach, spread along any little stream that gullied its way down to the river. And on the opposite bank under some cedars they saw what they were especially looking for – a long, low, stubborn snowbank, gray as stones.

Not off the ground.

So they would jump into the water and feel the cold hit them like ice daggers. Ice daggers shooting up behind their eyes and jabbing the tops of their skulls from the inside. Then they would move their arms and legs a few times and haul themselves out, quaking and letting their teeth rattle; they would push their numb limbs into their clothes and feel the painful recapture of their bodies by their startled blood and the relief of making their brag true.

The tracks that they didn't notice came right through the ditch – in which there was nothing growing now, there was only the flat dead straw-colored grass of the year before. Through the ditch and into the river without trying to turn around. The boys tramped over them. But by this time they were close enough to the water to have had their attention caught by something more extraordinary than car tracks.

There was a pale-blue shine to the water that was not a reflection of sky. It was a whole car, down in the pond on a slant, the front wheels and the nose of it poking into the mud on the bottom, and the bump of the trunk nearly breaking the surface. Light blue was in those days an unusual color for a car, and its bulgy shape was unusual, too. They knew it right away. The little English car, the Austin, the only one of its kind surely in the whole county. It belonged to Mr. Willens, the optometrist. He looked like a cartoon character when he drove it, because he was a short but thick man, with heavy shoulders and a large head. He always seemed to be crammed into his little car as if it was a bursting suit of clothes.

The car had a panel in its roof, which Mr. Willens opened in warm weather. It was open now. They could not see very well what was inside. The color of the car made its shape plain in the water, but the water was really not very clear, and it obscured what was not so bright. The boys squatted down on the bank, then lay on their stomachs and pushed their heads out like turtles, trying to see. There was something dark and furry, something like a big animal tail, pushed up through the hole in the roof and moving idly in the water. This was shortly seen to be an arm, covered by the sleeve of a dark jacket of some heavy and hairy material. It seemed that inside the car a man's body – it had to be the body of Mr. Willens – had got into a peculiar position. The force of the water – for even in the millpond there was a good deal of force in the water at this time of year – must have somehow lifted him from the seat and pushed him about, so that one shoulder was up near the car roof and one arm had got free. His head must have been shoved down against the driver's door and window. One front wheel was stuck deeper in the river bottom than the other, which meant that the car was on a slant from side to side as well as back to front. The window in fact must have been open and the head sticking out for the body to be lodged in that position. But they could not get to see that. They could picture

Mr. Willens's face as they knew it – a big square face, which often wore a theatrical sort of frown but was never seriously intimidating. His thin crinkly hair was reddish or brassy on top, and combed diagonally over his forehead. His eyebrows were darker than his hair, thick and fuzzy like caterpillars stuck above his eyes. This was a face already grotesque to them, in the way that many adult faces were, and they were not afraid to see it drowned. But all they got to see was that arm and his pale hand. They could see the hand quite plain once they got used to looking through the water. It rode there tremulously and irresolutely, like a feather, though it looked as solid as dough. And as ordinary, once you got used to its being there at all. The fingernails were all like neat little faces, with their intelligent everyday look of greeting, their sensible disowning of their circumstances.

"Son of a gun," these boys said. With gathering energy and a tone of deepening respect, even of gratitude. "*Son of a gun.*"

It was their first time out this year. They had come across the bridge over the Peregrine River, the single-lane double-span bridge known locally as Hell's Gate or the Death Trap – though the danger had really more to do with the sharp turn the road took at the south end of it than with the bridge itself.

There was a regular walkway for pedestrians, but they didn't use it. They never remembered using it. Perhaps years ago, when they were so young as to be held by the hand. But that time had vanished for them; they refused to recognize it even if they were shown the evidence in snapshots or forced to listen to it in family conversation.

They walked now along the iron shelf that ran on the opposite side of the bridge from the walkway. It was about eight inches wide and a foot or so above the bridge floor. The Peregrine River was rushing the winter load of ice and snow, now melted, out into Lake Huron. It was barely back within its banks after the yearly flood that turned the flats into a lake and tore out the young trees and bashed any boat or hut within its reach. With the runoff from the fields muddying the water and the pale sunlight on its surface, the water looked like butterscotch pudding on the boil. But if you fell into it, it would freeze your blood and fling you out into the lake, if it didn't brain you against the buttresses first.

Cars honked at them – a warning or a reproof – but they paid no attention. They proceeded single file, as self-possessed as sleepwalkers. Then, at the north end of the bridge, they cut down to the flats, locating the paths they remembered from the year before. The flood had been so recent that these paths were not easy to follow. You had to kick your way through beaten-down brush and jump from one hummock of mud-plastered grass to another. Sometimes they jumped carelessly and landed in mud or pools of leftover floodwater, and once their feet were wet they gave up caring where they landed. They squelched through the mud and splashed in the pools so that the water came in over the tops of their rubber boots. The wind was warm; it was pulling the clouds apart into threads of old wool, and the gulls and crows were quarrelling and diving over the river. Buzzards were circling over them, on the high lookout; the robins had just returned, and the red-winged blackbirds were darting in pairs, striking bright on your eyes as if they had been dipped in paint.

"Should've brought a twenty-two."

"Should've brought a twelve-gauge."

They were too old to raise sticks and make shooting noises. They spoke with casual regret, as if guns were readily available to them.

They climbed up the north banks to a place where there was bare sand. Turtles were supposed to lay their eggs in this sand. It was too early yet for that to happen, and in fact the story of turtle eggs dated from years back – none of these boys had ever seen any. But they kicked and stomped the sand, just in case. Then they looked around for the place where last year one of them, in company with another boy, had found a cow's hipbone, carried off by the flood from some slaughter pile. The river could be counted on every year to sweep off and deposit elsewhere a good number of surprising or cumbersome or bizarre or homely objects. Rolls of wire, an intact set of steps, a bent shovel, a corn kettle. The hipbone had been found caught on the branch of a sumac – which seemed proper, because all those smooth branches were like cow horns or deer antlers, some with rusty cone tips.

They crashed around for some time – Cece Ferns showed them the exact branch – but they found nothing.

It was Cece Ferns and Ralph Diller who had made that find, and when asked where it was at present Cece Ferns said, "Ralph took it." The two boys who were with him now – Jimmy Box and Bud Salter – knew why that would have to be. Cece could never take anything home unless it was of a size to be easily concealed from his father.

They talked of more useful finds that might be made or had been made in past years. Fence rails could be used to build a raft, pieces of stray lumber could be collected for a planned shack or boat. Real luck would be to get hold of some loose muskrat traps. Then you could go into business. You could pick up enough lumber for stretching boards and steal the knives for skinning. They spoke of taking over an empty shed they knew of, in the blind alley behind what used to be the livery barn. There was a padlock on it, but you could probably get in through the window, taking the boards off it at night and replacing them at daybreak. You could take a flashlight to work by. No – a lantern. You could skin the muskrats and stretch the pelts and sell them for a lot of money.

This project became so real to them that they started to worry about leaving valuable pelts in the shed all day. One of them would have to stand watch while the others went out on the traplines. (Nobody mentioned school.)

This was the way they talked when they got clear of town.

They talked as if they were free – or almost free – agents, as if they didn't go to school or live with families or suffer any of the indignities put on them because of their age. Also, as if the countryside and other people's establishments would provide them with all they needed for their undertakings and adventures, with only the smallest risk and effort on their part.

Another change in their conversation out here was that they practically gave up using names. They didn't use each other's real names much anyway – not even family nicknames such as Bud. But at school nearly everyone had another name, some of these having to do with the way people looked or talked, like Goggle or Jabber, and some, like Sore-arse and Chickenfucker, having to do with incidents real or fabulous in the lives of those named, or in the lives – such names were handed down for decades – of their brothers, fathers, or uncles. These were the names they let go of when they were out in the bush or on the river flats. If they had to get one another's attention, all they said was "Hey." Even the use of names that were outrageous and obscene and that grown-ups supposedly never heard would have spoiled a sense they had at these times, of taking each other's looks, habits, family, and personal history entirely for granted.

And yet they hardly thought of each other as friends. They would never have designated someone as a best friend or a next-best friend, or joggled people around in these positions, the way girls did. Any one of at least a dozen boys could have been substituted for any one of these three, and accepted by the others in exactly the same way. Most members of that company were between nine and twelve years old, too old to be bound by yards and neighborhoods but too young to have jobs – even jobs sweeping the sidewalk in front of stores or delivering groceries by bicycle. Most of them lived in the north end of town, which meant that they would be expected to get a job of that sort as soon as they were old enough, and that none of them would ever be sent away to Appleby or to

Upper Canada College. And none of them lived in a shack or had a relative in jail. Just the same, there were notable differences as to how they lived at home and what was expected of them in life. But these differences dropped away as soon as they were out of sight of the county jail and the grain elevator and the church steeples and out of range of the chimes of the courthouse clock.

On their way back they walked fast. Sometimes they trotted but did not run. Jumping, dallying, splashing, were all abandoned, and the noises they'd made on their way out, the hoots and howls, were put aside as well. Any windfall of the flood was taken note of but passed by. In fact they made their way as adults would do, at a fairly steady speed and by the most reasonable route, with the weight on them of where they had to go and what had to be done next. They had something close in front of them, a picture in front of their eyes that came between them and the world, which was the thing most adults seemed to have. The pond, the car, the arm, the hand. They had some idea that when they got to a certain spot they would start to shout. They would come into town yelling and waving their news around them and everybody would be stock-still, taking it in.

They crossed the bridge the same way as always, on the shelf. But they had no sense of risk or courage or nonchalance. They might as well have taken the walkway.

Instead of following the sharp-turning road from which you could reach both the harbor and the square, they climbed straight up the bank on a path that came out near the railway sheds. The clock played its quarter-after chimes. A quarter after twelve.

This was the time when people were walking home for dinner. People from offices had the afternoon off. But people who worked in stores were getting only their customary hour – the stores stayed open till ten or eleven o'clock on Saturday night.

Most people were going home to a hot, filling meal. Pork chops, or sausages, or boiled beef, or cottage roll. Potatoes for certain, mashed or fried; winter-stored root vegetables or cabbage or creamed onions. (A few housewives, richer or more feckless, might have opened a tin of peas or butter beans.) Bread, muffins, preserves, pie. Even those people who didn't have a home to go to, or who for some reason didn't want to go there, would be sitting down to much the same sort of food at the Duke of Cumberland, or the Merchants' Hotel, or for less money behind the foggy windows of Shervill's Dairy Bar.

Those walking home were mostly men. The women were already there – they were there all the time. But some women of middle age who worked in stores or offices for a reason that was not their fault – dead husbands or sick husbands or never any husband at all – were friends of the boys' mothers, and they called out greetings even across the street (it was worst for Bud Salter, whom they called Buddy) in a certain amused or sprightly way that brought to mind all they knew of family matters, or distant infancies.

Men didn't bother greeting boys by name, even if they knew them well, They called them "boys" or "young fellows" or, occasionally, "sirs."

"Good day to you, sirs."

"You boys going straight home now?"

"What monkey business you young fellows been up to this morning?"

All these greetings had a degree of jocularity, but there were differences. The men who said "young fellows" were better disposed – or wished to seem better disposed – than the ones who said "boys." "Boys" could be the signal that a telling off was to follow, for offenses that could be either vague or specific. "Young fellows" indicated that the speaker had once been young himself. "Sirs" was outright mockery and disparagement but didn't open the way to any scolding, because the person who said that could not be bothered.

When answering, the boys didn't look up past any lady's purse or any man's Adam's apple. They said "Hullo" clearly, because there might be some kind of trouble if you didn't, and in answer to queries they said "Yessir" and "Nosir" and "Nothing much." Even on this day, such voices speaking to them caused some alarm and confusion, and they replied with the usual reticence.

At a certain corner they had to separate. Cece Ferns, always the most anxious about getting home, pulled away first. He said, "See you after dinner."

Bud Salter said, "Yeah. We got to go downtown then."

This meant, as they all understood, "downtown to the Police Office." It seemed that without needing to consult each other they had taken up a new plan of operation, a soberer way of telling their news. But it wasn't clearly said that they wouldn't be telling anything at home. There wasn't any good reason why Bud Salter or Jimmy Box couldn't have done that.

Cece Ferns never told anything at home.

Cece Ferns was an only child. His parents were older than most boys' parents, or perhaps they only seemed older, because of the disabling life they lived together. When he got away from the other boys, Cece started to trot, as he usually did for the last block home. This was not because he was eager to get there or because he thought he could make anything better when he did. It may have been to make the time pass quickly, because the last block had to be full of apprehension.

His mother was in the kitchen. Good. She was out of bed though still in her wrapper. His father wasn't there, and that was good, too. His father worked at the grain elevator and got Saturday afternoon off and if he wasn't home by now it was likely that he had gone straight to the Cumberland. That meant it would be late in the day before they had to deal with him.

Cece's father's name was Cece Ferns, too. It was a well-known and generally an affectionately known name in Walley, and somebody telling a story even thirty or forty years later would take it for granted that everybody would know it was the father who was being talked about, not the son. If a person relatively new in town said, "That doesn't sound like Cece," he would be told that nobody meant *that* Cece.

"Not him, we're talking about his old man."

They talked about the time Cece Ferns went to the hospital – or was taken there – with pneumonia, or some other desperate thing, and the nurses wrapped him in wet towels or sheets to get the fever down. The fever sweated out of him, and all the towels and sheets turned brown. It was the nicotine in him. The nurses had never seen anything like it. Cece was delighted. He claimed to have been smoking tobacco and drinking alcohol since he was ten years old.

And the time he went to church. It was hard to imagine why, but it was the Baptist church, and his wife was a Baptist, so perhaps he went to please her, though that was even harder to imagine. They were serving Communion the Sunday he went, and in the Baptist church the bread is bread but the wine is grape juice. "What's this?" cried Cece Ferns aloud. "If this is the blood of the Lamb then he must've been pretty damn anemic."

Preparations for the noon meal were under way in the Fernses' kitchen. A loaf of sliced bread was sitting on the table and a can of diced beets had been opened. A few slices of bologna had been fried – before the eggs, though they should have been done after – and were being kept slightly warm on top of the stove. And now Cece's mother had started the eggs. She was bending over the stove with the egg lifter in one hand and the other hand pressed to her stomach, cradling a pain.

Cece took the egg lifter out of her hand and turned down the electric heat, which was way too high. He had to hold the pan off the burner while the burner cooled down, in order to keep the egg whites from getting too tough or burning at the edges. He hadn't been in time to wipe out the old grease and plop a bit of fresh lard in the pan. His mother never wiped out the old grease, just let it sit from one meal to the next and put in a bit of lard when she had to.

When the heat was more to his liking, he put the pan down and coaxed the lacy edges of the eggs into tidy circles. He found a clean spoon and dribbled a little hot fat over the yokes to set them. He and his mother liked their eggs cooked this way, but his mother often couldn't manage it right. His father liked his eggs turned over and flattened out like pancakes, cooked hard as shoe leather and blackened with pepper. Cece could cook them the way he wanted, too.

None of the other boys knew how practiced he was in the kitchen – just as none of them knew about the hiding place he had made outside the house in the blind corner past the dining-room window, behind the Japanese barberry.

His mother sat in the chair by the window while he was finishing up the eggs. She kept an eye on the street. There was still a chance that his father would come home for something to eat. He might not be drunk yet. But the way he behaved didn't always depend on how drunk he was. If he came into the kitchen now he might tell Cece to make him some eggs, too. Then he might ask him where his apron was and say that he would make some fellow a dandy wife. That would be how he'd behave if he was in a good mood. In another sort of mood he would start off by staring at Cece in a certain way – that is, with an exaggerated, absurdly threatening expression – and telling him he better watch out.

"Smart bugger, aren't you? Well, all I got to say to you is better watch out."

Then if Cece looked back at him, or maybe if he didn't look

back, or if he dropped the egg lifter or set it down with a clatter – or even if he was sliding around being extra cautious about not dropping anything and not making a noise – his father was apt to start showing his teeth and snarling like a dog. It would have been ridiculous – it was ridiculous – except that he meant business. A minute later the food and the dishes might be on the floor, and the chairs or the table overturned, and he might be chasing Cece around the room yelling how he was going to get him this time, flatten his face on the hot burner, how would he like that? You would be certain he'd gone crazy. But if at this moment a knock came at the door – if a friend of his arrived, say, to pick him up – his face would reassemble itself in no time and he would open the door and call out the friend's name in a loud bantering voice.

"I'll be with you in two shakes. I'd ask you in, but the wife's been pitching the dishes around again."

He didn't intend this to be believed. He said such things in order to turn whatever happened in his house into a joke.

Cece's mother asked him if the weather was warming up and where he had been that morning.

"Yeah," he said, and, "Out on the flats."

She said that she'd thought she could smell the wind on him.

"You know what I'm going to do right after we eat?" she said. "I'm going to take a hot-water bottle and go right back to bed and maybe I'll get my strength back and feel like doing something."

That was what she nearly always said she was going to do, but she always announced it as if it was an idea that had just occurred to her, a hopeful decision.

Bud Salter had two older sisters who never did anything useful unless his mother made them. And they never confined their hair arranging, nail polishing, shoe cleaning, making up, or even dressing activities to their bedrooms or the bathroom. They spread their combs and curlers and face powder and nail polish and shoe polish all over the house. Also they loaded every chair back with their newly ironed dresses and blouses and spread out their drying sweaters on towels on every clear space of floor. (Then they screamed at you if you walked near them.) They stationed themselves in front of various mirrors – the mirror in the hall coat stand, the mirror in the dining-room buffet, and the mirror beside the kitchen door with the shelf underneath always loaded with safety pins, bobby pins, pennies, buttons, bits of pencils. Sometimes one of them would stand in front of a mirror for twenty minutes or so, checking herself from various angles, inspecting her teeth and pulling her hair back then shaking it forward. Then she would walk away apparently satisfied or at least finished – but only as far as the next room, the next mirror, where she would begin all over again just as if she had been delivered a new head.

Right now his older sister, the one who was supposed to be good-looking, was taking the pins out of her hair in front of the kitchen mirror. Her head was covered with shiny curls like snails. His other sister, on orders from his mother, was mashing the potatoes. His five-year-old brother was sitting in place at the table, banging his knife and fork up and down and yelling, "Want some service. Want some service."

He got that from their father, who did it for a joke.

Bud passed by his brother's chair and said quietly, "Look. She's putting lumps in the mashed potatoes again."

He had his brother convinced that lumps were something you added, like raisins to rice pudding, from a supply in the cupboard.

His brother stopped chanting and began complaining.

"I won't eat none if she puts in lumps. Mama, I won't eat none if she puts lumps."

"Oh, don't be silly," Bud's mother said. She was frying apple slices and onion rings with the pork chops. "Quit whining like a baby."

"It was Bud got him started," the older sister said. "Bud went and told him she was putting lumps in. Bud always tells him that and he doesn't know any better."

"Bud ought to get his face smashed," said Doris, the sister who was mashing the potatoes. She didn't always say such things idly – she had once left a claw scar down the side of Bud's cheek.

Bud went over to the dresser, where there was a rhubarb pie cooling. He took a fork and began carefully, secretly prying at it, letting out delicious steam, a delicate smell of cinnamon. He was trying to open one of the vents in the top of it so that he could get a taste of the filling. His brother saw what he was doing but was too scared to say anything. His brother was spoiled and was defended by his sisters all the time – Bud was the only person in the house he respected.

"Want some service," he repeated, speaking now in a thoughtful undertone.

Doris came over to the dresser to get the bowl for the mashed potatoes. Bud made an incautious movement, and part of the top crust caved in.

"So now he's wrecking the pie," Doris said. "Mama – he's wrecking your pie."

"Shut your damn mouth," Bud said.

"Leave that pie alone," said Bud's mother with a practiced, almost serene severity. "Stop swearing. Stop tattle-telling. Grow up."

Jimmy Box sat down to dinner at a crowded table. He and his father and his mother and his four-year-old and six-year-old sisters lived in his grandmother's house with his grandmother and his great-aunt Mary and his bachelor uncle. His father had a bicycle-repair shop in the shed behind the house, and his mother worked in Honeker's Department Store.

Jimmy's father was crippled – the result of a polio attack when he was twenty-two years old. He walked bent forward from the hips, using a cane. This didn't show so much when he was working in the shop, because such work often means being bent over anyway. When he walked along the street he did look very strange, but nobody called him names or did an imitation of him. He had once been a notable hockey player and baseball player for the town, and some of the grace and valor of the past still hung around him, putting his present state into perspective, so that it could be seen as a phase (though a final one). He helped this perception along by cracking silly jokes and taking an optimistic tone, denying the pain that showed in his sunken eyes and kept him awake many nights. And, unlike Cece Ferns's father, he didn't change his tune when he came into his own house.

But, of course, it wasn't his own house. His wife had married him after he was crippled, though she had got engaged to him before, and it seemed the natural thing to do to move in with her mother, so that the mother could look after any children who came along while the wife went on working at her job. It seemed the natural thing to the wife's mother as well, to take on another family – just as it seemed natural that her sister Mary should move in with the rest of them when her eyesight failed, and that her son Fred, who was extraordinarily shy, should continue to live at home unless he found some place he liked better. This was a family who accepted burdens of one kind or another with even less fuss than they accepted the weather. In fact, nobody in that house would have spoken of Jimmy's father's condition or Aunt Mary's eyesight as burdens or problems, any more than they would of Fred's shyness. Drawbacks and adversity were not to be noticed, not to be distinguished from their opposites.

There was a traditional belief in the family that Jimmy's grandmother was an excellent cook, and this might have been true at one time, but in recent years there had been a falling off. Economies were practiced beyond what there was any need for now. Jimmy's mother and his uncle made decent wages and his aunt Mary got a pension and the bicycle shop was fairly busy, but one egg was used instead of three and the meat loaf got an extra cup of oatmeal. There was an attempt to compensate by overdoing the Worcestershire sauce or sprinkling too much nutmeg on the custard. But nobody complained. Everybody praised. Complaints were as rare as lightning balls in that house. And everybody said "Excuse me," even the little girls said "Excuse me," when they bumped into each other. Everybody passed and pleased and thank-you'd at the table as if there was company every day. This was the way they managed, all of them crammed so tight in the house, with clothes piled on every hook, coats hung over the banister, and cots set up permanently in the dining room for Jimmy and his uncle Fred, and the buffet hidden under a load of clothing waiting to be ironed or mended. Nobody pounded on the stairsteps or shut doors hard or turned the radio up loud or said anything disagreeable.

Did this explain why Jimmy kept his mouth shut that Saturday at dinnertime? They all kept their mouths shut, all three of them. In Cece's case it was easy to understand. His father would never have stood for Cece's claiming so important a discovery. He would have called him a liar as a matter of course. And Cece's mother, judging everything by the effect it would have on his father, would have understood – correctly – that even his going to the Police Office with his story would cause disruption at home, so she would have told him to please just keep quiet. But the two other boys lived in quite reasonable homes and they could have spoken. In Jimmy's house there would have been consternation and some disapproval, but soon enough they would have admitted that it was not Jimmy's fault.

Bud's sisters would have asked if he was crazy. They might even have twisted things around to imply that it was just like him, with his unpleasant habits, to come upon a dead body. His father, however, was a sensible, patient man, used to listening to many strange rigmaroles in his job as a freight agent at the railway station. He would have made Bud's sisters shut up, and after some serious talk to make sure Bud was telling the truth and not exaggerating he would have phoned the Police Office.

It was just that their houses seemed too full. Too much was going on already. This was true in Cece's house just as much as in the others, because even in his father's absence there was the threat and memory all the time of his haywire presence.

"Did you tell?"

"Did you?"

"Me neither."

They walked downtown, not thinking about the way they were going. They turned onto Shipka Street and found themselves going past the stucco bungalow where Mr. and Mrs. Willens lived. They were right in front of it before they recognized it. It had a small bay window on either side of the front door and a top step wide enough for two chairs, not there at present but occupied on summer evenings by Mr. Willens and his wife. There was a flat-roofed addition to one side of the house, with another door opening toward the street and a separate walk leading up to it. A sign beside that door said D.M. WILLENS, OPTOMETRIST. None of the boys themselves had visited that office, but Jimmy's aunt Mary went there regularly for her eyedrops, and his grandmother got her glasses there. So did Bud Salter's mother.

The stucco was a muddy pink color and the doors and window frames were painted brown. The storm windows had not been taken off yet, as they hadn't from most of the houses in town. There was nothing special at all about the house, but the front yard was famous for its flowers. Mrs. Willens was a renowned gardener who didn't grow her flowers in long rows beside the vegetable garden, as Jimmy's grandmother and Bud's mother grew theirs. She had them in round beds and crescent beds and all over, and in circles under the trees. In a couple of weeks daffodils would fill this lawn. But at present the only thing in bloom was a forsythia bush at the corner of the house. It was nearly as high as the eaves and it sprayed yellow into the air the way a fountain shoots water.

The forsythia shook, not with the wind, and out came a stooped brown figure. It was Mrs. Willens in her old gardening clothes, a lumpy little woman in baggy slacks and a ripped jacket and a peaked cap that might have been her husband's – it slipped down too low and almost hid her eyes. She was carrying a pair of shears.

They slowed right down – it was either that or run. Maybe they thought that she wouldn't notice them, that they could turn themselves into posts. But she had seen them already; that was why she came hastening through.

"I see you're gawking at my forsythia," said Mrs. Willens. "Would you like some to take home?"

What they had been gawking at was not the forsythia but the whole scene – the house looking just as usual, the sign by the office door, the curtains letting light in. Nothing hollow or ominous, nothing that said that Mr. Willens was not inside and that his car was not in the garage behind his office but in Jutland Pond. And Mrs. Willens out working in her yard, where anybody would expect her to be – everybody in town said so – the minute the snow was melted. And calling out in her familiar tobacco-roughened voice, abrupt and challenging but not unfriendly – a voice identifiable half a block away or coming from the back of any store.

"Wait," she said. "Wait, now, I'll get you some."

She began smartly, selectively snapping off the bright-yellow branches, and when she had all she wanted she came towards them behind a screen of flowers.

"Here you are," she said. "Take these home to your mothers. It's always good to see the forsythia, it's the very first thing in the spring." She was dividing the branches among them. "Like all Gaul," she said. "All Gaul is divided into three parts. You must know about that if you take Latin."

"We aren't in high school yet," said Jimmy, whose life at home had readied him, better than the others, for talking to ladies.

"Aren't you?" she said. "Well, you've got all sorts of things to look forward to. Tell your mothers to put them in lukewarm water. Oh, I'm sure they already know that. I've given you branches that aren't all the way out yet, so they should last and last."

They said thank you – Jimmy first and the others picking it up from him. They walked toward downtown with their arms loaded. They had no intention of turning back and taking the flowers home, and they counted on her not having any good idea of where their homes were. Half a block on, they sneaked looks back to see if she was watching.

She wasn't. The big house near the sidewalk blocked the view in any case.

The forsythia gave them something to think about. The embarrassment of carrying it, the problem of getting rid of it. Otherwise, they would have to think about Mr. Willens and Mrs. Willens. How she could be busy in her yard and he could be drowned in his car. Did she know where he was or did she not? It seemed that she couldn't. Did she even know that he was gone? She had acted as if there was nothing wrong, nothing at all, and when they were standing in front of her this had seemed to be the truth. What they knew, what they had seen, seemed actually to be pushed back, to be defeated, by her not knowing it.

Two girls on bicycles came wheeling around the corner. One was Bud's sister Doris. At once these girls began to hoot and yell.

"Oh, look at the flowers," they shouted. "Where's the wedding? Look at the beautiful bridesmaids."

Bud yelled back the worst thing he could think of.

"You got blood all over your arse."

Of course she didn't, but there had been an occasion when this had really been so – she had come home from school with blood on her skirt. Everybody had seen it, and it would never be forgotten.

He was sure she would tell on him at home, but she never did. Her shame about that other time was so great that she could not refer to it even to get him in trouble.

They realized then that they had to dump the flowers at once, so they simply threw the branches under a parked car. They brushed a few stray petals off their clothes as they turned onto the square.

Saturdays were still important then; they brought the country people into town. Cars were already parked around the square and on the side streets. Big country boys and girls and smaller children from the town and the country were heading for the movie matinee.

It was necessary to pass Honeker's in the first block. And there, in full view in one of the windows, Jimmy saw his mother. Back at work already, she was putting the hat straight on a female dummy, adjusting the veil, then fiddling with the shoulders of the dress. She was a short woman and she had to stand on tiptoe to do this properly. She had taken off her shoes to walk on the window carpet. You could see the rosy plump cushions of her heels through her stockings, and when she stretched you saw the back of her knee through the slit in her skirt. Above that was a wide but shapely behind and the line of her panties or girdle. Jimmy could hear in his mind the little grunts she would be making; also he could smell the stockings that she sometimes took off as soon as she got home, to save them from runs. Stockings and underwear, even clean female underwear, had a faint, private smell that was both appealing and disgusting.

He hoped two things. That the others hadn't noticed her (they had, but the idea of a mother dressed up every day and out in the public world of town was so strange to them that they couldn't comment, could only dismiss it) and that she would not, please not, turn around and spot him. She was capable, if she did that, of rapping on the glass and mouthing hello. At work she lost the hushed discretion, the studied gentleness, of home. Her obligingness turned from meek to pert. He used to be delighted by this other side of her, this friskiness, just as he was by Honeker's, with its extensive counters of glass and varnished wood, its big mirrors at the top of the staircase, in which he could see himself climbing up to Ladies' Wear, on the second floor.

"Here's my young mischief," his mother would say, and sometimes slip him a dime. He could never stay more than a minute; Mr. or Mrs. Honeker might be watching.

Young mischief.

Words that were once as pleasant to hear as the tinkle of dimes and nickels had now turned slyly shaming.

They were safely past.

In the next block they had to pass the Duke of Cumberland, but Cece had no worries. If his father had not come home at dinnertime, it meant he would be in there for hours yet. But the word "Cumberland" always fell across his mind heavily. From the days when he hadn't even known what it meant, he got a sense of sorrowful plummeting. A weight hitting dark water, far down.

Between the Cumberland and the Town Hall was an unpaved alley, and at the back of the Town Hall was the Police Office. They turned into this alley and soon a lot of new noise reached them, opposing the street noise. It was not from the Cumberland – the noise in there was all muffled up, the beer parlor having only small, high windows like a public toilet. It was coming from the Police Office. The door to that office was open on account of the mild weather, and even out in the alley you could smell the pipe tobacco and cigars. It wasn't just the policemen who sat in there, especially on Saturday afternoons, with the stove going in winter and the fan in summer and the door open to let in the pleasant air on an in-between day like today. Colonel Box would be there – in fact, they could already hear the wheeze he made, the long-drawn-out after-effects of his asthmatic laughter. He was a relative of Jimmy's, but there was a coolness in the family because he did not approve of Jimmy's father's marriage. He spoke to Jimmy, when he recognized him, in a surprised, ironic tone of voice. "If he ever offers you a quarter or anything, you say you don't need it," Jimmy's mother had told him. But Colonel Box had never made such an offer.

Also, Mr. Pollock would be there, who had retired from the drugstore, and Fergus Solley, who was not a half-wit but looked like one, because he had been gassed in the First World War. All day these men and others played cards, smoked, told stories, and drank coffee at the town's expense (as Bud's father said). Anybody wanting to make a complaint or a report had to do it within sight of them and probably within earshot.

Run the gauntlet.

They came almost to a stop outside the open door. Nobody had noticed them. Colonel Box said, "I'm not dead yet," repeating the final line of some story. They began to walk past slowly with their heads down, kicking at the gravel. Round the corner of the building they picked up speed. By the entry to the men's public toilet there was a recent streak of lumpy vomit on the wall and a couple of empty bottles on the gravel. They had to walk between the refuse bins and the high watchful windows of the town clerk's office, and then they were off the gravel, back on the square.

"I got money," Cece said. This matter-of-fact announcement brought them all relief. Cece jingled change in his pocket. It was the money his mother had given him after he washed up the dishes, when he went into the front bedroom to tell her he was going out. "Help yourself to fifty cents off the dresser," she had said. Sometimes she had money, though he never saw his father give her any. And whenever she said "Help yourself" or gave him a few coins, Cece understood that she was ashamed of their life, ashamed for him and in front of him, and these were the times when he hated the sight of her (though he was glad of the money). Especially if she said that he was a good boy and he was not to think she wasn't grateful for all he did.

They took the street that led down to the harbor. At the side of Paquette's Service Station there was a booth from which Mrs. Paquette sold hot dogs, ice cream, candy, and cigarettes. She had refused to sell them cigarettes even when Jimmy said they were for his uncle Fred. But she didn't hold it against them that they'd tried. She was a fat, pretty woman, a French Canadian.

They bought some licorice whips, black and red. They meant to buy some ice cream later when they weren't so full from dinner. They went over to where there were two old car seats set up by the fence under a tree that gave shade in summer. They shared out the licorice whips.

Captain Tervitt was sitting on the other seat.

Captain Tervitt had been a real captain, for many years, on the lake boats. Now he had a job as a special constable. He stopped the cars to let the children cross the street in front of the school and kept them from sledding down the side street in winter. He blew his whistle and held up one big hand, which looked like a clown's hand, in a white glove. He was still tall and straight and broad-shouldered, though old and white-haired. Cars would do what he said, and children, too.

At night he went around checking the doors of all the stores to see that they were locked and to make sure that there was nobody inside committing a burglary. During the day he often slept in public. When the weather was bad he slept in the library and when it was good he chose some seat out-of-doors. He didn't spend much time in the Police Office, probably because he was too deaf to follow the conversation without his hearing aid in, and like many deaf people he hated his hearing aid. And he was used to being solitary, surely, staring out over the bow of the lake boats.

His eyes were closed and his head tilted back so that he could get the sun in his face. When they went over to talk to him (and the decision to do this was made without any consultation, beyond one resigned and dubious look) they had to wake him from his doze. His face took a moment to register – where and when and who. Then he took a large old-fashioned watch out of his pocket, as if he counted on children always wanting to be told the time. But they went on talking to him, with their expressions agitated and slightly shamed. They were saying, "Mr. Willens is out in Jutland Pond," and "We seen the car," and "Drownded." He had to hold up his hand and make shushing motions while the other hand went rooting around in his pants pocket and came up with his hearing aid. He nodded his head seriously, encouragingly, as if to say, Patience, patience, while he got the device settled in his ear. Then both hands up – Be still, be still – while he was testing. Finally another nod, of a brisker sort, and in a stern voice but making a joke to some extent of his sternness – he said, "Proceed."

Cece, who was the quietest of the three – as Jimmy was the politest and Bud the mouthiest – was the one who turned everything around.

"Your fly's undone," he said.

Then they all whooped and ran away.

Their elation did not vanish right away. But it was not something that could be shared or spoken about: they had to pull apart.

Cece went home to work on his hideaway. The cardboard floor, which had been frozen through the winter, was sodden now and needed to be replaced. Jimmy climbed into the loft of the garage, where he had recently discovered a box of old Doc Savage magazines that had once belonged to his uncle Fred. Bud went home and found nobody there but his mother, who was waxing the dining-room floor. He looked at comic books for an hour or so and then he told her. He believed that his mother had no experience or authority outside their house and that she would not make up her mind about what to do until she had phoned his father. To his surprise, she immediately phoned the police. Then she phoned his father. And somebody went to round up Cece and Jimmy.

A police car drove into Jutland from the township road, and all was confirmed. A policeman and the Anglican minister went to see Mrs. Willens.

"I didn't want to bother you," Mrs. Willens was reported to have said. "I was going to give him till dark."

She told them that Mr. Willens had driven out to the country yesterday afternoon to take some drops to an old blind man. Sometimes he got held up, she said. He visited people, or the car got stuck.

Was he downhearted or anything like that? the policeman asked her.

"Oh, surely not," the minister said. "He was the bulwark of the choir."

"The word was not in his vocabulary," said Mrs. Willens.

Something was made of the boys' sitting down and eating their dinners and never saying a word. And then buying a bunch of licorice whips. A new nickname – Deadman – was found and settled on each of them. Jimmy and Bud bore it till they left town, and Cece – who married young and went to work in the elevator – saw it passed on to his two sons. By that time nobody thought of what it referred to.

The insult to Captain Tervitt remained a secret.

Each of them expected some reminder, some lofty look of injury or judgment, the next time they had to pass under his uplifted arm, crossing the street to the school. But he held up his gloved hand, his noble and clownish white hand, with his usual benevolent composure. He gave consent.

Proceed.

II. HEART FAILURE

"Glomerulonephritis," Enid wrote in her notebook. It was the first case that she had ever seen. The fact was that Mrs. Quinn's kidneys were failing, and nothing could be done about it. Her kidneys were drying up and turning into hard and useless granular lumps. Her urine at present was scanty and had a smoky look, and the smell that came out on her breath and through her skin was acrid and ominous. And there was another, fainter smell, like rotted fruit, that seemed to Enid related to the pale-lavender-brown stains appearing on her body. Her legs twitched in spasms of sudden pain and her skin was subject to a violent itching, so that Enid had to rub her with ice. She wrapped the ice in towels and pressed the packs to the spots in torment.

"How do you contract that kind of a disease anyhow?" said Mrs. Quinn's sister-in-law. Her name was Mrs. Green. Olive Green. (It had never occurred to her how that would sound, she said, until she got married and all of a sudden everybody was laughing at it.) She lived on a farm a few miles away, out on the highway, and every few days she came and took the sheets and towels and nightdresses home to wash. She did the children's washing as well, brought everything back freshly ironed and folded. She even ironed the ribbons on the nightdresses. Enid was grateful to her – she had been on jobs where she had to do the laundry herself, or, worse still, load it onto her mother, who would pay to have it done in town. Not wanting to offend but seeing which way the questions were tending, she said, "It's hard to tell."

"Because you hear one thing and another," Mrs. Green said. "You hear that sometimes a woman might take some pills. They get these pills to take for when their period is late and if they take them just like the doctor says and for a good purpose that's fine, but if they take too many and for a bad purpose their kidneys are wrecked. Am I right?"

"I've never come in contact with a case like that," Enid said.

Mrs. Green was a tall, stout woman. Like her brother Rupert, who was Mrs. Quinn's husband, she had a round, snub-nosed, agreeably wrinkled face – the kind that Enid's mother called "potato Irish." But behind Rupert's good-humored expression there was wariness and withholding. And behind Mrs. Green's there was yearning. Enid did not know for what. To the simplest conversation Mrs. Green brought a huge demand. Maybe it was just a yearning for news. News of something momentous. An event.

Of course, an event was coming, something momentous at least in this family. Mrs. Quinn was going to die, at the age of twenty-seven. (That was the age she gave herself – Enid would have put some years on it, but once an illness had progressed this far age was hard to guess.) When her kidneys stopped working altogether, her heart would give out and she would die. The doctor had said to Enid, "This'll take you into the summer, but the chances are you'll get some kind of a holiday before the hot weather's over."

"Rupert met her when he went up north," Mrs. Green said. "He went off by himself, he worked in the bush up there. She had some kind of a job in a hotel. I'm not sure what. Chambermaid job. She wasn't raised up there, though – she says she was raised in an orphanage in Montreal. She can't help that. You'd expect her to speak French, but if she does she don't let on."

Enid said, "An interesting life."

"You can say that again."

"An interesting life," said Enid. Sometimes she couldn't

help it – she tried a joke where it had hardly a hope of working. She raised her eyebrows encouragingly, and Mrs. Green did smile.

But was she hurt? That was just the way Rupert would smile, in high school, warding off some possible mockery.

"He never had any kind of a girlfriend before that," said Mrs. Green.

Enid had been in the same class as Rupert, though she did not mention that to Mrs. Green. She felt some embarrassment now because he was one of the boys – in fact, the main one – that she and her girlfriends had teased and tormented. "Picked on," as they used to say. They had picked on Rupert, following him up the street calling out, "Hello, Rupert. Hello, Ru-pert," putting him into a state of agony, watching his neck go red. "Rupert's got scarlet fever," they would say. "Rupert, you should be quarantined." And they would pretend that one of them – Enid, Joan McAuliffe, Marian Denny – had a case on him. "She wants to speak to you, Rupert. Why don't you ever ask her out? You could phone her up at least. She's dying to talk to you."

They did not really expect him to respond to these pleading overtures. But what joy if he had. He would have been rejected in short order and the story broadcast all over the school. Why? Why did they treat him this way, long to humiliate him? Simply because they could.

Impossible that he would have forgotten. But he treated Enid as if she were a new acquaintance, his wife's nurse, come into his house from anywhere at all. And Enid took her cue from him.

Things had been unusually well arranged here, to spare her extra work. Rupert slept at Mrs. Green's house, and ate his meals there. The two little girls could have been there as well, but it would have meant putting them into another school – there was nearly a month to go before school was out for the summer.

Rupert came into the house in the evenings and spoke to his children.

"Are you being good girls?" he said.

"Show Daddy what you made with your blocks," said Enid. "Show Daddy your pictures in the coloring book."

The blocks, the crayons, the coloring books, were all provided by Enid. She had phoned her mother and asked her to see what things she could find in the old trunks. Her mother had done that, and brought along as well an old book of cutout dolls which she had collected from someone – Princesses Elizabeth and Margaret Rose and their many outfits. Enid hadn't been able to get the little girls to say thank you until she put all these things on a high shelf and announced that they would stay there till thank you was said. Lois and Sylvie were seven and six years old, and as wild as little barn cats.

Rupert didn't ask where the playthings came from. He told his daughters to be good girls and asked Enid if there was anything she needed from town. Once she told him that she had replaced the lightbulb in the cellarway and that he could get her some spare bulbs.

"I could have done that," he said.

"I don't have any trouble with lightbulbs," said Enid. "Or fuses or knocking in nails. My mother and I have done without a man around the house for a long time now." She meant to tease a little, to be friendly, but it didn't work.

Finally Rupert would ask about his wife, and Enid would say that her blood pressure was down slightly, or that she had eaten and kept down part of an omelette for supper, or that the ice packs seemed to ease her itchy skin and she was sleeping better. And Rupert would say that if she was sleeping he'd better not go in.

Enid said, "Nonsense." To see her husband would do a woman more good than to have a little doze. She took the children up to bed then, to give man and wife a time of privacy. But Rupert never stayed more than a few minutes. And when

Enid came back downstairs and went into the front room – now the sickroom – to ready the patient for the night, Mrs. Quinn would be lying back against the pillows, looking agitated but not dissatisfied.

"Doesn't hang around here very long, does he?" Mrs. Quinn would say. "Makes me laugh. Ha-ha-ha, how-are-you? Ha-ha-ha, off-we-go. Why don't we take her out and throw her on the manure pile? Why don't we just dump her out like a dead cat? That's what he's thinking. Isn't he?"

"I doubt it," said Enid, bringing the basin and towels, the rubbing alcohol and the baby powder.

"I doubt it," said Mrs. Quinn quite viciously, but she submitted readily enough to having her nightgown removed, her hair smoothed back from her face, a towel slid under her hips. Enid was used to people making a fuss about being naked, even when they were very old or very ill. Sometimes she would have to tease them or badger them into common sense. "Do you think I haven't seen any bottom parts before?" she would say. "Bottom parts, top parts, it's pretty boring after a while. You know, there's just the two ways we're made." But Mrs. Quinn was without shame, opening her legs and raising herself a bit to make the job easier. She was a little bird-boned woman, queerly shaped now, with her swollen abdomen and limbs and her breasts shrunk to tiny pouches with dried-currant nipples.

"Swole up like some kind of pig," Mrs. Quinn said. "Except for my tits, and they always were kind of useless. I never had no big udders on me, like you. Don't you get sick of the sight of me? Won't you be glad when I'm dead?"

"If I felt like that I wouldn't be here," said Enid.

"Good riddance to bad rubbish," said Mrs. Quinn. "That's what you'll all say. Good riddance to bad rubbish. I'm no use to him anymore, am I? I'm no use to any man. He goes out of here every night and he goes to pick up women, doesn't he?"

"As far as I know, he goes to his sister's house."

"As far as you know. But you don't know much."

Enid thought she knew what this meant, this spite and venom, the energy saved for ranting. Mrs. Quinn was flailing about for an enemy. Sick people grew to resent well people, and sometimes that was true of husbands and wives, or even of mothers and their children. Both husband and children in Mrs. Quinn's case. On a Saturday morning, Enid called Lois and Sylvie from their games under the porch, to come and see their mother looking pretty. Mrs. Quinn had just had her morning wash, and was in a clean nightgown, with her fine, sparse, fair hair brushed and held back by a blue ribbon. (Enid took a supply of these ribbons with her when she went to nurse a female patient – also a bottle of cologne and a cake of scented soap.) She did look pretty – or you could see at least that she had once been pretty, with her wide forehead and cheekbones (they almost punched the skin now, like china doorknobs) and her large greenish eyes and childish translucent teeth and small stubborn chin.

The children came into the room obediently if unenthusiastically.

Mrs. Quinn said, "Keep them off of my bed, they're filthy."

"They just want to see you," said Enid.

"Well, now they've seen me," said Mrs. Quinn. "Now they can go."

This behavior didn't seem to surprise or disappoint the children. They looked at Enid, and Enid said, "All right, now, your mother better have a rest," and they ran out and slammed the kitchen door.

"Can't you get them to quit doing that?" Mrs. Quinn said. "Every time they do it, it's like a brick hits me in my chest."

You would think these two daughters of hers were a pair of rowdy orphans, wished on her for an indefinite visit. But that was the way some people were, before they settled down to their dying and sometimes even up to the event itself. People of a gentler nature – it would seem – than Mrs. Quinn might say that they knew how much their brothers, sisters, husbands, wives, and children had always hated them, how much of a disappointment they had been to others and others had been to them, and how glad they knew everybody would be to see them gone. They might say this at the end of peaceful, useful lives in the midst of loving families, where there was no explanation at all for such fits. And usually the fits passed. But often, too, in the last weeks or even days of life there was mulling over of old feuds and slights or whimpering about some unjust punishment suffered seventy years earlier. Once a woman had asked Enid to bring her a willow platter from the cupboard and Enid had thought that she wanted the comfort of looking at this one pretty possession for the last time. But it turned out that she wanted to use her last, surprising strength to smash it against the bedpost.

"Now I know my sister's never going to get her hands on that," she said.

And often people remarked that their visitors were only coming to gloat and that the doctor was responsible for their sufferings. They detested the sight of Enid herself, for her sleepless strength and patient hands and the way the juices of life were so admirably balanced and flowing in her. Enid was used to that, and she was able to understand the trouble they were in, the trouble of dying and also the trouble of their lives that sometimes overshadowed that.

But with Mrs. Quinn she was at a loss.

It was not just that she couldn't supply comfort here. It was that she couldn't want to. She could not conquer her dislike of this doomed, miserable young woman. She disliked this body that she had to wash and powder and placate with ice and alcohol rubs. She understood now what people meant when they said that they hated sickness and sick bodies; she understood the women who had said to her, I don't know how you do it, I could never be a nurse, that's the one thing I could never be. She disliked this particular body, all the particular signs of its disease. The smell of it and the discoloration, the malignant-looking little nipples and the pathetic ferretlike teeth. She saw all this as the sign of a willed corruption. She was as bad as Mrs. Green, sniffing out rampant impurity. In spite of being a nurse who knew better, and in spite of its being her job – and surely her nature – to be compassionate. She didn't know why this was happening. Mrs. Quinn reminded her somewhat of girls she had known in high school – cheaply dressed, sickly looking girls with dreary futures, who still displayed a hard-faced satisfaction with themselves. They lasted only a year or two – they got pregnant, most of them got married. Enid had nursed some of them in later years, in home childbirth, and found their confidence exhausted and their bold streak turned into meekness, or even piety. She was sorry for them, even when she remembered how determined they had been to get what they had got.

Mrs. Quinn was a harder case. Mrs. Quinn might crack and crack, but there would be nothing but sullen mischief, nothing but rot inside her.

Worse even than the fact that Enid should feel this revulsion was the fact that Mrs. Quinn knew it. No patience or gentleness or cheerfulness that Enid could summon would keep Mrs. Quinn from knowing. And Mrs. Quinn made knowing it her triumph.

Good riddance to bad rubbish.

When Enid was twenty years old, and had almost finished her nurse's training, her father was dying in the Walley hospital. That was when he said to her, "I don't know as I care for this career of yours. I don't want you working in a place like this."

Enid bent over him and asked what sort of place he thought he was in. "It's only the Walley hospital," she said.

"I know that," said her father, sounding as calm and reasonable as he had always done (he was an insurance and real-estate agent). "I know what I'm talking about. Promise me you won't."

"Promise you what?" said Enid.

"You won't do this kind of work," her father said. She could not get any further explanation out of him. He tightened up his mouth as if her questioning disgusted him. All he would say was "Promise."

"What is all this about?" Enid asked her mother, and her mother said, "Oh, go ahead. Go ahead and promise him. What difference is it going to make?"

Enid thought this a shocking thing to say, but made no comment. It was consistent with her mother's way of looking at a lot of things.

"I'm not going to promise anything I don't understand," she said. "I'm probably not going to promise anything anyway. But if you know what he's talking about you ought to tell me."

"It's just this idea he's got now," her mother said. "He's got an idea that nursing makes a woman coarse."

Enid said, "Coarse."

Her mother said that the part of nursing her father objected to was the familiarity nurses had with men's bodies. Her father thought – he had decided – that such familiarity would change a girl, and furthermore that it would change the way men thought about that girl. It would spoil her good chances and give her a lot of other chances that were not so good. Some men would lose interest and others would become interested in the wrong way.

"I suppose it's all mixed up with wanting you to get married," her mother said.

"Too bad if it is," said Enid.

But she ended up promising. And her mother said, "Well, I hope that makes you happy." Not "makes him happy." "Makes *you*." It seemed that her mother had known before

Enid did just how tempting this promise would be. The deathbed promise, the self-denial, the wholesale sacrifice. And the more absurd the better. This was what she had given in to. And not for love of her father, either (her mother implied), but for the thrill of it. Sheer noble perversity.

"If he'd asked you to give up something you didn't care one way or the other about, you'd probably have told him nothing doing," her mother said. "If for instance he'd asked you to give up wearing lipstick. You'd still be wearing it."

Enid listened to this with a patient expression.

"Did you pray about it?" said her mother sharply.

Enid said yes.

She withdrew from nursing school; she stayed at home and kept busy. There was enough money that she did not have to work. In fact, her mother had not wanted Enid to go into nursing in the first place, claiming that it was something poor girls did, it was a way out for girls whose parents couldn't keep them or send them to college. Enid did not remind her of this inconsistency. She painted a fence, she tied up the rosebushes for winter. She learned to bake and she learned to play bridge, taking her father's place in the weekly games her mother played with Mr. and Mrs. Willens from next door. In no time at all she became – as Mr. Willens said – a scandalously good player. He took to turning up with chocolates or a pink rose for her, to make up for his own inadequacies as a partner.

She went skating in the winter evenings. She played badminton.

She had never lacked friends, and she didn't now. Most of the people who had been in the last year of high school with her were finishing college now, or were already working at a distance, as teachers or nurses or chartered accountants. But she made friends with others who had dropped out before senior year to work in banks or stores or offices, to become plumbers or milliners. The girls in this group were dropping like flies, as they said of each other – they were dropping into matrimony. Enid was an organizer of bridal showers and a help at trousseau teas. In a couple of years would come the christenings, where she could expect to be a favorite godmother. Children not related to her would grow up calling her Aunt. And she was already a sort of honorary daughter to women of her mother's age and older, the only young woman who had time for the Book Club and the Horticultural Society. So, quickly and easily, still in her youth, she was slipping into this essential, central, yet isolated role.

But in fact it had been her role all along. In high school she was always the class secretary or class social convener. She was well liked and high-spirited and well dressed and good-looking, but she was slightly set apart. She had friends who were boys but never a boyfriend. She did not seem to have made a choice this way, but she was not worried about it, either. She had been preoccupied with her ambition – to be a missionary, at one embarrassing stage, and then to be a nurse. She had never thought of nursing as just something to do until she got married. Her hope was to be good, and do good, and not necessarily in the orderly, customary, wifely way.

At New Year's she went to the dance in the Town Hall. The man who danced with her most often, and escorted her home, and pressed her hand good night, was the manager of the creamery – a man in his forties, never married, an excellent dancer, an avuncular friend to girls unlikely to find partners. No woman ever took him seriously.

"Maybe you should take a business course," her mother said. "Or why shouldn't you go to college?"

Where the men might be more appreciative, she was surely thinking.

"I'm too old," said Enid.

Her mother laughed. "That only shows how young you are," she said. She seemed relieved to discover that her daughter had a touch of folly natural to her age – that she could think twenty-one was at a vast distance from eighteen.

"I'm not going to troop in with kids out of high school," Enid said. "I mean it. What do you want to get rid of me for anyway? I'm fine here." This sulkiness or sharpness also seemed to please and reassure her mother. But after a moment she sighed, and said, "You'll be surprised how fast the years go by."

That August there were a lot of cases of measles and a few of polio at the same time. The doctor who had looked after Enid's father, and had observed her competence around the hospital, asked her if she would be willing to help out for a while, nursing people at home. She said that she would think about it.

"You mean pray?" her mother said, and Enid's face took on a stubborn, secretive expression that in another girl's case might have had to do with meeting her boyfriend.

"That promise," she said to her mother the next day. "That was about working in a hospital, wasn't it?"

Her mother said that she had understood it that way, yes.

"And with graduating and being a registered nurse?"

Yes, yes.

So if there were people who needed nursing at home, who couldn't afford to go to the hospital or did not want to go, and if Enid went into their houses to nurse them, not as a registered nurse but as what they called a practical nurse, she would hardly be breaking her promise, would she? And since most of those needing her care would be children or women having babies, or old people dying, there would not be much danger of the coarsening effect, would there?

"If the only men you get to see are men who are never going to get out of bed again, you have a point," said her mother.

But she could not keep from adding that what all this meant was that Enid had decided to give up the possibility of a decent job in a hospital in order to do miserable backbreaking work in miserable primitive houses for next to no money. Enid would find herself pumping water from contaminated wells and breaking ice in winter washbasins and battling flies in summer and using an outdoor toilet. Scrub boards and coal-oil lamps instead of washing machines and electricity. Trying to look after sick people in those conditions and cope with housework and poor weaselly children as well.

"But if that is your object in life," she said, "I can see that the worse I make it sound the more determined you get to do it. The only thing is, I'm going to ask for a couple of promises myself. Promise me you'll boil the water you drink. And you won't marry a farmer."

Enid said, "Of all the crazy ideas."

That was sixteen years ago. During the first of those years people got poorer and poorer. There were more and more of them who could not afford to go to the hospital, and the houses where Enid worked had often deteriorated almost to the state that her mother had described. Sheets and diapers had to be washed by hand in houses where the washing machine had broken down and could not be repaired, or the electricity had been turned off, or where there had never been any electricity in the first place. Enid did not work without pay, because that would not have been fair to the other women who did the same kind of nursing, and who did not have the same options as she did. But she gave most of the money back, in the form of children's shoes and winter coats and trips to the dentist and Christmas toys.

Her mother went around canvassing her friends for old baby cots, and high chairs and blankets, and worn-out sheets, which she herself ripped up and hemmed to make diapers. Everybody said how proud she must be of Enid, and she said yes, she surely was.

"But sometimes it's a devil of a lot of work," she said. "This being the mother of a saint."

Then came the war, and the great shortage of doctors and nurses, and Enid was more welcome than ever. As she was for a while after the war, with so many babies being born. It was only now, with the hospitals being enlarged and many farms getting prosperous, that it looked as if her responsibilities might dwindle away to the care of those who had bizarre and hopeless afflictions, or were so irredeemably cranky that hospitals had thrown them out.

This summer there was a great downpour of rain every few days, and then the sun came out very hot, glittering off the drenched leaves and grass. Early mornings were full of mist – they were so close, here, to the river and even when the mist cleared off you could not see very far in any direction, because of the overflow and density of summer. The heavy trees, the bushes all bound up with wild grapevines and Virginia creeper, the crops of corn and barley and wheat and hay. Everything was ahead of itself, as people said. The hay was ready to cut in June, and Rupert had to rush to get it into the barn before a rain spoiled it.

He came into the house later and later in the evenings, having worked as long as the light lasted. One night when he came the house was in darkness, except for a candle burning on the kitchen table.

Enid hurried to unhook the screen door.

"Power out?" said Rupert.

Enid said, "Shhh." She whispered to him that she was letting the children sleep downstairs, because the upstairs rooms were so hot. She had pushed the chairs together and made beds on them with quilts and pillows. And of course she had had to turn the lights out so that they could get to sleep. She had found a candle in one of the drawers, and that was all she needed, to see to write by, in her notebook.

"They'll always remember sleeping here," she said. "You

always remember the times when you were a child and you slept somewhere different."

He set down a box that contained a ceiling fan for the sickroom. He had been into Walley to buy it. He had also bought a newspaper, which he handed to Enid.

"Thought you might like to know what's going on in the world," he said.

She spread the paper out beside her notebook, on the table. There was a picture of a couple of dogs playing in a fountain.

"It says there's a heat wave," she said. "Isn't it nice to find out about it?"

Rupert was carefully lifting the fan out of its box.

"That'll be wonderful," she said. "It's cooled off in there now, but it'll be such a comfort to her tomorrow."

"I'll be over early to put it up," he said. Then he asked how his wife had been that day.

Enid said that the pains in her legs had been easing off, and the new pills the doctor had her on seemed to be letting her get some rest.

"The only thing is, she goes to sleep so soon," she said. "It makes it hard for you to get a visit."

"Better she gets the rest," Rupert said.

This whispered conversation reminded Enid of conversations in high school, when they were both in their senior year and that earlier teasing, or cruel flirtation, or whatever it was, had long been abandoned. All that last year Rupert had sat in the seat behind hers, and they had often spoken to each other briefly, always to some immediate purpose. Have you got an ink eraser? How do you spell "incriminate"? Where is the Tyrrhenian Sea? Usually it was Enid, half turning in her seat and able only to sense, not see, how close Rupert was, who started these conversations. She did want to borrow an eraser, she was in need of information, but also she wanted to be sociable. And she wanted to make amends – she felt ashamed of the way she and her friends had treated him. It would do no good to apologize – that would just embarrass him all over again. He was only at ease when he sat behind her, and knew that she could not look him in the face. If they met on the street he would look away until the last minute, then mutter the faintest greeting while she sang out "Hello, Rupert," and heard an echo of the old tormenting tones she wanted to banish.

But when he actually laid a finger on her shoulder, tapping for attention, when he bent forward, almost touching or maybe really touching – she could not tell for sure – her thick hair that was wild even in a bob, then she felt forgiven. In a way, she felt honored. Restored to seriousness and to respect.

Where, where exactly, is the Tyrrhenian Sea?

She wondered if he remembered anything at all of that now.

She separated the back and front parts of the paper. Margaret Truman was visiting England, and had curtsied to the royal family. The King's doctors were trying to cure his Buerger's disease with vitamin E.

She offered the front part to Rupert. "I'm going to look at the crossword," she said. "I like to do the crossword – it relaxes me at the end of the day."

Rupert sat down and began to read the paper, and she asked him if he would like a cup of tea. Of course he said not to bother, and she went ahead and made it anyway, understanding that this reply might as well be yes in country speech.

"It's a South American theme," she said, looking at the crossword. "Latin American theme. First across is a musical ... *garment*. A musical garment? Garment. A lot of letters. Oh. Oh. I'm lucky tonight. Cape Horn!

"You see how silly they are, these things," she said, and rose and poured the tea.

If he did remember, did he hold anything against her? Maybe her blithe friendliness in their senior year had been as unwelcome, as superior-seeming to him, as that early taunting?

When she first saw him in this house, she thought that he had not changed much. He had been a tall, solid, round-faced boy, and he was a tall, heavy, round-faced man. He had worn his hair cut so short, always, that it didn't make much difference that there was less of it now and that it had turned from light brown to gray-brown. A permanent sunburn had taken the place of his blushes. And whatever troubled him and showed in his face might have been just the same old trouble – the problem of occupying space in the world and having a name that people could call you by, being somebody they thought they could know.

She thought of them sitting in the senior class. A small class, by that time – in five years the unstudious, the carefree, and the indifferent had been weeded out, leaving these overgrown, grave, and docile children learning trigonometry, learning Latin. What kind of life did they think they were preparing for? What kind of people did they think they were going to be?

She could see the dark-green, softened cover of a book called *History of the Renaissance and Reformation*. It was secondhand, or tenthhand – nobody ever bought a new textbook. Inside were written all the names of the previous owners, some of whom were middle-aged housewives or merchants around the town. You could not imagine them learning these things, or underlining "Edict of Nantes" with red ink and writing "N.B." in the margin.

Edict of Nantes. The very uselessness, the exotic nature, of the things in those books and in those students' heads, in her own head then and Rupert's, made Enid feel a tenderness and wonder. It wasn't that they had meant to be something that they hadn't become. Nothing like that. Rupert couldn't have imagined anything but farming this farm. It was a good farm, and he was an only son. And she herself had ended up doing exactly what she must have wanted to do. You couldn't say that they had chosen the wrong lives or chosen against their will or not understood their choices. Just that they had not understood how time would pass and leave them not more but maybe a little less than what they used to be.

"'Bread of the Amazon,'" she said. "'Bread of the Amazon'?"

Rupert said, "Manioc?"

Enid counted. "Seven letters," she said. "Seven."

He said, "Cassava?"

"Cassava? That's a double *s*? Cassava."

Mrs. Quinn became more capricious daily about her food. Sometimes she said she wanted toast, or bananas with milk on them. One day she said peanut-butter cookies. Enid prepared all these things – the children could eat them anyway – and when they were ready Mrs. Quinn could not stand the look or the smell of them. Even Jell-O had a smell she could not stand.

Some days she hated all noise; she would not even have the fan going. Other days she wanted the radio on, she wanted the station that played requests for birthdays and anniversaries and called people up to ask them questions. If you got the answer right you won a trip to Niagara Falls, a tankful of gas, or a load of groceries or tickets to a movie.

"It's all fixed," Mrs. Quinn said. "They just pretend to call somebody up – they're in the next room and already got the answer told to them. I used to know somebody that worked for a radio, that's the truth."

On these days her pulse was rapid. She talked very fast in a light, breathless voice. "What kind of car is that your mother's got?" she said.

"It's a maroon-colored car," said Enid.

"What *make*?" said Mrs. Quinn.

Enid said she did not know, which was the truth. She had known, but she had forgotten.

"Was it new when she got it?"

"Yes," said Enid. "Yes. But that was three or four years ago."

"She lives in that big rock house next door to Willenses?"

Yes, said Enid.

"How many rooms it got? Sixteen?"

"Too many."

"Did you go to Mr. Willens's funeral when he got drownded?"

Enid said no. "I'm not much for funerals."

"I was supposed to go. I wasn't awfully sick then, I was going with Herveys up the highway, they said I could get a ride with them and then her mother and her sister wanted to go and there wasn't enough room in back. Then Clive and Olive went in the truck and I could've scrunched up in their front seat but they never thought to ask me. Do you think he drownded himself?"

Enid thought of Mr. Willens handing her a rose. His jokey gallantry that made the nerves of her teeth ache, as from too much sugar.

"I don't know. I wouldn't think so."

"Did him and Mrs. Willens get along all right?"

"As far as I know, they got along beautifully."

"Oh, is that so?" said Mrs. Quinn, trying to imitate Enid's reserved tone. "Bee-you-tif-ley."

Enid slept on the couch in Mrs. Quinn's room. Mrs. Quinn's devastating itch had almost disappeared, as had her need to urinate. She slept through most of the night, though she would have spells of harsh and angry breathing. What woke Enid up and kept her awake was a trouble of her own. She had begun to have ugly dreams. These were unlike any dreams she had ever had before. She used to think that a bad dream was one of finding herself in an unfamiliar house where the rooms kept changing and there was always more work to do than she could handle, work undone that she thought she had done, innumerable distractions. And then, of course, she had what she thought of as romantic dreams, in which some man would have his arm around her or even be embracing her. It might be a stranger or a man she knew – sometimes a man whom it was quite a joke to think of in that way. These dreams made her thoughtful or a little sad but relieved in some way to know that such feelings were possible for her. They could be embarrassing, but were nothing, nothing at all compared with the dreams that she was having now. In the dreams that came to her now she would be copulating or trying to copulate (sometimes she was prevented by intruders or shifts of circumstances) with utterly forbidden and unthinkable partners. With fat squirmy babies or patients in bandages or her own mother. She would be slick with lust, hollow and groaning with it, and she would set to work with roughness and an attitude of evil pragmatism. "Yes, this will have to do," she would say to herself. "This will do if nothing better comes along." And this coldness of heart, this matter-of-fact depravity, simply drove her lust along. She woke up unrepentant, sweaty and exhausted, and lay like a carcass until her own self, her shame and disbelief, came pouring back into her. The sweat went cold on her skin. She lay there shivering in the warm night, with disgust and humiliation. She did not dare go back to sleep. She got used to the dark and the long rectangles of the net-curtained windows filled with a faint light. And the sick woman's breath grating and scolding and then almost disappearing.

If she were a Catholic, she thought, was this the sort of thing that could come out at confession? It didn't seem like the sort of thing she could even bring out in a private prayer. She didn't pray much anymore, except formally, and to bring the experiences she had just been through to the attention of God seemed absolutely useless, disrespectful. He would be insulted. She was insulted, by her own mind. Her religion was hopeful and sensible and there was no room in it for any sort of rubbishy drama, such as the invasion of the devil into her sleep. The filth in her mind was in her, and there was no point in dramatizing it and making it seem important. Surely not. It was nothing, just the mind's garbage.

In the little meadow between the house and the riverbank there were cows. She could hear them munching and jostling, feeding at night. She thought of their large gentle shapes in there with the money musk and chicory, the flowering grasses, and she thought, They have a lovely life, cows.

It ends, of course, in the slaughterhouse. The end is disaster.

For everybody, though, the same thing. Evil grabs us when we are sleeping; pain and disintegration lie in wait. Animal horrors, all worse than you can imagine beforehand. The comforts of bed and the cows' breath, the pattern of the stars at night – all that can get turned on its head in an instant. And here she was, here was Enid, working her life away pretending it wasn't so. Trying to ease people. Trying to be good. An angel of mercy, as her mother had said, with less and less irony as time went on. Patients and doctors, too, had said it.

And all the time how many thought that she was a fool? The people she spent her labors on might secretly despise her. Thinking they'd never do the same in her place. Never be fool enough. No.

Miserable offenders, came into her head. *Miserable offenders.*

Restore them that are penitent.

So she got up and went to work; as far as she was concerned, that was the best way to be penitent. She worked very quietly but steadily through the night, washing the cloudy glasses and sticky plates that were in the cupboards and establishing order where there was none before. None. Teacups had sat between the ketchup and the mustard and toilet paper on top of a pail of honey. There was no waxed paper or even newspaper laid out on the shelves. Brown sugar in the bag was as hard as rock. It was understandable that things should have gone downhill in the last few months, but it looked as if there had been no care, no organization here, ever. All the net curtains were gray with smoke and the windowpanes were greasy. The last bit of jam had been left to grow fuzz in the jar, and vile-smelling water that had held some ancient bouquet had never been dumped out of its jug. But this was a good house still, that scrubbing and painting could restore. Though what could you do about the ugly brown paint that had been recently and sloppily applied to the front-room floor?

When she had a moment later in the day she pulled the weeds out of Rupert's mother's flower beds, dug up the burdocks and twitch grass that were smothering the valiant perennials.

She taught the children to hold their spoons properly and to say grace.

Thank you for the world so sweet,
Thank you for the food we eat . . .

She taught them to brush their teeth and after that to say their prayers.

"God bless Mama and Daddy and Enid and Aunt Olive and Uncle Clive and Princess Elizabeth and Margaret Rose." After that each added the name of the other. They had been doing it for quite a while when Sylvie said, "What does it mean?"

Enid said, "What does what mean?"

"What does it mean 'God bless'?"

Enid made eggnogs, not flavoring them even with vanilla, and fed them to Mrs. Quinn from a spoon. She fed her a little of the rich liquid at a time, and Mrs. Quinn was able to hold down what was given to her in small amounts. If she could not do that, Enid spooned out flat, lukewarm ginger ale.

The sunlight, or any light, was as hateful as noise to Mrs. Quinn by now. Enid had to hang thick quilts over the windows, even when the blinds were pulled down. With the fan shut off, as Mrs. Quinn demanded, the room became very hot, and sweat dripped from Enid's forehead as she bent over the bed attending to the patient. Mrs. Quinn went into fits of shivering; she could never be warm enough.

"This is dragging out," the doctor said. "It must be those milkshakes you're giving her, keeping her going."

"Eggnogs," said Enid, as if it mattered.

Mrs. Quinn was often now too tired or weak to talk. Sometimes she lay in a stupor, with her breathing so faint and her pulse so lost and wandering that a person less experienced than Enid would have taken her for dead. But at other times she rallied, wanted the radio on, then wanted it off. She knew perfectly well who she was still, and who Enid was, and she sometimes seemed to be watching Enid with a speculative or inquiring look in her eyes. Color was long gone from her face and even from her lips, but her eyes looked greener than they had in the past – a milky, cloudy green. Enid tried to answer the look that was bent on her.

"Would you like me to get a priest to talk to you?"

Mrs. Quinn looked as if she wanted to spit.

"Do I look like a Mick?" she said.

"A minister?" said Enid. She knew this was the right thing to ask, but the spirit in which she asked it was not right – it was cold and faintly malicious.

No. This was not what Mrs. Quinn wanted. She grunted with displeasure. There was some energy in her still, and Enid had the feeling that she was building it up for a purpose. "Do you want to talk to your children?" she said, making herself speak compassionately and encouragingly. "Is that what you want?"

No.

"Your husband? Your husband will be here in a little while."

Enid didn't know that for sure. Rupert arrived so late some nights, after Mrs. Quinn had taken the final pills and gone to sleep. Then he sat with Enid. He always brought her the newspaper. He asked what she wrote in her notebooks – he noticed that there were two – and she told him. One for the doctor, with a record of blood pressure and pulse and temperature, a record of what was eaten, vomited, excreted, medicines taken, some general summing up of the patient's condition. In the other notebook, for herself, she wrote many of the same things, though perhaps not so exactly, but she added details about the weather and what was happening all around. And things to remember.

"For instance, I wrote something down the other day," she said. "Something that Lois said. Lois and Sylvie came in when Mrs. Green was here and Mrs. Green was mentioning how the berry bushes were growing along the lane and stretching across the road, and Lois said, 'It's like in "Sleeping Beauty."' Because I'd read them the story. I made a note of that."

Rupert said, "I'll have to get after those berry canes and cut them back."

Enid got the impression that he was pleased by what Lois had said and by the fact that she had written it down, but it wasn't possible for him to say so.

One night he told her that he would be away for a couple of days, at a stock auction. He had asked the doctor if it was all right, and the doctor had said to go ahead.

That night he had come before the last pills were given, and Enid supposed that he was making a point of seeing his wife awake before that little time away. She told him to go right into Mrs. Quinn's room, and he did, and shut the door after him. Enid picked up the paper and thought of going upstairs to read it, but the children probably weren't asleep yet; they would find excuses for calling her in. She could go out on the porch, but there were mosquitoes at this time of day, especially after a rain like the afternoon's.

She was afraid of overhearing some intimacy or perhaps the suggestion of a fight, then having to face him when he came out. Mrs. Quinn was building up to a display – of that Enid felt sure. And before she made up her mind where to go she did overhear something. Not the recriminations or (if it was possible) the endearments, or perhaps even weeping, that she had been half expecting, but a laugh. She heard Mrs.

Quinn weakly laughing, and the laughter had the mockery and satisfaction in it that Enid had heard before but also something she hadn't heard before, not in her life – something deliberately vile. She didn't move, though she should have, and she was at the table still, she was still there staring at the door of the room, when he came out a moment later. He didn't avoid her eyes – or she his. She couldn't. Yet she couldn't have said for sure that he saw her. He just looked at her and went on outside. He looked as if he had caught hold of an electric wire and begged pardon – who of? – that his body was given over to this stupid catastrophe.

The next day Mrs. Quinn's strength came flooding back, in that unnatural and deceptive way that Enid had seen once or twice in others. Mrs. Quinn wanted to sit up against the pillows. She wanted the fan turned on.

Enid said, "What a good idea."

"I could tell you something you wouldn't believe," Mrs. Quinn said.

"People tell me lots of things," said Enid.

"Sure. Lies," Mrs. Quinn said. "I bet it's all lies. You know Mr. Willens was right here in this room?"

III. MISTAKE

Mrs. Quinn had been sitting in the rocker getting her eyes examined and Mr. Willens had been close up in front of her with the thing up to her eyes, and neither one of them heard Rupert come in, because he was supposed to be cutting wood down by the river. But he had sneaked back. He sneaked back through the kitchen not making any noise – he must have seen Mr. Willens's car outside before he did that – then he opened the door to this room just easy, till he saw Mr. Willens there on his knees holding the thing up to her eye and he had the other hand on her leg to keep his balance. He had grabbed her leg to keep his balance and her skirt got scrunched up and her leg showed bare, but that was all there was to it and she couldn't do a thing about it, she had to concentrate on keeping still.

So Rupert got in the room without either of them hearing him come in and then he just gave one jump and landed on Mr. Willens like a bolt of lightning and Mr. Willens couldn't get up or turn around, he was down before he knew it. Rupert banged his head up and down on the floor, Rupert banged the life out of him, and she jumped up so fast the chair went over and Mr. Willens's box where he kept his eye things got knocked over and all the things flew out of it. Rupert just walloped him, and maybe he hit the leg of the stove, she didn't know what. She thought, It's me next. But she couldn't get round them to run out of the room. And then she saw Rupert wasn't going to go for her after all. He was out of wind and he just set the chair up and sat down in it. She went to Mr. Willens then and hauled him around, as heavy as he was, to get him right side up. His eyes were not quite open, not shut either, and there was dribble coming out of his mouth. But no skin broke on his face or bruise you could see – maybe it wouldn't have come up yet. The stuff coming out of his mouth didn't even look like blood. It was pink stuff, and if you wanted to know what it looked like it looked exactly like when the froth comes up when you're boiling the strawberries to make jam. Bright pink. It was smeared over his face from when Rupert had him facedown. He made a sound, too, when she was turning him over. *Glug-glug.* That was all there was to it. *Glug-glug* and he was laid out like a stone.

Rupert jumped out of the chair so it was still rocking, and he started picking up all the things and putting each one back where it went in Mr. Willens's box. Getting everything fitted in the way it should go. Wasting the time that way. It was a special box lined with red plush and a place in it for each one of his things that he used and you had to get everything in right or the top wouldn't go down. Rupert got it so the top went on and then he just sat down in the chair again and started pounding on his knees.

On the table there was one of those good-for-nothing cloths, it was a souvenir of when Rupert's mother and father went up north to see the Dionne Quintuplets. She took it off the table and wrapped it around Mr. Willens's head to soak up the pink stuff and so they wouldn't have to keep on looking at him.

Rupert kept banging his big flat hands. She said, Rupert, we got to bury him somewhere.

Rupert just looked at her, like to say, Why?

She said they could bury him down in the cellar, which had a dirt floor.

"That's right," said Rupert. "Where are we going to bury his car?"

She said they could put it in the barn and cover it up with hay.

He said too many people came poking around the barn.

Then she thought, Put him in the river. She thought of him sitting in his car right under the water. It came to her like a picture. Rupert didn't say anything at first, so she went into the kitchen and got some water and cleaned Mr. Willens up so he wouldn't dribble on anything. The goo was not coming up in his mouth anymore. She got his keys, which were in his pocket. She could feel, through the cloth of his pants, the fat of his leg still warm.

She said to Rupert, Get moving.

He took the keys.

They hoisted Mr. Willens up, she by the feet and Rupert by the head, and he weighed a ton. He was like lead. But as she carried him one of his shoes kind of kicked her between the legs, and she thought, There you are, you're still at it, you horny old devil. Even his dead old foot giving her the nudge. Not that she ever let him do anything, but he was always ready to get a grab if he could. Like grabbing her leg up under her skirt when he had the thing to her eye and she couldn't stop him and Rupert had to come sneaking in and get the wrong idea.

Over the doorsill and through the kitchen and across the porch and down the porch steps. All clear. But it was a windy day, and, first thing, the wind blew away the cloth she had wrapped over Mr. Willens's face.

Their yard couldn't be seen from the road, that was lucky. Just the peak of the roof and the upstairs window. Mr. Willens's car couldn't be seen.

Rupert had thought up the rest of what to do. Take him to Jutland, where it was deep water and the track going all the way back and it could look like he just drove in from the road and mistook his way. Like he turned off on the Jutland road, maybe it was dark and he just drove into the water before he knew where he was at. Like he just made a mistake.

He did. Mr. Willens certainly did make a mistake.

The trouble was it meant driving out their lane and along the road to the Jutland turn. But nobody lived down there and it was a dead end after the Jutland turn, so just the half mile or so to pray you never met anybody. Then Rupert would get Mr. Willens over in the driver's seat and push the car right off down the bank into the water. Push the whole works down into the pond. It was going to be a job to do that, but Rupert at least was a strong bugger. If he hadn't been so strong they wouldn't have been in this mess in the first place.

Rupert had a little trouble getting the car started because he had never driven one like that, but he did, and got turned around and drove off down the lane with Mr. Willens kind of bumping over against him. He had put Mr. Willens's hat on his head – the hat that had been sitting on the seat of the car.

Why take his hat off before he came into the house? Not just to be polite but so he could easier get a clutch on her and kiss her. If you could call that kissing, all that pushing up against her with the box still in one hand and the other grabbing on, and sucking away at her with his dribbly old mouth. Sucking and chewing away at her lips and her tongue and pushing himself up at her and the corner of the box sticking into her and digging her behind. She was so surprised and he got such a hold she didn't know how to get out of it. Pushing and sucking and dribbling and digging into her and hurting her all at the same time. He was a dirty old brute.

She went and got the Quintuplets cloth where it had blown onto the fence. She looked hard for blood on the steps or any mess on the porch or through the kitchen, but all she found was in the front room, also some on her shoes. She scrubbed up what was on the floor and scrubbed her shoes, which she took off, and not till she had all that done did she see a smear right down her front. How did she come by that? And the same time she saw it she heard a noise that turned her to stone. She heard a car and it was a car she didn't know and it was coming down the lane.

She looked through the net curtain and sure enough. A new-looking car and dark green. Her smeared-down front and shoes off and the floor wet. She moved back where she couldn't be seen, but she couldn't think of where to hide. The car stopped and a car door opened, but the engine didn't cut off. She heard the door shut and then the car turned around and she heard the sound of it driving back up the lane. And she heard Lois and Sylvie on the porch.

It was the teacher's boyfriend's car. He picked up the teacher every Friday afternoon, and this was a Friday. So the teacher said to him, Why don't we give these ones a lift home, they're the littlest and they got the farthest to go and it looks like it's going to rain.

It did rain, too. It had started by the time Rupert got back, walking home along the riverbank. She said, A good thing, it'll muddy up your tracks where you went to push it over. He said he'd took his shoes off and worked in his sock feet. So you must have got your brains going again, she said.

Instead of trying to soak the stuff out of that souvenir cloth or the blouse she had on, she decided to burn the both of them in the stove. They made a horrible smell and the smell made her sick. That was the whole beginning of her being sick. That and the paint. After she cleaned up the floor, she could still see where she thought there was a stain, so she got the brown paint left over from when Rupert painted the steps and she painted over the whole floor. That started her throwing up, leaning over and breathing in that paint. And the pains in her back – that was the start of them, too.

After she got the floor painted she just about quit going into the front room. But one day she thought she had better put some other cloth on that table. It would make things look more normal. If she didn't, then her sister-in-law was sure to come nosing around and say, Where's that cloth Mom and Dad brought back the time they went to see the Quints? If she had a different cloth on she could say, Oh, I just felt like a change. But no cloth would look funny.

So she got a cloth Rupert's mother had embroidered with flower baskets and took it in there and she could still smell the smell. And there on the table was sitting the dark-red box with Mr. Willens's things in it and his name on it and it had been sitting there all the time. She didn't even remember putting it there or seeing Rupert put it there. She had forgot all about it.

She took that box and hid it in one place and then she hid it in another. She never told where she hid it and she wasn't going to. She would have smashed it up, but how do you smash all those things in it? Examining things. Oh, Missus, would you like me to examine your eyes for you, just sit down here and just you relax and you just shut the one eye and keep the other one wide open. Wide open, now. It was like the same game every time, and she wasn't supposed to suspect what was going on, and when he had the thing out looking in her eye he wanted her to keep her panties on, him the dirty old cuss puffing away getting his fingers slicked in and puffing away. Her not supposed to say anything till he stops and gets the looker thing packed up in his box and all and then she's supposed to say, "Oh, Mr. Willens, now, how much do I owe you for today?"

And that was the signal for him to get her down and thump her like an old billy goat. Right on the bare floor to knock her up and down and try to bash her into pieces. Dingey on him like a blowtorch.

How'd you've liked that?

Then it was in the papers. Mr. Willens found drowned.

They said his head got bunged up knocking against the steering wheel. They said he was alive when he went in the water. What a laugh.

IV. LIES

Enid stayed awake all night – she didn't even try to sleep. She could not lie down in Mrs. Quinn's room. She sat in the kitchen for hours. It was an effort for her to move, even to make a cup of tea or go to the bathroom. Moving her body shook up the information that she was trying to arrange in her head and get used to. She had not undressed, or unrolled her hair, and when she brushed her teeth she seemed to be doing something laborious and unfamiliar. The moonlight came through the kitchen window – she was sitting in the dark – and she watched a patch of light shift through the night, on the linoleum, and disappear. She was surprised by its disappearance and then by the birds waking up, the new day starting. The night had seemed so long and then too short, because nothing had been decided.

She got up stiffly and unlocked the door and sat on the porch in the beginning light. Even that move jammed her thoughts together. She had to sort through them again and set them on two sides. What had happened – or what she had been told had happened – on one side. What to do about it on the other. What to do about it – that was what would not come clear to her.

The cows had been moved out of the little meadow between the house and the riverbank. She could open the gate if she wanted to and go in that direction. She knew that she should go back, instead, and check on Mrs. Quinn. But she found herself pulling open the gate bolt.

The cows hadn't cropped all the weeds. Sopping wet, they brushed against her stockings. The path was clear, though, under the riverbank trees, those big willows with the wild grape hanging on to them like monkeys' shaggy arms. Mist was rising so that you could hardly see the river. You had to fix your eyes, concentrate, and then a spot of water would show through, quiet as water in a pot. There must be a moving current, but she could not find it.

Then she saw a movement, and it wasn't in the water. There was a boat moving. Tied to a branch, a plain old rowboat was being lifted very slightly, lifted and let fall. Now that she had found it, she kept watching it, as if it could say something to her. And it did. It said something gentle and final.

You know. You know.

When the children woke up they found her in bountiful good spirits, freshly washed and dressed and with her hair loose. She had already made the Jell-O crammed with fruit that would be ready for them to eat at noon. And she was mixing batter for cookies that could be baked before it got too hot to use the oven.

"Is that your father's boat?" she said. "Down on the river?"

Lois said yes. "But we're not supposed to play in it." Then she said, "If you went down with us we could." They had caught on at once to the day's air of privilege, its holiday possibilities, Enid's unusual mix of languor and excitement.

"We'll see," said Enid. She wanted to make the day a special one for them, special aside from the fact – which she was already almost certain of – that it would be the day of their mother's death. She wanted them to hold something in their minds that could throw a redeeming light on whatever came later. On herself, that is, and whatever way she would affect their lives later.

That morning Mrs. Quinn's pulse had been hard to find and she had not been able, apparently, to raise her head or open her eyes. A great change from yesterday, but Enid was not surprised. She had thought that great spurt of energy, that wicked outpouring talk, would be the last. She held a spoon with water in it to Mrs. Quinn's lips, and Mrs. Quinn drew a little of the water in. She made a mewing sound – the last trace, surely, of all her complaints. Enid did not call the doctor, because he was due to visit anyway later that day, probably early in the afternoon.

She shook up soapsuds in a jar and bent a piece of wire, and then another piece, to make bubble wands. She showed the children how to make bubbles, blowing steadily and carefully until as large a shining bladder as possible trembled on the wire, then shaking it delicately free. They chased the bubbles around the yard and kept them afloat till breezes caught them and hung them in the trees or on the eaves of the porch. What kept them alive then seemed to be the cries of admiration, screams of joy, rising up from below. Enid put no restriction on the noise they could make, and when the soapsud mixture was all used up she made more.

The doctor phoned when she was giving the children their lunch – Jell-O and a plate of cookies sprinkled with colored sugar and glasses of milk into which she had stirred chocolate syrup. He said he had been held up by a child's falling out of a tree and he would probably not be out before suppertime. Enid said softly, "I think she may be going."

"Well, keep her comfortable if you can," the doctor said. "You know how as well as I do."

Enid didn't phone Mrs. Green. She knew that Rupert would not be back yet from the auction and she didn't think that Mrs. Quinn, if she ever had another moment of consciousness, would want to see or hear her sister-in-law in the room. Nor did it seem likely that she would want to see her children. And there would be nothing good about seeing her for them to remember.

She didn't bother trying to take Mrs. Quinn's blood pressure anymore, or her temperature – just sponged off her face and arms and offered the water, which was no longer noticed. She turned on the fan, whose noise Mrs. Quinn had so often objected to. The smell rising from the body seemed to be changing, losing its ammoniac sharpness. Changing into the common odor of death.

She went out and sat on the steps. She took off her shoes and stockings and stretched out her legs in the sun. The children began cautiously to pester her, asking if she would take them down to the river, if they could sit in the boat, or if they found the oars could she take them rowing. She knew enough not to go that far in the way of desertion, but she asked them, Would they like to have a swimming pool? Two swimming pools? And she brought out the two laundry tubs, set them on the grass, and filled them with water from the cistern pump. They stripped to their underpants and lolled in the water, becoming Princess Elizabeth and Princess Margaret Rose.

"What do you think," said Enid, sitting on the grass with her head back and her eyes shut, "what do you think, if a person does something very bad, do they have to be punished?"

"Yes," said Lois immediately. "They have to get a licking."

"Who did it?" said Sylvie.

"Just thinking of anybody," said Enid. "Now, what if it was a very bad thing but nobody knew they did it? Should they tell that they did and be punished?"

Sylvie said, "I would know they did it."

"You would not," said Lois. "How would you know?"

"I would've seed them."

"You would not."

"You know the reason I think they should be punished?" Enid said. "It's because of how bad they are going to feel, in themselves. Even if nobody did see them and nobody ever knew. If you do something very bad and you are not punished you feel worse, and feel far worse, than if you are."

"Lois stold a green comb," Sylvie said.

"I did not," said Lois.

"I want you to remember that," Enid said.

Lois said, "It was just laying the side the road."

Enid went into the sickroom every half hour or so to wipe Mrs. Quinn's face and hands with a damp cloth. She never spoke to her and never touched her hand, except with the cloth. She had never absented herself like this before with anybody who was dying. When she opened the door at around half past five she knew there was nobody alive in the room. The sheet was pulled out and Mrs. Quinn's head was hanging over the side of the bed, a fact that Enid did not record or mention to anybody. She had the body straightened out and cleaned and the bed put to rights before the doctor came. The children were still playing in the yard.

"July 5. Rain early a.m. L. and S. playing under porch. Fan off and on, complains noise. Half cup eggnog spoon at a time. B.P. up, pulse rapid, no complaints pain. Rain didn't cool off much. R.Q. in evening. Hay finished.

"July 6. Hot day, vy. close. Try fan but no. Sponge often. R.Q. in evening. Start to cut wheat tomorrow. Everything 1 or 2 wks ahead due to heat, rain.

"July 7. Cont'd heat. Won't take eggnog. Ginger ale from spoon. Vy. weak. Heavy rain last night, wind. R.Q. not able to cut, grain lodged some places.

"July 8. No eggnog. Ginger ale. Vomiting a.m. More alert. R.Q. to go to calf auction, gone 2 days. Dr. says go ahead.

"July 9. Vy. agitated. Terrible talk.

"July 10. Patient Mrs. Rupert (Jeanette) Quinn died today approx. 5 p.m. Heart failure due to uremia. (Glomerulonephritis.)"

Enid never made a practice of waiting around for the funerals of people she had nursed. It seemed to her a good idea to get out of the house as soon as she decently could. Her presence could not help being a reminder of the time just before the death, which might have been dreary and full of physical disaster, and was now going to be glossed over with ceremony and hospitality and flowers and cakes.

Also, there was usually some female relative who would be in place to take over the household completely, putting Enid suddenly in the position of unwanted guest.

Mrs. Green, in fact, arrived at the Quinns' house before the undertaker did. Rupert was not back yet. The doctor was in the kitchen drinking a cup of tea and talking to Enid about another case that she could take up now that this was finished. Enid was hedging, saying that she had thought of taking some time off. The children were upstairs. They had been told that their mother had gone to heaven, which for them had put the cap on this rare and eventful day.

Mrs. Green was shy until the doctor left. She stood at the window to see him turn his car around and drive away. Then she said, "Maybe I shouldn't say it right now, but I will. I'm glad it happened now and not later when the summer was over and they were started back to school. Now I'll have time to get them used to living at our place and used to the idea of the new school they'll be going to. Rupert, he'll have to get used to it, too."

This was the first time that Enid had realized that Mrs. Green meant to take the children to live with her, not just to stay for a while. Mrs. Green was eager to manage the move, had been looking forward to it, probably, for some time. Very likely she had the children's rooms ready and material bought to make them new clothes. She had a large house and no children of her own.

"You must be wanting to get off home yourself," she said to Enid. As long as there was another woman in the house it might look like a rival home, and it might be harder for her brother to see the necessity of moving the children out for good. "Rupert can run you in when he gets here."

Enid said that it was all right, her mother was coming out to pick her up.

"Oh, I forgot your mother," said Mrs. Green. "Her and her snappy little car."

She brightened up and began to open the cupboard doors, checking on the glasses and the teacups – were they clean for the funeral?

"Somebody's been busy," she said, quite relieved about Enid now and ready to be complimentary.

Mr. Green was waiting outside, in the truck, with the Greens' dog, General. Mrs. Green called upstairs for Lois and Sylvie, and they came running down with some clothes in brown paper bags. They ran through the kitchen and slammed the door, without taking any notice of Enid.

"That's something that's going to have to change," said Mrs. Green, meaning the door slamming. Enid could hear the children shouting their greetings to General and General barking excitedly in return.

Two days later Enid was back, driving her mother's car herself. She came late in the afternoon, when the funeral would have been well over. There were no extra cars parked outside, which meant that the women who had helped in the kitchen had all gone home, taking with them the extra chairs and teacups and the large coffeepot that belonged to their church. The grass was marked with car tracks and some dropped crushed flowers.

She had to knock on the door now. She had to wait to be asked in.

She heard Rupert's heavy, steady footsteps. She spoke some greeting to him when he stood in front of her on the other side of the screen door, but she didn't look into his face. He was in his shirtsleeves, but was wearing his suit trousers. He undid the hook of the door.

"I wasn't sure anybody would be here," Enid said. "I thought you might still be at the barn."

Rupert said, "They all pitched in with the chores."

She could smell whiskey when he spoke, but he didn't sound drunk.

"I thought you were one of the women come back to collect something you forgot," he said.

Enid said, "I didn't forget anything. I was just wondering, how are the children?"

"They're fine. They're at Olive's."

It seemed uncertain whether he was going to ask her in. It was bewilderment that stopped him, not hostility. She had not prepared herself for this first awkward part of the conversation. So that she wouldn't have to look at him, she looked around at the sky.

"You can feel the evenings getting shorter," she said. "Even if it isn't a month since the longest day."

"That's true," said Rupert. Now he opened the door and stood aside and she went in. On the table was a cup without a saucer. She sat down at the opposite side of the table from where he had been sitting. She was wearing a dark-green silk-crepe dress and suede shoes to match. When she put these things on she had thought how this might be the last time that she would dress herself and the last clothes she would ever wear. She had done her hair up in a French braid and powdered her face. Her care, her vanity, seemed foolish but were necessary to her. She had been awake now three nights in a row, awake every minute, and she had not been able to eat, even to fool her mother.

"Was it specially difficult this time?" her mother had said. She hated discussion of illness or deathbeds, and the fact that she had brought herself to ask this meant that Enid's upset was obvious.

"Was it the children you'd got fond of?" she said. "The poor little monkeys."

Enid said it was just the problem of settling down after a long case, and a hopeless case of course had its own strain. She did not go out of her mother's house in the daytime, but she did go for walks at night, when she could be sure of not meeting anybody and having to talk. She had found herself walking past the walls of the county jail. She knew there was a prison yard behind those walls where hangings had once taken place. But not for years and years. They must do it in some large central prison now, when they had to do it. And it was a long time since anybody from this community had committed a sufficiently serious crime.

Sitting across the table from Rupert, facing the door of Mrs. Quinn's room, she had almost forgotten her excuse, lost track of the way things were to go. She felt her purse in her lap, the weight of her camera in it – that reminded her.

"There is one thing I'd like to ask you," she said. "I thought I might as well now, because I wouldn't get another chance."

Rupert said, "What's that?"

"I know you've got a rowboat. So I wanted to ask you to row me out to the middle of the river. And I could get a picture. I'd like to get a picture of the riverbank. It's beautiful there, the willow trees along the bank."

"All right," said Rupert, with the careful lack of surprise that country people will show, regarding the frivolity – the rudeness, even – of visitors.

That was what she was now – a visitor.

Her plan was to wait until they got out to the middle of the river, then to tell him that she could not swim. First ask him how deep he thought the water would be there – and he would surely say, after all the rain they had been having, that it might be seven or eight, or even ten, feet. Then tell him that she could not swim. And that would not be a lie. She had grown up in Walley, on the lake, she had played on the beach every summer of her childhood, she was a strong girl and good at games, but she was frightened of the water, and no coaxing or demonstrating or shaming had ever worked with her – she had not learned to swim.

He would only have to give her a shove with one of the oars and topple her into the water and let her sink. Then leave the boat out on the water and swim to shore, change his clothes, and say that he had come in from the barn or from a walk and found the car there, and where was she? Even the camera if found would make it more plausible. She had taken the boat out to get a picture, then somehow fallen into the river.

Once he understood his advantage, she would tell him. She would ask, Is it true?

If it was not true, he would hate her for asking. If it was true – and didn't she believe all the time that it was true? – he would hate her in another, more dangerous way. Even if she said at once – and meant it, she would mean it – that she was never going to tell.

She would speak very quietly all the time, remembering how voices carry out on the water on a summer evening.

I am not going to tell, but you are. You can't live on with that kind of secret.

You cannot live in the world with such a burden. You will not be able to stand your life.

If she had got so far, and he had neither denied what she said nor pushed her into the river, Enid would know that she had won the gamble. It would take some more talking, more absolutely firm but quiet persuasion, to bring him to the point where he would start to row back to shore.

Or, lost, he would say, What will I do? and she would take him one step at a time, saying first, Row back.

The first step in a long, dreadful journey. She would tell him every step and she would stay with him for as many of them as she could. Tie up the boat now. Walk up the bank. Walk through the meadow. Open the gate. She would walk behind him or in front, whichever seemed better to him. Across the yard and up the porch and into the kitchen.

They will say goodbye and get into their separate cars and then it will be his business where he goes. And she will not phone the Police Office the next day. She will wait and they will phone her and she will go to see him in jail. Every day, or as often as they will let her, she will sit and talk to him in jail, and she will write him letters as well. If they take him to another jail she will go there; even if she is allowed to see him only once a month she will be close by. And in court – yes, every day in court, she will be sitting where he can see her.

She does not think anyone would get a death sentence for this sort of murder, which was in a way accidental, and was surely a crime of passion, but the shadow is there, to sober her when she feels that these pictures of devotion, of a bond that is like love but beyond love, are becoming indecent.

Now it has started. With her asking to be taken on the river, her excuse of the picture. Both she and Rupert are standing up, and she is facing the door of the sickroom – now again the front room – which is shut.

She says a foolish thing.

"Are the quilts taken down off the windows?"

He doesn't seem to know for a minute what she is talking about. Then he says, "The quilts. Yes. I think it was Olive took them down. In there was where we had the funeral."

"I was only thinking. The sun would fade them."

He opens the door and she comes around the table and they stand looking into the room. He says, "You can go in if you like. It's all right. Come in."

The bed is gone, of course. The furniture is pushed back against the walls. The middle of the room, where they would have set up the chairs for the funeral, is bare. So is the space in between the north windows – that must have been where they put the coffin. The table where Enid was used to setting the basin, and laying out cloths, cotton wool, spoons, medicine, is jammed into a corner and has a bouquet of delphiniums sitting on it. The tall windows still hold plenty of daylight.

"Lies" is the word that Enid can hear now, out of all the words that Mrs. Quinn said in that room. *Lies. I bet it's all lies.*

Could a person make up something so detailed and diabolical? The answer is yes. A sick person's mind, a dying person's mind, could fill up with all kinds of trash and organize that trash in a most convincing way. Enid's own mind, when she was asleep in this room, had filled up with the most disgusting inventions, with filth. Lies of that nature could be waiting around in the corners of a person's mind, hanging like bats in the corners, waiting to take advantage of any kind of darkness. You can never say, "Nobody could make that up. Look how elaborate dreams are, layer over layer in them, so that the part you can remember and put into words is just the bit you can scratch off the top."

When Enid was four or five years old she had told her mother that she had gone into her father's office and that she had seen him sitting behind his desk with a woman on his knee. All she could remember about this woman, then and now, was that she wore a hat with a great many flowers on it and a veil (a hat quite out of fashion even at that time), and that her blouse or dress was unbuttoned and there was one bare breast sticking out, the tip of it disappearing into Enid's father's mouth. She had told her mother about this in perfect certainty that she had seen it. She said, "One of her fronts was stuck in Daddy's mouth." She did not know the word for breasts, though she did know they came in pairs.

Her mother said, "Now, Enid. What are you talking about? What on earth is a front?"

"Like an ice-cream cone," Enid said.

And she saw it that way, exactly. She could see it that way still. The biscuit-colored cone with its mound of vanilla ice cream squashed against the woman's chest and the wrong end sticking into her father's mouth.

Her mother then did a very unexpected thing. She undid her own dress and took out a dull-skinned object that flopped over her hand. "Like this?" she said.

Enid said no. "An ice-cream cone," she said.

"Then that was a dream," her mother said. "Dreams are sometimes downright silly. Don't tell Daddy about it. It's too silly."

Enid did not believe her mother right away, but in a year or so she saw that such an explanation had to be right, because ice-cream cones did not ever arrange themselves in that way on ladies' chests and they were never so big. When she was older still she realized that the hat must have come from some picture.

Lies.

She hadn't asked him yet, she hadn't spoken. Nothing yet committed her to asking. It was still *before*. Mr. Willens had still driven himself into Jutland Pond, on purpose or by accident. Everybody still believed that, and as far as Rupert was concerned Enid believed it, too. And as long as that was so, this room and this house and her life held a different possibility, an entirely different possibility from the one she had been living with (or glorying in – however you wanted to put it) for the last few days. The different possibility was coming closer to her, and all she needed to do was to keep quiet and let it come. Through her silence, her collaboration in a silence, what benefits could bloom. For others, and for herself.

This was what most people knew. A simple thing that it had taken her so long to understand. This was how to keep the world habitable.

She had started to weep. Not with grief but with an onslaught of relief that she had not known she was looking for. Now she looked into Rupert's face and saw that his eyes were bloodshot and the skin around them puckered and dried out, as if he had been weeping, too.

He said, "She wasn't lucky in her life."

Enid excused herself and went to get her handkerchief, which was in her purse on the table. She was embarrassed now that she had dressed herself up in readiness for such a melodramatic fate.

"I don't know what I was thinking of," she said. "I can't walk down to the river in these shoes."

Rupert shut the door of the front room.

"If you want to go we can still go," he said. "There ought to be a pair of rubber boots would fit you somewhere."

Not hers, Enid hoped. No. Hers would be too small.

Rupert opened a bin in the woodshed, just outside the kitchen door. Enid had never looked into that bin. She had thought it contained firewood, which she had certainly had no need of that summer. Rupert lifted out several single rubber boots and even snow boots, trying to find a pair.

"These look like they might do," he said. "They maybe were Mother's. Or even mine before my feet got full size."

He pulled out something that looked like a piece of a tent, then, by a broken strap, an old school satchel.

"Forgot all the stuff that was in here," he said, letting these things fall back and throwing the unusable boots on top of them. He dropped the lid and gave a private, grieved, and formal-sounding sigh.

A house like this, lived in by one family for so long a time, and neglected for the past several years, would have plenty of bins, drawers, shelves, suitcases, trunks, crawl spaces full of things that it would be up to Enid to sort out, saving and labelling some, restoring some to use, sending others by the boxload to the dump. When she got that chance she wouldn't balk at it. She would make this house into a place that had no secrets from her and where all order was as she had decreed.

He set the boots down in front of her while she was bent over unbuckling her shoes. She smelled under the whiskey the bitter breath that came after a sleepless night and a long harsh day; she smelled the deeply sweat-soaked skin of a hard-worked man that no washing – at least the washing he did – could get quite fresh. No bodily smell – even the smell of semen – was unfamiliar to her, but there was something new and invasive about the smell of a body so distinctly not in her power or under her care.

That was welcome.

"See can you walk," he said.

She could walk. She walked in front of him to the gate. He bent over her shoulder to swing it open for her. She waited while he bolted it, then stood aside to let him walk ahead, because he had brought a little hatchet from the woodshed, to clear their path.

"The cows were supposed to keep the growth down," he said. "But there's things cows won't eat."

She said, "I was only down here once. Early in the morning."

The desperation of her frame of mind then had to seem childish to her now.

Rupert went along chopping at the big fleshy thistles. The sun cast a level, dusty light on the bulk of the trees ahead. The air was clear in some places, then suddenly you would enter a cloud of tiny bugs. Bugs no bigger than specks of dust that were constantly in motion yet kept themselves together in the shape of a pillar or a cloud. How did they manage to do that? And how did they choose one spot over another to do it in? It must have something to do with feeding. But they never seemed to be still enough to feed.

When she and Rupert went underneath the roof of summer leaves it was dusk, it was almost night. You had to watch that you didn't trip over roots that swelled up out of the path, or hit your head on the dangling, surprisingly tough-stemmed vines. Then a flash of water came through the black branches. The lit-up water near the opposite bank of the river, the trees over there still decked out in light. On this side – they were going down the bank now, through the willows – the water was tea-colored but clear.

And the boat waiting, riding in the shadows, just the same.

"The oars are hid," said Rupert. He went into the willows to locate them. In a moment she lost sight of him. She went closer to the water's edge, where her boots sank into the mud a little and held her. If she tried to, she could still hear Rupert's movements in the bushes. But if she concentrated on the motion of the boat, a slight and secretive motion, she could feel as if everything for a long way around had gone quiet.

Simon's Luck

ROSE GETS lonely in new places; she wishes she had invitations. She goes out and walks the streets and looks in the lighted windows at all the Saturday-night parties, the Sunday-night family suppers. It's no good telling herself she wouldn't be long inside there, chattering and getting drunk, or spooning up the gravy, before she'd wish she was walking the streets. She thinks she could take on any hospitality. She could go to parties in rooms hung with posters, lit by lamps with Coca-Cola shades, everything crumbly and askew; or else in warm professional rooms with lots of books, and brass rubbings, and maybe a skull or two; even in the recreation rooms she can just see the tops of, through the basement windows: rows of beer stems, hunting horns, drinking horns, guns. She could go and sit on lurex-threaded sofas under hangings of black velvet displaying mountains, galleons, polar bears, executed in brushed wool. She would like very much to be dishing up a costly *cabinet de diplomate* out of a cut-glass bowl in a rich dining room with a big gleaming belly of sideboard behind her, and a dim picture of horses feeding, cows feeding, sheep feeding, on badly painted purple grass. Or she could do as well with batter pudding in the eating nook of a kitchen in a little stucco house by the bus stop, plaster pears and peaches decorating the wall, ivy curling out of little brass pots. Rose is an actress; she can fit in anywhere.

She does get asked to parties. About two years ago, she was at a party in a high-rise apartment building in Kingston. The windows looked out on Lake Ontario and Wolfe Island. Rose didn't live in Kingston. She lived up-country; she had been teaching drama for two years at a community college. Some people were surprised that she would do this. They did not know how little money an actress might make; they thought that being well-known automatically meant being well-off.

She had driven down to Kingston just for this party, a fact which slightly shamed her. She had not met the hostess before. She had known the host last year, when he was teaching at the community college and living with another girl.

The hostess, whose name was Shelley, took Rose into the bedroom to put down her coat. Shelley was a thin, solemn-looking girl, a true blonde, with nearly white eyebrows, hair long and thick and straight as if cut from a block of wood. It seemed that she took her waif style seriously. Her voice was low and mournful, making Rose's own voice, her greeting of a moment ago, sound altogether too sprightly in her own ears.

In a basket at the foot of the bed a tortoiseshell cat was suckling four tiny, blind kittens.

"That's Tasha," the hostess said. "We can look at her kittens but we can't touch them, else she wouldn't feed them anymore."

She knelt down by the basket, crooning, talking to the mother cat with an intense devotion that Rose thought affected. The shawl around her shoulders was black, trimmed with jet beads. Some beads were crooked, some were missing. It was a genuine old shawl, not an imitation. Her limp, slightly yellowed, eyelet-embroidered dress was genuine too, though probably a petticoat in the first place. Such clothes took looking for.

On the other side of the spool bed was a large mirror,

hung suspiciously high, and tilted. Rose tried to get a look at herself when the girl was bent over the basket. It is very hard to look in the mirror when there is another, and particularly a younger, woman in the room. Rose was wearing a flowered cotton dress, a long dress with a tucked bodice and puffed sleeves, which was too short in the waist and too tight in the bust to be comfortable. There was something wrongly youthful or theatrical about it; perhaps she was not slim enough to wear that style. Her reddish-brown hair was dyed at home. Lines ran both ways under her eyes, trapping little diamonds of darkened skin.

Rose knew by now that when she found people affected, as she did this girl, and their rooms coyly decorated, their manner of living irritating (that mirror, the patchwork quilt, the Japanese erotic drawings over the bed, the African music coming from the living room), it was usually because she, Rose, hadn't received and was afraid she wouldn't receive the attention she wanted, hadn't penetrated the party, felt that she might be doomed to hang around on the fringes of things, making judgments.

She felt better in the living room, where there were some people she knew, and some faces as old as her own. She drank quickly at first, and before long was using the newborn kittens as a springboard for her own story. She said that something dreadful had happened to her cat that very day.

"The worst of it is," she said, "that I never liked my cat much. It wasn't my idea to have a cat. It was his. He followed me home one day and insisted on being taken in. He was just like some big sneering hulk of an unemployable, set on convincing me I owed him a living. Well, he always had a fondness for the clothes dryer. He liked to jump in when it was warm, as soon as I'd taken the clothes out. Usually I just have one load but today I had two, and when I reached in to take the second load out, I thought I felt something. I thought, what do I have that's fur?"

People moaned or laughed, in a sympathetically horrified way. Rose looked around at them appealingly. She felt much better. The living room, with its lake view, its careful decor (a jukebox, barbershop mirrors, turn-of-the-century advertisements – *Smoke, for your throat's sake* – old silk lampshades, farmhouse bowls and jugs, primitive masks and sculptures), no longer seemed so hostile. She took another drink of her gin and knew there was a limited time coming now when she would feel light and welcome as a hummingbird, convinced that many people in the room were witty and many were kind, and some were both together.

"Oh, *no*, I thought. But it was. It was. Death in the dryer."

"A warning to all pleasure seekers," said a little sharp-faced man at her elbow, a man she had known slightly for years. He taught in the English department of the university, where the host taught now, and the hostess was a graduate student.

"That's terrible," said the hostess, with her cold, fixed look of sensitivity. Those who had laughed looked a bit abashed, as if they thought they might have seemed heartless. "Your cat. That's terrible. How could you come tonight?"

As a matter of fact the incident had not happened today at all; it had happened last week. Rose wondered if the girl meant to put her at a disadvantage. She said sincerely and regretfully that she hadn't been very fond of the cat and that had made it seem worse, somehow. That's what she was trying to explain, she said.

"I felt as if maybe it was my fault. Maybe if I'd been fonder, it wouldn't have happened."

"Of course it wouldn't," said the man beside her. "It was warmth he was seeking in the dryer. It was love. Ah, Rose!"

"Now you won't be able to fuck the cat anymore," said a tall boy Rose hadn't noticed before. He seemed to have sprung up, right in front of her. "Fuck the dog, fuck the cat, I don't know what you do, Rose."

She was searching for his name. She had recognized him as a student, or former student.

"David," she said. "Hello, David." She was so pleased at coming up with the name that she was slow in registering what he had said.

"Fuck the dog, fuck the cat," he repeated, swaying over her.

"I beg your pardon," Rose said, and put on a quizzical, indulgent, charming expression. The people around her were finding it as hard to adjust to what the boy said as she was. The mood of sociability, sympathy, expectation of goodwill was not easy to halt; it rolled on in spite of signs that there was plenty here it wasn't going to be able to absorb. Almost everyone was still smiling, as if the boy was telling an anecdote or playing a part, the point of which would be made clear in a moment. The hostess cast down her eyes and slipped away.

"Beg yours," said the boy in a very ugly tone. "Up yours, Rose." He was white and brittle-looking, desperately drunk. He had probably been brought up in a gentle home, where people talked about answering Nature's call and blessed each other for sneezing.

A short, strong man with black curly hair took hold of the boy's arm just below the shoulder.

"Move it along," he said, almost maternally. He spoke with a muddled European accent, mostly French, Rose thought, though she was not good about accents. She did tend to think, in spite of knowing better, that such accents spring from a richer and more complicated masculinity than the masculinity to be found in North America and in places like Hanratty, where she had grown up. Such an accent promised masculinity tinged with suffering, tenderness, and guile.

The host appeared in a velvet jumpsuit and took hold of the other arm, more or less symbolically, at the same time kissing Rose's cheek, because he hadn't seen her when she came in. "Must talk to you," he murmured, meaning he hoped he wouldn't have to, because there was so much tricky territory; the girl he had lived with last year, for one thing, and a night he had spent with Rose toward the end of term, when there had been a lot of drinking and bragging and lamenting about faithlessness, as well as some curiously insulting though pleasurable sex. He was looking very brushed and tended, thinner but softened, with his flowing hair and suit of bottle-green velvet. Only three years younger than Rose, but look at him. He had shed a wife, a family, a house, a discouraging future, set himself up with new clothes and new furniture and a succession of student mistresses. Men can do it.

"My, my," Rose said and leaned against the wall. "What was that all about?"

The man beside her, who had smiled all the time and looked into his glass, said, "Ah, the sensitive youth of our time! Their grace of language, their depth of feeling! We must bow before them."

The man with the black curly hair came back, didn't say a word, but handed Rose a fresh drink and took her glass.

The host came back too.

"Rose baby. I don't know how he got in. I said no bloody students. There's got to be some place safe from them."

"He was in one of my classes last year," Rose said. That really was all she could remember. She supposed they were thinking there must be more to it.

"Did he want to be an actor?" said the man beside her. "I'll bet he did. Remember the good old days when they all wanted to be lawyers and engineers and business executives? They tell me that's coming back. I hope so. I devoutly hope so. Rose, I bet you listened to his problems. You must never do that. I bet that's what you did."

"Oh, I suppose."

"They come along looking for a parent-substitute. It's banal as can be. They trail around worshiping you and bothering you and then bam! It's parent-substitute rejecting time!"

Rose drank, and leaned against the wall, and heard them take up the theme of what students expected nowadays, how they broke down your door to tell you about their abortions, their suicide attempts, their creativity crises, their weight problems. Always using the same words: personhood, values, rejection.

"I'm not rejecting you, you silly bugger, I'm flunking you!" said the little sharp man, recalling a triumphant confrontation he had had with one such student. They laughed at that and at the young woman who said, "God, the difference when I was at university! You wouldn't have mentioned an abortion in a professor's office any more than you would have shit on the floor. *Shat* on the floor."

Rose was laughing too, but felt smashed, under the skin. It would be better, in a way, if there were something behind this such as they suspected. If she had slept with that boy. If she had promised him something, if she had betrayed him, humiliated him. She could not remember anything. He had sprung out of the floor to accuse her. She must have done something, and she could not remember it. She could not remember anything to do with her students; that was the truth. She was solicitous and charming, all warmth and acceptance; she listened and advised; then she could not get their names straight. She could not remember a thing she had said to them.

A woman touched her arm. "Wake up," she said, in a tone of sly intimacy that made Rose think she must know her. Another student? But no, the woman introduced herself.

"I'm doing a paper on female suicide," she said. "I mean, the suicide of female artists." She said she had seen Rose on television and was longing to talk to her. She mentioned Diane Arbus, Virginia Woolf, Sylvia Plath, Anne Sexton, Christiane Pflug. She was well informed. She looked like a prime candidate herself, Rose thought: emaciated, bloodless, obsessed. Rose said she was hungry, and the woman followed her out to the kitchen.

"And too many actresses to count –" the woman said. "Margaret Sullavan –"

"I'm just a teacher now."

"Oh, nonsense. I'm sure you are an actress to the marrow of your bones."

The hostess had made bread: glazed and braided and decorated loaves. Rose wondered at the pains taken here. The bread, the pâté, the hanging plants, the kittens, all on behalf of a most precarious and temporary domesticity. She wished, she often wished, that she could take such pains, that she could make ceremonies, impose herself, make bread.

She noticed a group of younger members of the faculty – she would have thought them students, except for what the host had said about students not being let in – who were sitting on the counters and standing in front of the sink. They were talking in low, serious voices. One of them looked at her. She smiled. Her smile was not returned. A couple of others looked at her, and they went on talking. She was sure they were talking about her, about what had happened in the living room. She urged the woman to try some bread and pâté. Presumably that would keep her quiet, so that Rose could overhear what was being said.

"I never eat at parties."

The woman's manner toward her was turning dark and vaguely accusing. Rose had learned that this was a department wife. Perhaps it had been a political move, inviting her. And promising her Rose; had that been part of the move?

"Are you always so hungry?" the woman said. "Are you never ill?"

"I am when there's something this good to eat," Rose said. She was only trying to set an example, and could hardly chew or swallow, in her anxiety to hear what was being said of her. "No, I'm not often ill," she said. It surprised her to realize that was true. She used to get sick with colds and flu and cramps and headaches; those definite ailments had now disappeared, simmered down into a low, steady hum of uneasiness, fatigue, apprehension.

Fucked-up jealous establishment.

Rose heard that, or thought she heard it. They were giving her quick, despising looks. Or so she thought; she could not look directly at them. *Establishment.* That was Rose. Was it? Was that Rose? Was that Rose who had taken a teaching job because she wasn't getting enough acting jobs to support herself, was granted the teaching job because of her experience on stage and television, but had to accept a cut in pay because she lacked degrees? She wanted to go over and tell them that. She wanted to state her case. The years of work, the exhaustion, the traveling, the high school auditoriums, the nerves, the boredom, the never knowing where your next pay was coming from. She wanted to plead with them, so they would forgive her and love her and take her on their side. It was their side she wanted to be on, not the side of the people in the living room who had taken up her cause. But that was a choice made because of fear, not on principle. She feared them. She feared their hard-hearted virtue, their cool despising faces, their secrets, their laughter, their obscenities.

She thought of Anna, her own daughter. Anna was seventeen. She had long fair hair and wore a fine gold chain around her throat. It was so fine you had to look closely to make sure it was a chain, not just a glinting of her smooth bright skin. She was not like these young people but she was equally remote. She practiced ballet and rode her horse every day but she didn't plan to ride in competitions or be a ballerina. Why not?

"Because it would be silly."

Something about Anna's style, the fine chain, her silences, made Rose think of her grandmother, Patrick's mother. But then, she thought, Anna might not be so silent, so fastidious, so unforthcoming, with anybody but her mother.

The man with the black curly hair stood in the kitchen doorway giving her an impudent and ironic look.

"Do you know who that is?" Rose said to the suicide woman. "The man who took the drunk away?"

"That's Simon. I don't think the boy was drunk, I think he's on drugs."

"What does he do?"

"Well, I expect he's a student of sorts."

"No," said Rose. "That man – Simon?"

"Oh, Simon. He's in the classics department. I don't think he's always been a teacher."

"Like me," Rose said, and turned the smile she had tried on the young people on Simon. Tired and adrift and witless as she was, she was beginning to feel familiar twinges, tidal promises.

If he smiles back, things will start to be all right.

He did smile, and the suicide woman spoke sharply.

"Look, do you come to a party just to meet men?"

When Simon was fourteen, he and his older sister and another boy, a friend of theirs, were hidden in a freight car, traveling from occupied to unoccupied France. They were on their way to Lyons, where they would be looked after, redirected to safe places, by members of an organization that was trying to save Jewish children. Simon and his sister had already been sent out of Poland, at the beginning of the war, to stay with French relatives. Now they had to be sent away again.

The freight car stopped. The train was standing still, at night somewhere out in the country. They could hear French and German voices. There was some commotion in the cars ahead. They heard the doors grinding open, heard and felt the boots striking on the bare floors of those cars. An inspection of the train. They lay down under some sacks, but did not even try to cover their faces; they thought there was no hope. The voices were getting closer and they heard the boots on the gravel beside the track. Then the train began to move. It moved so slowly that they did not notice for a moment or so, and even then they thought it was just a shunting of the cars. They expected it to stop, so that the inspection could continue. But the train kept moving. It moved a little faster, then faster; it picked up its ordinary speed, which was nothing very great. They were moving, they were free of the inspection, they were being carried away. Simon never knew what had happened. The danger was past.

Simon said that when he realized they were safe he suddenly felt that they would get through, that nothing could happen to them now, that they were particularly blessed and lucky. He took what happened for a lucky sign.

Rose asked him, had he ever seen his friend and his sister again?

"No. Never. Not after Lyons."

"So, it was only lucky for you."

Simon laughed. They were in bed, in Rose's bed in an old house, on the outskirts of a crossroads village; they had driven there straight from the party. It was April, the wind was cold, and Rose's house was chilly. The furnace was inadequate. Simon put a hand to the wallpaper behind the bed, made her feel the draft.

"What it needs is some insulation."

"I know. It's awful. And you should see my fuel bills."

Simon said she should get a wood stove. He told her about various kinds of firewood. Maple, he said, was a lovely wood to burn. Then he held forth on different kinds of insulation. Styrofoam, Micafil, fiberglass. He got out of bed and padded around naked, looking at the walls of her house. Rose shouted after him.

"Now I remember. It was a grant."

"What? I can't hear you."

She got out of bed and wrapped herself in a blanket. Standing at the top of the stairs, she said, "That boy came to me with an application for a grant. He wanted to be a playwright. I just this minute remembered."

"What boy?" said Simon. "Oh."

"But I recommended him. I know I did." The truth was she recommended everybody. If she could not see their merits, she believed it might just be a case of their having merits she was unable to see.

"He must not have got it. So he thought I shafted him."

"Well, suppose you had," said Simon, peering down the cellarway. "That would be your right."

"I know. I'm a coward about that lot. I hate their disapproval. They are so virtuous."

"They are not virtuous at all," said Simon. "I'm going to put my shoes on and look at your furnace. You probably need the filters cleaned. That is just their style. They are not much to be feared, they are just as stupid as anybody. They want a chunk of the power. Naturally."

"But would you get such venomous –" Rose had to stop and start the word again – "such *venomousness*, simply from ambition?"

"What else?" said Simon, climbing the stairs. He made a grab for the blanket, wrapped himself up with her, pecked her nose. "Enough of that, Rose. Have you no shame? I'm a poor fellow come to look at your furnace. Your basement furnace. Sorry to bump into you like this, ma'am." She already knew a few of his characters. This was The Humble Workman. Some others were The Old Philosopher, who bowed low to her, Japanese style, as he came out of the bathroom, murmuring *memento mori, memento mori*; and, when appropriate, The Mad Satyr, nuzzling and leaping, making triumphant smacking noises against her navel.

At the crossroads store she bought real coffee instead of instant, real cream, bacon, frozen broccoli, a hunk of local cheese, canned crabmeat, the best-looking tomatoes they had, mushrooms, long-grained rice. Cigarettes as well. She was in that state of happiness which seems perfectly natural and unthreatened. If asked, she would have said it was because of the weather – the day was bright, in spite of the harsh wind – as much as because of Simon.

"You must've brought home company," said the woman who kept the store. She spoke with no surprise or malice or censure, just a comradely sort of envy.

"When I wasn't expecting it." Rose dumped more groceries on the counter. "What a lot of bother they are. Not to mention expense. Look at that bacon. And cream."

"I could stand a bit of it," the woman said.

Simon cooked a remarkable supper from the resources provided, while Rose did nothing much but stand around watching, and change the sheets.

"Country life," she said. "I came here with some ideas about how I would live. I thought I would go for long walks on the deserted country roads. And the first time I did, I heard a car coming tearing along on the gravel behind me. I got well off. Then I heard shots. I was terrified. I hid in the bushes and a car came roaring past, weaving all over the road – and they were shooting out of the windows. I cut back through the fields and told the woman at the store I thought we should call the police. She said oh, yes, weekends the boys get a case of beer in the car and they go out shooting groundhogs. Then she said, what were you doing up that road anyway? I could see she thought going for walks by yourself was a lot more suspicious than shooting groundhogs. There were lots of things like that. I don't think I'd stay, but the job's here and the rent's cheap. Not that she isn't nice, the woman in the store. She tells fortunes. Cards and teacups."

Simon said that he had been sent from Lyons to work on a farm in the mountains of Provence. The people there lived and farmed very much as in the Middle Ages. They could not read or write or speak French. When they got sick they waited either to die or to get better. They had never seen a doctor, though a veterinarian came once a year to inspect the cows.

Simon ran a pitchfork into his foot, the wound became infected, he was feverish and had the greatest difficulty in persuading them to send for the veterinarian, who was then in the next village. At last they did, and the veterinarian came and gave Simon a shot with a great horse needle, and he got better. The household was bewildered and amused to see such measures taken on behalf of human life.

"Country life."

"But here it is not so bad. This house could be made very comfortable," said Simon, musing. "You should have a garden."

"That was another idea I had, I tried to have a garden. Nothing did very well. I was looking forward to the cabbages, I think cabbages are beautiful, but some worm got into them. It ate up the leaves till they looked like lace, and then they all turned yellow and lay on the ground."

"Cabbages are a very hard thing to grow. You should try with something easier." Simon left the table and went to the window. "Point me out where you had your garden."

"Along the fence. That's where they had it before."

"That is no good, it's too close to the walnut tree. Walnut trees are bad for the soil."

"I didn't know that."

"Well, it's true. You should have it nearer the house. Tomorrow I will dig up a garden for you. You'll need a lot of fertilizer. Now. Sheep manure is the very best fertilizer. Do you know anyone around here who has sheep? We will get several sacks of sheep manure and draw up a plan of what to plant, though it's too early yet, there could still be frost. You can start some things indoors, from seed. Tomatoes."

"I thought you had to go back on the morning bus," Rose said. They had driven up in her car.

"Monday is a light day. I will phone up and cancel. I'll tell the girls in the office to say I have a sore throat."

"Sore throat?"

"Something like that."

"It's good that you're here," said Rose truthfully. "Otherwise I'd be spending my time thinking about that boy. I'd be trying not to, but it would keep coming at me. In unprotected moments. I would have been in a state of humiliation."

"That's a pretty small thing to get into a state of humiliation about."

"So I see. It doesn't take much with me."

"Learn not to be so thin-skinned," said Simon, as if he were taking her over, in a sensible way, along with the house and garden. "Radishes. Leaf lettuce. Onions. Potatoes. Do you eat potatoes?"

Before he left they drew up a plan of the garden. He dug and worked the soil for her, though he had to content himself with cow manure. Rose had to go to work, on Monday, but kept him in her mind all day. She saw him digging in the garden. She saw him naked peering down the cellarway. A short, thick man, hairy, warm, with a crumpled comedian's face. She knew what he would say when she got home. He would say, "I hope I done it to your satisfaction, mum," and yank a forelock.

That was what he did, and she was so delighted she cried out, "Oh Simon, you idiot, you're the man for my life!" Such was the privilege, the widespread sunlight of the moment, that she did not reflect that saying this might be unwise.

In the middle of the week she went to the store, not to buy anything, but to get her fortune told. The woman looked in her cup and said, "Oh, you! You've met the man who will change everything."

"Yes, I think so."

"He will change your life. Oh Lord. You won't stay here. I see fame. I see water."

"I don't know about that. I think he wants to insulate my house."

"The change has begun already."

"Yes. I know it has. Yes."

She could not remember what they had said about Simon coming again. She thought that he was coming on the weekend. She expected him, and she went out and bought groceries, not at the local store this time but at a supermarket several miles away. She hoped the woman at the store wouldn't see her carrying the grocery bags into the house. She had wanted fresh vegetables and steak and imported black cherries, and Camembert and pears. She had bought wine, too, and a pair of sheets covered with stylish garlands of blue and yellow flowers. She was thinking her pale haunches would show up well against them.

On Friday night she put the sheets on the bed and the cherries in a blue bowl. The wine was chilling, the cheese was getting soft. Around nine o'clock came the loud knock, the expected joking knock on the door. She was surprised that she hadn't heard his car.

"Felt lonesome," said the woman from the store. "So I just thought I'd drop in and – oh-oh. You're expecting your company."

"Not really," Rose said. Her heart had started thumping joyfully when she heard the knock and was thumping still. "I don't know when he's arriving here," she said. "Maybe tomorrow."

"Bugger of a rain."

The woman's voice sounded hearty and practical, as if Rose might need distracting or consoling.

"I just hope he isn't driving in it, then," Rose said.

"No sir, you wouldn't want him driving in it."

The woman ran her fingers through her short gray hair, shaking the rain out, and Rose knew she ought to offer her something. A glass of wine? She might become mellow and talkative, wanting to stay and finish the bottle. Here was a person Rose had talked to, plenty of times, a friend of sorts, somebody she would have claimed to like, and she could hardly be bothered to acknowledge her. It would have been the same at that moment with anyone who was not Simon. Anyone else seemed accidental and irritating.

Rose could see what was coming. All the ordinary delights, consolations, diversions, of life would be rolled up and packed away; the pleasure found in food, lilacs, music, thunder in the night, would vanish. Nothing would do any more but to lie under Simon, nothing would do but to give way to pangs and convulsions.

She decided on tea. She thought she might as well put the time to use by having another go at her future.

"It's not clear," the woman said.

"What's not?"

"I'm not able to get anything in focus tonight. That happens. No, to be honest, I can't locate him."

"Can't locate him?"

"In your future. I'm beat."

Rose thought she was saying this out of ill-will, out of jealousy.

"Well, I'm not just concerned about him."

"Maybe I could do better if you had any possessions of his, just let me have it to hang on to. Anything he had his hands on, do you have that?"

"Me," said Rose. A cheap boast, at which the fortune-teller was obliged to laugh.

"No, seriously."

"I don't think so. I threw his cigarette butts out."

After the woman had gone Rose sat up waiting. Soon it was midnight. The rain came down hard. The next time she looked it was twenty to two. How could time so empty pass so quickly? She put out the lights because she didn't want to be caught sitting up. She undressed, but couldn't lie down on the fresh sheets. She sat on in the kitchen, in the dark. From time to time she made fresh tea. Some light from the street light at the corner came into the room. The village had bright new mercury vapor lights. She could see that light, a bit of the store, the church steps across the road. The church no longer served the discreet and respectable Protestant sect that had built it, but proclaimed itself a Temple of Nazareth, also a Holiness Center, whatever that might be. Things were more askew here than Rose had noticed before. No retired farmers lived in these houses; in fact there were no farms to retire from, just the poor fields covered with juniper. People worked thirty or forty miles away, in factories, in the Provincial Mental Hospital, or they didn't work at all, they lived a mysterious life on the borders of criminality or a life of orderly craziness in the shade of the Holiness Center. People's lives were surely more desperate than they used to be, and what could be more desperate than a woman of Rose's age, sitting up all night in her dark kitchen waiting for her lover? And this was a situation she had created, she had done it all herself, it seemed she never learned any lessons at all. She had turned Simon into the peg on which her hopes were hung and she could never manage now to turn him back into himself.

The mistake was in buying the wine, she thought, and the sheets and the cheese and the cherries. Preparations court disaster. She hadn't realized that till she opened the door and the commotion of her heart turned from merriment to dismay, like the sound of a tower full of bells turned comically (but not for Rose) into a rusty foghorn.

Hour after hour in the dark and the rain she foresaw what could happen. She could wait through the weekend, fortifying herself with excuses and sickening with doubt, never leaving the house in case the phone might ring. Back at work on Monday, dazed but slightly comforted by the real world, she would get up the courage to write him a note, in care of the classics department.

"I was thinking we might plant the garden next weekend. I have bought a great array of seeds (a lie, but she would buy them, if she heard from him). Do let me know if you're coming, but don't worry if you've made other plans."

Then she would worry: did it sound too off-hand, with that mention of other plans? Wouldn't it be too pushy, if she hadn't tacked that on? All her confidence, her lightness of heart, would have leaked away, but she would try to counterfeit it.

"If it's too wet to work in the garden we could always go for a drive. Maybe we could shoot some groundhogs. Best, Rose."

Then a further time of waiting, for which the weekend would have been only a casual trial run, a haphazard introduction to the serious, commonplace, miserable ritual. Putting her hand into the mailbox and drawing the mail out without looking at it, refusing to leave the college until five o'clock, putting a cushion against the telephone to block her view of it; pretending inattention. Watch-pot thinking. Sitting up late at night, drinking, never getting quite sick enough of this foolishness to give up on it because the waiting would be interspersed with such green and springlike reveries, such convincing arguments as to his intentions. These would be enough, at some point, to make her decide that he must have been taken ill, he would never have deserted her otherwise. She would phone the Kingston Hospital, ask about his condition, be told that he was not a patient. After that would come the day she went into the college library, picked up back copies of the Kingston paper, searched the obituaries to discover if he had by any chance dropped dead. Then, giving in utterly, cold and shaking, she would call him at the University. The girl in his office would say he was gone. Gone to Europe, gone to California; he had only been teaching there for a single term. Gone on a camping trip, gone to get married.

Or she might say, "Just a minute, please," and turn Rose over to him, just like that.

"Yes?"

"Simon?"

"Yes."

"It's Rose."

"Rose?"

It wouldn't be as drastic as that. It would be worse.

"I've been meaning to call you," he would say, or, "Rose, how *are* you?" or even, "How is that garden?"

Better lose him now. But going by the phone she put her hand on it, to see if it was warm, maybe, or to encourage it.

Before it began to get light Monday morning she packed what she thought she would need into the back of the car, and locked the house, with the Camembert still weeping on the kitchen counter; she drove off in a westerly direction. She meant to be gone a couple of days, until she came to her senses and could face the sheets and the patch of readied earth and the place behind the bed where she had put her hand to feel the draft. (Why did she bring her boots and her winter coat, if this was the case?) She wrote a letter to the college – she could lie beautifully in letters, though not on the phone – in which she said that she had been called to Toronto by the terminal illness of a dear friend. (Perhaps she didn't lie so beautifully after all, perhaps she overdid it.) She had been awake almost the whole weekend, drinking, not so very much, but steadily. *I'm not having any of it*, she said out loud, very seriously and emphatically, as she loaded the car. And as she crouched in the front seat, writing the letter, which she could more comfortably have written in the house, she thought how many crazy letters she had written, how many overblown excuses she had found, having to leave a place, or being afraid to leave a place, on account of some man. Nobody knew the extent of her foolishness, friends who had known her twenty years didn't know half of the flights she had been on, the money she had spent, and the risks she had taken. Here she was, she thought a bit later, driving a car, shutting down the windshield wipers as the rain finally let up on a Monday morning at ten o'clock, stopping for gas, stopping to get a transfer of money, now that the banks were open; she was competent and cheery, she remembered what to do, who would guess what mortifications, memories of mortification, predictions, were beating in her head? The most mortifying thing of all was simply hope, which burrows so deceitfully at first, masks itself cunningly, but not for long. In a week's time it can be out trilling and twittering and singing hymns at heaven's gate. And it was busy even now, telling her that Simon might be turning into her driveway at this very moment, might be standing at her door with his hands together, praying, mocking, apologizing. *Memento mori.*

Even so, even if that were true, what would happen some day, some morning? Some morning she could wake up and she would know by his breathing that he was awake beside her and not touching her, and that she was not supposed to touch him. So much female touching is asking (this is what she would have learned, or learned again, from him); women's tenderness is greedy, their sensuality is dishonest. She would lie there wishing she had some plain defect, something her shame could curl around and protect. As it was, she would have to be ashamed of, burdened by, the whole physical fact of herself, the whole outspread naked digesting putrefying fact. Her flesh could seem disastrous; thick and porous, gray and spotty. His body would not be in question, it never would be; he would be the one who condemned and forgave and how could she ever know if he would forgive her again? *Come here*, he could tell her, or *go away*. Never since Patrick had she been the free person, the one with that power; maybe she had used it all up, all that was coming to her.

Or she might hear him at a party, saying, "And then I knew I'd be all right, I knew it was a lucky sign." Telling his story to some tarty unworthy girl in a leopard-spotted silk, or – far worse – to a gentle long-haired girl in an embroidered smock, who would lead him by the hand, sooner or later, through a doorway into a room or landscape where Rose couldn't follow.

Yes, but wasn't it possible nothing like that would happen, wasn't it possible there'd be nothing but kindness, and sheep manure, and deep spring nights with the frogs singing? A failure to appear, on the first weekend, or to telephone, might have meant nothing but a different timetable; no ominous sign at all. Thinking like this, every twenty miles or so, she slowed, even looked for a place to turn around. Then she did not do it, she speeded up, thinking she would drive a little further to make sure her head was clear. Thoughts of herself sitting in the kitchen, images of loss, poured over her again. And so it was, back and forth, as if the rear end of the car was held by a magnetic force, which ebbed and strengthened, ebbed and strengthened again, but the strength was never quite enough to make her turn, and after a while she became almost impersonally curious, seeing it as a real physical force and wondering if it was getting weaker, as she drove, if at some point far ahead the car and she would leap free of it, and she would recognize the moment when she left its field.

So she kept driving. Muskoka; the Lakehead; the Manitoba border. Sometimes she slept in the car, pulled off to the side of the road for an hour or so. In Manitoba it was too cold to do that; she checked into a motel. She ate in roadside restaurants. Before she entered a restaurant she combed her hair and made up her face and put on that distant, dreamy, short-sighted look women wear when they think some man may be watching them. It was too much to say that she really expected Simon to be there, but it seemed she did not entirely rule him out.

The force did weaken, with distance. It was as simple as that, though the distance, she thought afterwards, would have to be covered by car, or by bus, or bicycle; you couldn't get the same results by flying. In a prairie town within sight of the Cypress Hills she recognized the change. She had driven all night until the sun came up behind her and she felt calm and clearheaded as you do at such times. She went into a café and ordered coffee and fried eggs. She sat at the counter looking at the usual things there are behind café counters – the coffee-pots and the bright, probably stale pieces of lemon and raspberry pie, the thick glass dishes they put ice-cream or Jell-O in. It was those dishes that told her of her changed state. She could not have said she found them shapely, or eloquent, without misstating the case. All she could have said was that she saw them in a way that wouldn't be possible to a person in any stage of love. She felt their solidity with a convalescent gratitude whose weight settled comfortably into her brains and feet. She realized then that she had come into this café without the least far-fetched idea of Simon, so it seemed the world had stopped being a stage where she might meet him, and gone back to being itself. During that bountifully clear half-hour before her breakfast made her so sleepy she had to get to a motel, where she fell asleep with her clothes on and the curtains open to the sun, she thought how love removes the world for you, and just as surely when it's going well as when it's going badly. This shouldn't have been, and wasn't, a surprise to her; the surprise was that she so much wanted, required, everything to be there for her, thick and plain as ice-cream dishes, so that it seemed to her it might not be the disappointment, the losses, the dissolution, she had been running from, any more than the opposite of those things; the celebration and shock of love, the dazzling alteration. Even if that was safe, she couldn't accept it. Either way you were robbed of something – a private balance spring, a little dry kernel of probity. So she thought.

She wrote to the college that while in Toronto attending the deathbed of her friend she had run into an old acquaintance who had offered her a job on the west coast, and that she was going there immediately. She supposed they could make trouble for her but she also supposed, rightly, that they would not bother, since the terms of her employment, and particularly her pay, were not quite regular. She wrote to the agency from which she rented the house; she wrote to the woman at the store, good luck and good-bye. On the Hope-Princeton highway she got out of the car and stood in the cool rain of the coastal mountains. She felt relatively safe, and exhausted, and sane, though she knew she had left some people behind who would not agree with that.

Luck was with her. In Vancouver she met a man she knew who was casting a new television series. It was to be produced on the west coast and concerned a family, or pseudo-family, of eccentrics and drifters using an old house on Salt Spring Island as their home or headquarters. Rose got the role of the woman who owned the house, the pseudo-mother. Just as she had said in the letter; a job on the west coast, possibly the best job she had ever had. Some special make-up techniques, aging techniques, had to be used on her face; the make-up man joked that if the series was a success, and ran for a few years, these techniques would not be necessary.

A word everybody at the coast was using was *fragile*. They spoke of feeling fragile today, of being in a fragile state. Not me, Rose said, I am getting a distinct feeling of being made of old horsehide. The wind and sun on the prairies had browned and roughened her skin. She slapped her creased brown neck, to emphasize the word horsehide. She was already beginning to adopt some of the turns of phrase, the mannerisms, of the character she was to play.

A year or so later Rose was out on the deck of one of the B.C. ferries, wearing a dingy sweater and a head scarf. She had to creep around among the lifeboats, keeping an eye on a pretty young girl who was freezing in cut-off jeans and a halter. According to the script, the woman Rose played was afraid this young girl meant to jump off the boat because she was pregnant.

Filming this scene, they collected a sizeable crowd. When they broke and walked towards the sheltered part of the deck, to put on their coats and drink coffee, a woman in the crowd reached out and touched Rose's arm.

"You won't remember me," she said, and in fact Rose did not remember her. Then this woman began to talk about Kingston, the couple who had given the party, even about the death of Rose's cat. Rose recognized her as the woman who had been doing the paper on suicide. But she looked quite different; she was wearing an expensive beige pant-suit, a beige and white scarf around her hair; she was no longer fringed and soiled and stringy and mutinous-looking. She introduced a husband, who grunted at Rose as if to say that if she expected him to make a big fuss about her, she had another think coming. He moved away and the woman said, "Poor Simon. You know he died."

Then she wanted to know if they were going to be shooting any more scenes. Rose knew why she asked. She wanted to get into the background or even the foreground of these scenes so that she could call up her friends and tell them to watch her. If she called the people who had been at that party she would have to say that she knew the series was utter tripe but that she had been persuaded to be in a scene, for the fun of it.

"Died?"

The woman took off her scarf and the wind blew her hair across her face.

"Cancer of the pancreas," she said, and turned to face the wind so that she could put the scarf on again, more to her satisfaction. Her voice seemed to Rose knowledgeable and sly. "I don't know how well you knew him," she said. Was that to make Rose wonder how well *she* knew him? That slyness could ask for help, as well as measure victories and surprises. She tucked her chin in, knotting the scarf.

"So sad," she said, business-like now. "Sad. He had it for a long time."

Somebody was calling Rose's name; she had to go back to the scene. The girl didn't throw herself into the sea. They didn't have things like that happening in the series. Such things always threatened to happen but they didn't happen, except now and then to peripheral and unappealing characters. People watching trusted that they would be protected from predictable disasters, also from those shifts of emphasis that throw the story line open to question, the disarrangements which demand new judgments and solutions, and throw the windows open on inappropriate unforgettable scenery.

Simon's dying struck Rose as that kind of disarrangement. It was preposterous, it was unfair, that such a chunk of information should have been left out, and that Rose even at this late date could have thought herself the only person who could seriously lack power.

Hateship, Friendship, Courtship, Loveship, Marriage

YEARS AGO, before the trains stopped running on so many of the branch lines, a woman with a high, freckled forehead and a frizz of reddish hair came into the railway station and inquired about shipping furniture.

The station agent often tried a little teasing with women, especially the plain ones who seemed to appreciate it.

"Furniture?" he said, as if nobody had ever had such an idea before. "Well. Now. What kind of furniture are we talking about?"

A dining-room table and six chairs. A full bedroom suite, a sofa, a coffee table, end tables, a floor lamp. Also a china cabinet and a buffet.

"Whoa there. You mean a houseful."

"It shouldn't count as that much," she said. "There's no kitchen things and only enough for one bedroom."

Her teeth were crowded to the front of her mouth as if they were ready for an argument.

"You'll be needing the truck," he said.

"No. I want to send it on the train. It's going out west, to Saskatchewan."

She spoke to him in a loud voice as if he was deaf or stupid, and there was something wrong with the way she pronounced her words. An accent. He thought of Dutch – the Dutch were moving in around here – but she didn't have the heft of the Dutch women or the nice pink skin or the fair hair. She might have been under forty, but what did it matter? No beauty queen, ever.

He turned all business.

"First you'll need the truck to get it to here from wherever you got it. And we better see if it's a place in Saskatchewan where the train goes through. Otherways you'd have to arrange to get it picked up, say, in Regina."

"It's Gdynia," she said. "The train goes through."

He took down a greasy-covered directory that was hanging from a nail and asked how she would spell that. She helped herself to the pencil that was also on a string and wrote on a piece of paper from her purse: *G D Y N I A*.

"What kind of nationality would that be?"

She said she didn't know.

He took back the pencil to follow from line to line.

"A lot of places out there it's all Czechs or Hungarians or Ukrainians," he said. It came to him as he said this that she might be one of those. But so what, he was only stating a fact.

"Here it is, all right, it's on the line."

"Yes," she said. "I want to ship it Friday – can you do that?"

"We can ship it, but I can't promise what day it'll get there," he said. "It all depends on the priorities. Somebody going to be on the lookout for it when it comes in?"

"Yes."

"It's a mixed train Friday, two-eighteen p.m. Truck picks it up Friday morning. You live here in town?"

She nodded, writing down the address. 106 Exhibition Road.

It was only recently that the houses in town had been numbered, and he couldn't picture the place, though he knew where Exhibition Road was. If she'd said the name McCauley at that time he might have taken more of an interest, and things might have turned out differently. There were new houses out there, built since the war, though they were called "wartime houses." He supposed it must be one of those.

"Pay when you ship," he told her.

"Also, I want a ticket for myself on the same train. Friday afternoon."

"Going same place?"

"Yes."

"You can travel on the same train to Toronto, but then you have to wait for the Transcontinental, goes out ten-thirty at night. You want sleeper or coach? Sleeper you get a berth, coach you sit up in the day car."

She said she would sit up.

"Wait in Sudbury for the Montreal train, but you won't get off there, they'll just shunt you around and hitch on the Montreal cars. Then on to Port Arthur and then to Kenora. You don't get off till Regina, and there you have to get off and catch the branch-line train."

She nodded as if he should just get on and give her the ticket.

Slowing down, he said, "But I won't promise your furniture'll arrive when you do, I wouldn't think it would get in till a day or two after. It's all the priorities. Somebody coming to meet you?"

"Yes."

"Good. Because it won't likely be much of a station. Towns out there, they're not like here. They're mostly pretty rudimentary affairs."

She paid for the passenger ticket now, from a roll of bills in a cloth bag in her purse. Like an old lady. She counted her change, too. But not the way an old lady would count it – she held it in her hand and flicked her eyes over it, but you could tell she didn't miss a penny. Then she turned away rudely, without a good-bye.

"See you Friday," he called out.

She wore a long, drab coat on this warm September day, also a pair of clunky laced-up shoes, and ankle socks.

He was getting a coffee out of his thermos when she came back and rapped on the wicket.

"The furniture I'm sending," she said. "It's all good furniture, it's like new. I wouldn't want it to get scratched or banged up or in any way damaged. I don't want it to smell like livestock, either."

"Oh, well," he said. "The railway's pretty used to shipping things. And they don't use the same cars for shipping furniture they use for shipping pigs."

"I'm concerned that it gets there in just as good a shape as it leaves here."

"Well, you know, when you buy your furniture, it's in the store, right? But did you ever think how it got there? It wasn't made in the store, was it? No. It was made in some factory someplace, and it got shipped to the store, and that was done quite possibly by train. So that being the case, doesn't it stand to reason the railway knows how to look after it?"

She continued to look at him without a smile or any admission of her female foolishness.

"I hope so," she said. "I hope they do."

The station agent would have said, without thinking about it, that he knew everybody in town. Which meant that he knew about half of them. And most of those he knew were the core people, the ones who really were "in town" in the sense that they had not arrived yesterday and had no plans to move on. He did not know the woman who was going to Saskatchewan because she did not go to his church or teach his children in school or work in any store or restaurant or office that he went into. Nor was she married to any of the men he knew in the Elks or the Oddfellows or the Lions Club or the Legion. A look at her left hand while she was getting the money out had told him – and he was not surprised – that she was not married to anybody. With those shoes, and ankle socks instead of stockings, and no hat or gloves in the afternoon, she might have been a farm woman. But she didn't have the hesitation they generally had, the embarrassment. She didn't have country manners – in fact, she had no manners at all. She had treated him as if he was an information machine. Besides, she had written a town address – Exhibition Road. The person she really reminded him of was a plainclothes nun he had seen on television, talking about the missionary work she did somewhere in the jungle – probably they had got out of their nuns' clothes there because it made it easier for them to clamber around. This nun had smiled once in a while to show that her religion was supposed to make people happy, but most of the time she looked out at her audience as if she believed that other people were mainly in the world for her to boss around.

One more thing Johanna meant to do she had been putting off doing. She had to go into the dress shop called Milady's and buy herself an outfit. She had never been inside that shop – when she had to buy anything, like socks, she went to Callaghans Mens Ladies and Childrens Wear. She had lots of clothes inherited from Mrs. Willets, things like this coat that would never wear out. And Sabitha – the girl she looked after, in Mr. McCauley's house – was showered with costly hand-me-downs from her cousins.

In Milady's window there were two mannequins wearing suits with quite short skirts and boxy jackets. One suit was a rusty-gold color and the other a soft deep green. Big gaudy paper maple leaves were scattered round the mannequins' feet and pasted here and there on the window. At the time of year when most people's concern was to rake up leaves and burn them, here they were the chosen thing. A sign written in flowing black script was stuck diagonally across the glass. It said: *Simple Elegance, the Mode for Fall.*

She opened the door and went inside.

Right ahead of her, a full-length mirror showed her in Mrs. Willets's high-quality but shapeless long coat, with a few inches of lumpy bare legs above the ankle socks.

They did that on purpose, of course. They set the mirror there so you could get a proper notion of your deficiencies, right away, and then – they hoped – you would jump to the conclusion that you had to buy something to alter the picture. Such a transparent trick that it would have made her walk out, if she had not come in determined, knowing what she had to get.

Along one wall was a rack of evening dresses, all fit for belles of the ball with their net and taffeta, their dreamy colors. And beyond them, in a glass case so no profane fingers could get at them, half a dozen wedding gowns, pure white froth or vanilla satin or ivory lace, embroidered in silver beads or seed pearls. Tiny bodices, scalloped necklines, lavish skirts. Even when she was younger she could never have contemplated such extravagance, not just in the matter of money but in expectations, in the preposterous hope of transformation, and bliss.

It was two or three minutes before anybody came. Maybe they had a peephole and were eyeing her, thinking she wasn't their kind of customer and hoping she would go away.

She would not. She moved beyond the mirror's reflection – stepping from the linoleum by the door to a plushy rug – and at long last the curtain at the back of the store opened and out stepped Milady herself, dressed in a black suit with glittery buttons. High heels, thin ankles, girdle so tight her nylons rasped, gold hair skinned back from her made-up face.

"I thought I could try on the suit in the window," Johanna said in a rehearsed voice. "The green one."

"Oh, that's a lovely suit," the woman said. "The one in the window happens to be a size ten. Now you look to be – maybe a fourteen?"

She rasped ahead of Johanna back to the part of the store where the ordinary clothes, the suits and daytime dresses, were hung.

"You're in luck. Fourteen coming up."

The first thing Johanna did was look at the price tag. Easily twice what she'd expected, and she was not going to pretend otherwise.

"It's expensive enough."

"It's very fine wool." The woman monkeyed around till she found the label, then read off a description of the material that Johanna wasn't really listening to because she had caught at the hem to examine the workmanship.

"It feels as light as silk, but it wears like iron. You can see it's lined throughout, lovely silk-and-rayon lining. You won't find it bagging in the seat and going out of shape the way the cheap suits do. Look at the velvet cuffs and collar and the little velvet buttons on the sleeve."

"I see them."

"That's the kind of detail you pay for, you just do not get it otherwise. I love the velvet touch. It's only on the green one, you know – the apricot one doesn't have it, even though they're exactly the same price."

Indeed it was the velvet collar and cuffs that gave the suit, in Johanna's eyes, its subtle look of luxury and made her long to buy it. But she was not going to say so.

"I might as well go ahead and try it on."

This was what she'd come prepared for, after all. Clean underwear and fresh talcum powder under her arms.

The woman had enough sense to leave her alone in the bright cubicle. Johanna avoided the glass like poison till she'd got the skirt straight and the jacket done up.

At first she just looked at the suit. It was all right. The fit was all right – the skirt shorter than what she was used to, but then what she was used to was not the style. There was no problem with the suit. The problem was with what stuck out of it. Her neck and her face and her hair and her big hands and thick legs.

"How are you getting on? Mind if I take a peek?"

Peek all you want to, Johanna thought, it's a case of a sow's ear, as you'll soon see.

The woman tried looking from one side, then the other.

"Of course, you'll need your nylons on and your heels. How does it feel? Comfortable?"

"The suit feels fine," Johanna said. "There's nothing the matter with the suit."

The woman's face changed in the mirror. She stopped smiling. She looked disappointed and tired, but kinder.

"Sometimes that's just the way it is. You never really know until you try something on. The thing is," she said, with a new, more moderate conviction growing in her voice, "the thing is you have a fine figure, but it's a strong figure. You have large bones and what's the matter with that? Dinky little velvet-covered buttons are not for you. Don't bother with it anymore. Just take it off."

Then when Johanna had got down to her underwear there was a tap and a hand through the curtain.

"Just slip this on, for the heck of it."

A brown wool dress, lined, with a full skirt gracefully gathered, three-quarter sleeves and a plain round neckline. About as plain as you could get, except for a narrow gold belt. Not as expensive as the suit, but still the price seemed like a lot, when you considered all there was to it.

At least the skirt was a more decent length and the fabric made a noble swirl around her legs. She steeled herself and looked in the glass.

This time she didn't look as if she'd been stuck into the garment for a joke.

The woman came and stood beside her, and laughed, but with relief.

"It's the color of your eyes. You don't need to wear velvet. You've got velvet eyes."

That was the kind of soft-soaping Johanna would have felt bound to scoff at, except that at the moment it seemed to be true. Her eyes were not large, and if asked to describe their color she would have said, "I guess they're a kind of a brown." But now they looked to be a really deep brown, soft and shining.

It wasn't that she had suddenly started thinking she was pretty or anything. Just that her eyes were a nice color, if they had been a piece of cloth.

"Now, I bet you don't wear dress shoes very often," the woman said. "But if you had nylons on and just a minimum kind of pump – And I bet you don't wear jewelry, and you're quite right, you don't need to, with that belt."

To cut off the sales spiel Johanna said, "Well, I better take it off so you can wrap it up." She was sorry to lose the soft weight of the skirt and the discreet ribbon of gold around her waist. She had never in her life had this silly feeling of being enhanced by what she had put on herself.

"I just hope it's for a special occasion," the woman called out as Johanna was hastening into her now dingy-looking regular clothes.

"It'll likely be what I get married in," said Johanna.

She was surprised at that coming out of her mouth. It wasn't a major error – the woman didn't know who she was and would probably not be talking to anybody who did know. Still, she had meant to keep absolutely quiet. She must have felt she owed this person something – that they'd been through the disaster of the green suit and the discovery of the brown dress together and that was a bond. Which was nonsense. The woman was in the business of selling clothes, and she'd just succeeded in doing that.

"Oh!" the woman cried out. "Oh, that's wonderful."

Well, it might be, Johanna thought, and then again it might not. She might be marrying anybody. Some miserable farmer who wanted a workhorse around the place, or some wheezy old half-cripple looking for a nurse. This woman had no idea what kind of man she had lined up, and it wasn't any of her business anyway.

"I can tell it's a love match," the woman said, just as if she had read these disgruntled thoughts. "That's why your eyes were shining in the mirror. I've wrapped it all in tissue paper, all you have to do is take it out and hang it up and the material will fall out beautifully. Just give it a light press if you want, but you probably won't even need to do that."

Then there was the business of handing over the money. They both pretended not to look, but both did.

"It's worth it," the woman said. "You only get married the once. Well, that's not always strictly true –"

"In my case it'll be true," Johanna said. Her face was hotly flushed because marriage had not, in fact, been mentioned. Not even in the last letter. She had revealed to this woman what she was counting on, and that had perhaps been an unlucky thing to do.

"Where did you meet him?" said the woman, still in that tone of wistful gaiety. "What was your first date?"

"Through family," Johanna said truthfully. She wasn't meaning to say any more but heard herself go on. "The Western Fair. In London."

"The Western Fair," the woman said. "In London." She could have been saying "the Castle Ball."

"We had his daughter and her friend with us," said Johanna, thinking that in a way it would have been more accurate to say that he and Sabitha and Edith had her, Johanna, with them.

"Well, I can say my day has not been wasted. I've provided the dress for somebody to be a happy bride in. That's enough to justify my existence." The woman tied a narrow pink ribbon around the dress box, making a big, unnecessary bow, then gave it a wicked snip with the scissors.

"I'm here all day," she said. "And sometimes I just wonder what I think I'm doing. I ask myself, What do you think you're doing here? I put up a new display in the window and I do this and that to entice the people in, but there are days – there are *days* – when I do not see one soul come in that door. I know – people think these clothes are too expensive – but they're *good*. They're good clothes. If you want the quality you have to pay the price."

"They must come in when they want something like those," said Johanna, looking towards the evening dresses. "Where else could they go?"

"That's just it. They don't. They go to the city – that's where they go. They'll drive fifty miles, a hundred miles, never mind the gas, and tell themselves that way they get something better than I've got here. And they haven't. Not better quality, not better selection. Nothing. Just that they'd be ashamed to say they bought their wedding outfits in town. Or they'll come in and try something on and say they have to think about it. I'll be back, they say. And I think, Oh, yes, I know what that means. It means they'll try to find the same thing cheaper in London or Kitchener, and even if it isn't cheaper, they'll buy it there once they've driven all that way and got sick of looking.

"I don't know," she said. "Maybe if I was a local person it would make a difference. It's very clique-y here, I find. You're not local, are you?"

Johanna said, "No."

"Don't you find it clique-y?"

Cleeky.

"Hard for an outsider to break in, is what I mean."

"I'm used to being on my own," Johanna said.

"But you found somebody. You won't be on your own anymore and isn't that lovely? Some days I think how grand it would be, to be married and stay at home. Of course, I used to be married, and I worked anyway. Ah, well. Maybe the man in the moon will walk in here and fall in love with me and then I'll be all set!"

Johanna had to hurry – that woman's need for conversation had delayed her. She was hurrying to be back at the house, her purchase stowed away, before Sabitha got home from school.

Then she remembered that Sabitha wasn't there, having been carried off on the weekend by her mother's cousin, her Aunt Roxanne, to live like a proper rich girl in Toronto and go to a rich girl's school. But she continued to walk fast – so fast some smart aleck holding up the wall of the drugstore called out to her, "Where's the fire?" and she slowed down a bit, not to attract attention.

The dress box was awkward – how could she have known the store would have its own pink cardboard boxes, with *Milady's* written across them in purple handwriting? A dead giveaway.

She felt a fool for mentioning a wedding, when he hadn't mentioned it and she ought to remember that. So much else had been said – or written – such fondness and yearning expressed, that the actual marrying seemed just to have been overlooked. The way you might speak about getting up in the morning and not about having breakfast, though you certainly intended to have it.

Nevertheless she should have kept her mouth shut.

She saw Mr. McCauley walking in the opposite direction up the other side of the street. That was all right – even if he had met her head-on he would never have noticed the box she carried. He would have raised a finger to his hat and passed her by, presumably noticing that she was his housekeeper but possibly not. He had other things on his mind, and for all anybody knew might be looking at some town other than the one they saw. Every working day – and sometimes, forgetfully, on holidays or Sundays – he got dressed in one of his three-piece suits and his light overcoat or his heavy overcoat, and his gray fedora and his well-polished shoes, and walked from Exhibition Road uptown to the office he still maintained over what had been the harness and luggage store. It was spoken of as an Insurance Office, though it was quite a long time since he had actively sold insurance. Sometimes people climbed the stairs to see him, maybe to ask some question about their policies or more likely about lot boundaries, the history of some piece of real estate in town or farm out in the country. His office was full of maps old and new, and he liked nothing better than to lay them out and get into a discussion that expanded far beyond the question asked. Three or four times a day he emerged and walked the street, as now. During the war he had put the McLaughlin-Buick up on blocks in the barn, and walked everywhere to set an example. He still seemed to be setting an example, fifteen years later. Hands clasped behind his back, he was like a kind landlord inspecting his property or a preacher happy to observe his flock. Of course, half the people that he met had no idea who he was.

The town had changed, even in the time Johanna had been here. Trade was moving out to the highway, where there was a new discount store and a Canadian Tire and a motel with a lounge and topless dancers. Some downtown shops had tried to spruce themselves up with pink or mauve or olive paint, but already that paint was curling on the old brick and some of the interiors were empty. Milady's was almost certain to follow suit.

If Johanna was the woman in there, what would she have done? She'd never have gotten in so many elaborate evening dresses, for a start. What instead? If you made the switch to cheaper clothes you'd only be putting yourself in competition with Callaghans and the discount place, and there probably wasn't trade enough to go around. So what about going into fancy baby clothes, children's clothes, trying to pull in the grandmothers and aunts who had the money and would spend it for that kind of thing? Forget about the mothers, who would go to Callaghans, having less money and more sense.

But if it was her in charge – Johanna – she would never be able to pull in anybody. She could see what needed to be done, and how, and she could round up and supervise people to do it, but she could never charm or entice. Take it or leave it, would be her attitude. No doubt they would leave it.

It was the rare person who took to her, and she'd been aware of that for a long time. Sabitha certainly hadn't shed any tears when she said good-bye – though you could say Johanna was the nearest thing Sabitha had to a mother, since her own mother had died. Mr. McCauley would be upset when she left because she'd given good service and it would be hard to replace her, but that would be all he thought about. Both he and his granddaughter were spoiled and self-centered. As for the neighbors, they would no doubt rejoice. Johanna had had problems on both sides of the property. On one side it was the neighbors' dog digging in her garden, burying and retrieving his supply of bones, which he could better have done at home. And on the other it was the black cherry tree, which was on the McCauleys' property but bore most of its cherries on the branches hanging over into the next yard. In both cases she had raised a fuss, and won. The dog was tied up and the other neighbors left the cherries alone. If she got up on the stepladder she could reach well over into their yard, but they no longer chased the birds out of the branches and it made a difference to the crop.

Mr. McCauley would have let them pick. He would have let the dog dig. He would let himself be taken advantage of. Part of the reason was that these were new people and lived in new houses and so he preferred not to pay attention to them. At one time there had been just three or four large houses on Exhibition Road. Across from them were the fair-grounds, where the fall fair was held (officially called the

Agricultural Exhibition, hence the name), and in between were orchard trees, small meadows. A dozen years ago or so that land had been sold off in regular lot sizes and houses had been put up – small houses in alternating styles, one kind with an upstairs and the other kind without. Some were already getting to look pretty shabby.

There were only a couple of houses whose occupants Mr. McCauley knew and was friendly with – the schoolteacher, Miss Hood, and her mother, and the Shultzes, who ran the Shoe Repair shop. The Shultzes' daughter, Edith, was or had been Sabitha's great friend. It was natural, with their being in the same grade at school – at least last year, once Sabitha had been held back – and living near each other. Mr. McCauley hadn't minded – maybe he had some idea that Sabitha would be removed before long to live a different sort of life in Toronto. Johanna would not have chosen Edith, though the girl was never rude, never troublesome when she came to the house. And she was not stupid. That might have been the problem – she was smart and Sabitha was not so smart. She had made Sabitha sly.

That was all over now. Now that the cousin, Roxanne – Mrs. Huber – had shown up, the Schultz girl was all part of Sabitha's childish past.

I am going to arrange to get all your furniture out to you on the train as soon as they can take it and prepaid as soon as they tell me what it will cost. I have been thinking you will need it now. I guess it will not be that much of a surprise that I thought you would not mind it if I went along to be of help to you as I hope I can be.

This was the letter she had taken to the Post Office, before she went to make arrangements at the railway station. It was the first letter she had ever sent to him directly. The others had been slipped in with the letters she made Sabitha write.

And his to her had come in the same way, tidily folded and with her name, Johanna, typed on the back of the page so there would be no mistaking. That kept the people in the Post Office from catching on, and it never hurt to save a stamp. Of course, Sabitha could have reported to her grandfather, or even read what was written to Johanna, but Sabitha was no more interested in communicating with the old man than she was in letters – the writing or the receiving of them.

The furniture was stored back in the barn, which was just a town barn, not a real barn with animals and a granary. When Johanna got her first look at everything a year or so ago, she found it grimy with dust and splattered with pigeon droppings. The pieces had been piled in carelessly without anything to cover them. She had hauled what she could carry out into the yard, leaving space in the barn to get at the big pieces she couldn't carry – the sofa and buffet and china cabinet and dining table. The bedstead she could take apart. She went at the wood with soft dustrags, then lemon oil, and when she was finished it shone like candy. Maple candy – it was bird's-eye maple wood. It looked glamorous to her, like satin bedspreads and blond hair. Glamorous and modern, a total contrast to all the dark wood and irksome carving of the furniture she cared for in the house. She thought of it as *his* furniture then, and still did when she got it out this Wednesday. She had put old quilts over the bottom layer to protect everything there from what was piled on top, and sheets over what was on top to protect that from the birds, and as a result there was only a light dust. But she wiped everything and lemon-oiled it before she put it back, protected in the same way, to wait for the truck on Friday.

Dear Mr. McCauley,

I am leaving on the train this afternoon (Friday). I realize this is without giving my notice to you, but I will wave my last pay, which would be three weeks owing this coming

Monday. There is a beef stew on the stove in the double boiler that just needs warming up. Enough there for three meals or maybe could be stretched to a fourth. As soon as it is hot and you have got all you want, put the lid on and put it away in the fridge. Remember, put the lid on at once not to take chances with it getting spoiled. Regards to you and to Sabitha and will probably be in touch when I am settled. Johanna Parry.

P.S. I have shipped his furniture to Mr. Boudreau as he may need it. Remember to make sure when you reheat there is enough water in bottom part of the double boiler.

Mr. McCauley had no trouble finding out that the ticket Johanna had bought was to Gdynia, Saskatchewan. He phoned the station agent and asked. He could not think how to describe Johanna – was she old or young-looking, thin or moderately heavy, what was the color of her coat? – but that was not necessary when he mentioned the furniture.

When this call came through there were a couple of people in the station waiting for the evening train. The agent tried to keep his voice down at first, but he became excited when he heard about the stolen furniture (what Mr. McCauley actually said was "and I believe she took some furniture with her"). He swore that if he had known who she was and what she was up to he would never have let her set foot on the train. This assertion was heard and repeated and believed, nobody asking how he could have stopped a grown woman who had paid for her ticket, unless he had some proof right away that she was a thief. Most people who repeated his words believed that he could and would have stopped her – they believed in the authority of station agents and of upright-walking fine old men in three-piece suits like Mr. McCauley.

The beef stew was excellent, as Johanna's cooking always was, but Mr. McCauley found he could not swallow it. He disregarded the instruction about the lid and left the pot sitting open on the stove and did not even turn off the burner until the water in the bottom pot boiled away and he was alerted by a smell of smoking metal.

This was the smell of treachery.

He told himself to be thankful at least that Sabitha was taken care of and he did not have that to worry about. His cousin – his wife's cousin, actually, Roxanne – had written to tell him that from what she had seen of Sabitha on her summer visit to Lake Simcoe the girl was going to take some handling.

"Frankly I don't think you and that woman you've hired are going to be up to it when the boys come swarming around."

She did not go so far as to ask him whether he wanted another Marcelle on his hands, but that was what she meant. She said she would get Sabitha into a good school where she could be taught manners at least.

He turned on the television for a distraction, but it was no use.

It was the furniture that galled him. It was Ken Boudreau.

The fact was that three days before – on the very day that Johanna had bought her ticket, as the station agent had now told him – Mr. McCauley had received a letter from Ken Boudreau asking him to (a) advance some money against the furniture belonging to him (Ken Boudreau) and his dead wife, Marcelle, which was stored in Mr. McCauley's barn, or (b) if he could not see his way to doing that, to sell the furniture for as much as he could get and send the money as quickly as he could to Saskatchewan. There was no mention of the loans that had already been made by father-in-law to son-in-law, all against the value of this furniture and amounting to more than it could ever be sold for. Could Ken Boudreau have forgotten all about that? Or did he simply hope – and this was more probable – that his father-in-law would have forgotten?

He was now, it seemed, the owner of a hotel. But his letter was full of diatribes against the fellow who had formerly owned it and who had misled him as to various particulars.

"If I can just get over this hurdle," he said, "then I am convinced I can still make a go of it." But what was the hurdle? A need for immediate money, but he did not say whether it was owing to the former owner, or to the bank, or to a private mortgage holder, or what. It was the same old story – a desperate, wheedling tone mixed in with some arrogance, some sense of its being what was owed him, because of the wounds inflicted on him, the shame suffered, on account of Marcelle.

With many misgivings but remembering that Ken Boudreau was after all his son-in-law and had fought in the war and been through God-knows-what trouble in his marriage, Mr. McCauley had sat down and written a letter saying that he did not have any idea how to go about getting the best price for the furniture and it would be very difficult for him to find out and that he was enclosing a check, which he would count as an outright personal loan. He wished his son-in-law to acknowledge it as such and to remember the number of similar loans made in the past – already, he believed, exceeding any value of the furniture. He was enclosing a list of dates and amounts. Apart from fifty dollars paid nearly two years ago (with a promise of regular payments to follow), he had received nothing. His son-in-law must surely understand that as a result of these unpaid and interest-free loans Mr. McCauley's income had declined, since he would otherwise have invested the money.

He had thought of adding, "I am not such a fool as you seem to think," but decided not to, since that would reveal his irritation and perhaps his weakness.

And now look. The man had jumped the gun and enlisted Johanna in his scheme – he would always be able to get around women – and got hold of the furniture as well as the check. She had paid for the shipping herself, the station agent had said. The flashy-looking modern maple stuff had been overvalued in the deals already made and they would not get much for it, especially when you counted what the railway had charged. If they had been cleverer they would simply have taken something from the house, one of the old cabinets or parlor settees too uncomfortable to sit on, made and bought in the last century. That, of course, would have been plain stealing. But what they had done was not far off.

He went to bed with his mind made up to prosecute.

He woke in the house alone, with no smell of coffee or breakfast coming from the kitchen – instead, there was a whiff of the burned pot still in the air. An autumn chill had settled in all the high-ceilinged, forlorn rooms. It had been warm last evening and on preceding evenings – the furnace had not been turned on yet, and when Mr. McCauley did turn it on the warm air was accompanied by a blast of cellar damp, of mold and earth and decay. He washed and dressed slowly, with forgetful pauses, and spread some peanut butter on a piece of bread for his breakfast. He belonged to a generation in which there were men who were said not to be able even to boil water, and he was one of them. He looked out the front windows and saw the trees on the other side of the racetrack swallowed up in the morning fog, which seemed to be advancing, not retreating as it should at this hour, across the track itself. He seemed to see in the fog the looming buildings of the old Exhibition Grounds – homely, spacious buildings, like enormous barns. They had stood for years and years unused – all through the war – and he forgot what happened to them in the end. Were they torn down, or did they fall down? He abhorred the races that took place now, the crowds and the loudspeaker and the illegal drinking and the ruinous uproar of the summer Sundays. When he thought of that he thought of his poor girl Marcelle, sitting on the veranda steps and calling out to grown schoolmates who had got out of their parked cars and were hurrying to see the races. The fuss she made, the joy she expressed at being back in town, the hugging and holding people up, talking a mile a minute, rattling on about childhood days and how she'd missed everybody. She had said that the only thing not perfect about life was missing her husband, Ken, left out west because of his work.

She went out there in her silk pajamas, with straggly, uncombed, dyed-blond hair. Her arms and legs were thin, but her face was somewhat bloated, and what she claimed was her tan seemed a sickly brown color not from the sun. Maybe jaundice.

The child had stayed inside and watched television – Sunday cartoons that she was surely too old for.

He couldn't tell what was wrong, or be sure that anything was. Marcelle went away to London to have some female thing done and died in the hospital. When he phoned her husband to tell him, Ken Boudreau said, "What did she take?"

If Marcelle's mother had been alive still, would things have been any different? The fact was that her mother, when she was alive, had been as bewildered as he was. She had sat in the kitchen crying while their teenage daughter, locked into her room, had climbed out the window and slid down the veranda roof to be welcomed by carloads of boys.

The house was full of a feeling of callous desertion, of deceit. He and his wife had surely been kind parents, driven to the wall by Marcelle. When she had eloped with an airman, they had hoped that she would be all right, at last. They had been generous to the two of them as to the most proper young couple. But it all fell apart. To Johanna Parry he had likewise been generous, and look how she too had gone against him.

He walked to town and went into the hotel for his breakfast. The waitress said, "You're bright and early this morning."

And while she was still pouring out his coffee he began to tell her about how his housekeeper had walked out on him without any warning or provocation, not only left her job with no notice but taken a load of furniture that had belonged to his daughter, that now was supposed to belong to his son-in-law but didn't really, having been bought with his daughter's wedding money. He told her how his daughter had married an airman, a good-looking, plausible fellow who wasn't to be trusted around the corner.

"Excuse me," the waitress said. "I'd love to chat, but I got people waiting on their breakfast. Excuse me –"

He climbed the stairs to his office, and there, spread out on his desk, were the old maps he had been studying yesterday in an effort to locate exactly the very first burying ground in the county (abandoned, he believed, in 1839). He turned on the light and sat down, but he found he could not concentrate. After the waitress's reproof – or what he took for a reproof – he hadn't been able to eat his breakfast or enjoy his coffee. He decided to go out for a walk to calm himself down.

But instead of walking along in his usual way, greeting people and passing a few words with them, he found himself bursting into speech. The minute anybody asked him how he was this morning he began in a most uncharacteristic, even shameful way to blurt out his woes, and like the waitress, these people had business to attend to and they nodded and shuffled and made excuses to get away. The morning didn't seem to be warming up in the way foggy fall mornings usually did; his jacket wasn't warm enough, so he sought the comfort of the shops.

People who had known him the longest were the most dismayed. He had never been anything but reticent – the well-mannered gentleman, his mind on other times, his courtesy a deft apology for privilege (which was a bit of a joke, because the privilege was mostly in his recollections and not apparent to others). He should have been the last person to air wrongs or ask for sympathy – he hadn't when his wife died, or even when his daughter died – yet here he was, pulling out some letter, asking if it wasn't a shame the way this fellow had taken him for money over and over again, and even now when he'd taken pity on him once more the fellow had connived with his housekeeper to steal the furniture. Some thought it was his own furniture he was talking about – they believed the old man had been left without a bed or a chair in his house. They advised him to go to the police.

"That's no good, that's no good," he said. "How can you get blood from a stone?"

He went into the Shoe Repair shop and greeted Herman Shultz.

"Do you remember those boots you resoled for me, the ones I got in England? You resoled them four or five years ago."

The shop was like a cave, with shaded bulbs hanging down over various workplaces. It was abominably ventilated, but its manly smells – of glue and leather and shoe-blacking and fresh-cut felt soles and rotted old ones – were comfortable to Mr. McCauley. Here his neighbor Herman Shultz, a sallow, expert, spectacled workman, bent-shouldered, was occupied in all seasons – driving in iron nails and clinch nails and, with a wicked hooked knife, cutting the desired shapes out of leather. The felt was cut by something like a miniature circular saw. The buffers made a scuffing noise and the sandpaper wheel made a rasp and the emery stone on a tool's edge sang high like a mechanical insect and the sewing machine punched the leather in an earnest industrial rhythm. All the sounds and smells and precise activities of the place had been familiar to Mr. McCauley for years but never identified or reflected upon before. Now Herman, in his blackened leather apron with a boot on one hand, straightened up, smiled, nodded, and Mr. McCauley saw the man's whole life in this cave. He wished to express sympathy or admiration or something more that he didn't understand.

"Yes, I do," Herman said. "They were nice boots."

"Fine boots. You know I got them on my wedding trip. I got them in England. I can't remember now where, but it wasn't in London."

"I remember you telling me."

"You did a fine job on them. They're still doing well. Fine job, Herman. You do a good job here. You do honest work."

"That's good." Herman took a quick look at the boot on his hand. Mr. McCauley knew that the man wanted to get back to his work, but he couldn't let him.

"I've just had an eye-opener. A shock."

"Have you?"

The old man pulled out the letter and began to read bits of it aloud, with interjections of dismal laughter.

"Bronchitis. He says he's sick with bronchitis. He doesn't know where to turn. *I don't know who to turn to.* Well he always knows who to turn to. When he's run through everything else, turn to me. *A few hundred just till I get on my feet.* Begging and pleading with me and all the time he's conniving with my housekeeper. Did you know that? She stole a load of furniture and went off out west with it. They were hand in glove. This is a man I've saved the skin of time and time again. And never a penny back. No, no, I have to be honest and say fifty dollars. Fifty out of hundreds and hundreds. Thousands. He was in the Air Force in the war, you know. Those shortish fellows, they were often in the Air Force. Strutting around thinking they were war heroes. Well, I guess I shouldn't say that, but I think the war spoiled some of those fellows, they never could adjust to life afterwards. But that's not enough of an excuse. Is it? I can't excuse him forever because of the war."

"No you can't."

"I knew he wasn't to be trusted the first time I met him. That's the extraordinary thing. I knew it and I let him rook me all the same. There are people like that. You take pity on them just for being the crooks they are. I got him his insurance job out there, I had some connections. Of course he mucked it up. A bad egg. Some just are."

"You're right about that."

Mrs. Shultz was not in the store that day. Usually she was the one at the counter, taking in the shoes and showing them to her husband and reporting back what he said, making out the slips, and taking the payment when the restored shoes were handed back. Mr. McCauley remembered that she had had some kind of operation during the summer.

"Your wife isn't in today? Is she well?"

"She thought she'd better take it easy today. I've got my girl in."

Herman Shultz nodded towards the shelves to the right of the counter, where the finished shoes were displayed. Mr. McCauley turned his head and saw Edith, the daughter, whom he hadn't noticed when he came in. A childishly thin girl with straight black hair, who kept her back to him, rearranging the shoes. That was just the way she had seemed to slide in and out of sight when she came to his house as Sabitha's friend. You never got a good look at her face.

"You're going to help your father out now?" Mr. McCauley said. "You're through with school?"

"It's Saturday," said Edith, half turning, faintly smiling.

"So it is. Well, it's a good thing to help your father, anyway. You must take care of your parents. They've worked hard and they're good people." With a slight air of apology, as if he knew he was being sententious, Mr. McCauley said, "Honor thy father and thy mother, that thy days may be long in the –"

Edith said something not for him to hear. She said, "Shoe Repair shop."

"I'm taking up your time, I'm imposing on you," said Mr. McCauley sadly. "You have work to do."

"There's no need for you to be sarcastic," said Edith's father when the old man had gone.

He told Edith's mother all about Mr. McCauley at supper.

"He's not himself," he said. "Something's come over him."

"Maybe a little stroke," she said. Since her own operation – for gallstones – she spoke knowledgeably and with a placid satisfaction about the afflictions of other people.

Now that Sabitha had gone, vanished into another sort of life that had, it seemed, always been waiting for her, Edith had reverted to being the person she had been before Sabitha came here. "Old for her age," diligent, critical. After three weeks at high school she knew that she was going to be very good at all the new subjects – Latin, Algebra, English Literature. She believed that her cleverness was going to be recognized and acclaimed and an important future would open out for her. The past year's silliness with Sabitha was slipping out of sight.

Yet when she thought about Johanna's going off out west she felt a chill from her past, an invasive alarm. She tried to bang a lid down on that, but it wouldn't stay.

As soon as she had finished washing the dishes she went off to her room with the book they had been assigned for literature class. *David Copperfield.*

She was a child who had never received more than tepid reproofs from her parents – old parents to have a child of her age, which was said to account for her being the way she was – but she felt in perfect accord with David in his unhappy situation. She felt that she was one like him, one who might as well have been an orphan, because she would probably have to run away, go into hiding, fend for herself, when the truth became known and her past shut off her future.

It had all begun with Sabitha saying, on the way to school, "We have to go by the Post Office. I have to send a letter to my dad."

They walked to and from school together every day. Sometimes they walked with their eyes closed, or backwards. Sometimes when they met people they gabbled away softly in a nonsense language, to cause confusion. Most of their good ideas were Edith's. The only idea Sabitha introduced was the writing down of a boy's name and your own, and the stroking out of all letters that were duplicated and the counting of the remainder. Then you ticked off the counted number on your fingers, saying, *Hateship, friendship, courtship, loveship, marriage*, till you got the verdict on what could happen between you and that boy.

"That's a fat letter," said Edith. She noticed everything, and she remembered everything, quickly memorizing whole pages of the textbooks in a way the other children found sinister. "Did you have a lot of things to write to your dad?" she said, surprised, because she could not credit this – or at least could not credit that Sabitha would get them on paper.

"I only wrote on one page," Sabitha said, feeling the letter.

"A-ha," said Edith. "Ah. Ha."

"Aha what?"

"I bet she put something else in. Johanna did."

The upshot of this was that they did not take the letter directly to the Post Office, but saved it and steamed it open at Edith's house after school. They could do such things at Edith's house because her mother worked all day at the Shoe Repair shop.

Dear Mr. Ken Boudreau,

I just thought I would write and send my thanks to you for the nice things you said about me in your letter to your daughter. You do not need to worry about me leaving. You say that I am a person you can trust. That is the meaning I take and as far as I know it is true. I am grateful to you for saying that, since some people feel that a person like me that they do not know the background of is Beyond the Pale. So I thought I would tell you something about myself. I was born in Glasgow, but my mother had to give me up when she got married. I was taken to the Home at the age of five. I looked for her to come back, but she didn't and I got used to it there and they weren't Bad. At the age of eleven I was brought to Canada on a Plan and lived with the Dixons, working on their Market Gardens. School was in the Plan, but I didn't see much of it. In winter I worked in the house for the Mrs. but circumstances made me think of leaving, and being big and strong for my age got taken on at a Nursing Home looking after the old people. I did not mind the work, but for better money went and worked in a Broom Factory. Mr. Willets that owned it had an old mother that came in to see how things were going, and she and I took to each other some way. The atmosphere was giving me breathing troubles so she said I should come and work for her and I did. I lived with her 12 yrs. on a lake called Mourning Dove Lake up north. There was only the two of us, but I could take care of everything outside and in, even running the motorboat and driving the car. I learned to read properly because her eyes were going bad and she liked me to read to her. She died at the age of 96. You might say what a life for a young person, but I was happy. We ate together every meal and I slept in her room the last year and a half. But after she died the family gave me one wk. to pack up. She had left me some money and I guess they did not like that. She wanted me to use it for Education but I would have to go in with kids. So when I saw the ad Mr. McCauley put in the Globe and Mail I came to see about it. I needed work to get over missing Mrs. Willets. So I guess I have bored you long enough with my History and you'll be relieved I have got up to the Present. Thank you for your good opinion and for taking me along to the Fair. I am not one for the rides or for eating the stuff but it was still certainly a pleasure to be included.

Your friend, Johanna Parry.

Edith read Johanna's words aloud, in an imploring voice and with a woebegone expression.

"I was born in Glasgow, but my mother had to give me up when she took one look at me –"

"Stop," said Sabitha. "I'm laughing so hard I'll be sick."

"How did she get her letter in with yours without you knowing?"

"She just takes it from me and puts it in an envelope and writes on the outside because she doesn't think my writing is good enough."

Edith had to put Scotch tape on the flap of the envelope to make it stick, since there wasn't enough sticky stuff left. "She's in love with him," she said.

"Oh, puke-puke," said Sabitha, holding her stomach. "She can't be. Old Johanna."

"What did he say about her, anyway?"

"Just about how I was supposed to respect her and it would be too bad if she left because we were lucky to have her and he didn't have a home for me and Grandpa couldn't raise a girl by himself and blah-blah. He said she was a lady. He said he could tell."

"So then she falls in lo-ove."

The letter remained with Edith overnight, lest Johanna discover that it hadn't been posted and was sealed with Scotch tape. They took it to the Post Office the next morning.

"Now we'll see what he writes back. Watch out," said Edith.

No letter came for a long time. And when it did, it was a disappointment. They steamed it open at Edith's house, but found nothing inside for Johanna.

Dear Sabitha,

Christmas finds me a bit short this year, sorry I don't have more than a two-dollar bill to send you. But I hope you are in good health and have a Merry Christmas and keep up your schoolwork. I have not been feeling so well myself having got Bronchitis, which I seem to do every winter, but this is the first time it landed me in bed before Christmas.

As you see by the address I am in a new place. The apartment was in a very noisy location and too many people dropping in hoping for a party. This is a boardinghouse, which suits me fine as I was never good at the shopping and the cooking.

Merry Christmas and love, Dad.

"Poor Johanna," said Edith. "Her heart will be bwoken."

Sabitha said, "Who cares?"

"Unless we do it," Edith said.

"What?"

"*Answer* her."

They would have to type their letter, because Johanna would notice that it was not in Sabitha's father's handwriting. But the typing was not difficult. There was a typewriter in Edith's house, on a card table in the front room. Her mother had worked in an office before she was married and she sometimes earned a little money still by writing the sort of letters that people wanted to look official. She had taught Edith the basics of typing, in the hope that Edith too might get an office job someday.

"Dear Johanna," said Sabitha, "I am sorry I cannot be in love with you because you have got those ugly spots all over your face."

"I'm going to be serious," said Edith. "So shut up."

She typed, "I was so glad to get the letter –" speaking the words of her composition aloud, pausing while she thought up more, her voice becoming increasingly solemn and tender. Sabitha sprawled on the couch, giggling. At one point she turned on the television, but Edith said, "Pul-eeze. How can I concentrate on my e-motions with all that shit going on?"

Edith and Sabitha used the words "shit" and "bitch" and "Jesus Christ" when they were alone together.

Dear Johanna,

I was so glad to get the letter you put in with Sabitha's and to find out about your life. It must often have been a sad and lonely one though Mrs. Willets sounds like a lucky person for you to find. You have remained industrious and uncomplaining and I must say that I admire you very much. My own life has been a checkered one and I have never exactly settled down. I do not know why I have this inner restlessness and loneliness, it just seems to be my fate. I am always meeting people and talking to people but sometimes I ask myself, Who is my friend? Then comes your letter and you write at the end of it, Your friend. So I think, Does she really mean that? And what a very nice Christmas present it would be for me if Johanna would tell me that she is my friend. Maybe you just thought it was a nice way to end a letter and you don't really know me well enough. Merry Christmas anyway.

Your friend, Ken Boudreau.

The letter went home to Johanna. The one to Sabitha had ended up being typed as well because why would one be typed and not the other? They had been sparing with the steam this time and opened the envelope very carefully so there would be no telltale Scotch tape.

"Why couldn't we type a new envelope? Wouldn't he do that if he typed the letter?" said Sabitha, thinking she was being clever.

"Because a new *envelope* wouldn't have a *postmark* on it. Dumb-dumb."

"What if she answers it?"

"We'll read it."

"Yah, what if she answers it and sends it direct to *him*?"

Edith didn't like to show she had not thought of that.

"She won't. She's sly. Anyway, you write him back right away to give her the idea she can slip it in with yours."

"I hate writing stupid letters."

"Go on. It won't kill you. Don't you want to see what she says?"

Dear Friend,

You ask me do I know you well enough to be your friend and my answer is that I think I do. I have only had one Friend in my life, Mrs. Willets who I loved and she was so good to me but she is dead. She was a lot older than me and the trouble with Older Friends is they die and leave you. She was so old she would call me sometimes by another person's name. I did not mind it though.

I will tell you a strange thing. That picture that you got the photographer at the Fair to take, of you and Sabitha and her friend Edith and me, I had it enlarged and framed and set in the living room. It is not a very good picture and he certainly charged you enough for what it is, but it is better than nothing. So the day before yesterday I was dusting around it and I imagined I could hear you say Hello to me. Hello, you said, and I looked at your face as well as you can see it in the picture and I thought, Well, I must be losing my mind. Or else it is a sign of a letter coming. I am just fooling, I don't really believe in anything like that. But yesterday there was a letter. So you see it is not asking too much of me to be your friend. I can always find a way to keep busy but a true Friend is something else again.

Your Friend, Johanna Parry.

Of course, that could not be replaced in the envelope. Sabitha's father would spot something fishy in the references to a letter he had never written. Johanna's words had to be torn into tiny pieces and flushed down the toilet at Edith's house.

When the letter came telling about the hotel it was months and months later. It was summer. And it was just by luck that Sabitha had picked that letter up, since she had been away for three weeks, staying at the cottage on Lake Simcoe that belonged to her Aunt Roxanne and her Uncle Clark.

Almost the first thing Sabitha said, coming into Edith's house, was, "Ugga-ugga. This place stinks."

"Ugga-ugga" was an expression she had picked up from her cousins.

Edith sniffed the air. "I don't smell anything."

"It's like your dad's shop, only not so bad. They must bring it home on their clothes and stuff."

Edith attended to the steaming and opening. On her way from the Post Office, Sabitha had bought two chocolate eclairs at the bakeshop. She was lying on the couch eating hers.

"Just one letter. For you," said Edith. "Pore old Johanna. Of course he never actually *got* hers."

"Read it to me," said Sabitha resignedly. "I've got sticky guck all over my hands."

Edith read it with businesslike speed, hardly pausing for the periods.

> Well, Sabitha, my fortunes have taken a different turn, as you can see I am not in Brandon anymore but in a place called Gdynia. And not in the employ of my former bosses. I have had an exceptionally hard winter with my chest troubles and they, that is my bosses, thought I should be out on the road even if I was in danger of developing pneumonia so this developed into quite an argument so we all decided to say farewell. But luck is a strange thing and just about that time I came into possession of a Hotel. It is too

complicated to explain the ins and outs but if your grandfather wants to know about it just tell him a man who owed me money which he could not pay let me have this hotel instead. So here I am moved from one room in a boardinghouse to a twelve-bedroom building and from not even owning the bed I slept in to owning several. It's a wonderful thing to wake up in the morning and know you are your own boss. I have some fixing up to do, actually plenty, and will get to it as soon as the weather warms up. I will need to hire somebody to help and later on I will hire a good cook to have a restaurant as well as the beverage room. That ought to go like hotcakes as there is none in this town. Hope you are well and doing your schoolwork and developing good habits.

Love, Your Dad.

Sabitha said, "Have you got some coffee?"

"Instant," said Edith. "Why?"

Sabitha said that iced coffee was what everybody had been drinking at the cottage and they were all crazy about it. She was crazy about it too. She got up and messed around in the kitchen, boiling the water and stirring up the coffee with milk and ice cubes. "What we really ought to have is vanilla ice cream," she said. "Oh, my Gad, is it ever wonderful. Don't you want your eclair?"

Oh, my Gad.

"Yes. All of it," said Edith meanly.

All these changes in Sabitha in just three weeks – during the time Edith had been working in the shop and her mother recovering at home from her operation. Sabitha's skin was an appetizing golden-brown color, and her hair was cut shorter and fluffed out around her face. Her cousins had cut it and given her a permanent. She wore a sort of playsuit, with shorts cut like a skirt and buttons down the front and frills over the shoulders in a becoming blue color. She had got plumper, and when she leaned over to pick up her glass of iced coffee, which was on the floor, she displayed a smooth, glowing cleavage.

Breasts. They must have started growing before she went away, but Edith had not noticed. Maybe they were just something you woke up with one morning. Or did not.

However they came, they seemed to indicate a completely unearned and unfair advantage.

Sabitha was full of talk about her cousins and life at the cottage. She would say, "Listen, I've got to tell you about this, it's a scream –" and then ramble on about what Aunt Roxanne said to Uncle Clark when they had the fight, how Mary Jo drove with the top down and without a license in Stan's car (who was Stan?) and took them all to a drive-in – and what was the scream or the point of the story somehow never became clear.

But after a while other things did. The real adventures of the summer. The older girls – that included Sabitha – slept in the upstairs of the boathouse. Sometimes they had tickling fights – they would all gang up on someone and tickle her till she shrieked for mercy and agreed to pull her pajama pants down to show if she had hair. They told stories about girls at boarding school who did things with hairbrush handles, toothbrush handles. *Ugga-ugga.* Once a couple of cousins put on a show – one girl got on top of the other and pretended to be the boy and they wound their legs around each other and groaned and panted and carried on.

Uncle Clark's sister and her husband came to visit on their honeymoon, and he was seen to put his hand inside her swimsuit.

"They really loved each other, they were at it day and night," said Sabitha. She hugged a cushion to her chest. "People can't help it when they're in love like that."

One of the cousins had already done it with a boy. He was one of the summer help in the gardens of the resort down the road. He took her out in a boat and threatened to push her out until she agreed to let him do it. So it wasn't her fault.

"Couldn't she swim?" said Edith.

Sabitha pushed the cushion between her legs. "Oooh," she said. "Feels so nice."

Edith knew all about the pleasurable agonies Sabitha was feeling, but she was appalled that anybody would make them public. She herself was frightened of them. Years ago, before she knew what she was doing, she had gone to sleep with the blanket between her legs and her mother had discovered her and told her about a girl she had known who did things like that all the time and had eventually been operated on for the problem.

"They used to throw cold water on her, but it didn't cure her," her mother had said. "So she had to be cut."

Otherwise her organs would get congested and she might die.

"Stop," she said to Sabitha, but Sabitha moaned defiantly and said, "It's nothing. We all did it like this. Haven't you got a cushion?"

Edith got up and went to the kitchen and filled her empty iced-coffee glass with cold water. When she got back Sabitha was lying limp on the couch, laughing, the cushion flung on the floor.

"What did you think I was doing?" she said. "Didn't you know I was kidding?"

"I was thirsty," Edith said.

"You just drank a whole glass of iced coffee."

"I was thirsty for water."

"Can't have any fun with you." Sabitha sat up. "If you're so thirsty why don't you drink it?"

They sat in a moody silence until Sabitha said, in a conciliatory but disappointed tone, "Aren't we going to write Johanna another letter? Let's write her a lovey-dovey letter."

Edith had lost a good deal of her interest in the letters, but she was gratified to see that Sabitha had not. Some sense of having power over Sabitha returned, in spite of Lake Simcoe and the breasts. Sighing, as if reluctantly, she got up and took the cover off the typewriter.

"My darlingest Johanna –" said Sabitha.

"No. That's too sickening."

"She won't think so."

"She will so," said Edith.

She wondered whether she should tell Sabitha about the danger of congested organs. She decided not to. For one thing, that information fell into a category of warnings she had received from her mother and never known whether to wholly trust or distrust. It had not fallen as low, in credibility, as the belief that wearing foot-rubbers in the house would ruin your eyesight, but there was no telling – someday it might.

And for another thing – Sabitha would just laugh. She laughed at warnings – she would laugh even if you told her that chocolate eclairs would make her fat.

"Your last letter made me so happy –"

"Your last letter filled me with rap-ture –" said Sabitha.

"– made me so happy to think I did have a true friend in the world, which is you –"

"I could not sleep all night because I was longing to crush you in my arms –" Sabitha wrapped her arms around herself and rocked back and forth.

"*No.* Often I have felt so lonely in spite of a gregarious life and not known where to turn –"

"What does that mean – 'gregarious'? She won't know what it means."

"*She* will."

That shut Sabitha up and perhaps hurt her feelings. So at the end Edith read out, "I must say good-bye and the only way I can do it is to imagine you reading this and blushing –" "Is that more what you want?"

"Reading it in bed with your nightgown on," said Sabitha, always quickly restored, "and thinking how I would crush you in my arms and I would suck your titties –"

My Dear Johanna,
Your last letter made me so happy to think I have a true friend in the world, which is you. Often I have felt so lonely in spite of a gregarious life and not known where to turn.

Well, I have told Sabitha in my letter about my good fortune and how I am going into the hotel business. I did not tell her actually how sick I was last winter because I did not want to worry her. I do not want to worry you, either, dear Johanna, only to tell you that I thought of you so often and longed to see your dear sweet face. When I was feverish I thought that I really did see it bending over me and I heard your voice telling me I would soon be better and I felt the ministrations of your kind hands. I was in the boardinghouse and when I came to out of my fever there was a lot of teasing going on as to, who is this Johanna? But I was sad as could be to wake and find you were not there. I really wondered if you could have flown through the air and been with me, even though I knew that could not have happened. Believe me, believe me, the most beautiful movie star could not have been as welcome to me as you. I don't know if I should tell you the other things you were saying to me because they were very sweet and intimate but they might embarrass you. I hate to end this letter because it feels now as if I have my arms around you and I am talking to you quietly in the dark privacy of our room, but I must say good-bye and the only way I can do it is to imagine you reading this and blushing. It would be wonderful if you were reading it in bed with your nightgown on and thinking how I would like to crush you in my arms.

L-v-, Ken Boudreau.

Somewhat surprisingly, there was no reply to this letter. When Sabitha had written her half-page, Johanna put it in the envelope and addressed it and that was that.

When Johanna got off the train there was nobody to meet her. She did not let herself worry about that – she had been thinking that her letter might not, after all, have got here before she did. (In fact it had, and was lying in the Post Office, uncollected, because Ken Boudreau, who had not been seriously sick last winter, really did have bronchitis now and for several days had not come in for his mail. On this day it had been joined by another envelope, containing the check from Mr. McCauley. But payment on that had already been stopped.)

What was of more concern to her was that there did not appear to be a town. The station was an enclosed shelter with benches along the walls and a wooden shutter pulled down over the window of the ticket office. There was also a freight shed – she supposed it was a freight shed – but the sliding door to it would not budge. She peered through a crack between the planks until her eyes got used to the dark in there, and she saw that it was empty, with a dirt floor. No crates of furniture there. She called out, "Anybody here? Anybody here?" several times, but she did not expect a reply.

She stood on the platform and tried to get her bearings.

About half a mile away there was a slight hill, noticeable at once because it had a crown of trees. And the sandy-looking track that she had taken, when she saw it from the train, for a back lane into a farmer's field – that must be the road. Now she saw the low shapes of buildings here and there in the trees – and a water tower, which looked from this distance like a toy, a tin soldier on long legs.

She picked up her suitcase – this would not be too difficult; she had carried it, after all, from Exhibition Road to the other railway station – and set out.

There was a wind blowing, but this was a hot day – hotter than the weather she had left in Ontario – and the wind seemed hot as well. Over her new dress she was wearing her same old coat, which would have taken up too much room in the suitcase. She looked with longing to the shade of the town ahead, but when she got there she found that the trees were either spruce, which were too tight and narrow to give much shade, or raggedy thin-leaved cottonwoods, which blew about and let the sun through anyway.

There was a discouraging lack of formality, or any sort of organization, to this place. No sidewalks, or paved streets, no imposing buildings except a big church like a brick barn. A painting over its door, showing the Holy Family with clay-colored faces and staring blue eyes. It was named for an unheard-of saint – Saint Voytech.

The houses did not show much forethought in their situation or planning. They were set at different angles to the road, or street, and most of them had mean-looking little windows stuck here and there, with snow porches like boxes round the doors. Nobody was out in the yards, and why should they be? There was nothing to tend, only clumps of brown grass and once a big burst of rhubarb, gone to seed.

The main street, if that's what it was, had a raised wooden walk on one side only, and some unconsolidated buildings, of which a grocery store (containing the Post Office) and a garage seemed to be the only ones functioning. There was one two-story building that she thought might be the hotel, but it was a bank and it was closed.

The first human being she saw – though two dogs had barked at her – was a man in front of the garage, busy loading chains into the back of his truck.

"Hotel?" he said. "You come too far."

He told her that it was down by the station, on the other side of the tracks and along a bit, it was painted blue and you couldn't miss it.

She set the suitcase down, not from discouragement but because she had to have a moment's rest.

He said he would ride her down there if she wanted to wait a minute. And though it was a new kind of thing for her to accept such an offer, she soon found herself riding in the hot, greasy cab of his truck, rocking down the dirt road that she had just walked up, with the chains making a desperate racket in the back.

"So – where'd you bring this heat wave from?" he said.

She said Ontario, in a tone that promised nothing further.

"Ontario," he said regretfully. "Well. There 'tis. Your hotel." He took one hand off the wheel. The truck gave an accompanying lurch as he waved to a two-story flat-roofed building that she hadn't missed but had seen from the train, as they came in. She had taken it then for a large and fairly derelict, perhaps abandoned, family home. Now that she had seen the houses in town, she knew that she should not have dismissed it so readily. It was covered with sheets of tin stamped to look like bricks and painted a light blue. There was the one word HOTEL, in neon tubing, no longer lit, over the doorway.

"I am a dunce," she said, and offered the man a dollar for the ride.

He laughed. "Hang on to your money. You never know when you'll need it."

Quite a decent-looking car, a Plymouth, was parked outside this hotel. It was very dirty, but how could you help that, with these roads?

There were signs on the door advertising a brand of cigarettes, and of beer. She waited till the truck had turned before she knocked – knocked because it didn't look as if the place could in any way be open for business. Then she tried the door to see if it was open, and walked into a little dusty room with a staircase, and then into a large dark room in which there was a billiard table and a bad smell of beer and an unswept floor. Off in a side room she could see the glimmer of a mirror, empty shelves, a counter. These rooms had the blinds pulled tightly down. The only light she saw was coming through two small round windows, which turned out to be set in double swinging doors. She went on through these into a kitchen. It was lighter, because of a row of high – and dirty – windows, uncovered, in the opposite wall. And here were the first signs of life – somebody had been eating at the table and had left a plate smeared with dried ketchup and a cup half full of cold black coffee.

One of the doors off the kitchen led outside – this one was locked – and one to a pantry in which there were several cans of food, one to a broom closet, and one to an enclosed stairway. She climbed the steps, bumping her suitcase along in front of her because the space was narrow. Straight ahead of her on the second floor she saw a toilet with the seat up.

The door of the bedroom at the end of the hall was open, and in there she found Ken Boudreau.

She saw his clothes before she saw him. His jacket hanging up on a corner of the door and his trousers on the doorknob, so that they trailed on the floor. She thought at once that this was no way to treat good clothes, so she went boldly into the room – leaving her suitcase in the hall – with the idea of hanging them up properly.

He was in bed, with only a sheet over him. The blanket and his shirt were lying on the floor. He was breathing restlessly as if about to wake up, so she said, "Good morning. Afternoon."

The bright sunlight was coming in the window, hitting him almost in the face. The window was closed and the air horribly stale – smelling, for one thing, of the full ashtray on the chair he used as a bed table.

He had bad habits – he smoked in bed.

He did not wake up at her voice – or he woke only part way. He began to cough.

She recognized this as a serious cough, a sick man's cough. He struggled to lift himself up, still with his eyes closed, and she went over to the bed and hoisted him. She looked for a handkerchief or a box of tissues, but she saw nothing so she reached for his shirt on the floor, which she could wash later. She wanted to get a good look at what he spat up.

When he had hacked up enough, he muttered and sank down into the bed, gasping, the charming cocky-looking face she remembered crumpled up in disgust. She knew from the feel of him that he had a fever.

The stuff that he had coughed out was greenish-yellow – no rusty streaks. She carried the shirt to the toilet sink, where rather to her surprise she found a bar of soap, and washed it out and hung it on the door hook, then thoroughly washed her hands. She had to dry them on the skirt of her new brown dress. She had put that on in another little toilet – the *Ladies* on the train – not more than a couple of hours ago. She had been wondering then if she should have got some makeup.

In a hall closet she found a roll of toilet paper and took it into his room for the next time he had to cough. She picked up the blanket and covered him well, pulled the blind down to the sill and raised the stiff window an inch or two, propping it open with the ashtray she had emptied. Then she changed, out in the hall, from the brown dress into old clothes from her suitcase. A lot of use a nice dress or any makeup in the world would be now, in these surroundings.

She was not sure how sick he was, but she had nursed Mrs. Willets – also a heavy smoker – through several bouts of bronchitis, and she thought she could manage for a while without having to think about getting a doctor. In the same hall closet was a pile of clean, though worn and faded, towels, and she wet one of these and wiped his arms and legs, to try to get his fever down. He came half awake at this and began to cough again. She held him up and made him spit into the toilet paper, examined it once more and threw it down the toilet and washed her hands. She had a towel now to dry them on. She went downstairs and found a glass in the kitchen, also an empty, large ginger-ale bottle, which she filled with water. This she attempted to make him drink. He took a little, protested, and she let him lie down. In five minutes or so she tried again. She kept doing this until she believed he had swallowed as much as he could hold without throwing up.

Time and again he coughed and she lifted him up, held him with one arm while the other hand pounded on his back to help loosen the load in his chest. He opened his eyes several times and seemed to take in her presence without alarm or surprise – or gratitude, for that matter. She sponged him once more, being careful to cover immediately with the blanket the part that had just been cooled.

She noticed that it had begun to get dark, and she went down into the kitchen, found the light switch. The lights and the old electric stove were working. She opened and heated a can of chicken-with-rice soup, carried it upstairs and roused him. He swallowed a little from the spoon. She took advantage of his momentary wakefulness to ask if he had a bottle of aspirin. He nodded yes, then became very confused when trying to tell her where. "In the wastebasket," he said.

"No, no," she said. "You don't mean wastebasket."

"In the – in the –"

He tried to shape something with his hands. Tears came into his eyes.

"Never mind," Johanna said. "Never mind."

His fever went down anyway. He slept for an hour or more without coughing. Then he grew hot again. By that time she had found the aspirin – they were in a kitchen drawer with such things as a screwdriver and some lightbulbs and a ball of twine – and she got a couple into him. Soon he had a violent coughing fit, but she didn't think he threw them up. When he lay down she put her ear to his chest and listened to the wheezing. She had already looked for mustard to make a plaster with, but apparently there wasn't any. She went downstairs again and heated some water and brought it in a basin. She tried to make him lean over it, tenting him with towels, so that he could breathe the steam. He would cooperate only for a moment or so, but perhaps it helped – he hacked up quantities of phlegm.

His fever went down again and he slept more calmly. She dragged in an armchair she had found in one of the other rooms and she slept too, in snatches, waking and wondering where she was, then remembering and getting up and touching him – his fever seemed to be staying down – and tucking in the blanket. For her own cover she used the everlasting old tweed coat that she had Mrs. Willets to thank for.

He woke. It was full morning. "What are you doing here?" he said, in a hoarse, weak voice.

"I came yesterday," she said. "I brought your furniture. It isn't here yet, but it's on its way. You were sick when I got here and you were sick most of the night. How do you feel now?"

He said, "Better," and began to cough. She didn't have to lift him, he sat up on his own, but she went to the bed and pounded his back. When he finished, he said, "Thank you."

His skin now felt as cool as her own. And smooth – no rough moles, no fat on him. She could feel his ribs. He was like a delicate, stricken boy. He smelled like corn.

"You swallowed the phlegm," she said. "Don't do that, it's not good for you. Here's the toilet paper, you have to spit it out. You could get trouble with your kidneys, swallowing it."

"I never knew that," he said. "Could you find the coffee?"

The percolator was black on the inside. She washed it as well as she could and put the coffee on. Then she washed and tidied herself, wondering what kind of food she should give him. In the pantry there was a box of biscuit mix. At first she thought she would have to mix it with water, but she found a can of milk powder as well. When the coffee was ready she had a pan of biscuits in the oven.

As soon as he heard her busy in the kitchen, he got up to go to the toilet. He was weaker than he'd thought – he had to lean over and put one hand on the tank. Then he found some underwear on the floor of the hall closet where he kept clean clothes. He had figured out by now who this woman was and recalled her writing him some kind of friendly letter he couldn't take the time to answer. She had said she came to bring him his furniture, though he hadn't asked her or anybody to do that – hadn't asked for the furniture at all, just the money. He should know her name, but he couldn't remember it. That was why he opened her purse, which was on the floor of the hall beside her suitcase. There was a name tag sewn to the lining.

Johanna Parry, and the address of his father-in-law, on Exhibition Road.

Some other things. A cloth bag with a few bills in it. Twenty-seven dollars. Another bag with change, which he didn't bother to count. A bright blue bankbook. He opened it up automatically, without expectations of anything unusual.

A couple of weeks ago Johanna had been able to transfer the whole of her inheritance from Mrs. Willets into her bank account, adding it to the amount of money she had saved. She had explained to the bank manager that she did not know when she might need it.

The sum was not dazzling, but it was impressive. It gave her substance. In Ken Boudreau's mind, it added a sleek upholstery to the name Johanna Parry.

"Were you wearing a brown dress?" he said, when she came up with the coffee.

"Yes, I was. When I first got here."

"I thought it was a dream. It was you."

"Like in your other dream," Johanna said, her speckled forehead turning fiery. He didn't know what that was all about and hadn't the energy to inquire. Possibly a dream he'd wakened from when she was here in the night – one he couldn't now remember. He coughed again in a more reasonable way, with her handing him some toilet paper.

"Now," she said, "where are you going to set your coffee?" She pushed up the wooden chair that she had moved to get at him more easily. "There," she said. She lifted him under the arms and wedged the pillow in behind him. A dirty pillow, without a case, but she had covered it last night with a towel.

"Could you see if there's any cigarettes downstairs?"

She shook her head, but said, "I'll look. I've got biscuits in the oven."

Ken Boudreau was in the habit of lending money, as well as borrowing it. Much of the trouble that had come upon him – or that he had got into, to put it another way – had to do with not being able to say no to a friend. Loyalty. He had not been drummed out of the peacetime Air Force, but had resigned out of loyalty to the friend who had been hauled up for offering insults to the C.O. at a mess party. At a mess party, where everything was supposed to be a joke and no offense taken – it was not fair. And he had lost the job with the fertilizer company because he took a company truck across the American border without permission, on a Sunday, to pick up a buddy who had got into a fight and was afraid of being caught and charged.

Part and parcel of the loyalty to friends was the difficulty with bosses. He would confess that he found it hard to knuckle under. "Yes, sir," and "no, sir" were not ready words in his vocabulary. He had not been fired from the insurance company, but he had been passed over so many times that it seemed they were daring him to quit, and eventually he did.

Drink had played a part, you had to admit that. And the idea that life should be a more heroic enterprise than it ever seemed to be nowadays.

He liked to tell people he'd won the hotel in a poker game. He was not really much of a gambler, but women liked the sound of that. He didn't want to admit that he'd taken it sight unseen in payment of a debt. And even after he saw it, he told himself it could be salvaged. The idea of being his own boss did appeal to him. He did not see it as a place where people would stay – except perhaps hunters, in the fall. He saw it as a drinking establishment and a restaurant. If he could get a good cook. But before anything much could happen money would have to be spent. Work had to be done – more than he could possibly do himself though he was not unhandy. If he could live through the winter doing what he could by himself, proving his good intentions, he thought maybe he could get a loan from the bank. But he needed a smaller loan just to get through the winter, and that was where his father-in-law came into the picture. He would rather have tried somebody else, but nobody else could so easily spare it.

He had thought it a good idea to put the request in the form of a proposal to sell the furniture, which he knew the old man would never bestir himself enough to do. He was aware, not very specifically, of loans still outstanding from the past – but he was able to think of those as sums he'd been entitled to, for supporting Marcelle during a period of bad behavior (hers, at a time when his own hadn't started) and for accepting Sabitha as his child when he had his doubts. Also, the McCauleys were the only people he knew who had money that nobody now alive had earned.

I brought your furniture.

He was unable to figure out what that could mean for him, at present. He was too tired. He wanted to sleep more than he wanted to eat when she came with the biscuits (and no cigarettes). To satisfy her he ate half of one. Then he fell dead asleep. He came only half awake when she rolled him on one side, then the other, getting the dirty sheet out from under him, then spreading the clean one and rolling him onto that, all without making him get out of bed or really wake up.

"I found a clean sheet, but it's thin as a rag," she said. "It didn't smell too good, so I hung it on the line awhile."

Later he realized that a sound he'd been hearing for a long time in a dream was really the sound of the washing machine. He wondered how that could be – the hot-water tank was defunct. She must have heated tubs of water on the stove. Later still, he heard the unmistakable sound of his own car starting up and driving away. She would have got the keys from his pants pocket.

She might be driving away in his only worthwhile possession, deserting him, and he could not even phone the police to nab her. The phone was cut off, even if he'd been able to get to it.

That was always a possibility – theft and desertion – yet he turned over on the fresh sheet, which smelled of prairie wind and grass, and went back to sleep, knowing for certain that she had only gone to buy milk and eggs and butter and bread and other supplies – even cigarettes – that were necessary for a decent life, and that she would come back and be busy downstairs and that the sound of her activity would be like a net beneath him, heaven-sent, a bounty not to be questioned.

There was a woman problem in his life right now. Two women, actually, a young one and an older one (that is, one of about his own age) who knew about each other and were ready to tear each other's hair out. All he had got from them recently was howling and complaining, punctuated with their angry assertions that they loved him.

Perhaps a solution had arrived for that, as well.

When she was buying groceries in the store, Johanna heard a train, and driving back to the hotel, she saw a car parked at the railway station. Before she had even stopped Ken Boudreau's car she saw the furniture crates piled up on the platform. She talked to the agent – it was his car there – and he was very surprised and irritated by the arrival of all these big crates. When she had got out of him the name of a man with a truck – a clean truck, she insisted – who lived twenty miles away and sometimes did hauling, she used the station phone to call the man and half bribed, half ordered him to come right away. Then she impressed upon the agent that he must stay with the crates till the truck arrived. By suppertime the truck had come, and the man and his son had unloaded all the furniture and carried it into the main room of the hotel.

The next day she took a good look around. She was making up her mind.

The day after that she judged Ken Boudreau to be able to sit up and listen to her, and she said, "This place is a sinkhole for money. The town is on its last legs. What should be done is to take out everything that can bring in any cash and sell it. I don't mean the furniture that was shipped in, I mean things like the pool table and the kitchen range. Then we ought to sell the building to somebody who'll strip the tin off it for junk. There's always a bit to be made off stuff you'd never think had any value. Then – What was it you had in mind to do before you got hold of the hotel?"

He said that he had had some idea of going to British Columbia, to Salmon Arm, where he had a friend who had told him one time he could have a job managing orchards. But he couldn't go because the car needed new tires and work done on it before he could undertake a long trip, and he was spending all he had just to live. Then the hotel had fallen into his lap.

"Like a ton of bricks," she said. "Tires and fixing the car would be a better investment than sinking anything into this place. It would be a good idea to get out there before the snow comes. And ship the furniture by rail again, to make use of it when we get there. We have got all we need to furnish a home."

"It's maybe not all that firm of an offer."

She said, "I know. But it'll be all right."

He understood that she did know, and that it was, it would be, all right. You could say that a case like his was right up her alley.

Not that he wouldn't be grateful. He'd got to a point where

gratitude wasn't a burden, where it was natural – especially when it wasn't demanded.

Thoughts of regeneration were starting. *This is the change I need.* He had said that before, but surely there was one time when it would be true. The mild winters, the smell of the evergreen forests and the ripe apples. *All we need to make a home.*

He has his pride, she thought. That would have to be taken account of. It might be better never to mention the letters in which he had laid himself open to her. Before she came away, she had destroyed them. In fact she had destroyed each one as soon as she'd read it over well enough to know it by heart, and that didn't take long. One thing she surely didn't want was for them ever to fall into the hands of young Sabitha and her shifty friend. Especially the part in the last letter, about her nightgown, and being in bed. It wasn't that such things wouldn't go on, but it might be thought vulgar or sappy or asking for ridicule, to put them on paper.

She doubted they'd see much of Sabitha. But she would never thwart him, if that was what he wanted.

This wasn't really a new experience, this brisk sense of expansion and responsibility. She'd felt something the same for Mrs. Willets – another fine-looking, flighty person in need of care and management. Ken Boudreau had turned out to be a bit more that way than she was prepared for, and there were the differences you had to expect with a man, but surely there was nothing in him that she couldn't handle.

After Mrs. Willets her heart had been dry, and she had considered it might always be so. And now such a warm commotion, such busy love.

Mr. McCauley died about two years after Johanna's departure. His funeral was the last one held in the Anglican church. There was a good turnout for it. Sabitha – who came with her mother's cousin, the Toronto woman – was now self-contained and pretty and remarkably, unexpectedly slim. She wore a sophisticated black hat and did not speak to anybody unless they spoke to her first. Even then, she did not seem to remember them.

The death notice in the paper said that Mr. McCauley was survived by his granddaughter Sabitha Boudreau and his son-in-law Ken Boudreau, and Mr. Boudreau's wife Johanna, and their infant son Omar, of Salmon Arm, B.C.

Edith's mother read this out – Edith herself never looked at the local paper. Of course, the marriage was not news to either of them – or to Edith's father, who was around the corner in the front room, watching television. Word had got back. The only news was Omar.

"Her with a *baby*," Edith's mother said.

Edith was doing her Latin translation at the kitchen table. *Tu ne quaesieris, scire nefas, quem mihi, quem tibi* –

In the church she had taken the precaution of not speaking to Sabitha first, before Sabitha could not speak to her.

She was not really afraid, anymore, of being found out – though she still could not understand why they hadn't been. And in a way, it seemed only proper that the antics of her former self should not be connected with her present self – let alone with the real self that she expected would take over once she got out of this town and away from all the people who thought they knew her. It was the whole twist of consequence that dismayed her – it seemed fantastical, but dull. Also insulting, like some sort of joke or inept warning, trying to get its hooks into her. For where, on the list of things she planned to achieve in her life, was there any mention of her being responsible for the existence on earth of a person named Omar?

Ignoring her mother, she wrote, "You must not ask, it is forbidden for us to know –"

She paused, chewing her pencil, then finished off with a chill of satisfaction, "– what fate has in store for me, or for you –"

The Bear Came Over the Mountain

FIONA LIVED in her parents' house, in the town where she and Grant went to university. It was a big, bay-windowed house that seemed to Grant both luxurious and disorderly, with rugs crooked on the floors and cup rings bitten into the table varnish. Her mother was Icelandic – a powerful woman with a froth of white hair and indignant far-left politics. The father was an important cardiologist, revered around the hospital but happily subservient at home, where he would listen to strange tirades with an absentminded smile. All kinds of people, rich or shabby-looking, delivered these tirades, and kept coming and going and arguing and conferring, sometimes in foreign accents. Fiona had her own little car and a pile of cashmere sweaters, but she wasn't in a sorority, and this activity in her house was probably the reason.

Not that she cared. Sororities were a joke to her, and so was politics, though she liked to play "The Four Insurgent Generals" on the phonograph, and sometimes also she played the "Internationale," very loud, if there was a guest she thought she could make nervous. A curly-haired, gloomy-looking foreigner was courting her – she said he was a Visigoth – and so were two or three quite respectable and uneasy young interns. She made fun of them all and of Grant as well. She would drolly repeat some of his small-town phrases. He thought maybe she was joking when she proposed to him, on a cold bright day on the beach at Port Stanley. Sand was stinging their faces and the waves delivered crashing loads of gravel at their feet.

"Do you think it would be fun –" Fiona shouted. "Do you think it would be fun if we got married?"

He took her up on it, he shouted yes. He wanted never to be away from her. She had the spark of life.

Just before they left their house Fiona noticed a mark on the kitchen floor. It came from the cheap black house shoes she had been wearing earlier in the day.

"I thought they'd quit doing that," she said in a tone of ordinary annoyance and perplexity, rubbing at the gray smear that looked as if it had been made by a greasy crayon.

She remarked that she would never have to do this again, since she wasn't taking those shoes with her.

"I guess I'll be dressed up all the time," she said. "Or semi dressed up. It'll be sort of like in a hotel."

She rinsed out the rag she'd been using and hung it on the rack inside the door under the sink. Then she put on her golden-brown fur-collared ski jacket over a white turtle-necked sweater and tailored fawn slacks. She was a tall, narrow-shouldered woman, seventy years old but still upright and trim, with long legs and long feet, delicate wrists and ankles and tiny, almost comical-looking ears. Her hair, which was light as milkweed fluff, had gone from pale blond to white somehow without Grant's noticing exactly when, and she still wore it down to her shoulders, as her mother had done. (That was the thing that had alarmed Grant's own mother, a small-town widow who worked as a doctor's receptionist. The long white hair on Fiona's mother, even more than the state of the house, had told her all she needed to know about attitudes and politics.)

Otherwise Fiona with her fine bones and small sapphire

eyes was nothing like her mother. She had a slightly crooked mouth which she emphasized now with red lipstick – usually the last thing she did before she left the house. She looked just like herself on this day – direct and vague as in fact she was, sweet and ironic.

Over a year ago Grant had started noticing so many little yellow notes stuck up all over the house. That was not entirely new. She'd always written things down – the title of a book she'd heard mentioned on the radio or the jobs she wanted to make sure she did that day. Even her morning schedule was written down – he found it mystifying and touching in its precision.

7 a.m. Yoga. 7:30–7:45 teeth face hair. 7:45–8:15 walk. 8:15 Grant and Breakfast.

The new notes were different. Taped onto the kitchen drawers – Cutlery, Dishtowels, Knives. Couldn't she have just opened the drawers and seen what was inside? He remembered a story about the German soldiers on border patrol in Czechoslovakia during the war. Some Czech had told him that each of the patrol dogs wore a sign that said *Hund*. Why? said the Czechs, and the Germans said, Because that is a *hund*.

He was going to tell Fiona that, then thought he'd better not. They always laughed at the same things, but suppose this time she didn't laugh?

Worse things were coming. She went to town and phoned him from a booth to ask him how to drive home. She went for her walk across the field into the woods and came home by the fence line – a very long way round. She said that she'd counted on fences always taking you somewhere.

It was hard to figure out. She said that about fences as if it was a joke, and she had remembered the phone number without any trouble.

"I don't think it's anything to worry about," she said. "I expect I'm just losing my mind."

He asked if she had been taking sleeping pills.

"If I have I don't remember," she said. Then she said she was sorry to sound so flippant.

"I'm sure I haven't been taking anything. Maybe I should be. Maybe vitamins."

Vitamins didn't help. She would stand in doorways trying to figure out where she was going. She forgot to turn on the burner under the vegetables or put water in the coffeemaker. She asked Grant when they'd moved to this house.

"Was it last year or the year before?"

He said that it was twelve years ago.

She said, "That's shocking."

"She's always been a bit like this," Grant said to the doctor. "Once she left her fur coat in storage and just forgot about it. That was when we were always going somewhere warm in the winters. Then she said it was unintentionally on purpose, she said it was like a sin she was leaving behind. The way some people made her feel about fur coats."

He tried without success to explain something more – to explain how Fiona's surprise and apologies about all this seemed somehow like routine courtesy, not quite concealing a private amusement. As if she'd stumbled on some adventure that she had not been expecting. Or was playing a game that she hoped he would catch on to. They had always had their games – nonsense dialects, characters they invented. Some of Fiona's made-up voices, chirping or wheedling (he couldn't tell the doctor this), had mimicked uncannily the voices of women of his that she had never met or known about.

"Yes, well," the doctor said. "It might be selective at first. We don't know, do we? Till we see the pattern of the deterioration, we really can't say."

In a while it hardly mattered what label was put on it. Fiona, who no longer went shopping alone, disappeared from the supermarket while Grant had his back turned. A policeman picked her up as she walked down the middle of the road, blocks away. He asked her name and she answered readily. Then he asked her the name of the prime minister of the country.

"If you don't know that, young man, you really shouldn't be in such a responsible job."

He laughed. But then she made the mistake of asking if he'd seen Boris and Natasha.

These were the Russian wolfhounds she had adopted some years ago as a favor to a friend, then devoted herself to for the rest of their lives. Her taking them over might have coincided with the discovery that she was not likely to have children. Something about her tubes being blocked, or twisted – Grant could not remember now. He had always avoided thinking about all that female apparatus. Or it might have been after her mother died. The dogs' long legs and silky hair, their narrow, gentle, intransigent faces made a fine match for her when she took them out for walks. And Grant himself, in those days, landing his first job at the university (his father-in-law's money welcome in spite of the political taint), might have seemed to some people to have been picked up on another of Fiona's eccentric whims, and groomed and tended and favored. Though he never understood this, fortunately, until much later.

She said to him, at suppertime on the day of the wandering-off at the supermarket, "You know what you're going to have to do with me, don't you? You're going to have to put me in that place. Shallowlake?"

Grant said, "Meadowlake. We're not at that stage yet."

"Shallowlake, Shillylake," she said, as if they were engaged in a playful competition. "Sillylake. Sillylake it is."

He held his head in his hands, his elbows on the table. He said that if they did think of it, it must be as something that need not be permanent. A kind of experimental treatment. A rest cure.

There was a rule that nobody could be admitted during the month of December. The holiday season had so many emotional pitfalls. So they made the twenty-minute drive in January. Before they reached the highway the country road dipped through a swampy hollow now completely frozen over. The swamp-oaks and maples threw their shadows like bars across the bright snow.

Fiona said, "Oh, remember."

Grant said, "I was thinking about that too."

"Only it was in the moonlight," she said.

She was talking about the time that they had gone out skiing at night under the full moon and over the black-striped snow, in this place that you could get into only in the depths of winter. They had heard the branches cracking in the cold.

So if she could remember that so vividly and correctly, could there really be so much the matter with her?

It was all he could do not to turn around and drive home.

There was another rule which the supervisor explained to him. New residents were not to be visited during the first thirty days. Most people needed that time to get settled in. Before the rule had been put in place, there had been pleas and tears and tantrums, even from those who had come in willingly. Around the third or fourth day they would start lamenting and begging to be taken home. And some relatives could be susceptible to that, so you would have people being carted home who would not get on there any better than they had before. Six months later or sometimes only a few weeks later, the whole upsetting hassle would have to be gone through again.

"Whereas we find," the supervisor said, "we find that if they're left on their own they usually end up happy as clams. You have to practically lure them into a bus to take a trip to town. The same with a visit home. It's perfectly okay to take them home then, visit for an hour or two – they're the ones that'll worry about getting back in time for supper. Meadowlake's their home then. Of course, that doesn't apply to the ones on the second floor, we can't let them go. It's too difficult, and they don't know where they are anyway."

"My wife isn't going to be on the second floor," Grant said.

"No," said the supervisor thoughtfully. "I just like to make everything clear at the outset."

They had gone over to Meadowlake a few times several years ago, to visit Mr. Farquar, the old bachelor farmer who had been their neighbor. He had lived by himself in a drafty brick house unaltered since the early years of the century, except for the addition of a refrigerator and a television set. He had paid Grant and Fiona unannounced but well-spaced visits and, as well as local matters, he liked to discuss books he had been reading – about the Crimean War or Polar explorations or the history of firearms. But after he went to Meadowlake he would talk only about the routines of the place, and they got the idea that their visits, though gratifying, were a social burden for him. And Fiona in particular hated the smell of urine and bleach that hung about, hated the perfunctory bouquets of plastic flowers in niches in the dim, low-ceilinged corridors.

Now that building was gone, though it had dated only from the fifties. Just as Mr. Farquar's house was gone, replaced by a gimcrack sort of castle that was the weekend home of some people from Toronto. The new Meadowlake was an airy, vaulted building whose air was faintly pleasantly pine-scented. Profuse and genuine greenery sprouted out of giant crocks.

Nevertheless, it was the old building that Grant would find himself picturing Fiona in during the long month he had to get through without seeing her. It was the longest month of his life, he thought – longer than the month he had spent with his mother visiting relatives in Lanark County, when he was thirteen, and longer than the month that Jacqui Adams spent on holiday with her family, near the beginning of their affair. He phoned Meadowlake every day and hoped that he would get the nurse whose name was Kristy. She seemed a little amused at his constancy, but she would give him a fuller report than any other nurse he got stuck with.

Fiona had caught a cold, but that was not unusual for newcomers.

"Like when your kids start school," Kristy said. "There's a whole bunch of new germs they're exposed to, and for a while they just catch everything."

Then the cold got better. She was off the antibiotics, and she didn't seem as confused as she had been when she came in. (This was the first time Grant had heard about either the antibiotics or the confusion.) Her appetite was pretty good, and she seemed to enjoy sitting in the sunroom. She seemed to enjoy watching television.

One of the things that had been so intolerable about the old Meadowlake had been the way the television was on everywhere, overwhelming your thoughts or conversation wherever you chose to sit down. Some of the inmates (that was what he and Fiona called them then, not residents) would raise their eyes to it, some talked back to it, but most just sat and meekly endured its assault. In the new building, as far as he could recall, the television was in a separate sitting room, or in the bedrooms. You could make a choice to watch it.

So Fiona must have made a choice. To watch what?

During the years that they had lived in this house, he and Fiona had watched quite a bit of television together. They had spied on the lives of every beast or reptile or insect or sea creature that a camera was able to reach, and they had followed the plots of what seemed like dozens of rather similar fine nineteenth-century novels. They had slid into an infatuation with an English comedy about life in a department store and had watched so many reruns that they knew the dialogue by heart. They mourned the disappearance of actors who died in real life or went off to other jobs, then welcomed those same actors back as the characters were born again. They watched the floorwalker's hair going from black to gray and finally back to black, the cheap sets never changing. But these, too, faded; eventually the sets and the blackest hair faded as if dust from the London streets was getting in under the elevator doors, and there was a sadness about this that seemed to affect Grant and Fiona more than any of the tragedies on *Masterpiece Theatre*, so they gave up watching before the final end.

Fiona was making some friends, Kristy said. She was definitely coming out of her shell.

What shell was that? Grant wanted to ask, but checked himself, to remain in Kristy's good graces.

If anybody phoned, he let the message go onto the machine. The people they saw socially, occasionally, were not close neighbors but people who lived around the countryside, who were retired, as they were, and who often went away without notice. The first years that they had lived here Grant and Fiona had stayed through the winter. A country winter was a new experience, and they had plenty to do, fixing up the house. Then they had gotten the idea that they too should travel while they could, and they had gone to Greece, to Australia, to Costa Rica. People would think that they were away on some such trip at present.

He skied for exercise but never went as far as the swamp. He skied around and around in the field behind the house as the sun went down and left the sky pink over a countryside that seemed to be bound by waves of blue-edged ice. He counted off the times he went round the field, and then he came back to the darkening house, turning the television news on while he got his supper. They had usually prepared supper together. One of them made the drinks and the other the fire, and they talked about his work (he was writing a study of legendary Norse wolves and particularly of the great

Fenris wolf who swallows up Odin at the end of the world) and about whatever Fiona was reading and what they had been thinking during their close but separate day. This was their time of liveliest intimacy, though there was also, of course, the five or ten minutes of physical sweetness just after they got into bed – something that did not often end up in sex but reassured them that sex was not over yet.

In a dream Grant showed a letter to one of his colleagues whom he had thought of as a friend. The letter was from the roommate of a girl he had not thought of for a while. Its style was sanctimonious and hostile, threatening in a whining way – he put the writer down as a latent lesbian. The girl herself was someone he had parted from decently, and it seemed unlikely that she would want to make a fuss, let alone try to kill herself, which was what the letter was apparently, elaborately, trying to tell him.

The colleague was one of those husbands and fathers who had been among the first to throw away their neckties and leave home to spend every night on a floor mattress with a bewitching young mistress, coming to their offices, their classes, bedraggled and smelling of dope and incense. But now he took a dim view of such shenanigans, and Grant recollected that he had in fact married one of those girls, and that she had taken to giving dinner parties and having babies, just as wives used to do.

"I wouldn't laugh," he said to Grant, who did not think he had been laughing. "And if I were you I'd try to prepare Fiona."

So Grant went off to find Fiona in Meadowlake – the old Meadowlake – and got into a lecture theater instead. Everybody was waiting there for him to teach his class. And sitting in the last, highest row was a flock of cold-eyed young women all in black robes, all in mourning, who never took their bitter stares off him and conspicuously did not write down, or care about, anything he was saying.

Fiona was in the first row, untroubled. She had transformed the lecture room into the sort of corner she was always finding at a party – some high-and-dry spot where she drank wine with mineral water, and smoked ordinary cigarettes and told funny stories about her dogs. Holding out there against the tide, with some people who were like herself, as if the dramas that were being played out in other corners, in bedrooms and on the dark veranda, were nothing but childish comedy. As if chastity was chic, and reticence a blessing.

"Oh, phooey," Fiona said. "Girls that age are always going around talking about how they'll kill themselves."

But it wasn't enough for her to say that – in fact, it rather chilled him. He was afraid that she was wrong, that something terrible had happened, and he saw what she could not – that the black ring was thickening, drawing in, all around his windpipe, all around the top of the room.

He hauled himself out of the dream and set about separating what was real from what was not.

There had been a letter, and the word "RAT" had appeared in black paint on his office door, and Fiona, on being told that a girl had suffered from a bad crush on him, had said pretty much what she said in the dream. The colleague hadn't come into it, the black-robed women had never appeared in his classroom, and nobody had committed suicide. Grant hadn't been disgraced, in fact he had got off easily when you thought of what might have happened just a couple of years later. But word got around. Cold shoulders became conspicuous. They had few Christmas invitations and spent New Year's Eve alone. Grant got drunk, and without its being required of him – also, thank God, without making the error of a confession – he promised Fiona a new life.

The shame he felt then was the shame of being duped, of not having noticed the change that was going on. And not one woman had made him aware of it. There had been the change in the past when so many women so suddenly became available – or it seemed that way to him – and now this new change, when they were saying that what had happened was not what they had had in mind at all. They had collaborated because they were helpless and bewildered, and they had been injured by the whole thing, rather than delighted. Even when they had taken the initiative they had done so only because the cards were stacked against them.

Nowhere was there any acknowledgment that the life of a philanderer (if that was what Grant had to call himself – he who had not had half as many conquests or complications as the man who had reproached him in his dream) involved acts of kindness and generosity and even sacrifice. Not in the beginning, perhaps, but at least as things went on. Many times he had catered to a woman's pride, to her fragility, by offering more affection – or a rougher passion – than anything he really felt. All so that he could now find himself accused of wounding and exploiting and destroying self-esteem. And of deceiving Fiona – as of course he had deceived her – but would it have been better if he had done as others had done with their wives and left her?

He had never thought of such a thing. He had never stopped making love to Fiona in spite of disturbing demands elsewhere. He had not stayed away from her for a single night. No making up elaborate stories in order to spend a weekend in San Francisco or in a tent on Manitoulin Island. He had gone easy on the dope and the drink and he had continued to publish papers, serve on committees, make progress in his career. He had never had any intention of throwing up work and marriage and taking to the country to practice carpentry or keep bees.

But something like that had happened after all. He took an early retirement with a reduced pension. The cardiologist had died, after some bewildered and stoical time alone in the big house, and Fiona had inherited both that property and the farmhouse where her father had grown up, in the country near Georgian Bay. She gave up her job, as a hospital coordinator of volunteer services (in that everyday world, as she said, where people actually had troubles that were not related to drugs or sex or intellectual squabbles). A new life was a new life.

Boris and Natasha had died by this time. One of them got sick and died first – Grant forgot which one – and then the other died, more or less out of sympathy.

He and Fiona worked on the house. They got cross-country skis. They were not very sociable, but they gradually made some friends. There were no more hectic flirtations. No bare female toes creeping up under a man's pants leg at a dinner party. No more loose wives.

Just in time, Grant was able to think, when the sense of injustice wore down. The feminists and perhaps the sad silly girl herself and his cowardly so-called friends had pushed him out just in time. Out of a life that was in fact getting to be more trouble than it was worth. And that might eventually have cost him Fiona.

On the morning of the day when he was to go back to Meadowlake for the first visit, Grant woke early. He was full of a solemn tingling, as in the old days on the morning of his first planned meeting with a new woman. The feeling was not precisely sexual. (Later, when the meetings had become routine, that was all it was.) There was an expectation of discovery, almost a spiritual expansion. Also timidity, humility, alarm.

He left home too early. Visitors were not allowed before two o'clock. He did not want to sit out in the parking lot, waiting, so he made himself turn the car in a wrong direction.

There had been a thaw. Plenty of snow was left, but the dazzling hard landscape of earlier winter had crumbled. These pocked heaps under a gray sky looked like refuse in the fields.

In the town near Meadowlake he found a florist's shop and

bought a large bouquet. He had never presented flowers to Fiona before. Or to anyone else. He entered the building feeling like a hopeless lover or a guilty husband in a cartoon.

"Wow. Narcissus this early," Kristy said. "You must've spent a fortune." She went along the hall ahead of him and snapped on the light in a closet, or sort of kitchen, where she searched for a vase. She was a heavy young woman who looked as if she had given up in every department except her hair. That was blond and voluminous. All the puffed-up luxury of a cocktail waitress's style, or a stripper's, on top of such a workaday face and body.

"There, now," she said, and nodded him down the hall. "Name's right on the door."

So it was, on a nameplate decorated with bluebirds. He wondered whether to knock, and did, then opened the door and called her name.

She wasn't there. The closet door was closed, the bed smoothed. Nothing on the bedside table, except a box of Kleenex and a glass of water. Not a single photograph or picture of any kind, not a book or a magazine. Perhaps you had to keep those in a cupboard.

He went back to the nurses' station, or reception desk, or whatever it was. Kristy said "No?" with a surprise that he thought perfunctory.

He hesitated, holding the flowers. She said, "Okay, okay – let's set the bouquet down here." Sighing, as if he was a backward child on his first day at school, she led him along a hall, into the light of the huge sky windows in the large central space, with its cathedral ceiling. Some people were sitting along the walls, in easy chairs, others at tables in the middle of the carpeted floor. None of them looked too bad. Old – some of them incapacitated enough to need wheelchairs – but decent. There used to be some unnerving sights when he and Fiona went to visit Mr. Farquar. Whiskers on old women's chins, somebody with a bulged-out eye like a rotted plum. Dribblers, head wagglers, mad chatterers. Now it looked as if there'd been some weeding out of the worst cases. Or perhaps drugs, surgery had come into use, perhaps there were ways of treating disfigurement, as well as verbal and other kinds of incontinence – ways that hadn't existed even those few years ago.

There was, however, a very disconsolate woman sitting at the piano, picking away with one finger and never achieving a tune. Another woman, staring out from behind a coffee urn and a stack of plastic cups, looked bored to stone. But she had to be an employee – she wore a pale-green pants outfit like Kristy's.

"See?" said Kristy in a softer voice. "You just go up and say hello and try not to startle her. Remember she may not – Well. Just go ahead."

He saw Fiona in profile, sitting close up to one of the card tables, but not playing. She looked a little puffy in the face, the flab on one cheek hiding the corner of her mouth, in a way it hadn't done before. She was watching the play of the man she sat closest to. He held his cards tilted so that she could see them. When Grant got near the table she looked up. They all looked up – all the players at the table looked up, with displeasure. Then they immediately looked down at their cards, as if to ward off any intrusion.

But Fiona smiled her lopsided, abashed, sly, and charming smile and pushed back her chair and came round to him, putting her fingers to her mouth.

"Bridge," she whispered. "Deadly serious. They're quite rabid about it." She drew him towards the coffee table, chatting. "I can remember being like that for a while at college. My friends and I would cut class and sit in the common room and smoke and play like cutthroats. One's name was Phoebe, I don't remember the others."

"Phoebe Hart," Grant said. He pictured the little hollow-chested, black-eyed girl, who was probably dead by now. Wreathed in smoke, Fiona and Phoebe and those others, rapt as witches.

"You knew her too?" said Fiona, directing her smile now towards the stone-faced woman. "Can I get you anything? A cup of tea? I'm afraid the coffee isn't up to much here."

Grant never drank tea.

He could not throw his arms around her. Something about her voice and smile, familiar as they were, something about the way she seemed to be guarding the players and even the coffee woman from him – as well as him from their displeasure – made that not possible.

"I brought you some flowers," he said. "I thought they'd do to brighten up your room. I went to your room, but you weren't there."

"Well, no," she said. "I'm here."

Grant said, "You've made a new friend." He nodded towards the man she'd been sitting next to. At this moment that man looked up at Fiona and she turned, either because of what Grant had said or because she felt the look at her back.

"It's just Aubrey," she said. "The funny thing is I knew him years and years ago. He worked in the store. The hardware store where my grandpa used to shop. He and I were always kidding around and he could not get up the nerve to ask me out. Till the very last weekend and he took me to a ball game. But when it was over my grandpa showed up to drive me home. I was up visiting for the summer. Visiting my grandparents – they lived on a farm."

"Fiona. I know where your grandparents lived. It's where we live. Lived."

"Really?" she said, not paying full attention because the card-player was sending her his look, which was not one of supplication but command. He was a man of about Grant's age, or a little older. Thick coarse white hair fell over his forehead, and his skin was leathery but pale, yellowish-white like an old wrinkled-up kid glove. His long face was dignified and melancholy, and he had something of the beauty of a powerful, discouraged, elderly horse. But where Fiona was concerned he was not discouraged.

"I better go back," Fiona said, a blush spotting her newly fattened face. "He thinks he can't play without me sitting there. It's silly, I hardly know the game anymore. I'm afraid you'll have to excuse me."

"Will you be through soon?"

"Oh, we should be. It depends. If you go and ask that grim-looking lady nicely she'll get you some tea."

"I'm fine," Grant said.

"So I'll leave you then, you can entertain yourself? It must all seem strange to you, but you'll be surprised how soon you get used to it. You'll get to know who everybody is. Except that some of them are pretty well off in the clouds, you know – you can't expect them all to get to know who *you* are."

She slipped back into her chair and said something into Aubrey's ear. She tapped her fingers across the back of his hand.

Grant went in search of Kristy and met her in the hall. She was pushing a cart on which there were pitchers of apple juice and grape juice.

"Just one sec," she said to him, as she stuck her head through a doorway. "Apple juice in here? Grape juice? Cookies?"

He waited while she filled two plastic glasses and took them into the room. Then she came back and put two arrowroot cookies on paper plates.

"Well?" she said. "Aren't you glad to see her participating and everything?"

Grant said, "Does she even know who I am?"

He could not decide. She could have been playing a joke. It would not be unlike her. She had given herself away by that little pretense at the end, talking to him as if she thought perhaps he was a new resident.

If that was what she was pretending. If it was a pretense.

But would she not have run after him and laughed at him then, once the joke was over? She would not have just gone back to the game, surely, and pretended to forget about him. That would have been too cruel.

Kristy said, "You just caught her at sort of a bad moment. Involved in the game."

"She's not even playing," he said.

"Well, but her friend's playing. Aubrey."

"So who is Aubrey?"

"That's who he is. Aubrey. Her friend. Would you like a juice?"

Grant shook his head.

"Oh, look," said Kristy. "They get these attachments. That takes over for a while. Best buddy sort of thing. It's kind of a phase."

"You mean she really might not know who I am?"

"She might not. Not today. Then tomorrow – you never know do you? Things change back and forth all the time and there's nothing you can do about it. You'll see the way it is once you've been coming here for a while. You'll learn not to take it all so serious. Learn to take it day by day."

Day by day. But things really didn't change back and forth, and he didn't get used to the way they were. Fiona was the one who seemed to get used to him, but only as some persistent visitor who took a special interest in her. Or perhaps even as a nuisance who must be prevented, according to her old rules of courtesy, from realizing that he was one. She treated him with a distracted, social sort of kindness that was successful in holding him back from the most obvious, the most necessary question. He could not demand of her whether she did or did not remember him as her husband of nearly fifty years. He got the impression that she would be embarrassed by such a question – embarrassed not for herself but for him. She would have laughed in a fluttery way and mortified him with her politeness and bewilderment, and somehow she would have ended up not saying either yes or no. Or she would have said either one in a way that gave not the least satisfaction.

Kristy was the only nurse he could talk to. Some of the others treated the whole thing as a joke. One tough old stick laughed in his face. "That Aubrey and that Fiona? They've really got it bad, haven't they?"

Kristy told him that Aubrey had been the local representative of a company that sold weed killer – "and all that kind of stuff" – to farmers.

"He was a fine person," she said, and Grant did not know whether this meant that Aubrey was honest and openhanded and kind to people, or that he was well spoken and well dressed and drove a good car. Probably both.

And then when he was not very old or even retired – she said – he had suffered some unusual kind of damage.

"His wife is the one takes care of him usually. She takes care of him at home. She just put him in here on temporary care so she could get a break. Her sister wanted her to go to Florida. See, she's had a hard time, you wouldn't ever have expected a man like him – They just went on a holiday somewhere and he got something, like some bug, that gave him a terrible high fever. And it put him in a coma and left him like he is now."

He asked her about these affections between residents. Did they ever go too far? He was able now to take a tone of indulgence that he hoped would save him from any lectures.

"Depends what you mean," she said. She kept writing in her record book while deciding how to answer him. When she finished what she was writing she looked up at him with a frank smile.

"The trouble we have in here, it's funny, it's often with some of the ones that haven't been friendly with each other at all. They maybe won't even know each other, beyond knowing, like, is it a man or a woman? You'd think it'd be the old guys trying to crawl in bed with the old women, but you know half the time it's the other way round. Old women going after the old men. Could be they're not so wore out, I guess."

Then she stopped smiling, as if she was afraid she had said too much, or spoken callously.

"Don't take me wrong," she said. "I don't mean Fiona. Fiona is a lady."

Well, what about Aubrey? Grant felt like saying. But he remembered that Aubrey was in a wheelchair.

"She's a real lady," Kristy said, in a tone so decisive and reassuring that Grant was not reassured. He had in his mind a picture of Fiona, in one of her long eyelet-trimmed blue-ribboned nightgowns, teasingly lifting the covers of an old man's bed.

"Well, I sometimes wonder –" he said.

Kristy said sharply, "You wonder what?"

"I wonder whether she isn't putting on some kind of a charade."

"A what?" said Kristy.

Most afternoons the pair could be found at the card table. Aubrey had large, thick-fingered hands. It was difficult for him to manage his cards. Fiona shuffled and dealt for him and sometimes moved quickly to straighten a card that seemed to be slipping from his grasp. Grant would watch from across the room her darting move and quick, laughing apology. He could see Aubrey's husbandly frown as a wisp of her hair touched his cheek. Aubrey preferred to ignore her as long as she stayed close.

But let her smile her greeting at Grant, let her push back her chair and get up to offer him tea – showing that she had accepted his right to be there and possibly felt a slight responsibility for him – and Aubrey's face took on its look of sombre consternation. He would let the cards slide from his fingers and fall on the floor, to spoil the game.

So that Fiona had to get busy and put things right.

If they weren't at the bridge table they might be walking along the halls, Aubrey hanging on to the railing with one hand and clutching Fiona's arm or shoulder with the other. The nurses thought that it was a marvel, the way she had got him out of his wheelchair. Though for longer trips – to the conservatory at one end of the building or the television room at the other – the wheelchair was called for.

The television seemed to be always turned to the sports channel and Aubrey would watch any sport, but his favorite appeared to be golf. Grant didn't mind watching that with them. He sat down a few chairs away. On the large screen a small group of spectators and commentators followed the players around the peaceful green, and at appropriate moments broke into a formal sort of applause. But there was silence everywhere as the player made his swing and the ball took its lonely, appointed journey across the sky. Aubrey and Fiona and Grant and possibly others sat and held their breaths, and then Aubrey's breath broke out first, expressing satisfaction or disappointment. Fiona's chimed in on the same note a moment later.

In the conservatory there was no such silence. The pair found themselves a seat among the most lush and thick and tropical-looking plants – a bower, if you like – which Grant had just enough self-control to keep from penetrating. Mixed in with the rustle of the leaves and the sound of splashing water was Fiona's soft talk and her laughter.

Then some sort of chortle. Which of them could it be?

Perhaps neither – perhaps it came from one of the impudent flashy-looking birds who inhabited the corner cages.

Aubrey could talk, though his voice probably didn't sound the way it used to. He seemed to say something now – a couple of thick syllables. *Take care. He's here. My love.*

On the blue bottom of the fountain's pool lay some wishing coins. Grant had never seen anybody actually throwing money in. He stared at these nickels and dimes and quarters, wondering if they had been glued to the tiles – another feature of the building's encouraging decoration.

Teenagers at the baseball game, sitting at the top of the bleachers out of the way of the boy's friends. A couple of inches of bare wood between them, darkness falling, quick chill of the evening late in the summer. The skittering of their hands, the shift of haunches, eyes never lifted from the field. He'll take off his jacket, if he's wearing one, to lay it around her narrow shoulders. Underneath it he can pull her closer to him, press his spread fingers into her soft arm.

Not like today when any kid would probably be into her pants on the first date.

Fiona's skinny soft arm. Teenage lust astonishing her and flashing along all the nerves of her tender new body, as the night thickens beyond the lighted dust of the game.

Meadowlake was short on mirrors, so he did not have to catch sight of himself stalking and prowling. But every once in a while it came to him how foolish and pathetic and perhaps unhinged he must look, trailing around after Fiona and Aubrey. And having no luck in confronting her, or him. Less and less sure of what right he had to be on the scene but unable to withdraw. Even at home, while he worked at his desk or cleaned up the house or shovelled snow when necessary, some ticking metronome in his mind was fixed on Meadowlake, on his next visit. Sometimes he seemed to himself like a mulish boy conducting a hopeless courtship, sometimes like one of those wretches who follow celebrated women through the streets, convinced that one day these women will turn around and recognize their love.

He made a great effort, and cut his visits down to Wednesdays and Saturdays. Also he set himself to observing other things about the place, as if he was a sort of visitor at large, a person doing an inspection or a social study.

Saturdays had a holiday bustle and tension. Families arrived in clusters. Mothers were usually in charge, they were like cheerful but insistent sheepdogs herding the men and children. Only the smallest children were without apprehension. They noticed right away the green and white squares on the hall floors and picked one color to walk on, the other to jump over. The bolder ones might try to hitch rides on the back of wheelchairs. Some persisted in these tricks in spite of scolding, and had to be removed to the car. And how happily, then, how readily, some older child or father volunteered to do the removing, and thus opt out of the visit.

It was the women who kept the conversation afloat. Men seemed cowed by the situation, teenagers affronted. Those being visited rode in a wheelchair or stumped along with a cane, or walked stiffly, unaided, at the procession's head, proud of the turnout but somewhat blank-eyed, or desperately babbling, under the stress of it. And now surrounded by a variety of outsiders these insiders did not look like such regular people after all. Female chins might have had their bristles shaved to the roots and bad eyes might be hidden by patches or dark lenses, inappropriate utterances might be controlled by medication, but some glaze remained, a haunted rigidity – as if people were content to become memories of themselves, final photographs.

Grant understood better now how Mr. Farquar must have felt. People here – even the ones who did not participate in any activities but sat around watching the doors or looking out the windows – were living a busy life in their heads (not to mention the life of their bodies, the portentous shifts in their bowels, the stabs and twinges everywhere along the line), and that was a life that in most cases could not very well be described or alluded to in front of visitors. All they could do was wheel or somehow propel themselves about and hope to come up with something that could be displayed or talked about.

There was the conservatory to be shown off and the big television screen. Fathers thought that was really something. Mothers said the ferns were gorgeous. Soon everybody sat down around the little tables and ate ice cream – refused only by the teenagers, who were dying of disgust. Women wiped away the dribble from shivery old chins and men looked the other way.

There must be some satisfaction in this ritual, and perhaps even the teenagers would be glad, one day, that they had come. Grant was no expert on families.

No children or grandchildren appeared to visit Aubrey, and since they could not play cards – the tables being taken over for the ice cream parties – he and Fiona stayed clear of the Saturday parade. The conservatory was far too popular then for any of their intimate conversations.

Those might be going on, of course, behind Fiona's closed door. Grant could not manage to knock, though he stood there for some time staring at the Disney birds with an intense, a truly malignant dislike.

Or they might be in Aubrey's room. But he did not know where that was. The more he explored this place, the more corridors and seating spaces and ramps he discovered, and in his wanderings he was still apt to get lost. He would take a certain picture or chair as a landmark, and the next week whatever he had chosen seemed to have been placed somewhere else. He didn't like to mention this to Kristy, lest she think he was suffering some mental dislocations of his own. He supposed this constant change and rearranging might be for the sake of the residents – to make their daily exercise more interesting.

He did not mention either that he sometimes saw a woman at a distance that he thought was Fiona, but then thought it couldn't be, because of the clothes the woman was wearing. When had Fiona ever gone in for bright flowered blouses and electric blue slacks? One Saturday he looked out a window and saw Fiona – it must be her – wheeling Aubrey along one of the paved paths now cleared of snow and ice, and she was wearing a silly woolly hat and a jacket with swirls of blue and purple, the sort of thing he had seen on local women at the supermarket.

The fact must be that they didn't bother to sort out the wardrobes of the women who were roughly the same size. And counted on the women not recognizing their own clothes anyway.

They had cut her hair, too. They had cut away her angelic halo. On a Wednesday, when everything was more normal and card games were going on again, and the women in the Crafts Room were making silk flowers or costumed dolls without anybody hanging around to pester or admire them, and when Aubrey and Fiona were again in evidence so that it was possible for Grant to have one of his brief and friendly and maddening conversations with his wife, he said to her, "Why did they chop off your hair?"

Fiona put her hands up to her head, to check.

"Why – I never missed it," she said.

He thought he should find out what went on on the second floor, where they kept the people who, as Kristy said, had really lost it. Those who walked around down here holding conversations with themselves or throwing out odd questions at a passerby ("Did I leave my sweater in the church?") had apparently lost only some of it.

Not enough to qualify.

There were stairs, but the doors at the top were locked and only the staff had the keys. You could not get into the elevator unless somebody buzzed for it to open, from behind the desk.

What did they do, after they lost it?

"Some just sit," said Kristy. "Some sit and cry. Some try to holler the house down. You don't really want to know."

Sometimes they got it back.

"You go in their rooms for a year and they don't know you from Adam. Then one day, it's oh, hi, when are we going home. All of a sudden they're absolutely back to normal again."

But not for long.

"You think, wow, back to normal. And then they're gone again." She snapped her fingers. "Like so."

In the town where he used to work there was a bookstore that he and Fiona had visited once or twice a year. He went back there by himself. He didn't feel like buying anything, but he had made a list and picked out a couple of the books on it, and then bought another book that he noticed by chance. It was about Iceland. A book of nineteenth-century watercolors made by a lady traveller to Iceland.

Fiona had never learned her mother's language and she had never shown much respect for the stories that it preserved – the stories that Grant had taught and written about, and still did write about, in his working life. She referred to their heroes as "old Njal" or "old Snorri." But in the last few years she had developed an interest in the country itself and looked at travel guides. She read about William Morris's trip, and Auden's. She didn't really plan to travel there. She said the weather was too dreadful. Also – she said – there ought to be one place you thought about and knew about and maybe longed for – but never did get to see.

When Grant first started teaching Anglo-Saxon and Nordic Literature he got the regular sort of students in his classes. But after a few years he noticed a change. Married women started going back to school. Not with the idea of qualifying for a better job or for any job but simply to give themselves something more interesting to think about than their usual housework and hobbies. To enrich their lives. And perhaps it followed naturally that the men who taught them these things would become part of the enrichment, that these men would seem to these women more mysterious and desirable than the men they still cooked for and slept with.

The studies chosen were usually Psychology or Cultural History or English Literature. Archaeology or Linguistics was picked sometimes but dropped when it turned out to be heavy going. Those who signed up for Grant's courses might have a Scandinavian background, like Fiona, or they might have learned something about Norse mythology from Wagner or historical novels. There were also a few who thought he was teaching a Celtic language and for whom everything Celtic had a mystic allure.

He spoke to such aspirants fairly roughly from his side of the desk.

"If you want to learn a pretty language, go and learn Spanish. Then you can use it if you go to Mexico."

Some took his warning and drifted away. Others seemed to be moved in a personal way by his demanding tone. They worked with a will and brought into his office, into his regulated, satisfactory life, the great surprising bloom of their mature female compliance, their tremulous hope of approval.

He chose the woman named Jacqui Adams. She was the opposite of Fiona – short, cushiony, dark-eyed, effusive. A stranger to irony. The affair lasted for a year, until her husband was transferred. When they were saying good-bye, in her car, she began to shake uncontrollably. It was as if she had hypothermia. She wrote to him a few times, but he found the tone of her letters overwrought and could not decide how to answer. He let the time for answering slip away while he became magically and unexpectedly involved with a girl who was young enough to be her daughter.

For another and more dizzying development had taken place while he was busy with Jacqui. Young girls with long hair and sandalled feet were coming into his office and all but declaring themselves ready for sex. The cautious approaches, the tender intimations of feeling required with Jacqui were out the window. A whirlwind hit him, as it did many others, wish becoming action in a way that made him wonder if there wasn't something missed. But who had time for regrets? He heard of simultaneous liaisons, savage and risky encounters. Scandals burst wide open, with high and painful drama all round but a feeling that somehow it was better so. There were reprisals – there were firings. But those fired went off to teach at smaller, more tolerant colleges or Open Learning Centers, and many wives left behind got over the shock and took up the costumes, the sexual nonchalance of the girls who had tempted their men. Academic parties, which used to be so predictable, became a minefield. An epidemic had broken out, it was spreading like the Spanish flu. Only this time people ran after contagion, and few between sixteen and sixty seemed willing to be left out.

Fiona appeared to be quite willing, however. Her mother was dying, and her experience in the hospital led her from her routine work in the registrar's office into her new job. Grant himself did not go overboard, at least in comparison with some people around him. He never let another woman get as close to him as Jacqui had been. What he felt was mainly a gigantic increase in well-being. A tendency to pudginess that he had had since he was twelve years old disappeared. He ran up steps two at a time. He appreciated as never before a pageant of torn clouds and winter sunset seen from his office window, the charm of antique lamps glowing between his neighbors' living-room curtains, the cries of children in the park at dusk, unwilling to leave the hill where they'd been tobogganing. Come summer, he learned the names of flowers. In his classroom, after coaching by his nearly voiceless mother-in-law (her affliction was cancer of the throat), he risked reciting and then translating the majestic and gory ode, the head-ransom, the Hofuolausn, composed to honor King Eric Blood-axe by the skald whom that king had condemned to death. (And who was then, by the same king – and by the power of poetry – set free.) All applauded – even the peaceniks in the class whom he'd cheerfully taunted earlier, asking if they would like to wait in the hall. Driving home that day or maybe another he found an absurd and blasphemous quotation running around in his head.

And so he increased in wisdom and stature –

And in favor with God and man.

That embarrassed him at the time and gave him a superstitious chill. As it did yet. But so long as nobody knew, it seemed not unnatural.

He took the book with him, the next time he went to Meadowlake. It was a Wednesday. He went looking for Fiona at the card tables and did not see her.

A woman called out to him, "She's not here. She's sick." Her voice sounded self-important and excited – pleased with herself for having recognized him when he knew nothing about her. Perhaps also pleased with all she knew about Fiona, about Fiona's life here, thinking it was maybe more than he knew.

"He's not here either," she said.

Grant went to find Kristy.

"Nothing, really," she said, when he asked what was the matter with Fiona. "She's just having a day in bed today, just a bit of an upset."

Fiona was sitting straight up in the bed. He hadn't noticed, the few times that he had been in this room, that this was a hospital bed and could be cranked up in such a way. She was wearing one of her high-necked maidenly gowns, and her face had a pallor that was not like cherry blossoms but like flour paste.

Aubrey was beside her in his wheelchair, pushed as close to the bed as it could get. Instead of the nondescript open-necked shirts he usually wore, he was wearing a jacket and a tie. His natty-looking tweed hat was resting on the bed. He looked as if he had been out on important business.

To see his lawyer? His banker? To make arrangements with the funeral director?

Whatever he'd been doing, he looked worn out by it. He too was gray in the face.

They both looked up at Grant with a stony, grief-ridden apprehension that turned to relief, if not to welcome, when they saw who he was.

Not who they thought he'd be.

They were hanging on to each other's hands and they did not let go.

The hat on the bed. The jacket and tie.

It wasn't that Aubrey had been out. It wasn't a question of where he'd been or whom he'd been to see. It was where he was going.

Grant set the book down on the bed beside Fiona's free hand.

"It's about Iceland," he said. "I thought maybe you'd like to look at it."

"Why, thank you," said Fiona. She didn't look at the book. He put her hand on it.

"Iceland," he said.

She said, "Ice-land." The first syllable managed to hold a tinkle of interest, but the second fell flat. Anyway, it was necessary for her to turn her attention back to Aubrey, who was pulling his great thick hand out of hers.

"What is it?" she said. "What is it, dear heart?"

Grant had never heard her use this flowery expression before.

"Oh, all right," she said. "Oh, here." And she pulled a handful of tissues from the box beside her bed.

Aubrey's problem was that he had begun to weep. His nose had started to run, and he was anxious not to turn into a sorry spectacle, especially in front of Grant.

"Here. Here," said Fiona. She would have tended to his nose herself and wiped his tears – and perhaps if they had been alone he would have let her do it. But with Grant there Aubrey would not permit it. He got hold of the Kleenex as well as he could and made a few awkward but lucky swipes at his face.

While he was occupied, Fiona turned to Grant.

"Do you by any chance have any influence around here?" she said in a whisper. "I've seen you talking to them –"

Aubrey made a noise of protest or weariness or disgust. Then his upper body pitched forward as if he wanted to throw himself against her. She scrambled half out of bed and caught him and held on to him. It seemed improper for Grant to help her, though of course he would have done so if he'd thought Aubrey was about to tumble to the floor.

"Hush," Fiona was saying. "Oh, honey. Hush. We'll get to see each other. We'll have to. I'll go and see you. You'll come and see me."

Aubrey made the same sound again with his face in her chest, and there was nothing Grant could decently do but get out of the room.

"I just wish his wife would hurry up and get here," Kristy said. "I wish she'd get him out of here and cut the agony short. We've got to start serving supper before long and how are we supposed to get her to swallow anything with him still hanging around?"

Grant said, "Should I stay?"

"What for? She's not sick, you know."

"To keep her company," he said.

Kristy shook her head.

"They have to get over these things on their own. They've got short memories usually. That's not always so bad."

Kristy was not hard-hearted. During the time he had known her Grant had found out some things about her life. She had four children. She did not know where her husband was but thought he might be in Alberta. Her younger boy's asthma was so bad that he would have died one night in January if she had not got him to the emergency ward in time. He was not on any illegal drugs, but she was not so sure about his brother.

To her, Grant and Fiona and Aubrey too must seem lucky. They had got through life without too much going wrong. What they had to suffer now that they were old hardly counted.

Grant left without going back to Fiona's room. He noticed that the wind was actually warm that day and the crows were making an uproar. In the parking lot a woman wearing a tartan pants suit was getting a folded-up wheelchair out of the trunk of her car.

The street he was driving down was called Black Hawks Lane. All the streets around were named for teams in the old National Hockey League. This was in an outlying section of the town near Meadowlake. He and Fiona had shopped in the town regularly but had not become familiar with any part of it except the main street.

The houses looked to have been built all around the same time, perhaps thirty or forty years ago. The streets were wide and curving and there were no sidewalks – recalling the time when it was thought unlikely that anybody would do much walking ever again. Friends of Grant's and Fiona's had moved to places something like this when they began to have their children. They were apologetic about the move at first. They called it "going out to Barbecue Acres."

Young families still lived here. There were basketball hoops over garage doors and tricycles in the driveways. But some of the houses had gone downhill from the sort of family homes they were surely meant to be. The yards were marked by car tracks, the windows were plastered with tinfoil or hung with faded flags.

Rental housing. Young male tenants – single still, or single again.

A few properties seemed to have been kept up as well as possible by the people who had moved into them when they were new – people who hadn't had the money or perhaps hadn't felt the need to move on to someplace better. Shrubs had grown to maturity, pastel vinyl siding had done away with the problem of repainting. Neat fences or hedges gave the sign that the children in the houses had all grown up and gone away, and that their parents no longer saw the point of letting the yard be a common run-through for whatever new children were loose in the neighborhood.

The house that was listed in the phone book as belonging to Aubrey and his wife was one of these. The front walk was paved with flagstones and bordered by hyacinths that stood as stiff as china flowers, alternately pink and blue.

Fiona had not got over her sorrow. She did not eat at mealtimes, though she pretended to, hiding food in her napkin. She was being given a supplementary drink twice a day – someone stayed and watched while she swallowed it down. She got out of bed and dressed herself, but all she wanted to do then was sit in her room. She wouldn't have taken any exercise at all if Kristy or one of the other nurses, and Grant during visiting hours, had not walked her up and down in the corridors or taken her outside.

In the spring sunshine she sat, weeping weakly, on a bench by the wall. She was still polite – she apologized for her tears, and never argued with a suggestion or refused to answer a question. But she wept. Weeping had left her eyes raw-edged and dim. Her cardigan – if it was hers – would be buttoned crookedly. She had not got to the stage of leaving her hair unbrushed or her nails uncleaned, but that might come soon.

Kristy said that her muscles were deteriorating, and that if she didn't improve soon they would put her on a walker.

"But you know once they get a walker they start to depend on it and they never walk much anymore, just get wherever it is they have to go."

"You'll have to work at her harder," she said to Grant. "Try and encourage her."

But Grant had no luck at that. Fiona seemed to have taken a dislike to him, though she tried to cover it up. Perhaps she was reminded, every time she saw him, of her last minutes with Aubrey, when she had asked him for help and he hadn't helped her.

He didn't see much point in mentioning their marriage, now.

She wouldn't go down the hall to where most of the same people were still playing cards. And she wouldn't go into the television room or visit the conservatory.

She said that she didn't like the big screen, it hurt her eyes. And the birds' noise was irritating and she wished they would turn the fountain off once in a while.

So far as Grant knew, she never looked at the book about Iceland, or at any of the other – surprisingly few – books that she had brought from home. There was a reading room where she would sit down to rest, choosing it probably because there was seldom anybody there, and if he took a book off the shelves she would allow him to read to her. He suspected that she did that because it made his company easier for her – she was able to shut her eyes and sink back into her own grief. Because if she let go of her grief even for a minute it would only hit her harder when she bumped into it again. And sometimes he thought she closed her eyes to hide a look of informed despair that it would not be good for him to see.

So he sat and read to her out of one of these old novels about chaste love, and lost-and-regained fortunes, that could have been the discards of some long-ago village or Sunday school library. There had been no attempt, apparently, to keep the contents of the reading room as up-to-date as most things in the rest of the building.

The covers of the books were soft, almost velvety, with designs of leaves and flowers pressed into them, so that they resembled jewelry boxes or chocolate boxes. That women – he supposed it would be women – could carry home like treasure.

The supervisor called him into her office. She said that Fiona was not thriving as they had hoped.

"Her weight is going down even with the supplement. We're doing all we can for her."

Grant said that he realized they were.

"The thing is, I'm sure you know, we don't do any prolonged bed care on the first floor. We do it temporarily if someone isn't feeling well, but if they get too weak to move around and be responsible we have to consider upstairs."

He said he didn't think that Fiona had been in bed that often.

"No. But if she can't keep up her strength, she will be. Right now she's borderline."

He said that he had thought the second floor was for people whose minds were disturbed.

"That too," she said.

He hadn't remembered anything about Aubrey's wife except the tartan suit he had seen her wearing in the parking lot. The tails of the jacket had flared open as she bent into the trunk of the car. He had got the impression of a trim waist and wide buttocks.

She was not wearing the tartan suit today. Brown belted slacks and a pink sweater. He was right about the waist – the tight belt showed she made a point of it. It might have been better if she hadn't, since she bulged out considerably above and below.

She could be ten or twelve years younger than her husband. Her hair was short, curly, artificially reddened. She had blue eyes – a lighter blue than Fiona's, a flat robin's-egg or turquoise blue – slanted by a slight puffiness. And a good many wrinkles made more noticeable by a walnut-stain makeup. Or perhaps that was her Florida tan.

He said that he didn't quite know how to introduce himself. "I used to see your husband at Meadowlake. I'm a regular visitor there myself."

"Yes," said Aubrey's wife, with an aggressive movement of her chin.

"How is your husband doing?"

The "doing" was added on at the last moment. Normally he would have said, "How is your husband?"

"He's okay," she said.

"My wife and he struck up quite a close friendship."

"I heard about that."

"So. I wanted to talk to you about something if you had a minute."

"My husband did not try to start anything with your wife, if that's what you're getting at," she said. "He did not molest her in any way. He isn't capable of it and he wouldn't anyway. From what I heard it was the other way round."

Grant said, "No. That isn't it at all. I didn't come here with any complaints about anything."

"Oh," she said. "Well, I'm sorry. I thought you did."

That was all she was going to give by way of apology. And she didn't sound sorry. She sounded disappointed and confused.

"You better come in, then," she said. "It's blowing cold in through the door. It's not as warm out today as it looks."

So it was something of a victory for him even to get inside. He hadn't realized it would be as hard as this. He had expected a different sort of wife. A flustered homebody, pleased by an unexpected visit and flattered by a confidential tone.

She took him past the entrance to the living room, saying, "We'll have to sit in the kitchen where I can hear Aubrey." Grant caught sight of two layers of front-window curtains, both blue, one sheer and one silky, a matching blue sofa and a daunting pale carpet, various bright mirrors and ornaments.

Fiona had a word for those sort of swooping curtains – she said it like a joke, though the women she'd picked it up from used it seriously. Any room that Fiona fixed up was bare and bright – she would have been astonished to see so much fancy stuff crowded into such a small space. He could not think what that word was.

From a room off the kitchen – a sort of sunroom, though the blinds were drawn against the afternoon brightness – he could hear the sounds of television.

Aubrey. The answer to Fiona's prayers sat a few feet away, watching what sounded like a ball game. His wife looked in at him. She said, "You okay?" and partly closed the door.

"You might as well have a cup of coffee," she said to Grant.

He said, "Thanks."

"My son got him on the sports channel a year ago Christmas, I don't know what we'd do without it."

On the kitchen counters there were all sorts of contrivances and appliances – coffeemaker, food processor, knife sharpener, and some things Grant didn't know the names or uses of. All looked new and expensive, as if they had just been taken out of their wrappings, or were polished daily.

He thought it might be a good idea to admire things. He admired the coffeemaker she was using and said that he and Fiona had always meant to get one. This was absolutely untrue – Fiona had been devoted to a European contraption that made only two cups at a time.

"They gave us that," she said. "Our son and his wife. They live in Kamloops. B.C. They send us more stuff than we can handle. It wouldn't hurt if they would spend the money to come and see us instead."

Grant said philosophically, "I suppose they're busy with their own lives."

"They weren't too busy to go to Hawaii last winter. You could understand it if we had somebody else in the family, closer at hand. But he's the only one."

The coffee being ready, she poured it into two brown-and-green ceramic mugs that she took from the amputated branches of a ceramic tree trunk that sat on the table.

"People do get lonely," Grant said. He thought he saw his chance now. "If they're deprived of seeing somebody they care about, they do feel sad. Fiona, for instance. My wife."

"I thought you said you went and visited her."

"I do," he said. "That's not it."

Then he took the plunge, going on to make the request he'd come to make. Could she consider taking Aubrey back to Meadowlake maybe just one day a week, for a visit? It was only a drive of a few miles, surely it wouldn't prove too difficult. Or if she'd like to take the time off – Grant hadn't thought of this before and was rather dismayed to hear himself suggest it – then he himself could take Aubrey out there, he wouldn't mind at all. He was sure he could manage it. And she could use a break.

While he talked she moved her closed lips and her hidden tongue as if she was trying to identify some dubious flavor. She brought milk for his coffee, and a plate of ginger cookies.

"Homemade," she said as she set the plate down. There was challenge rather than hospitality in her tone. She said nothing more until she had sat down, poured milk into her coffee and stirred it.

Then she said no.

"No. I can't do that. And the reason is, I'm not going to upset him."

"Would it upset him?" Grant said earnestly.

"Yes, it would. It would. That's no way to do. Bringing him home and taking him back. Bringing him home and taking him back, that's just confusing him."

"But wouldn't he understand that it was just a visit? Wouldn't he get into the pattern of it?"

"He understands everything all right." She said this as if he had offered an insult to Aubrey. "But it's still an interruption. And then I've got to get him all ready and get him into the car, and he's a big man, he's not so easy to manage as you might think. I've got to maneuver him into the car and pack his chair along and all that and what for? If I go to all that trouble I'd prefer to take him someplace that was more fun."

"But even if I agreed to do it?" Grant said, keeping his tone hopeful and reasonable. "It's true, you shouldn't have the trouble."

"You couldn't," she said flatly. "You don't know him. You couldn't handle him. He wouldn't stand for you doing for him. All that bother and what would he get out of it?"

Grant didn't think he should mention Fiona again.

"It'd make more sense to take him to the mall," she said. "Where he could see kids and whatnot. If it didn't make him sore about his own two grandsons he never gets to see. Or now the lake boats are starting to run again, he might get a charge out of going and watching that."

She got up and fetched her cigarettes and lighter from the window above the sink.

"You smoke?" she said.

He said no thanks, though he didn't know if a cigarette was being offered.

"Did you never? Or did you quit?"

"Quit," he said.

"How long ago was that?"

He thought about it.

"Thirty years. No – more."

He had decided to quit around the time he started up with Jacqui. But he couldn't remember whether he quit first, and thought a big reward was coming to him for quitting, or thought that the time had come to quit, now that he had such a powerful diversion.

"I've quit quitting," she said, lighting up. "Just made a resolution to quit quitting, that's all."

Maybe that was the reason for the wrinkles. Somebody – a woman – had told him that women who smoked developed a special set of fine facial wrinkles. But it could have been from the sun, or just the nature of her skin – her neck was noticeably wrinkled as well. Wrinkled neck, youthfully full and up-tilted breasts. Women of her age usually had these contradictions. The bad and good points, the genetic luck or lack of it, all mixed up together. Very few kept their beauty whole, though shadowy, as Fiona had done.

And perhaps that wasn't even true. Perhaps he only thought that because he'd known Fiona when she was young. Perhaps to get that impression you had to have known a woman when she was young.

So when Aubrey looked at his wife did he see a high-school girl full of scorn and sass, with an intriguing tilt to her robin's-egg blue eyes, pursing her fruity lips around a forbidden cigarette?

"So your wife's depressed?" Aubrey's wife said. "What's your wife's name? I forget."

"It's Fiona."

"Fiona. And what's yours? I don't think I ever was told that."

Grant said, "It's Grant."

She stuck her hand out unexpectedly across the table.

"Hello, Grant. I'm Marian."

"So now we know each other's name," she said, "there's no point in not telling you straight out what I think. I don't know if he's still so stuck on seeing your – on seeing Fiona. Or not. I don't ask him and he's not telling me. Maybe just a passing fancy. But I don't feel like taking him back there in case it turns out to be more than that. I can't afford to risk it. I don't want him getting hard to handle. I don't want him upset and carrying on. I've got my hands full with him as it is. I don't have any help. It's just me here. I'm it."

"Did you ever consider – it *is* very hard for you –" Grant said – "did you ever consider his going in there for good?"

He had lowered his voice almost to a whisper, but she did not seem to feel a need to lower hers.

"No," she said. "I'm keeping him right here."

Grant said, "Well. That's very good and noble of you."

He hoped the word "noble" had not sounded sarcastic. He had not meant it to be.

"You think so?" she said. "Noble is not what I'm thinking about."

"Still. It's not easy."

"No, it isn't. But the way I am, I don't have much choice. If I put him in there I don't have the money to pay for him unless I sell the house. The house is what we own outright. Otherwise I don't have anything in the way of resources. I get the pension next year, and I'll have his pension and my pension, but even so I could not afford to keep him there and hang on to the house. And it means a lot to me, my house does."

"It's very nice," said Grant.

"Well, it's all right. I put a lot into it. Fixing it up and keeping it up."

"I'm sure you did. You do."

"I don't want to lose it."

"No."

"I'm not *going* to lose it."

"I see your point."

"The company left us high and dry," she said. "I don't know all the ins and outs of it, but basically he got shoved out. It ended up with them saying he owed them money and when I tried to find out what was what he just went on saying it's none of my business. What I think is he did something pretty stupid. But I'm not supposed to ask, so I shut up. You've been married. You are married. You know how it is. And in the middle of me finding out about this we're supposed to go on this trip with these people and can't get out of it. And on the trip he takes sick from this virus you never heard of and goes into a coma. So that pretty well gets *him* off the hook."

Grant said, "Bad luck."

"I don't mean exactly that he got sick on purpose. It just happened. He's not mad at me anymore and I'm not mad at him. It's just life."

"That's true."

"You can't beat life."

She flicked her tongue in a cat's businesslike way across her top lip, getting the cookie crumbs. "I sound like I'm quite the philosopher, don't I? They told me out there you used to be a university professor."

"Quite a while ago," Grant said.

"I'm not much of an intellectual," she said.

"I don't know how much I am, either."

"But I know when my mind's made up. And it's made up. I'm not going to let go of the house. Which means I'm keeping him here and I don't want him getting it in his head he wants to move anyplace else. It was probably a mistake putting him in there so I could get away, but I wasn't going to get another chance, so I took it. So. Now I know better."

She shook out another cigarette.

"I bet I know what you're thinking," she said. "You're thinking there's a mercenary type of a person."

"I'm not making judgments of that sort. It's your life."

"You bet it is."

He thought they should end on a more neutral note. So he asked her if her husband had worked in a hardware store in the summers, when he was going to school.

"I never heard about it," she said. "I wasn't raised here."

Driving home, he noticed that the swamp hollow that had been filled with snow and the formal shadows of tree trunks was now lighted up with skunk lilies. Their fresh, edible-looking leaves were the size of platters. The flowers sprang straight up like candle flames, and there were so many of them, so pure a yellow, that they set a light shooting up from the earth on this cloudy day. Fiona had told him that they generated a heat of their own as well. Rummaging around in one of her concealed pockets of information, she said that you were supposed to be able to put your hand inside the curled petal and feel the heat. She said that she had tried it, but she couldn't be sure if what she felt was heat or her imagination. The heat attracted bugs.

"Nature doesn't fool around just being decorative."

He had failed with Aubrey's wife. Marian. He had foreseen that he might fail, but he had not in the least foreseen why. He had thought that all he'd have to contend with would be a woman's natural sexual jealousy – or her resentment, the stubborn remains of sexual jealousy.

He had not had any idea of the way she might be looking at things. And yet in some depressing way the conversation had not been unfamiliar to him. That was because it reminded him of conversations he'd had with people in his own family. His uncles, his relatives, probably even his mother, had thought the way Marian thought. They had believed that when other people did not think that way it was because they were kidding themselves – they had got too airy-fairy, or stupid, on account of their easy and protected lives or their education. They had lost touch with reality. Educated people, literary people, some rich people like Grant's socialist in-laws had lost touch with reality. Due to an unmerited good fortune or an innate silliness. In Grant's case, he suspected, they pretty well believed it was both.

That was how Marian would see him, certainly. A silly person, full of boring knowledge and protected by some fluke from the truth about life. A person who didn't have to worry about holding on to his house and could go around thinking his complicated thoughts. Free to dream up the fine, generous schemes that he believed would make another person happy.

What a jerk, she would be thinking now.

Being up against a person like that made him feel hopeless, exasperated, finally almost desolate. Why? Because he couldn't be sure of holding on to himself against that person? Because he was afraid that in the end they'd be right? Fiona wouldn't feel any of that misgiving. Nobody had beat her down, narrowed her in, when she was young. She'd been amused by his upbringing, able to think its harsh notions quaint.

Just the same, they have their points, those people. (He could hear himself now arguing with somebody. Fiona?) There's some advantage to the narrow focus. Marian would probably be good in a crisis. Good at survival, able to scrounge for food and able to take the shoes off a dead body in the street.

Trying to figure out Fiona had always been frustrating. It could be like following a mirage. No – like living in a mirage. Getting close to Marian would present a different problem. It would be like biting into a litchi nut. The flesh with its oddly artificial allure, its chemical taste and perfume, shallow over the extensive seed, the stone.

He might have married her. Think of it. He might have married some girl like that. If he'd stayed back where he belonged. She'd have been appetizing enough, with her choice breasts. Probably a flirt. The fussy way she had of shifting her buttocks on the kitchen chair, her pursed mouth, a slightly contrived air of menace – that was what was left of the more or less innocent vulgarity of a small-town flirt.

She must have had some hopes, when she picked Aubrey. His good looks, his salesman's job, his white-collar expectations. She must have believed that she would end up better off than she was now. And so it often happened with those practical people. In spite of their calculations, their survival instincts, they might not get as far as they had quite reasonably expected. No doubt it seemed unfair.

In the kitchen the first thing he saw was the light blinking on his answering machine. He thought the same thing he always thought now. Fiona.

He pressed the button before he got his coat off.

"Hello, Grant. I hope I got the right person. I just thought of something. There is a dance here in town at the Legion supposed to be for singles on Saturday night, and I am on the supper committee, which means I can bring a free guest. So I wondered whether you would happen to be interested in that? Call me back when you get a chance."

A woman's voice gave a local number. Then there was a beep, and the same voice started talking again.

"I just realized I'd forgot to say who it was. Well you probably recognized the voice. It's Marian. I'm still not so used to these machines. And I wanted to say I realize you're not a single and I don't mean it that way. I'm not either, but it doesn't hurt to get out once in a while. Anyway, now I've said all this I really hope it's you I'm talking to. It did sound like your voice. If you are interested you can call me and if you are not you don't need to bother. I just thought you might like the chance to get out. It's Marian speaking. I guess I already said that. Okay, then. Good-bye."

Her voice on the machine was different from the voice he'd heard a short time ago in her house. Just a little different in the first message, more so in the second. A tremor of nerves there, an affected nonchalance, a hurry to get through and a reluctance to let go.

Something had happened to her. But when had it happened? If it had been immediate, she had concealed it very successfully all the time he was with her. More likely it came on her gradually, maybe after he'd gone away. Not necessarily as a blow of attraction. Just the realization that he was a possibility, a man on his own. More or less on his own. A possibility that she might as well try to follow up.

But she'd had the jitters when she made the first move. She had put herself at risk. How much of herself, he could not yet tell. Generally a woman's vulnerability increased as time went on, as things progressed. All you could tell at the start was that if there was an edge of it now, there'd be more later.

It gave him a satisfaction – why deny it? – to have brought that out in her. To have roused something like a shimmer, a blurring, on the surface of her personality. To have heard in her testy, broad vowels this faint plea.

He set out the eggs and mushrooms to make himself an omelette. Then he thought he might as well pour a drink.

Anything was possible. Was that true – was anything possible? For instance, if he wanted to, would he be able to break her down, get her to the point where she might listen to him about taking Aubrey back to Fiona? And not just for visits, but for the rest of Aubrey's life. Where could that tremor lead them? To an upset, to the end of her self-preservation? To Fiona's happiness?

It would be a challenge. A challenge and a creditable feat. Also a joke that could never be confided to anybody – to think that by his bad behavior he'd be doing good for Fiona.

But he was not really capable of thinking about it. If he did think about it, he'd have to figure out what would become of him and Marian, after he'd delivered Aubrey to Fiona. It would not work – unless he could get more satisfaction that he foresaw, finding the stone of blameless self-interest inside her robust pulp.

You never quite knew how such things would turn out. You almost knew, but you could never be sure.

She would be sitting in her house now, waiting for him to call. Or probably not sitting. Doing things to keep herself busy. She seemed to be a woman who would keep busy. Her house had certainly shown the benefits of nonstop attention. And there was Aubrey – care of him had to continue as usual. She might have given him an early supper – fitting his meals to a Meadowlake timetable in order to get him settled for the night earlier and free herself of his routine for the day. (What would she do about him when she went to the dance? Could he be left alone or would she get a sitter? Would she tell him where she was going, introduce her escort? Would her escort pay the sitter?)

She might have fed Aubrey while Grant was buying the mushrooms and driving home. She might now be preparing him for bed. But all the time she would be conscious of the phone, of the silence of the phone. Maybe she would have calculated how long it would take Grant to drive home. His address in the phone book would have given her a rough idea of where he lived. She would calculate how long, then add to that time for possible shopping for supper (figuring that a man alone would shop every day). Then a certain amount of time for him to get around to listening to his messages. And as the silence persisted she would think of other things. Other errands he might have had to do before he got home. Or perhaps a dinner out, a meeting that meant he would not get home at suppertime at all.

She would stay up late, cleaning her kitchen cupboards, watching television, arguing with herself about whether there was still a chance.

What conceit on his part. She was above all things a sensible woman. She would go to bed at her regular time thinking that he didn't look as if he'd be a decent dancer anyway. Too stiff, too professorial.

He stayed near the phone, looking at magazines, but he didn't pick it up when it rang again.

"Grant. This is Marian. I was down in the basement putting the wash in the dryer and I heard the phone and when I got upstairs whoever it was had hung up. So I just thought I ought to say I was here. If it was you and if you are even home. Because I don't have a machine obviously, so you couldn't leave a message. So I just wanted. To let you know.

"'Bye."

The time was now twenty-five after ten.

'Bye.

He would say that he'd just got home. There was no point in bringing to her mind the picture of his sitting here, weighing the pros and cons.

Drapes. That would be her word for the blue curtains – drapes. And why not? He thought of the ginger cookies so perfectly round that she'd had to announce they were home-made, the ceramic coffee mugs on their ceramic tree. A plastic runner, he was sure, protecting the hall carpet. A high-gloss exactness and practicality that his mother had never achieved but would have admired – was that why he could feel this twinge of bizarre and unreliable affection? Or was it because he'd had two more drinks after the first?

The walnut-stain tan – he believed now that it was a tan – of her face and neck would most likely continue into her cleavage, which would be deep, crepey-skinned, odorous and hot. He had that to think of, as he dialled the number that he had already written down. That and the practical sensuality of her cat's tongue. Her gemstone eyes.

Fiona was in her room but not in bed. She was sitting by the open window, wearing a seasonable but oddly short and bright dress. Through the window came a heady, warm blast of lilacs in bloom and the spring manure spread over the fields.

She had a book open in her lap.

She said, "Look at this beautiful book I found, it's about Iceland. You wouldn't think they'd leave valuable books lying around in the rooms. The people staying here are not necessarily honest. And I think they've got the clothes mixed up. I never wear yellow."

"Fiona . . .," he said.

"You've been gone a long time. Are we all checked out now?"

"Fiona, I've brought a surprise for you. Do you remember Aubrey?"

She stared at him for a moment, as if waves of wind had come beating into her face. Into her face, into her head, pulling everything to rags.

"Names elude me," she said harshly.

Then the look passed away as she retrieved, with an effort, some bantering grace. She set the book down carefully and stood up and lifted her arms to put them around him. Her skin or her breath gave off a faint new smell, a smell that seemed to him like that of the stems of cut flowers left too long in their water.

"I'm happy to see you," she said, and pulled his earlobes.

"You could have just driven away," she said. "Just driven away without a care in the world and forsook me. Forsooken me. Forsaken."

He kept his face against her white hair, her pink scalp, her sweetly shaped skull. He said, Not a chance.

The Albanian Virgin

IN THE MOUNTAINS, in Maltsia e madhe, she must have tried to tell them her name, and "Lottar" was what they made of it. She had a wound in her leg, from a fall on sharp rocks when her guide was shot. She had a fever. How long it took them to carry her through the mountains, bound up in a rug and strapped to a horse's back, she had no idea. They gave her water to drink now and then, and sometimes *raki*, which was a kind of brandy, very strong. She could smell pines. At one time they were on a boat and she woke up and saw the stars, brightening and fading and changing places – unstable clusters that made her sick. Later she understood that they must have been on the lake. Lake Scutari, or Sckhoder, or Skodra. They pulled up among the reeds. The rug was full of vermin, which got under the rag tied around her leg.

At the end of her journey, though she did not know it was the end, she was lying in a small stone hut that was an outbuilding of the big house, called the *kula*. It was the hut of the sick and dying. Not of giving birth, which these women did in the cornfields, or beside the path when they were carrying a load to market.

She was lying, perhaps for weeks, on a heaped-up bed of ferns. It was comfortable, and had the advantage of being easily changed when fouled or bloodied. The old woman named Tima looked after her. She plugged up the wound with a paste made of beeswax and olive oil and pine resin. Several times a day the dressing was removed, the wound washed out with *raki*. Lottar could see black lace curtains hanging from the rafters, and she thought she was in her room at home, with her mother (who was dead) looking after her. "Why have you hung up those curtains?" she said. "They look horrible."

She was really seeing cobwebs, all thick and furry with smoke – ancient cobwebs, never disturbed from year to year.

Also, in her delirium, she had the sensation of some wide board being pushed against her face – something like a coffin plank. But when she came to her senses she learned that it was nothing but a crucifix, a wooden crucifix that a man was trying to get her to kiss. The man was a priest, a Franciscan. He was a tall, fierce-looking man with black eyebrows and mustache and a rank smell, and he carried, besides the crucifix, a gun that she learned later was a Browning revolver. He knew by the look of her that she was a giaour – not a Muslim – but he did not understand that she might be a heretic. He knew a little English but pronounced it in a way that she could not make out. And she did not then know any of the language of the Ghegs. But after her fever subsided, when he tried a few words of Italian on her, they were able to talk, because she had learned Italian at school and had been travelling for six months in Italy. He understood so much more than anyone else around her that she expected him, at first, to understand everything. What is the nearest city? she asked him, and he said, Skodra. So go there, please, she said – go and find the British Consulate, if there is one. I belong to the British Empire. Tell them I am here. Or if there is no British Consul, go to the police.

She did not understand that under no circumstances would anybody go to the police. She didn't know that she belonged now to this tribe, this *kula*, even though taking her prisoner had not been their intention and was an embarrassing mistake.

It is shameful beyond belief to attack a woman. When they had shot and killed her guide, they had thought that she would turn her horse around and fly back down the mountain road, back to Bar. But her horse took fright at the shot and stumbled among the boulders and she fell, and her leg was injured. Then they had no choice but to carry her with them, back across the border between the Crna Gora (which means Black Rock, or Montenegro) and Maltsia e madhe.

"But why rob the guide and not me?" she said, naturally thinking robbery to be the motive. She thought of how starved they looked, the man and his horse, and of the fluttering white rags of his headdress.

"Oh, they are not robbers!" said the Franciscan, shocked. "They are honest men. They shot him because they were in blood with him. With his house. It is their law."

He told her that the man who had been shot, her guide, had killed a man of this *kula*. He had done that because the man he had killed had killed a man of his *kula*. This would go on, it had been going on for a long time now, there were always more sons being born. They think they have more sons than other people in the world, and it is to serve this necessity.

"Well, it is terrible," the Franciscan concluded. "But it is for their honor, the honor of their family. They are always ready to die for their honor."

She said that her guide did not seem to be so ready, if he had fled to Crna Gora.

"But it did not make any difference, did it?" said the Franciscan. "Even if he had gone to America, it would not have made any difference."

At Trieste she had boarded a steamer, to travel down the Dalmatian Coast. She was with her friends Mr. and Mrs. Cozzens, whom she had met in Italy, and their friend Dr. Lamb, who had joined them from England. They put in at the little port of Bar, which the Italians call Antivari, and stayed the night at the European Hotel. After dinner they walked on the terrace, but Mrs. Cozzens was afraid of a chill, so they went indoors and played cards. There was rain in the night. She woke up and listened to the rain and was full of disappointment, which gave rise to a loathing for these middle-aged people, particularly for Dr. Lamb, whom she believed the Cozzenses had summoned from England to meet her. They probably thought she was rich. A transatlantic heiress whose accent they could almost forgive. These people ate too much and then they had to take pills. And they worried about being in strange places – what had they come for? In the morning she would have to get back on the boat with them or they would make a fuss. She would never take the road over the mountains to Cetinge, Montenegro's capital city – they had been told that it was not wise. She would never see the bell tower where the heads of Turks used to hang, or the plane tree under which the Poet-Prince held audience with the people. She could not get back to sleep, so she decided to go downstairs with the first light, and, even if it was still raining, to go a little way up the road behind the town, just to see the ruins that she knew were there, among the olive trees, and the Austrian fortress on its rock and the dark face of Mount Lovchen.

The weather obliged her, and so did the man at the hotel desk, producing almost at once a tattered but cheerful guide and his underfed horse. They set out – she on the horse, the man walking ahead. The road was steep and twisting and full of boulders, the sun increasingly hot and the intervening shade cold and black. She became hungry and thought she must turn back soon. She would have breakfast with her companions, who got up late.

No doubt there was some sort of search for her, after the guide's body was found. The authorities must have been notified – whoever the authorities were. The boat must have sailed on time, her friends must have gone with it. The hotel had not taken their passports. Nobody back in Canada would think of investigating. She was not writing regularly to anyone, she had had a falling-out with her brother, her parents were dead. You won't come home till all your inheritance is spent, her brother had said, and then who will look after you?

When she was being carried through the pine forest, she awoke and found herself suspended, lulled – in spite of the pain and perhaps because of the *raki* – into a disbelieving surrender. She fastened her eyes on the bundle that was hanging from the saddle of the man ahead of her and knocking against the horse's back. It was something about the size of a cabbage, wrapped in a stiff and rusty-looking cloth.

I heard this story in the old St. Joseph's Hospital in Victoria from Charlotte, who was the sort of friend I had in my early days there. My friendships then seemed both intimate and uncertain. I never knew why people told me things, or what they meant me to believe.

I had come to the hospital with flowers and chocolates. Charlotte lifted her head, with its clipped and feathery white hair, toward the roses. "Bah!" she said. "They have no smell! Not to me, anyway. They are beautiful, of course.

"You must eat the chocolates yourself," she said. "Everything tastes like tar to me. I don't know how I know what tar tastes like, but this is what I think."

She was feverish. Her hand, when I held it, felt hot and puffy. Her hair had all been cut off, and this made her look as if she had actually lost flesh around her face and neck. The part of her under the hospital covers seemed as extensive and lumpy as ever.

"But you must not think I am ungrateful," she said. "Sit down. Bring that chair from over there – she doesn't need it."

There were two other women in the room. One was just a

thatch of yellow-gray hair on the pillow, and the other was tied into a chair, wriggling and grunting.

"This is a terrible place," said Charlotte. "But we must just try our best to put up with it. I am so glad to see you. That one over there yells all night long," she said, nodding toward the window bed. "We must thank Christ she's asleep now. I don't get a wink of sleep, but I have been putting the time to very good use. What do you think I've been doing? I've been making up a story, for a movie! I have it all in my head and I want you to hear it. You will be able to judge if it will make a good movie. I think it will. I would like Jennifer Jones to act in it. I don't know, though. She does not seem to have the same spirit anymore. She married that mogul.

"Listen," she said. "(Oh, could you haul that pillow up more, behind my head?) It takes place in Albania, in northern Albania, which is called Maltsia e madhe, in the nineteen-twenties, when things were very primitive. It is about a young woman travelling alone. Lottar is her name in the story."

I sat and listened. Charlotte would lean forward, even rock a little on her hard bed, stressing some point for me. Her puffy hands flew up and down, her blue eyes widened commandingly, and then from time to time she sank back onto the pillows, and she shut her eyes to get the story in focus again. Ah, yes, she said. Yes, yes. And she continued.

"Yes, yes," she said at last. "I know how it goes on, but that is enough for now. You will have to come back. Tomorrow. Will you come back?"

I said, yes, tomorrow, and she appeared to have fallen asleep without hearing me.

The *kula* was a great, rough stone house with a stable below and the living quarters above. A veranda ran all the way around, and there would always be an old woman sitting there, with a bobbin contraption that flew like a bird from one hand to the other and left a trail of shiny black braid, mile after mile of black braid, which was the adornment of all the men's trousers. Other women worked at the looms or sewed together the leather sandals. Nobody sat there knitting, because nobody would think to sit down to knit. Knitting was what they did while they trotted back and forth to the spring with their water barrels strapped to their backs, or took the path to the fields or to the beech wood, where they collected the fallen branches. They knitted stockings – black and white, red and white, with zigzag patterns like lightning strokes. Women's hands must never be idle. Before dawn they pounded the bread dough in its blackened wooden trough, shaped it into loaves on the backs of shovels, and baked it on the hearth. (It was corn bread, unleavened and eaten hot, which would swell up like a puffball in your stomach.) Then they had to sweep out the *kula* and dump the dirty ferns and pile up armloads of fresh ferns for the next night's sleep. This was often one of Lottar's jobs, since she was so unskilled at everything else. Little girls stirred the yogurt so that lumps would not form as it soured. Older girls might butcher a kid and sew up its stomach, which they had stuffed with wild garlic and sage and apples. Or they would go together, girls and women, all ages, to wash the men's white head scarves in the cold little river nearby, whose waters were clear as glass. They tended the tobacco crop and hung the ripe leaves to dry in the darkened shed. They hoed the corn and cucumbers, milked the ewes.

The women looked stern but they were not so, really. They were only preoccupied, and proud of themselves, and eager for competition. Who could carry the heaviest load of wood, knit the fastest, hoe the most rows of cornstalks? Tima, who had looked after Lottar when she was sick, was the most spectacular worker of all. She would run up the slope to the *kula* with a load of wood bound to her back that looked ten times as big as herself. She would leap from rock to rock in the river and pound the scarves as if they were the bodies of enemies.

"Oh, Tima, Tima!" the other women cried out in ironic admiration, and "Oh, Lottar, Lottar!" in nearly the same tones, when Lottar, at the other end of a scale of usefulness, let the clothes drift away downstream. Sometimes they whacked Lottar with a stick, as they would a donkey, but this had more exasperation in it than cruelty. Sometimes the young ones would say, "Talk your talk!" and for their entertainment she would speak English. They wrinkled up their faces and spat, at such peculiar sounds. She tried to teach them words – "hand," "nose," and so on. But these seemed to them jokes, and they would repeat them to each other and fall about laughing.

Women were with women and men were with men, except at times in the night (women teased about such times were full of shame and denial, and sometimes there would be a slapping) and at meals, when the women served the men their food. What the men did all day was none of women's business. Men made their ammunition, and gave a lot of care to their guns, which were in some cases very beautiful, decorated with engraved silver. They also dynamited rocks to clear the road, and were responsible for the horses. Wherever they were, there was a lot of laughing, and sometimes singing and firing off of blanks. While they were at home they seemed to be on holiday, and then some of them would have to ride off on an expedition of punishment, or to attend a council called to put an end to some particular bout of killing. None of the women believed it would work – they laughed and said that it would only mean twenty more shot. When a young man was going off on his first killing, the women made a great fuss over his clothes and his haircut, to encourage him. If he didn't succeed, no woman would marry him – a woman of any worth would be ashamed to marry a man who had not killed – and everyone was anxious to have new brides in the house, to help with the work.

One night, when Lottar served one man his food – a guest; there were always guests invited for meals around the low table, the *sofra* – she noticed what small hands he had, and hairless wrists. Yet he was not young, he was not a boy. A wrinkled, leathery face, without a mustache. She listened for his voice in the talk, and it seemed to her hoarse but womanish. But he smoked, he ate with the men, he carried a gun.

"Is that a man?" Lottar said to the woman serving with her. The woman shook her head, not willing to speak where the men might hear them. But the young girls who overheard the question were not so careful. "Is that a man? Is that a man?" they mimicked Lottar. "Oh, Lottar, you are so stupid! Don't you know when you see a Virgin?"

So she did not ask them anything else. But the next time she saw the Franciscan, she ran after him to ask him her question. What is a Virgin? She had to run after him, because he did not stop and talk to her now as he had when she was sick in the little hut. She was always working when he came to the *kula*, and he could not spend much time with the women anyway – he sat with the men. She ran after him when she saw him leaving, striding down the path among the sumac trees, heading for the bare wooden church and the lean-to church house, where he lived.

He said it was a woman, but a woman who had become like a man. She did not want to marry, and she took an oath in front of witnesses that she never would, and then she put on men's clothes and had her own gun, and her horse if she could afford one, and she lived as she liked. Usually she was poor, she had no woman to work for her. But nobody troubled her, and she could eat at the *sofra* with the men.

Lottar no longer spoke to the priest about going to Skodra. She understood now that it must be a long way away. Sometimes she asked if he had heard anything, if anybody was looking for her, and he would say, sternly, no one. When she thought of how she had been during those first weeks – giving orders, speaking English without embarrassment, sure that her special case merited attention – she was ashamed at how little she had understood. And the longer she stayed at the *kula*, the better she spoke the language and became accustomed to the work, the stranger was the thought of leaving. Someday she must go, but how could it be now? How could she leave in the middle of the tobacco-picking or the sumac harvest, or during the preparations for the feast of the Translation of St. Nicholas?

In the tobacco fields they took off their jerkins and blouses and worked half naked in the sun, hidden between the rows of tall plants. The tobacco juice was black and sticky, like molasses, and it ran down their arms and was smeared over their breasts. At dusk they went down to the river and scrubbed themselves clean. They splashed in the cold water, girls and big, broad women together. They tried to push each other off balance, and Lottar heard her name cried then, in warning and triumph, without contempt, like any other name: "Lottar, watch out! Lottar!"

They told her things. They told her that children died here because of the *Striga*. Even grown-up people shrivel and die sometimes, when the *Striga* has put her spell on them. The *Striga* looks like a normal woman, so you do not know who she is. She sucks blood. To catch her, you must lay a cross on the threshold of the church on Easter Sunday when everybody is inside. Then the woman who is the *Striga* cannot come out. Or you can follow the woman you suspect, and you may see her vomit up the blood. If you can manage to scrape up some of this blood on a silver coin, and carry that coin with you, no *Striga* can touch you, ever.

Hair cut at the time of the full moon will turn white.

If you have pains in your limbs, cut some hair from your head and your armpits and burn it – then the pains will go away.

The *oras* are the devils that come out at night and flash false lights to bewilder travellers. You must crouch down and cover your head, else they will lead you over a cliff. Also they will catch the horses and ride them to death.

The tobacco had been harvested, the sheep brought down from the slopes, animals and humans shut up in the *kula* through the weeks of snow and cold rain, and one day, in the early warmth of the spring sun, the women brought Lottar to a chair on the veranda. There, with great ceremony and delight, they shaved off the hair above her forehead. Then they combed some black, bubbling dye through the hair that remained. The dye was greasy – the hair became so stiff that they could shape it into wings and buns as firm as blood puddings. Everybody thronged about, criticizing and admiring. They put flour on her face and dressed her up in clothes they had pulled out of one of the great carved chests. What for, she asked, as she found herself disappearing into a white blouse with gold embroidery, a red bodice with fringed epaulets, a sash of striped silk a yard wide and a dozen yards long, a black-and-red wool skirt, with chain after chain of false gold being thrown over her hair and around her neck. For beauty, they said. And they said when they had finished, "See! She is beautiful!" Those who said it seemed triumphant, challenging others who must have doubted that the transformation could be made. They squeezed the muscles in her arms, which she had got from hoeing and wood-carrying, and patted her broad, floured forehead. Then they shrieked, because they had forgotten a very important thing – the black paint that joins the eyebrows in a single line over the nose.

"The priest is coming!" shouted one of the girls, who must have been placed as a lookout, and the woman who was painting the black line said, "Ha, he will not stop it!" But the others drew aside.

The Franciscan shot off a couple of blanks, as he always did to announce his arrival, and the men of the house fired off blanks also, to welcome him. But he did not stay with the men this time. He climbed at once to the veranda, calling, "Shame! Shame! Shame on you all! Shame!

"I know what you have dyed her hair for," he said to the women. "I know why you have put bride's clothes on her. All for a pig of a Muslim!

"You! You sitting there in your paint," he said to Lottar. "Don't you know what it is for? Don't you know they have sold you to a Muslim? He is coming from Vuthaj. He will be here by dark!"

"So what of it?" said one of the women boldly. "All they could get for her was three napoleons. She has to marry somebody."

The Franciscan told her to hold her tongue. "Is this what you want?" he said to Lottar. "To marry an infidel and go to live with him in Vuthaj?"

Lottar said no. She felt as if she could hardly move or open her mouth, under the weight of her greased hair and her finery. Under this weight she struggled as you do to rouse yourself to a danger, out of sleep. The idea of marrying the Muslim was still too distant to be the danger – what she understood was that she would be separated from the priest, and would never be able to claim an explanation from him again.

"Did you know you were being married?" he asked her. "Is it something you want, to be married?"

No, she said. No. And the Franciscan clapped his hands. "Take off that gold trash!" he said. "Take those clothes off her! I am going to make her a Virgin!

"If you become a Virgin, it will be all right," he said to her. "The Muslim will not have to shoot anybody. But you must swear you will never go with a man. You must swear in front of witnesses. *Per quri e per kruch.* By the stone and by the Cross. Do you understand that? I am not going to let them marry you to a Muslim, but I do not want more shooting to start on this land."

It was one of the things the Franciscan tried so hard to prevent – the selling of women to Muslim men. It put him into a frenzy, that their religion could be so easily set aside. They sold girls like Lottar, who would bring no price anywhere else, and widows who had borne only girls.

Slowly and sulkily the women removed all the rich clothes. They brought out men's trousers, worn and with no braid, and a shirt and head scarf. Lottar put them on. One woman with an ugly pair of shears chopped off most of what remained of Lottar's hair, which was difficult to cut because of the dressing.

"Tomorrow you would have been a bride," they said to her. Some of them seemed mournful, some contemptuous. "Now you will never have a son."

The little girls snatched up the hair that had been cut off and struck it on their heads, arranging various knots and fringes.

Lottar swore her oath in front of twelve witnesses. They were, of course, all men, and looked as sullen as the women about the turn things had taken. She never saw the Muslim. The Franciscan berated the men and said that if this sort of thing did not stop he would close up the churchyard and make them bury their dead in unholy ground. Lottar sat at a distance from them all, in her unaccustomed clothes. It was strange and unpleasant to be idle. When the Franciscan had finished his harangue, he came over and stood looking down at her. He was breathing hard because of his rage, or the exertions of the lecture.

"Well, then," he said. "Well." He reached into some inner fold of his clothing and brought out a cigarette and gave it to her. It smelled of his skin.

A nurse brought in Charlotte's supper, a light meal of soup and canned peaches. Charlotte took the cover off the soup, smelled it, and turned her head away. "Go away, don't look at this slop," she said. "Come back tomorrow – you know it's not finished yet."

The nurse walked with me to the door, and once we were in the corridor she said, "It's always the ones with the least at home who turn the most critical. She's not the easiest in the world, but you can't help kind of admiring her. You're not related, are you?"

Oh, no, I said. No.

"When she came in it was amazing. We were taking her things off and somebody said, oh, what lovely bracelets, and right away she wanted to sell them! Her *husband* is something else. Do you know him? They are really quite the characters."

Charlotte's husband, Gjurdhi, had come to my bookstore by himself one cold morning less than a week earlier. He was pulling a wagon full of books, which he had wrapped up in a blanket. He had tried to sell me some books once before, in their apartment, and I thought perhaps these were the same ones. I had been confused then, but now that I was on my own ground I was able to be more forceful. I said no, I did not handle secondhand books, I was not interested. Gjurdhi nodded brusquely, as if I had not needed to tell him this and it was of no importance to our conversation. He continued to pick up the books one by one, urging me to run my hands over the bindings, insisting that I note the beauty of the illustrations and be impressed by the dates of publication. I had to repeat my refusal over and over again, and I heard myself begin to attach some apologies to it, quite against my own will. He chose to understand each rejection as applying to an individual book and would simply fetch out another, saying vehemently, "This, too! This is very beautiful. You will notice. And it is very old. Look what a beautiful old book!"

They were travel books, some of them, from the turn of the century. Not so very old, and not so beautiful, either, with their dim, grainy photographs. *A Trek Through the Black Peaks. High Albania. Secret Lands of Southern Europe.*

"You will have to go to the Antiquarian Bookstore," I said. "The one on Fort Street. It isn't far to take them."

He made a sound of disgust, maybe indicating that he knew well enough where it was, or that he had already made an unsuccessful trip there, or that most of these books had come from there, one way or another, in the first place.

"How is Charlotte?" I said warmly. I had not seen her for a while, although she used to visit the store quite often. She would bring me little presents – coffee beans coated with chocolate to give me energy; a bar of pure glycerine soap to counteract the drying effects, on the skin, of having to handle so much paper. A paperweight embedded with samples of rocks found in British Columbia, a pencil that lit up in the dark (so that I could see to write up bills if the lights should go out). She drank coffee with me, talked, and strolled about the store, discreetly occupied, when I was busy. Through the dark, blustery days of fall she wore the velvet cloak that I had first seen her in, and kept the rain off with an oversized, ancient black umbrella. She called it her tent. If she saw that I had become too involved with a customer, she would tap me on the shoulder and say, "I'll just silently steal away with my tent now. We'll talk another day."

Once, a customer said to me bluntly, "Who is that woman? I've seen her around town with her husband. I guess he's her husband. I thought they were peddlers."

Could Charlotte have heard that, I wondered. Could she have detected a coolness in the attitude of my new clerk? (Charlotte was certainly cool to her.) There might have been just too many times when I was busy. I did not actually think that the visits had stopped. I preferred to think that an interval had grown longer, for a reason that might have nothing to do with me. I was busy and tired, anyway, as Christmas loomed. The number of books I was selling was a pleasant surprise.

"I don't want to be any kind of character assassin," the clerk had said to me. "But I think you should know that that woman and her husband have been banned from a lot of stores in town. They're suspected of lifting things. I don't know. He wears that rubber coat with the big sleeves and she's got her cloak. I do know for sure that they used to go around at Christmastime and snip off holly that was growing in people's gardens. Then they took it round and tried to sell it in apartment buildings."

On that cold morning, after I had refused all the books in his wagon, I asked Gjurdhi again how Charlotte was. He said that she was sick. He spoke sullenly, as if it were none of my business.

"Take her a book," I said. I picked out a Penguin light verse. "Take her this – tell her I hope she enjoys it. Tell her I hope she'll be better very soon. Perhaps I can get around to see her."

He put the book into his bundle in the wagon. I thought that he would probably try to sell it immediately.

"Not at home," he said. "In the hospital."

I had noticed, each time he bent over the wagon, a large, wooden crucifix that swung down outside his coat and had to be tucked back inside. Now this happened again, and I said, thoughtlessly, in my confusion and contrition, "Isn't that beautiful! What beautiful dark wood! It looks medieval."

He pulled it over his head, saying, "Very old. Very beautiful. Oak wood. Yes."

He pushed it into my hand, and as soon as I realized what was happening I pushed it back.

"*Wonderful* wood," I said. As he put it away I felt rescued, though full of irritable remorse.

"Oh, I hope Charlotte is not very sick!" I said.

He smiled disdainfully, tapping himself on the chest – perhaps to show me the source of Charlotte's trouble, perhaps only to feel for himself the skin that was newly bared there.

Then he took himself, the crucifix, the books, and the wagon out of my store. I felt that insults had been offered, humiliations suffered, on both sides.

Up past the tobacco field was a beech wood, where Lottar had often gone to get sticks for the fire. Beyond that was a grassy slope – a high meadow – and at the top of the meadow, about half an hour's climb from the *kula*, was a small stone shelter, a primitive place with no window, a low doorway and no door, a corner hearth without a chimney. Sheep took cover there; the floor was littered with their droppings.

That was where she went to live after she became a Virgin. The incident of the Muslim bridegroom had taken place in the spring, just about a year after she first came to Maltsia e madhe, and it was time for the sheep to be driven to their higher pastures. Lottar was to keep count of the flock and see that they did not fall into ravines or wander too far away. And she was to milk the ewes every evening. She was expected to shoot wolves, if any came near. But none did, no one alive now at the *kula* had ever seen a wolf. The only wild animals Lottar saw were a red fox, once, by the stream, and the rabbits, which were plentiful and unwary. She learned to shoot and skin and cook them, cleaning them out as she had seen the butcher girls do at the *kula* and stewing the meatier parts in her pot over the fire, with some bulbs of wild garlic.

She did not want to sleep inside the shelter, so she fixed up a roof of branches outside, against the wall, this roof an extension of the roof of the building. She had her heap of ferns underneath, and a felt rug she had been given, to spread on the ferns when she slept. She no longer took any notice of the bugs. There were some spikes pushed into the wall between the dry stones. She did not know why they were there, but they served her well for hanging up the milk pails and the few pots she had been provided with. She brought her water from the stream, in which she washed her own head scarf, and herself sometimes, more for relief from the heat than out of concern about her dirtiness.

Everything was changed. She no longer saw the women. She lost her habits of constant work. The little girls came up in the evenings to get the milk. This far away from the *kula* and their mothers, they became quite wild. They climbed up on the roof, often smashing through the arrangement of branches which Lottar had contrived. They jumped into the ferns and sometimes snatched an armful of them to bind into a crude ball, which they threw at one another until it fell apart. They enjoyed themselves so much that Lottar had to chase them away at dusk, reminding them of how frightened they got in the beech wood after dark. She believed that they ran all the way through it and spilled half the milk on their way.

Now and then they brought her corn flour, which she mixed with water and baked on her shovel by the fire. Once they had a treat, a sheep's head – she wondered if they had stolen it – for her to boil in her pot. She was allowed to keep some of the milk, and instead of drinking it fresh she usually let it go sour, and stirred it to make yogurt to dip her bread in. That was how she preferred it now.

The men often came up through the wood shortly after the little girls had run through it on their way down. It seemed that this was a custom of theirs, in the summer. They liked to sit on the banks of the stream and fire off blanks and drink *raki* and sing, or sometimes just smoke and talk. They were not making this expedition to see how she was getting on. But since they were coming anyway, they brought her presents of coffee and tobacco and were full of competing advice on how to fix up the roof of her shelter so it wouldn't fall down, how to keep her fire going all night, how to use her gun.

Her gun was an old Italian Martini, which had been given to her when she left the *kula*. Some of the men said that gun was unlucky, since it had belonged to a boy who had been killed before he himself had even shot anybody. Others said that Martinis in general were unlucky, hardly any use at all.

Mausers were what you needed, for accuracy and repeating power.

But Mauser bullets were too small to do enough damage. There were men walking around full of Mauser holes – you could hear them whistle as they passed by.

Nothing can really compare with a heavy flintlock that has a good packing of powder, a bullet, and nails.

When they weren't talking about guns, the men spoke of recent killings, and told jokes. One of them told a joke about a wizard. There was a wizard held in prison by a Pasha. The Pasha brought him out to do tricks in front of guests. Bring a bowl of water, said the wizard. Now, this water is the sea. And what port shall I show you on the sea? Show a port on the island of Malta, they said. And there it was. Houses and churches and a steamer ready to sail. Now would you like to see me step on board that steamer? And the Pasha laughed. Go ahead! So the wizard put his foot in the bowl of water and stepped on board the steamer and went to America! What do you think of that!

"There are no wizards, anyway," said the Franciscan, who had climbed up with the men on this evening, as he often did. "If you had said a saint, you might have made some sense." He spoke severely, but Lottar thought he was happy, as they all were, as she, too, was permitted to be, in their presence and in his, though he paid no attention to her. The strong tobacco that they gave her to smoke made her dizzy and she had to lie down on the grass.

The time came when Lottar had to think about moving inside her house. The mornings were cold, the ferns were soaked with dew, and the grape leaves were turning yellow. She took the shovel and cleaned the sheep droppings off the floor, in preparation for making up her bed inside. She began to stuff grass and leaves and mud into the chinks between the stones.

When the men came they asked her what she was doing that for. For the winter, she said, and they laughed.

"Nobody can stay here in the winter," they said. They showed her how deep the snow was, putting hands against their breastbones. Besides, all the sheep would have been taken down.

"There will be no work for you – and what will you eat?" they said. "Do you think the women will let you have bread and yogurt for nothing?"

"How can I go back to the *kula*?" Lottar said. "I am a Virgin, where would I sleep? What kind of work would I do?"

"That is right," they said kindly, speaking to her and then to each other. "When a Virgin belongs to the *kula* she gets a bit of land, usually, where she can live on her own. But this one doesn't really belong to the *kula*, she has no father to give her anything. What will she do?"

Shortly after this – and in the middle of the day, when visitors never came – the Franciscan climbed the meadow, all alone.

"I don't trust them," he said. "I think they will try again to sell you to a Muslim. Even though you have been sworn. They will try to make some money out of you. If they could find you a Christian, it might not be so bad, but I am sure it will be an infidel."

They sat on the grass and drank coffee. The Franciscan said, "Do you have any belongings to take with you? No. Soon we will start."

"Who will milk the ewes?" said Lottar. Some of the ewes were already working their way down the slope; they would stand and wait for her.

"Leave them," said the Franciscan.

In this way she left not only the sheep but her shelter, the meadow, the wild grape and the sumac and mountain ash and juniper bushes and scrub oak she had looked at all summer, the rabbit pelt she had used as a pillow and the pan she had boiled her coffee in, the heap of wood she had gathered only that morning, the stones around her fire – each one of them known to her by its particular shape and color. She understood that she was leaving, because the Franciscan was so stern, but she did not understand it in a way that would make her look around, to see everything for the last time. That was not necessary, anyway. She would never forget any of it.

As they entered the beech wood the Franciscan said, "Now we must be very quiet. I am going to take another path, which does not go so near the *kula*. If we hear anybody on the path, we will hide."

Hours, then, of silent walking, between the beech trees with their smooth elephant bark, and the black-limbed oaks and the dry pines. Up and down, crossing the ridges, choosing paths that Lottar had not known existed. The Franciscan never hesitated and never spoke of a rest. When they came out of the trees at last, Lottar was very surprised to see that there was still so much light in the sky.

The Franciscan pulled a loaf of bread and a knife from some pocket in his garment, and they ate as they walked.

They came to a dry riverbed, paved with stones that were not flat and easily walkable but a torrent, a still torrent of stones between fields of corn and tobacco. They could hear dogs barking, and sometimes people's voices. The corn and tobacco plants, still unharvested, were higher than their heads, and they walked along the dry river in this shelter, while the daylight entirely faded. When they could not walk anymore and the darkness would conceal them, they sat down on the white stones of the riverbed.

"Where are you taking me?" Lottar finally asked. At the start she had thought they must be going in the direction of the church and the priest's house, but now she saw that this could not be so. They had come much too far.

"I am taking you to the Bishop's house," said the Franciscan. "He will know what to do with you."

"Why not to your house?" said Lottar. "I could be a servant in your house."

"It isn't allowed – to have a woman servant in my house. Or in any priest's house. This Bishop now will not allow even an old woman. And he is right, trouble comes from having a woman in the house."

After the moon rose they went on. They walked and rested, walked and rested, but never fell asleep, or even looked for a comfortable place to lie down. Their feet were tough and their sandals well worn, and they did not get blisters. Both of them were used to walking long distances – the Franciscan in his far-flung parish and Lottar when she was following the sheep.

The Franciscan became less stern – perhaps less worried – after a while and talked to her almost as he had done in the first days of their acquaintance. He spoke Italian, though she was now fairly proficient in the language of the Ghegs.

"I was born in Italy," he said. "My parents were Ghegs, but I lived in Italy when I was young, and that was where I became a priest. Once I went back for a visit, years ago, and I shaved off my mustache, I do not know why. Oh, yes, I do know – it was because they laughed at me in the village. Then when I got back I did not dare show my face in the *madhe*. A hairless man there is a disgrace. I sat in a room in Skodra until it grew again."

"It is Skodra we are going to?" said Lottar.

"Yes, that is where the Bishop is. He will send a message that it was right to take you away, even if it is an act of stealing. They are barbarians, in the *madhe*. They will come up and pull on your sleeve in the middle of Mass and ask you to write a letter for them. Have you seen what they put up on the graves? The crosses? They make the cross into a very thin man with a rifle across his arms. Haven't you seen that?" He laughed and shook his head and said, "I don't know what to do with them. But they are good people all the same – they will never betray you."

"But you thought they might sell me in spite of my oath."

"Oh, yes. But to sell a woman is a way to get some money. And they are so poor."

Lottar now realized that in Skodra she would be in an unfamiliar position – she would not be powerless. When they got there, she could run away from him. She could find someone who spoke English, she could find the British Consulate. Or, if not that, the French.

The grass was soaking wet before dawn and the night got very cold. But when the sun came up Lottar stopped shivering and within an hour she was hot. They walked on all day. They ate the rest of the bread and drank from any stream they found that had water in it. They had left the dry river and the mountains far behind. Lottar looked back and saw a wall of jagged rocks with a little green clinging around their bases. That green was the woods and meadows which she had thought so high. They followed paths through the hot fields and were never out of the sound of barking dogs. They met people on the paths.

At first the Franciscan said, "Do not speak to anybody – they will wonder who you are." But he had to answer when greetings were spoken.

"Is this the way to Skodra? We are going to Skodra to the Bishop's house. This is my servant with me, who has come from the mountains.

"It is all right, you look like a servant in these clothes," he said to Lottar. "But do not speak – they will wonder, if you speak."

I had painted the walls of my bookstore a clear, light yellow. Yellow stands for intellectual curiosity. Somebody must have told me that. I opened the store in March of 1964. This was in Victoria, in British Columbia.

I sat there at the desk, with my offerings spread out behind me. The publishers' representatives had advised me to stock books about dogs and horses, sailing and gardening, bird books and flower books – they said that was all anybody in Victoria would buy. I flew against their advice and brought in novels and poetry and books that explained about Sufism and relativity and Linear B. And I had set out these books, when they came, so that Political Science could shade into Philosophy and Philosophy into Religion without a harsh break, so that compatible poets could nestle together, the arrangement of the shelves of books – I believed – reflecting a more or less natural ambling of the mind, in which treasures new and forgotten might be continually surfacing. I had taken all this care, and now what? Now I waited, and I felt like somebody who had got dramatically dressed up for a party, maybe even fetching jewels from the pawnshop or the family vault, only to discover that it was just a few neighbors playing cards. It was just meat loaf and mashed potatoes in the kitchen, and a glass of fizzy pink wine.

The store was often empty for a couple of hours at a time, and then when somebody did come in, it would be to ask about a book remembered from the Sunday-school library or a grandmother's bookcase or left behind twenty years ago in a foreign hotel. The title was usually forgotten, but the person would tell me the story. It is about this little girl who goes out to Australia with her father to mine the gold claims they have inherited. It is about the woman who had a baby all alone in Alaska. It is about a race between one of the old clipper ships and the first steamer, way back in the 1840s.

Oh, well. I just thought I'd ask.

They would leave without a glance at the riches around them.

A few people did exclaim in gratitude, said what a glorious addition to the town. They would browse for half an hour, an hour, before spending seventy-five cents.

It takes time.

I had found a one-room apartment with a kitchenette in an old building at a corner called the Dardanelles. The bed folded up into the wall. But I did not usually bother to fold it up, because I never had any company. And the hook seemed unsafe to me. I was afraid that the bed might leap out of the wall sometime when I was eating my tinned soup or baked-potato supper. It might kill me. Also, I kept the window open all the time, because I believed I could smell a whiff of escaping gas, even when the two burners and the oven were shut off. With the window open at home and the door open at the store, to entice the customers, it was necessary for me to be always bundled up in my black woolly sweater or my red corduroy dressing gown (a garment that had once left its pink tinge on all my forsaken husband's handkerchiefs and underwear). I had difficulty separating myself from these comforting articles of clothing so that they might be washed. I was sleepy much of the time, underfed and shivering.

But I was not despondent. I had made a desperate change in my life, and in spite of the regrets I suffered every day, I was proud of that. I felt as if I had finally come out into the world in a new true skin. Sitting at the desk, I made a cup of coffee or of thin red soup last an hour, clasping my hands around the cup while there was still any warmth to be got from it. I read, but without purpose or involvement. I read stray sentences from the books that I had always meant to read. Often these sentences seemed so satisfying to me, or so elusive and lovely, that I could not help abandoning all the surrounding words and giving myself up to a peculiar state. I was alert and dreamy, closed off from all particular people but conscious all the time of the city itself – which seemed a strange place.

A small city, here at the western edge of the country. Pockets of fakery for tourists. The Tudor shop fronts and double-decker buses and flowerpots and horse-drawn rides: almost insulting. But the sea light in the street, the spare and healthy old people leaning into the wind as they took their daily walks along the broom-topped cliffs, the shabby, slightly bizarre bungalows with their monkey-puzzle trees and ornate shrubs in the gardens. Chestnut trees blossom as spring comes on, hawthorn trees along the streets bear red-and-white flowers, oily-leaved bushes put out lush pink and rose-red blooms such as you would never see in the hinterlands. Like a town in a story, I thought – like the transplanted seaside town of the story set in New Zealand, in Tasmania. But something North American persists. So many people, after all, have come here from Winnipeg or Saskatchewan. At noon a smell of dinners cooking drifts out of poor, plain apartment buildings. Frying meat, boiling vegetables – farm dinners being cooked, in the middle of the day, in cramped kitchenettes.

How could I tell what I liked so much? Certainly it was not what a new merchant might be looking for – bustle and energy to raise the hope of commercial success. *Not much doing* was the message the town got across to me. And when a person who is opening a store doesn't mind hearing the message *Not much doing*, you could ask, What's going on? People open shops in order to sell things, they hope to become busy so that they will have to enlarge the shop, then to sell more things, and grow rich, and eventually not have to come into the shop at all. Isn't that true? But are there other people who open a shop with the hope of being sheltered there, among such things as they most value – the yarn or the teacups or the books – and with the idea only of making a comfortable assertion? They will become a part of the block, a part of the street, part of everybody's map of the town, and eventually of everybody's memories. They will sit and drink coffee in the middle of the morning, they will get out the familiar bits of tinsel at Christmas, they will wash the windows in spring before spreading out the new stock. Shops, to these people, are what a cabin in the woods might be to somebody else – a refuge and a justification.

Some customers are necessary, of course. The rent comes due and the stock will not pay for itself. I had inherited a little money – that was what had made it possible for me to come out here and get the shop going – but unless business picked up to some extent I could not last beyond the summer. I understood that. I was glad that more people started coming in as the weather warmed up. More books were sold, survival began to seem possible. Book prizes were due to be awarded in the schools at the end of term, and that brought the school-teachers with their lists and their praise and their unfortunate expectation of discounts. The people who came to browse were buying regularly, and some of them began to turn into friends – or the sort of friends I had here, where it seemed I would be happy to talk to people day after day and never learn their names.

When Lottar and the priest first saw the town of Skodra, it seemed to float above the mud flats, its domes and steeples shining as if they were made of mist. But when they entered it in the early evening all this tranquillity vanished. The streets were paved with big, rough stones and were full of people and donkey carts, roving dogs, pigs being driven somewhere, and smells of fires and cooking and dung and something terrible – like rotten hides. A man came along with a parrot on his shoulder. The bird seemed to be shrieking curses in an unknown language. Several times the Franciscan stopped people and asked the way to the Bishop's house, but they pushed by him without answering or laughed at him or said some words he didn't understand. A boy said that he would show the way, for money.

"We have no money," the Franciscan said. He pulled Lottar into a doorway and there they sat down to rest. "In Maltsia e madhe," he said, "many of these who think so well of themselves would soon sing a different tune."

Lottar's notion of running away and leaving him had

vanished. For one thing, she could not manage to ask directions any better than he could. For another, she felt that they were allies who could not survive in this place out of sight of each other. She had not understood how much she depended on the smell of his skin, the aggrieved determination of his long strides, the flourish of his black mustache.

The Franciscan jumped up and said he had remembered – he had remembered now the way to the Bishop's house. He hurried ahead of her through narrow, high-walled back streets where nothing of houses or courtyards could be seen – just walls and gates. The paving stones were thrust up so that walking here was as difficult as in the dry riverbed. But he was right, he gave a shout of triumph, they had come to the gate of the Bishop's house.

A servant opened the gate and let them in, but only after some high-pitched argument. Lottar was told to sit on the ground just inside the gate, and the Franciscan was led into the house to see the Bishop. Soon someone was sent through the streets to the British Consulate (Lottar was not told this), and he came back with the Consul's manservant. It was dark by then, and the Consul's servant carried a lantern. And Lottar was led away again. She followed the servant and his lantern to the consulate.

A tub of hot water for her to bathe in, in the courtyard. Her clothes taken away. Probably burned. Her greasy black, vermin-infested hair cut off. Kerosene poured on her scalp. She had to tell her story – the story of how she came to Maltsia e madhe – and this was difficult, because she was not used to speaking English, also because that time seemed so far away and unimportant. She had to learn to sleep on a mattress, to sit on a chair, to eat with a knife and fork.

As soon as possible they put her on a boat.

Charlotte stopped. She said, "That part is not of interest."

I had come to Victoria because it was the farthest place I could get to from London, Ontario, without going out of the country. In London, my husband, Donald, and I had rented a basement apartment in our house to a couple named Nelson and Sylvia. Nelson was an English major at the university and Sylvia was a nurse. Donald was a dermatologist, and I was doing a thesis on Mary Shelley – not very quickly. I had met Donald when I went to see him about a rash on my neck. He was eight years older than I was – a tall, freckled, blushing man, cleverer than he looked. A dermatologist sees grief and despair, though the problems that bring people to him may not be in the same class as tumors and blocked arteries. He sees sabotage from within, and truly unlucky fate. He sees how matters like love and happiness can be governed by a patch of riled-up cells. Experience of this sort had made Donald kind, in a cautious, impersonal way. He said that my rash was probably due to stress, and that he could see that I was going to be a wonderful woman, once I got a few problems under control.

We invited Sylvia and Nelson upstairs for dinner, and Sylvia told us about the tiny town they both came from, in Northern Ontario. She said that Nelson had always been the smartest person in their class and in their school and possibly in the whole town. When she said this, Nelson looked at her with a perfectly flat and devastating expression, an expression that seemed to be waiting with infinite patience and the mildest curiosity for some explanation, and Sylvia laughed and said, "Just kidding, of course."

When Sylvia was working late shifts at the hospital, I sometimes asked Nelson to share a meal with us in a more informal way. We got used to his silences and his indifferent table manners and to the fact that he did not eat rice or noodles, eggplant, olives, shrimp, peppers, or avocados, and no doubt a lot of other things, because those had not been familiar foods in the town in Northern Ontario.

Nelson looked older than he was. He was short and sturdily built, sallow-skinned, unsmiling, with a suggestion of mature scorn and handy pugnaciousness laid over his features, so that it seemed he might be a hockey coach, or an intelligent, uneducated, fair-minded, and foul-mouthed foreman of a construction gang, rather than a shy, twenty-two-year-old student.

He was not shy in love. I found him resourceful and determined. The seduction was mutual, and it was a first affair for both of us. I had once heard somebody say, at a party, that one of the nice things about marriage was that you could have real affairs – an affair before marriage could always turn out to be nothing but courtship. I was disgusted by this speech, and frightened to think that life could be so bleak and trivial. But once my own affair with Nelson started, I was amazed all the time. There was no bleakness or triviality about it, only ruthlessness and clarity of desire, and sparkling deception.

Nelson was the one who first faced up to things. One afternoon he turned on his back and said hoarsely and defiantly, "We are going to have to leave."

I thought he meant that he and Sylvia would have to leave, they could not go on living in this house. But he meant himself and me. "We" meant himself and me. Of course he and I had said "we" of our arrangements, of our transgression. Now he had made it the "we" of our decision – perhaps of a life together.

My thesis was supposed to be on Mary Shelley's later novels, the ones nobody knows about. *Lodore*, *Perkin Warbeck*, *The Last Man*. But I was really more interested in Mary's life before she learned her sad lessons and buckled down to raising her son to be a baronet. I loved to read about the other women who had hated or envied or traipsed along: Harriet, Shelley's first wife, and Fanny Imlay, who was Mary's half-sister and may have been in love with Shelley herself, and

Mary's stepsister, Mary Jane Clairmont, who took my own name – Claire – and joined Mary and Shelley on their unwed honeymoon so that she could keep on chasing Byron. I had often talked to Donald about impetuous Mary and married Shelley and their meetings at Mary's mother's grave, about the suicides of Harriet and Fanny and the persistence of Claire, who had a baby by Byron. But I never mentioned any of this to Nelson, partly because we had little time for talk and partly because I did not want him to think that I drew some sort of comfort or inspiration from this mishmash of love and despair and treachery and self-dramatizing. I did not want to think so myself. And Nelson was not a fan of the nineteenth century or the Romantics. He said so. He said that he wanted to do something on the Muckrakers. Perhaps he meant that as a joke.

Sylvia did not behave like Harriet. Her mind was not influenced or impeded by literature, and when she found out what had been going on, she went into a wholesome rage.

"You blithering idiot," she said to Nelson.

"You two-faced twit," she said to me.

The four of us were in our living room. Donald went on cleaning and filling his pipe, tapped it and lit it, nursed and inspected it, drew on it, lit it again – all so much the way someone would do in a movie that I was embarrassed for him. Then he put some books and the latest copy of *Maclean's* into his briefcase, went to the bathroom to get his razor and to the bedroom to get his pajamas, and walked out.

He went straight to the apartment of a young widow who worked as a secretary at his clinic. In a letter he wrote to me later, he said that he had never thought of this woman except as a friend until that night, when it suddenly dawned on him what a pleasure it would be to love a kind and sensible, *unwracked-up* sort of person.

Sylvia had to be at work at eleven o'clock. Nelson usually walked her over to the hospital – they did not have a car. On this night she told him that she would rather be escorted by a skunk.

That left Nelson and me alone together. The scene had lasted a much shorter time than I had expected. Nelson seemed gloomy but relieved, and if I felt that short shrift had been given to the notion of love as a capturing tide, a glorious and harrowing event, I knew better than to show it.

We lay down on the bed to talk about our plans and ended up making love, because that was what we were used to doing. Sometime during the night Nelson woke up and thought it best to go downstairs to his own bed.

I got up in the dark, dressed, packed a suitcase, wrote a note, and walked to the phone at the corner, where I called a taxi. I took the six-o'clock train to Toronto, connecting with the train to Vancouver. It was cheaper to take the train, if you were willing to sit up for three nights, which I was.

So there I sat, in the sad, shambling morning in the day coach, coming down the steep-walled Fraser Canyon into the sodden Fraser Valley, where smoke hung over the small, dripping houses, the brown vines, the thorny bushes and huddled sheep. It was in December that this earthquake in my life had arrived. Christmas was cancelled for me. Winter with its snowdrifts and icicles and invigorating blizzards was cancelled by this blurred season of muck and rain. I was constipated, I knew that I had bad breath, my limbs were cramped, and my spirits utterly bleak. And did I not think then, What nonsense it is to suppose one man so different from another when all that life really boils down to is getting a decent cup of coffee and room to stretch out in? Did I not think that even if Nelson were sitting here beside me, he would have turned into a gray-faced stranger whose desolation and unease merely extended my own?

No. No. Nelson would still be Nelson to me. I had not changed, with regard to his skin and his smell and his forbidding eyes. It seemed to be the outside of Nelson which came most readily to my mind, and in the case of Donald it was his inner quakes and sympathies, the labored-at kindness and those private misgivings that I had got knowledge of by wheedling and conniving. If I could have my love of these two men together, and settle it on one man, I would be a happy woman. If I could care for everybody in the world as minutely as I did for Nelson, and as calmly, as uncarnally as I now did for Donald, I would be a saint. Instead, I had dealt a twofold, a wanton-seeming, blow.

The regular customers who had changed into something like friends were: a middle-aged woman who was a chartered accountant but preferred such reading as *Six Existentialist Thinkers* and *The Meaning of Meaning*; a provincial civil servant who ordered splendid, expensive works of pornography such as I had not known existed (their elaborate Oriental, Etruscan connections seemed to me grotesque and uninteresting, compared to the simple, effective, longed-for rituals of myself and Nelson); a Notary Public who lived behind his office at the foot of Johnson Street ("I live in the slums," he told me. "Some night I expect a big bruiser of a fellow to lurch around the corner hollering '*Ste-el-la.*'"); and the woman I knew later as Charlotte – the Notary Public called her the Duchess. None of these people cared much for one another, and an early attempt that I made to bring the accountant and the Notary Public into conversation was a fizzle.

"Spare me the females with the withered, painted faces," the Notary Public said, the next time he came in. "I hope you haven't got her lurking around anywhere tonight."

It was true that the accountant painted her thin, intelligent, fifty-year-old face with a heavy hand, and drew on eyebrows that were like two strokes of India ink. But who was the Notary Public to talk, with his stumpy, nicotined teeth and pocked cheeks?

"I got the impression of a rather superficial fellow," the accountant said, as if she had guessed and bravely discounted the remarks made about herself.

So much for trying to corral people into couples, I wrote to Donald. *And who am I to try?* I wrote to Donald regularly, describing the store, and the city, and even, as well as I could, my own unaccountable feelings. He was living with Helen, the secretary. I wrote also to Nelson, who might or might not be living alone, might or might not be reunited with Sylvia. I didn't think he was. I thought she would believe in inexcusable behavior and definite endings. He had a new address. I had looked it up in the London phone book at the public library. Donald, after a grudging start, was writing back. He wrote impersonal, mildly interesting letters about people we both knew, events at the clinic. Nelson did not write at all. I started sending registered letters. Now I knew at least that he picked them up.

Charlotte and Gjurdhi must have come into the store together, but I did not understand that they were a couple until it was time for them to leave. Charlotte was a heavy, shapeless, but quick-moving woman, with a pink face, bright blue eyes, and a lot of glistening white hair, worn like a girl's, waving down over her shoulders. Though the weather was fairly warm, she was wearing a cape of dark-gray velvet with a scanty gray fur trim – a garment that looked as if it belonged, or had once belonged, on the stage. A loose shirt and a pair of plaid wool slacks showed underneath, and there were open sandals on her broad, bare, dusty feet. She clanked as if she wore hidden armor. An arm reaching up to get a book showed what caused the clanking. Bracelets – any number of them, heavy or slender, tarnished or bright. Some were set with large, square stones, the color of toffee or blood.

"Imagine this old fraud being still on the go," she said to me, as if continuing some desultory and enjoyable conversation.

She had picked up a book by Anaïs Nin.

"Don't pay any attention," she said. "I say terrible things. I'm quite fond of the woman, really. It's him I can't stand."

"Henry Miller?" I said, beginning to follow this.

"That's right." She went on talking about Henry Miller, Paris, California, in a scoffing, energetic, half-affectionate way. She seemed to have been neighbors, at least, with the people she was talking about. Finally, naïvely, I asked her if this was the case.

"No, no. I just feel I know them all. Not personally. Well – personally. Yes, personally. What other way is there to know them? I mean, I haven't met them, face-to-face. But in their books? Surely that's what they intend? I know them. I know them to the point where they bore me. Just like anybody you know. Don't you find that?"

She drifted over to the table where I had laid out the New Directions paperbacks.

"Here's the new bunch, then," she said. "Oh, my," she said, widening her eyes at the photographs of Ginsberg and Corso and Ferlinghetti. She began reading, so attentively that I thought the next thing she said must be part of some poem.

"I've gone by and I've seen you here," she said. She put the book down and I realized she meant me. "I've seen you sitting in here, and I've thought a young woman would probably like to be outside some of the time. In the sun. I don't suppose you'd consider hiring me to sit there, so you could get out?"

"Well, I would like to –" I said.

"I'm not so dumb. I'm fairly knowledgeable, really. Ask me who wrote Ovid's *Metamorphoses*. It's all right, you don't have to laugh."

"I would like to, but I really can't afford to."

"Oh, well. You're probably right. I'm not very chic. And I would probably foul things up. I would argue with people if they were buying books I thought were dreadful." She did not seem disappointed. She picked up a copy of *The Dud Avocado* and said, "There! I have to buy this, for the title."

She gave a little whistle, and the man it seemed to be meant for looked up from the table of books he had been staring at, near the back of the store. I had known he was there but had not connected him with her. I thought he was just one of those men who wander in off the street, alone, and stand looking about, as if trying to figure out what sort of place this is or what the books are for. Not a drunk or a panhandler, and certainly not anybody to be worried about – just one of a number of shabby, utterly uncommunicative old men who belong to the city somewhat as the pigeons do, moving restlessly all day within a limited area, never looking at people's faces. He was wearing a coat that came down to his ankles, made of some shiny, rubberized, liver-colored material, and a brown velvet cap with a tassel. The sort of cap a doddery old scholar or a clergyman might wear in an English movie. There was, then, a similarity between them – they were both wearing things that might have been discards from a costume box. But close up he looked years older than she. A long, yellowish face, drooping tobacco-brown eyes, an unsavory, straggling mustache. Some faint remains of handsomeness, or potency. A quenched ferocity. He came at her whistle – which seemed half serious, half a joke – and stood by, mute and self-respecting as a dog or a donkey, while the woman prepared to pay.

At that time, the government of British Columbia applied a sales tax to books. In this case it was four cents.

"I can't pay that," she said. "A tax on books. I think it is immoral. I would rather go to jail. Don't you agree?"

I agreed. I did not point out – as I would have done with anybody else – that the store would not be let off the hook on that account.

"Don't I sound appalling?" she said. "See what this government can do to people? It makes them into *orators*."

She put the book in her bag without paying the four cents, and never paid the tax on any future occasion.

I described the two of them to the Notary Public. He knew at once who I meant.

"I call them the Duchess and the Algerian," he said. "I don't know what the background is. I think maybe he's a retired terrorist. They go around the town with a wagon, like scavengers."

I got a note asking me to supper on a Sunday evening. It was signed *Charlotte*, without a surname, but the wording and handwriting were quite formal.

My husband Gjurdhi and I would be delighted –

Up until then I had not wished for any invitations of this sort and would have been embarrassed and disturbed to get one. So the pleasure I felt surprised me. Charlotte held out a decided promise; she was unlike the others whom I wanted to see only in the store.

The building where they lived was on Pandora Street. It was covered with mustard stucco and had a tiny, tiled vestibule that reminded me of a public toilet. It did not smell, though, and the apartment was not really dirty, just horrendously untidy. Books were stacked against the walls, and pieces of patterned cloth were hung up droopily to hide the wallpaper. There were bamboo blinds on the window, sheets of colored paper – surely flammable – pinned over the light bulbs.

"What a darling you are to come," cried Charlotte. "We were afraid you would have tons more interesting things to do than visiting ancient old us. Where can you sit down? What about here?" She took a pile of magazines off a wicker chair. "Is that comfortable? It makes such interesting noises, wicker. Sometimes I'll be sitting here alone and that chair will start creaking and cracking exactly as if someone were shifting around in it. I could say it was a presence, but I'm no good at believing in that rubbish. I've tried."

Gjurdhi poured out a sweet yellow wine. For me a long-stemmed glass that had not been dusted, for Charlotte a glass tumbler, for himself a plastic cup. It seemed impossible that any dinner could come out of the little kitchen alcove, where foodstuffs and pots and dishes were piled helter-skelter, but there was a good smell of roasting chicken, and in a little while Gjurdhi brought out the first course – platters of sliced cucumber, dishes of yogurt. I sat in the wicker chair and Charlotte in the single armchair. Gjurdhi sat on the floor. Charlotte was wearing her slacks, and a rose-colored T-shirt which clung to her unsupported breast. She had painted her toenails to match the T-shirt. Her bracelets clanked against the plate as she picked up the slices of cucumber. (We were eating with our fingers.) Gjurdhi wore his cap and a dark-red silky dressing gown over his trousers. Stains had mingled with its pattern.

After the cucumber, we ate chicken cooked with raisins in golden spices, and sour bread, and rice. Charlotte and I were provided with forks, but Gjurdhi scooped the rice up with the bread. I would often think of this meal in the years that followed, when this kind of food, this informal way of sitting and eating, and even some version of the style and the untidiness of the room, would become familiar and fashionable. The people I knew, and I myself, would give up – for a while – on dining-room tables, matching wineglasses, to some extent on cutlery or chairs. When I was being entertained, or making a stab at entertaining people, in this way, I would think of Charlotte and Gjurdhi and the edge of true privation, the risky authenticity that marked them off from all these later imitations. At the time, it was all new to me, and I was both uneasy and delighted. I hoped to be worthy of such exoticism but not to be tried too far.

Mary Shelley came to light shortly. I recited the titles of the later novels, and Charlotte said dreamily, "Per-kin War-beck. Wasn't he the one – wasn't he the one who pretended to be a little Prince who was murdered in the Tower?"

She was the only person I had ever met – not a historian, not a *Tudor* historian – who had known this.

"That would make a movie," she said. "Don't you think? The question I always think about Pretenders like that is who do *they* think they are? Do they believe it's true, or what? But Mary Shelley's own life is the movie, isn't it? I wonder there hasn't been one made. Who would play Mary, do you think? No. No, first of all, start with Harriet. Who would play Harriet?

"Someone who would look well drowned," she said, ripping off a golden chunk of chicken. "Elizabeth Taylor? Not a big enough part. Susannah York?

"Who was the father?" she wondered, referring to Harriet's unborn baby. "I don't think it was Shelley. I've never thought so. Do you?"

This was all very well, very enjoyable, but I had hoped we would get to explanations – personal revelations, if not exactly confidences. You did expect some of that, on occasions like this. Hadn't Sylvia, at my own table, told about the town in Northern Ontario and about Nelson's being the smartest person in the school? I was surprised at how eager I found myself, at last, to tell my story. Donald and Nelson – I was looking forward to telling the truth, or some of it, in all its wounding complexity, to a person who would not be surprised or outraged by it. I would have liked to puzzle over my behavior, in good company. Had I taken on Donald as a father figure – or as a parent figure, since both my parents were dead? Had I deserted him because I was angry at *them* for deserting *me*? What did Nelson's silence mean, and was it now permanent? (But I did not think, after all, that I would tell anybody about the letter that had been returned to me last week, marked "Not Known at This Address.")

This was not what Charlotte had in mind. There was no opportunity, no exchange. After the chicken, the wineglass and the tumbler and cup were taken away and filled with an extremely sweet pink sherbet that was easier to drink than to eat with a spoon. Then came small cups of desperately strong coffee. Gjurdhi lit two candles as the room grew darker, and I was given one of these to carry to the bathroom, which turned out to be a toilet with a shower. Charlotte said the lights were not working.

"Some repairs going on," she said. "Or else they have taken a whim. I really think they take whims. But fortunately we have our gas stove. As long as we have a gas stove we can laugh at their whims. My only regret is that we cannot play any music. I was going to play some old political songs – 'I dreamed I saw Joe Hill last night,'" she sang in a mocking baritone. "Do you know that one?"

I did know it. Donald used to sing it when he was a little drunk. Usually the people who sang "Joe Hill" had certain vague but discernible political sympathies, but with Charlotte I did not think this would be so. She would not operate from sympathies, from principles. She would be playful about what other people took seriously. I was not certain what I felt about her. It was not simple liking or respect. It was more like a wish to move in her element, unsurprised. To be buoyant, self-mocking, gently malicious, unquenchable.

Gjurdhi, meanwhile, was showing me some of the books. How had this started? Probably from a comment I made – how many of them there were, something of that sort – when I stumbled over some on my way back from the toilet. He was bringing forward books with bindings of leather or imitation leather – how could I know the difference? – with marbled endpapers, watercolor frontispieces, steel engravings. At first, I believed admiration might be all that was required, and I admired everything. But close to my ear I heard the mention of money – was that the first distinct thing I had ever heard Gjurdhi say?

"I only handle new books," I said. "These are marvelous, but I don't really know anything about them. It's a completely different business, books like these."

Gjurdhi shook his head as if I had not understood and he would now try, firmly, to explain again. He repeated the price in a more insistent voice. Did he think I was trying to haggle with him? Or perhaps he was telling me what he had paid for the book? We might be having a speculative conversation about the price it might be sold for – not about whether I should buy it.

I kept saying no, and yes, trying to juggle these responses appropriately. *No*, I cannot take them for my store. *Yes*, they are very fine. *No*, truly, I'm sorry, I am not the one to judge.

"If we had been living in another country, Gjurdhi and I might have done something," Charlotte was saying. "Or even if the movies in this country had ever got off the ground. That's what I would love to have done. Got work in the movies. As extras. Or maybe we are not bland enough types to be extras, maybe they would have found bit parts for us. I believe extras have to be the sort that don't stand out in a crowd, so you can use them over and over again. Gjurdhi and I are more memorable than that. Gjurdhi in particular – you could *use* that face."

She paid no attention to the second conversation that had developed, but continued talking to me, shaking her head indulgently at Gjurdhi now and then, to suggest that he was behaving in a way she found engaging, though perhaps importunate. I had to talk to him softly, sideways, nodding all the while in response to her.

"Really you should take them to the Antiquarian Bookstore," I said. "Yes, they are quite beautiful. Books like these are out of my range."

Gjurdhi did not whine, his manner was not ingratiating. Peremptory, rather. It seemed as if he would give me orders, and would be most disgusted if I did not capitulate. In my confusion I helped myself to more of the yellow wine, pouring it into my unwashed sherbet glass. This was probably a dire offense. Gjurdhi looked horridly displeased.

"Can you imagine illustrations in modern novels?" said Charlotte, finally consenting to tie the two conversations together. "For instance, in Norman Mailer? They would have to be abstracts. Don't you think? Sort of barbed wire and blotches?"

I went home with a headache and a feeling of jangled inadequacy. I was a prude, that was all, when it came to mixing up buying and selling with hospitality. I had perhaps behaved clumsily, I had disappointed them. And they had disappointed me. Making me wonder why I had been asked.

I was homesick for Donald, because of "Joe Hill."

I also had a longing for Nelson, because of an expression on Charlotte's face as I was leaving. A savoring and contented look that I knew had to do with Gjurdhi, though I hardly wanted to believe that. It made me think that after I walked downstairs and left the building and went into the street, some hot and skinny, slithery, yellowish, indecent old beast, some mangy but urgent old tiger, was going to pounce among the books and the dirty dishes and conduct a familiar rampage.

A day or so later I got a letter from Donald. He wanted a divorce, so that he could marry Helen.

I hired a clerk, a college girl, to come in for a couple of hours in the afternoon, so I could get to the bank, and do some office work. The first time Charlotte saw her she went up to the desk and patted a stack of books sitting there, ready for quick sale.

"Is this what the office managers are telling their minions to buy?" she said. The girl smiled cautiously and didn't answer.

Charlotte was right. It was a book called *Psycho-Cybernetics*, about having a positive self-image.

"You were smart to hire her instead of me," Charlotte said. "She is much niftier-looking, and she won't shoot her mouth off and scare the customers away. She won't have *opinions*."

"There's something I ought to tell you about that woman," the clerk said, after Charlotte left.

That part is not of interest.

"What do you mean?" I said. But my mind had been wandering, that third afternoon in the hospital. Just at the last part of Charlotte's story I had thought of a special-order book that hadn't come in, on Mediterranean cruises. Also I had been thinking about the Notary Public, who had been beaten about the head the night before, in his office on Johnson Street. He was not dead but he might be blinded. Robbery? Or an act of revenge, outrage, connected with a layer of his life that I hadn't guessed at?

Melodrama and confusion made this place seem more ordinary to me, but less within my grasp.

"Of course it is of interest," I said. "All of it. It's a fascinating story."

"Fascinating," repeated Charlotte in a mincing way. She made a face, so she looked like a baby vomiting out a spoonful of pap. Her eyes, still fixed on me, seemed to be losing color, losing their childish, bright, and self-important blue. Fretfulness was changing into disgust. An expression of vicious disgust, she showed, of unspeakable weariness such as people might show to the mirror but hardly ever to one another. Perhaps because of the thoughts that were already in my head, it occurred to me that Charlotte might die. She might die at any moment. At this moment. Now.

She motioned at the water glass, with its crooked plastic straw. I held the glass so that she could drink, and supported her head. I could feel the heat of her scalp, a throbbing at the base of her skull. She drank thirstily, and the terrible look left her face.

She said, "Stale."

"I think it would make an excellent movie," I said, easing her back onto the pillows. She grabbed my wrist, then let it go.

"Where did you get the idea?" I said.

"From life," said Charlotte indistinctly. "Wait a moment." She turned her head away, on the pillow, as if she had to arrange something in private. Then she recovered, and she told a little more.

Charlotte did not die. At least she did not die in the hospital. When I came in rather late, the next afternoon, her bed was empty and freshly made up. The nurse who had talked to me before was trying to take the temperature of the woman tied in the chair. She laughed at the look on my face.

"Oh, no!" she said. "Not that. She checked out of here this morning. Her husband came and got her. We were transferring her to a long-term place out in Saanich, and he was supposed to be taking her there. He said he had the taxi outside. Then we get this phone call that they never showed up! They were in great spirits when they left. He brought her a pile of money, and she was throwing it up in the air. I don't know – maybe it was only dollar bills. But we haven't a clue where they've got to."

I walked around to the apartment building on Pandora Street. I thought they might simply have gone home. They might have lost the instructions about how to get to the nursing home and not wanted to ask. They might have decided to stay together in their apartment no matter what. They might have turned on the gas.

At first I could not find the building and thought that I must be in the wrong block. But I remembered the corner store and some of the houses. The building had been changed – that was what had happened. The stucco had been painted pink; large, new windows and French doors had been put in; little balconies with wrought-iron railings had been attached. The fancy balconies had been painted white, the whole place had the air of an ice-cream parlor. No doubt it had been renovated inside as well, and the rents increased, so that people like Charlotte and Gjurdhi could have no hope of living there. I checked the names by the door, and of course theirs were gone. They must have moved out some time ago.

The change in the apartment building seemed to have some message for me. It was about vanishing. I knew that Charlotte and Gjurdhi had not actually vanished – they were somewhere, living or dead. But for me they had vanished. And because of this fact – not really because of any loss of them – I was tipped into dismay more menacing than any of the little eddies of regret that had caught me in the past year. I had lost my bearings. I had to get back to the store so my clerk could go home, but I felt as if I could as easily walk another way, just any way at all. My connection was in danger – that was all. Sometimes our connection is frayed, it is in danger, it seems almost lost. Views and streets deny knowledge of us, the air grows thin. Wouldn't we rather have a destiny to submit to, then, something that claims us, anything, instead of such flimsy choices, arbitrary days?

I let myself slip, then, into imagining a life with Nelson. If I had done so accurately, this is how it would have gone.

He comes to Victoria. But he does not like the idea of working in the store, serving the public. He gets a job teaching at a boys' school, a posh place where his look of lower-class toughness, his bruising manners, soon make him a favorite.

We move from the apartment at the Dardanelles to a roomy bungalow a few blocks from the sea. We marry.

But this is the beginning of a period of estrangement. I become pregnant. Nelson falls in love with the mother of a student. I fall in love with an intern I meet in the hospital during labor.

We get over all this – Nelson and I do. We have another child. We acquire friends, furniture, rituals. We go to too many parties at certain seasons of the year, and talk regularly about starting a new life, somewhere far away, where we don't know anybody.

We become distant, close – distant, close – over and over again.

As I entered the store, I was aware of a man standing near the door, half looking in the window, half looking up the street, then looking at me. He was a short man dressed in a trenchcoat and a fedora. I had the impression of someone disguised. Jokingly disguised. He moved toward me and bumped my shoulder, and I cried out as if I had received the shock of my life, and indeed it was true that I had. For this really was Nelson, come to claim me. Or at least to accost me, and see what would happen.

We have been very happy.
I have often felt completely alone.
There is always in this life something to discover.
The days and the years have gone by in some sort of blur.
On the whole, I am satisfied.

When Lottar was leaving the Bishop's courtyard, she was wrapped in a long cloak they had given her, perhaps to conceal her ragged clothing, or to contain her smell. The Consul's servant spoke to her in English, telling her where they were going. She could understand him but could not reply. It was not quite dark. She could still see the pale shapes of roses and oranges in the Bishop's garden.

The Bishop's man was holding the gate open.

She had never seen the Bishop at all. And she had not seen the Franciscan since he had followed the Bishop's man into the house. She called out for him now as she was leaving. She had no name to call, so she called, "*Xoti! Xoti! Xoti,*" which means "leader" or "master" in the language of the Ghegs. But no answer came, and the Consul's servant swung his lantern impatiently, showing her the way to go. Its light fell by accident on the Franciscan standing half concealed by a tree. It was a little orange tree he stood behind. His face, pale as the oranges were in that light, looked out of the branches, all its swarthiness drained away. It was a wan face hanging in the tree, its melancholy expression quite impersonal and undemanding, like the expression you might see on the face of a devout but proud apostle in a church window. Then it was gone, taking the breath out of her body, as she knew too late.

She called him and called him, and when the boat came into the harbor at Trieste he was waiting on the dock.

Meneseteung

I

Columbine, bloodroot,
And wild bergamot,
Gathering armfuls,
Giddily we go.

Offerings the book is called. Gold lettering on a dull-blue cover. The author's full name underneath: Almeda Joynt Roth. The local paper, the *Vidette*, referred to her as "our poetess." There seems to be a mixture of respect and contempt, both for her calling and for her sex – or for their predictable conjuncture. In the front of the book is a photograph, with the photographer's name in one corner, and the date: 1865. The book was published later, in 1873.

The poetess has a long face; a rather long nose; full, sombre dark eyes, which seem ready to roll down her cheeks like giant tears; a lot of dark hair gathered around her face in droopy rolls and curtains. A streak of gray hair plain to see, although she is, in this picture, only twenty-five. Not a pretty girl but the sort of woman who may age well, who probably won't get fat. She wears a tucked and braid-trimmed dark dress or jacket, with a lacy, floppy arrangement of white material –

frills or a bow – filling the deep V at the neck. She also wears a hat, which might be made of velvet, in a dark color to match the dress. It's the untrimmed, shapeless hat, something like a soft beret, that makes me see artistic intentions, or at least a shy and stubborn eccentricity, in this young woman, whose long neck and forward-inclining head indicate as well that she is tall and slender and somewhat awkward. From the waist up, she looks like a young nobleman of another century. But perhaps it was the fashion.

"In 1854," she writes in the preface to her book, "my father brought us – my mother, my sister Catherine, my brother William, and me – to the wilds of Canada West (as it then was). My father was a harness-maker by trade, but a cultivated man who could quote by heart from the Bible, Shakespeare, and the writings of Edmund Burke. He prospered in this newly opened land and was able to set up a harness and leather-goods store, and after a year to build the comfortable house in which I live (alone) today. I was fourteen years old, the eldest of the children, when we came into this country from Kingston, a town whose handsome streets I have not seen again but often remember. My sister was eleven and my brother nine. The third summer that we lived here, my brother and sister were taken ill of a prevalent fever and died within a few days of each other. My dear mother did not regain her spirits after this blow to our family. Her health declined, and after another three years she died. I then became housekeeper to my father and was happy to make his home for twelve years, until he died suddenly one morning at his shop.

"From my earliest years I have delighted in verse and I have occupied myself – and sometimes allayed my griefs, which have been no more, I know, than any sojourner on earth must encounter – with many floundering efforts at its composition. My fingers, indeed, were always too clumsy for crochetwork, and those dazzling productions of embroidery which one sees often today – the overflowing fruit and flower baskets, the little Dutch boys, the bonneted maidens with their watering cans – have likewise proved to be beyond my skill. So I offer instead, as the product of my leisure hours, these rude posies, these ballads, couplets, reflections."

Titles of some of the poems: "Children at Their Games," "The Gypsy Fair," "A Visit to My Family," "Angels in the Snow," "Champlain at the Mouth of the Meneseteung," "The Passing of the Old Forest," and "A Garden Medley." There are other, shorter poems, about birds and wildflowers and snowstorms. There is some comically intentioned doggerel about what people are thinking about as they listen to the sermon in church.

"Children at Their Games": The writer, a child, is playing with her brother and sister – one of those games in which children on different sides try to entice and catch each other. She plays on in the deepening twilight, until she realizes that she is alone, and much older. Still she hears the (ghostly) voices of her brother and sister calling. *Come over, come over, let Meda come over.* (Perhaps Almeda was called Meda in the family, or perhaps she shortened her name to fit the poem.)

"The Gypsy Fair": The Gypsies have an encampment near the town, a "fair," where they sell cloth and trinkets, and the writer as a child is afraid that she may be stolen by them, taken away from her family. Instead, her family has been taken away from her, stolen by Gypsies she can't locate or bargain with.

"A Visit to My Family": A visit to the cemetery, a one-sided conversation.

"Angels in the Snow": The writer once taught her brother and sister to make "angels" by lying down in the snow and moving their arms to create wing shapes. Her brother always jumped up carelessly, leaving an angel with a crippled wing. Will this be made perfect in Heaven, or will he be flying with his own makeshift, in circles?

"Champlain at the Mouth of the Meneseteung": This poem celebrates the popular, untrue belief that the explorer sailed down the eastern shore of Lake Huron and landed at the mouth of the major river.

"The Passing of the Old Forest": A list of all the trees – their names, appearance, and uses – that were cut down in the original forest, with a general description of the bears, wolves, eagles, deer, waterfowl.

"A Garden Medley": Perhaps planned as a companion to the forest poem. Catalogue of plants brought from European countries, with bits of history and legend attached, and final Canadianness resulting from this mixture.

The poems are written in quatrains or couplets. There are a couple of attempts at sonnets, but mostly the rhyme scheme is simple – *a b a b* or *a b c b*. The rhyme used is what was once called "masculine" ("shore"/"before"), though once in a while it is "feminine" ("quiver"/"river"). Are those terms familiar anymore? No poem is unrhymed.

II

White roses cold as snow
Bloom where those "'angels" lie.
Do they but rest below
Or, in God's wonder, fly?

In 1879, Almeda Roth was still living in the house at the corner of Pearl and Dufferin streets, the house her father had built for his family. The house is there today; the manager of the liquor store lives in it. It's covered with aluminum siding; a closed-in porch has replaced the veranda. The woodshed, the fence, the gates, the privy, the barn – all these are gone. A photograph taken in the eighteen-eighties shows them all in place. The house and fence look a little shabby, in need of paint, but perhaps that is just because of the bleached-out look of the brownish photograph. The lace-curtained windows look like white eyes. No big shade tree is in sight, and, in fact, the tall elms that overshadowed the town until the nineteen-fifties, as well as the maples that shade it now, are skinny young trees with rough fences around them to protect them from the cows. Without the shelter of those trees, there is a great exposure – back yards, clotheslines, woodpiles, patchy sheds and barns and privies – all bare, exposed, provisional-looking. Few houses would have anything like a lawn, just a patch of plantains and anthills and raked dirt. Perhaps petunias growing on top of a stump, in a round box. Only the main street is gravelled; the other streets are dirt roads, muddy or dusty according to season. Yards must be fenced to keep animals out. Cows are tethered in vacant lots or pastured in back yards, but sometimes they get loose. Pigs get loose, too, and dogs roam free or nap in a lordly way on the boardwalks. The town has taken root, it's not going to vanish, yet it still has some of the look of an encampment. And, like an encampment, it's busy all the time – full of people, who, within the town, usually walk wherever they're going; full of animals, which leave horse buns, cow pats, dog turds that ladies have to hitch up their skirts for; full of the noise of building and of drivers shouting at their horses and of the trains that come in several times a day.

I read about that life in the *Vidette*.

The population is younger than it is now, than it will ever be again. People past fifty usually don't come to a raw, new place. There are quite a few people in the cemetery already, but most of them died young, in accidents or childbirth or epidemics. It's youth that's in evidence in town. Children – boys – rove through the streets in gangs. School is compulsory for only four months a year, and there are lots of occasional jobs that even a child of eight or nine can do – pulling flax, holding horses, delivering groceries, sweeping the boardwalk in front of stores. A good deal of time they spend looking for adventures. One day they follow an old woman, a drunk nicknamed Queen Aggie. They get her into a wheelbarrow and trundle her all over town, then dump her into a ditch to sober her up. They also spend a lot of time around the railway station. They jump on shunting cars and dart between them and dare each other to take chances, which once in a while result in their getting maimed or killed. And they keep an eye out for any strangers coming into town. They follow them, offer to carry their bags, and direct them (for a five-cent piece) to a hotel. Strangers who don't look so prosperous are taunted and tormented. Speculation surrounds all of them – it's like a cloud of flies. Are they coming to town to start up a new business, to persuade people to invest in some scheme, to sell cures or gimmicks, to preach on the street corners? All these things are possible any day of the week. Be on your guard, the *Vidette* tells people. These are times of opportunity and danger. Tramps, confidence men, hucksters, shysters, plain thieves are travelling the roads, and particularly the railroads. Thefts are announced: money invested and never seen again, a pair of trousers taken from the clothesline, wood from the woodpile, eggs from the henhouse. Such incidents increase in the hot weather.

Hot weather brings accidents, too. More horses run wild then, upsetting buggies. Hands caught in the wringer while doing the washing, a man lopped in two at the sawmill, a leaping boy killed in a fall of lumber at the lumberyard. Nobody sleeps well. Babies wither with summer complaint, and fat people can't catch their breath. Bodies must be buried in a hurry. One day a man goes through the streets ringing a cowbell and calling, "Repent! Repent!" It's not a stranger this time, it's a young man who works at the butcher shop. Take him home, wrap him in cold wet cloths, give him some nerve medicine, keep him in bed, pray for his wits. If he doesn't recover, he must go to the asylum.

Almeda Roth's house faces on Dufferin Street, which is a street of considerable respectability. On this street, merchants, a mill owner, an operator of salt wells have their houses. But Pearl Street, which her back windows overlook and her back gate opens onto, is another story. Workmen's houses are adjacent to hers. Small but decent row houses – that is all right. Things deteriorate toward the end of the block, and the next, last one becomes dismal. Nobody but the poorest people, the unrespectable and undeserving poor, would live there at the edge of a boghole (drained since then), called the Pearl Street Swamp. Bushy and luxuriant weeds grow there, makeshift shacks have been put up, there are piles of refuse and debris and crowds of runty children, slops are flung from doorways. The town tries to compel these people to build privies, but they would just as soon go in the bushes. If a gang of boys goes down there in search of adventure, it's likely they'll get more than they bargained for. It is said that even the town constable won't go down Pearl Street on a Saturday night. Almeda Roth has never walked past the row housing. In one of those houses lives the young girl Annie, who helps her with her housecleaning. That young girl herself, being a decent girl, has never walked down to the last block or the swamp. No decent woman ever would.

But that same swamp, lying to the east of Almeda Roth's house, presents a fine sight at dawn. Almeda sleeps at the back of the house. She keeps to the same bedroom she once shared with her sister Catherine – she would not think of moving to the large front bedroom, where her mother used to lie in bed all day, and which was later the solitary domain of her father. From her window she can see the sun rising, the swamp mist filling with light, the bulky, nearest trees floating against that mist and the trees behind turning transparent. Swamp oaks, soft maples, tamarack, bitternut.

III

Here where the river meets the inland sea,
Spreading her blue skirts from the solemn wood,
I think of birds and beasts and vanished men,
Whose pointed dwellings on these pale sands stood.

One of the strangers who arrived at the railway station a few years ago was Jarvis Poulter, who now occupies the next house to Almeda Roth's – separated from hers by a vacant lot, which he has bought, on Dufferin Street. The house is plainer than the Roth house and has no fruit trees or flowers planted around it. It is understood that this is a natural result of Jarvis Poulter's being a widower and living alone. A man may keep his house decent, but he will never – if he is a proper man – do much to decorate it. Marriage forces him to live with more ornament as well as sentiment, and it protects him, also, from the extremities of his own nature – from a frigid parsimony or a luxuriant sloth, from squalor, and from excessive sleeping or reading, drinking, smoking, or freethinking.

> *In the interests of economy, it is believed, a certain estimable gentleman of our town persists in fetching water from the public tap and supplementing his fuel supply by picking up the loose coal along the railway track. Does he think to repay the town or the railway company with a supply of free salt?*

This is the *Vidette*, full of shy jokes, innuendo, plain accusation that no newspaper would get away with today. It's Jarvis Poulter they're talking about – though in other passages he is spoken of with great respect, as a civil magistrate, an employer, a churchman. He is close, that's all. An eccentric, to a degree. All of which may be a result of his single condition, his widower's life. Even carrying his water from the town tap and filling his coal pail along the railway track. This is a decent citizen, prosperous: a tall – slightly paunchy? – man in a dark suit with polished boots. A beard? Black hair streaked with gray. A severe and self-possessed air, and a large pale wart among the bushy hairs of one eyebrow? People talk about a young, pretty, beloved wife, dead in childbirth or some horrible accident, like a house fire or a railway disaster. There is no ground for this, but it adds interest. All he has told them is that his wife is dead.

He came to this part of the country looking for oil. The first oil well in the world was sunk in Lambton County, south of here, in the eighteen-fifties. Drilling for oil, Jarvis Poulter discovered salt. He set to work to make the most of that. When he walks home from church with Almeda Roth, he tells her about his salt wells. They are twelve hundred feet deep. Heated water is pumped down into them, and that dissolves the salt. Then the brine is pumped to the surface. It is poured into great evaporator pans over slow, steady fires, so that the water is steamed off and the pure, excellent salt remains. A commodity for which the demand will never fail.

"The salt of the earth," Almeda says.

"Yes," he says, frowning. He may think this disrespectful. She did not intend it so. He speaks of competitors in other towns who are following his lead and trying to hog the market. Fortunately, their wells are not drilled so deep, or their evaporating is not done so efficiently. There is salt everywhere under this land, but it is not so easy to come by as some people think.

Does this not mean, Almeda says, that there was once a great sea?

Very likely, Jarvis Poulter says. Very likely. He goes on to tell her about other enterprises of his – a brickyard, a limekiln. And he explains to her how this operates, and where the good clay is found. He also owns two farms, whose woodlots supply the fuel for his operations.

Among the couples strolling home from church on a recent, sunny Sabbath morning we noted a certain salty gentleman and literary lady, not perhaps in their first youth but by no means blighted by the frosts of age. May we surmise?

This kind of thing pops up in the *Vidette* all the time.

May they surmise, and is this courting? Almeda Roth has a bit of money, which her father left her, and she has her house. She is not too old to have a couple of children. She is a good enough housekeeper, with the tendency toward fancy iced cakes and decorated tarts that is seen fairly often in old maids. (Honorable mention at the Fall Fair.) There is nothing wrong with her looks, and naturally she is in better shape than most married women of her age, not having been loaded down with work and children. But why was she passed over in her earlier, more marriageable years, in a place that needs women to be partnered and fruitful? She was a rather gloomy girl – that may have been the trouble. The deaths of her brother and sister, and then of her mother, who lost her reason, in fact, a year before she died, and lay in her bed talking nonsense – those weighed on her, so she was not lively company. And all that reading and poetry – it seemed more of a drawback, a barrier, an obsession, in the young girl than in the middle-aged woman, who needed something, after all, to fill her time. Anyway, it's five years since her book was published, so perhaps she has got over that. Perhaps it was the proud, bookish father encouraging her?

Everyone takes it for granted that Almeda Roth is thinking of Jarvis Poulter as a husband and would say yes if he asked her. And she is thinking of him. She doesn't want to get her hopes up too much, she doesn't want to make a fool of herself. She would like a signal. If he attended church on Sunday evenings, there would be a chance, during some months of the year, to walk home after dark. He would carry a lantern. (There is as yet no street lighting in town.) He would swing the lantern to light the way in front of the lady's feet and observe their narrow and delicate shape. He might catch her arm as they step off the boardwalk. But he does not go to church at night.

Nor does he call for her, and walk with her *to* church on Sunday mornings. That would be a declaration. He walks her home, past his gate as far as hers; he lifts his hat then and leaves her. She does not invite him to come in – a woman living alone could never do such a thing. As soon as a man and woman of almost any age are alone together within four walls, it is assumed that anything may happen. Spontaneous combustion, instant fornication, an attack of passion. Brute instinct, triumph of the senses. What possibilities men and women must see in each other to infer such dangers. Or, believing in the dangers, how often they must think about the possibilities.

When they walk side by side, she can smell his shaving soap, the barber's oil, his pipe tobacco, the wool and linen and leather smell of his manly clothes. The correct, orderly, heavy clothes are like those she used to brush and starch and iron for her father. She misses that job – her father's appreciation, his dark, kind authority. Jarvis Poulter's garments, his smell, his movements all cause the skin on the side of her body next to him to tingle hopefully, and a meek shiver raises the hairs on her arms. Is this to be taken as a sign of love? She thinks of him coming into her – *their* – bedroom in his long underwear and his hat. She knows this outfit is ridiculous, but in her mind he does not look so; he has the solemn effrontery of a figure in a dream. He comes into the room and lies down on the bed beside her, preparing to take her in his arms. Surely he removes his hat? She doesn't know, for at this point a fit of welcome and submission overtakes her, a buried gasp. He would be her husband.

One thing she has noticed about married women, and that is how many of them have to go about creating their husbands. They have to start ascribing preferences, opinions, dictatorial ways. Oh, yes, they say, my husband is very particular. He won't touch turnips. He won't eat fried meat. (Or he will only eat fried meat.) He likes me to wear blue (brown) all the time. He can't stand organ music. He hates to see a woman go out bareheaded. He would kill me if I took one puff of tobacco. This way, bewildered, sidelong-looking men are made over, made into husbands, heads of households. Almeda Roth cannot imagine herself doing that. She wants a man who doesn't have to be made, who is firm already and determined and mysterious to her. She does not look for companionship. Men – except for her father – seem to her deprived in some way, incurious. No doubt that is necessary, so that they will do what they have to do. Would she herself, knowing that there was salt in the earth, discover how to get it out and sell it? Not likely. She would be thinking about the ancient sea. That kind of speculation is what Jarvis Poulter has, quite properly, no time for.

Instead of calling for her and walking her to church, Jarvis Poulter might make another, more venturesome declaration. He could hire a horse and take her for a drive out to the country. If he did this, she would be both glad and sorry. Glad to be beside him, driven by him, receiving this attention from him in front of the world. And sorry to have the countryside removed for her – filmed over, in a way, by his talk and preoccupations. The countryside that she has written about in her poems actually takes diligence and determination to see. Some things must be disregarded. Manure piles, of course, and boggy fields full of high, charred stumps, and great heaps of brush waiting for a good day for burning. The meandering creeks have been straightened, turned into ditches with high, muddy banks. Some of the crop fields and pasture fields are fenced with big, clumsy uprooted stumps; others are held in a crude stitchery of rail fences. The trees have all been cleared back to the woodlots. And the woodlots are all second growth. No trees along the roads or lanes or around the farmhouses, except a few that are newly planted, young and weedy-looking. Clusters of log barns – the grand barns that are to dominate the countryside for the next hundred years are just beginning to be built – and mean-looking log houses, and every four or five miles a ragged little settlement with a church and school and store and a blacksmith shop. A raw countryside just wrenched from the forest, but swarming with people. Every hundred acres is a farm, every farm has a family, most families have ten or twelve children. (This is the country that will send out wave after wave of settlers – it's already starting to send them – to northern Ontario and the West.) It's true that you can gather wildflowers in spring in the woodlots, but you'd have to walk through herds of horned cows to get to them.

IV

The Gypsies have departed.
Their camping-ground is bare.
Oh, boldly would I bargain now
At the Gypsy Fair.

Almeda suffers a good deal from sleeplessness, and the doctor has given her bromides and nerve medicine. She takes the bromides, but the drops gave her dreams that were too vivid and disturbing, so she has put the bottle by for an emergency. She told the doctor her eyeballs felt dry, like hot glass, and her joints ached. Don't read so much, he said, don't study; get yourself good and tired out with housework, take exercise. He believes that her troubles would clear up if she got married. He believes this in spite of the fact that most of his nerve medicine is prescribed for married women.

So Almeda cleans house and helps clean the church, she lends a hand to friends who are wallpapering or getting ready for a wedding, she bakes one of her famous cakes for the

Sunday-school picnic. On a hot Saturday in August, she decides to make some grape jelly. Little jars of grape jelly will make fine Christmas presents, or offerings to the sick. But she started late in the day and the jelly is not made by nightfall. In fact, the hot pulp has just been dumped into the cheesecloth bag to strain out the juice. Almeda drinks some tea and eats a slice of cake with butter (a childish indulgence of hers), and that's all she wants for supper. She washes her hair at the sink and sponges off her body to be clean for Sunday. She doesn't light a lamp. She lies down on the bed with the window wide open and a sheet just up to her waist, and she does feel wonderfully tired. She can even feel a little breeze.

When she wakes up, the night seems fiery hot and full of threats. She lies sweating on her bed, and she has the impression that the noises she hears are knives and saws and axes – all angry implements chopping and jabbing and boring within her head. But it isn't true. As she comes further awake, she recognizes the sounds that she has heard sometimes before – the fracas of a summer Saturday night on Pearl Street. Usually the noise centers on a fight. People are drunk, there is a lot of protest and encouragement concerning the fight, somebody will scream, "Murder!" Once, there was a murder. But it didn't happen in a fight. An old man was stabbed to death in his shack, perhaps for a few dollars he kept in the mattress.

She gets out of bed and goes to the window. The night sky is clear, with no moon and with bright stars. Pegasus hangs straight ahead, over the swamp. Her father taught her that constellation – automatically, she counts its stars. Now she can make out distinct voices, individual contributions to the row. Some people, like herself, have evidently been wakened from sleep. "Shut up!" they are yelling. "Shut up that caterwauling or I'm going to come down and tan the arse off yez!"

But nobody shuts up. It's as if there were a ball of fire rolling up Pearl Street, shooting off sparks – only the fire is noise; it's yells and laughter and shrieks and curses, and the sparks are voices that shoot off alone. Two voices gradually distinguish themselves – a rising and falling howling cry and a steady throbbing, low-pitched stream of abuse that contains all those words which Almeda associates with danger and depravity and foul smells and disgusting sights. Someone – the person crying out, "Kill me! Kill me now!" – is being beaten. A woman is being beaten. She keeps crying, "Kill me! Kill me!" and sometimes her mouth seems choked with blood. Yet there is something taunting and triumphant about her cry. There is something theatrical about it. And the people around are calling out, "Stop it! Stop that!" or "Kill her! Kill her!" in a frenzy, as if at the theatre or a sporting match or a prizefight. Yes, thinks Almeda, she has noticed that before – it is always partly a charade with these people; there is a clumsy sort of parody, an exaggeration, a missed connection. As if anything they did – even a murder – might be something they didn't quite believe but were powerless to stop.

Now there is the sound of something thrown – a chair, a plank? – and of a woodpile or part of a fence giving way. A lot of newly surprised cries, the sound of running, people getting out of the way, and the commotion has come much closer. Almeda can see a figure in a light dress, bent over and running. That will be the woman. She has got hold of something like a stick of wood or a shingle, and she turns and flings it at the darker figure running after her.

"Ah, go get her!" the voices cry. "Go baste her one!"

Many fall back now; just the two figures come on and grapple, and break loose again, and finally fall down against Almeda's fence. The sound they make becomes very confused – gagging, vomiting, grunting, pounding. Then a long, vibrating, choking sound of pain and self-abasement, self-abandonment, which could come from either or both of them.

Almeda has backed away from the window and sat down on the bed. Is that the sound of murder she has heard? What is to be done, what is she to do? She must light a lantern, she must go downstairs and light a lantern – she must go out into the yard, she must go downstairs. Into the yard. The lantern. She falls over on her bed and pulls the pillow to her face. In a minute. The stairs, the lantern. She sees herself already down there, in the back hall, drawing the bolt of the back door. She falls asleep.

She wakes, startled, in the early light. She thinks there is a big crow sitting on her windowsill, talking in a disapproving but unsurprised way about the events of the night before. "Wake up and move the wheelbarrow!" it says to her, scolding, and she understands that it means something else by "wheelbarrow" – something foul and sorrowful. Then she is awake and sees that there is no such bird. She gets up at once and looks out the window.

Down against her fence there is a pale lump pressed – a body.

Wheelbarrow.

She puts a wrapper over her nightdress and goes downstairs. The front rooms are still shadowy, the blinds down in the kitchen. Something goes *plop, plup*, in a leisurely, censorious way, reminding her of the conversation of the crow. It's just the grape juice, straining overnight. She pulls the bolt and goes out the back door. Spiders have draped their webs over the doorway in the night, and the hollyhocks are drooping, heavy with dew. By the fence, she parts the sticky hollyhocks and looks down and she can see.

A woman's body heaped up there, turned on her side with her face squashed down into the earth. Almeda can't see her face. But there is a bare breast let loose, brown nipple pulled long like a cow's teat, and a bare haunch and leg, the haunch showing a bruise as big as a sunflower. The unbruised skin is grayish, like a plucked, raw drumstick. Some kind of nightgown or all-purpose dress she has on. Smelling of vomit. Urine, drink, vomit.

Barefoot, in her nightgown and flimsy wrapper, Almeda

runs away. She runs around the side of her house between the apple trees and the veranda; she opens the front gate and flees down Dufferin Street to Jarvis Poulter's house, which is the nearest to hers. She slaps the flat of her hand many times against the door.

"There is the body of a woman," she says when Jarvis Poulter appears at last. He is in his dark trousers, held up with braces, and his shirt is half unbuttoned, his face unshaven, his hair standing up on his head. "Mr. Poulter, excuse me. A body of a woman. At my back gate."

He looks at her fiercely. "Is she dead?"

His breath is dank, his face creased, his eyes bloodshot.

"Yes. I think murdered," says Almeda. She can see a little of his cheerless front hall. His hat on a chair. "In the night I woke up. I heard a racket down on Pearl Street," she says, struggling to keep her voice low and sensible. "I could hear this – pair. I could hear a man and a woman fighting."

He picks up his hat and puts it on his head. He closes and locks the front door, and puts the key in his pocket. They walk along the boardwalk and she sees that she is in her bare feet. She holds back what she feels a need to say next – that she is responsible, she could have run out with a lantern, she could have screamed (but who needed more screams?), she could have beat the man off. She could have run for help then, not now.

They turn down Pearl Street, instead of entering the Roth yard. Of course the body is still there. Hunched up, half bare, the same as before.

Jarvis Poulter doesn't hurry or halt. He walks straight over to the body and looks down at it, nudges the leg with the toe of his boot, just as you'd nudge a dog or a sow.

"You," he says, not too loudly but firmly, and nudges again.

Almeda tastes bile at the back of her throat.

"Alive," says Jarvis Poulter, and the woman confirms this. She stirs, she grunts weakly.

Almeda says, "I will get the doctor." If she had touched the woman, if she had forced herself to touch her, she would not have made such a mistake.

"Wait," says Jarvis Poulter. "Wait. Let's see if she can get up."

"Get up, now," he says to the woman. "Come on. Up, now. Up."

Now a startling thing happens. The body heaves itself onto all fours, the head is lifted – the hair all matted with blood and vomit – and the woman begins to bang this head, hard and rhythmically, against Almeda Roth's picket fence. As she bangs her head, she finds her voice and lets out an openmouthed yowl, full of strength and what sounds like an anguished pleasure.

"Far from dead," says Jarvis Poulter. "And I wouldn't bother the doctor."

"There's blood," says Almeda as the woman turns her smeared face.

"From her nose," he says. "Not fresh." He bends down and catches the horrid hair close to the scalp to stop the head-banging.

"You stop that, now," he says. "Stop it. Gwan home, now. Gwan home, where you belong." The sound coming out of the woman's mouth has stopped. He shakes her head slightly, warning her, before he lets go of her hair. "Gwan home!"

Released, the woman lunges forward, pulls herself to her feet. She can walk. She weaves and stumbles down the street, making intermittent, cautious noises of protest. Jarvis Poulter watches her for a moment to make sure that she's on her way. Then he finds a large burdock leaf, on which he wipes his hand. He says, "There goes your dead body!"

The back gate being locked, they walk around to the front. The front gate stands open. Almeda still feels sick. Her abdomen is bloated; she is hot and dizzy.

"The front door is locked," she says faintly. "I came out by the kitchen." If only he would leave her, she could go straight to the privy. But he follows. He follows her as far as the back door and into the back hall. He speaks to her in a tone of harsh joviality that she has never before heard from him. "No need for alarm," he says. "It's only the consequences of drink. A lady oughtn't to be living alone so close to a bad neighborhood." He takes hold of her arm just above the elbow. She can't open her mouth to speak to him, to say thank you. If she opened her mouth, she would retch.

What Jarvis Poulter feels for Almeda Roth at this moment is just what he has not felt during all those circumspect walks and all his own solitary calculations of her probable worth, undoubted respectability, adequate comeliness. He has not been able to imagine her as a wife. Now that is possible. He is sufficiently stirred by her loosened hair – prematurely gray but thick and soft – her flushed face, her light clothing, which nobody but a husband should see. And by her indiscretion, her agitation, her foolishness, her need?

"I will call on you later," he says to her. "I will walk with you to church."

At the corner of Pearl and Dufferin streets last Sunday morning there was discovered, by a lady resident there, the body of a certain woman of Pearl Street, thought to be dead but only, as it turned out, dead drunk. She was roused from her heavenly – or otherwise – stupor by the firm persuasion of Mr. Poulter, a neighbour and a Civil Magistrate, who had been summoned by the lady resident. Incidents of this sort, unseemly, troublesome, and disgraceful to our town, have of late become all too common.

V

I sit at the bottom of sleep,
As on the floor of the sea.

And fanciful Citizens of the Deep
Are graciously greeting me.

As soon as Jarvis Poulter has gone and she has heard her front gate close, Almeda rushes to the privy. Her relief is not complete, however, and she realizes that the pain and fullness in her lower body come from an accumulation of menstrual blood that has not yet started to flow. She closes and locks the back door. Then, remembering Jarvis Poulter's words about church, she writes on a piece of paper, "I am not well, and wish to rest today." She sticks this firmly into the outside frame of the little window in the front door. She locks that door, too. She is trembling, as if from a great shock or danger. But she builds a fire, so that she can make tea. She boils water, measures the tea leaves, makes a large pot of tea, whose steam and smell sicken her further. She pours out a cup while the tea is still quite weak and adds to it several dark drops of nerve medicine. She sits to drink it without raising the kitchen blind. There, in the middle of the floor, is the cheesecloth bag hanging on its broom handle between the two chairbacks. The grape pulp and juice has stained the swollen cloth a dark purple. *Plop, plup*, into the basin beneath. She can't sit and look at such a thing. She takes her cup, the teapot, and the bottle of medicine into the dining room.

She is still sitting there when the horses start to go by on the way to church, stirring up clouds of dust. The roads will be getting hot as ashes. She is there when the gate is opened and a man's confident steps sound on her veranda. Her hearing is so sharp she seems to hear the paper taken out of the frame and unfolded – she can almost hear him reading it, hear the words in his mind. Then the footsteps go the other way, down the steps. The gate closes. An image comes to her of tombstones – it makes her laugh. Tombstones are marching down the street on their little booted feet, their long bodies inclined forward, their expressions preoccupied and severe. The church bells are ringing.

Then the clock in the hall strikes twelve and an hour has passed.

The house is getting hot. She drinks more tea and adds more medicine. She knows that the medicine is affecting her. It is responsible for her extraordinary languor, her perfect immobility, her unresisting surrender to her surroundings. That is all right. It seems necessary.

Her surroundings – some of her surroundings – in the dining room are these: walls covered with dark-green garlanded wallpaper, lace curtains and mulberry velvet curtains on the windows, a table with a crocheted cloth and a bowl of wax fruit, a pinkish-gray carpet with nosegays of blue and pink roses, a sideboard spread with embroidered runners and holding various patterned plates and jugs and the silver tea things. A lot of things to watch. For every one of these patterns, decorations seems charged with life, ready to move and flow and alter. Or possibly to explode. Almeda Roth's occupation throughout the day is to keep an eye on them. Not to prevent their alteration so much as to catch them at it – to understand it, to be a part of it. So much is going on in this room that there is no need to leave it. There is not even the thought of leaving it.

Of course, Almeda in her observations cannot escape words. She may think she can, but she can't. Soon this glowing and swelling begins to suggest words – not specific words but a flow of words somewhere, just about ready to make themselves known to her. Poems, even. Yes, again, poems. Or one poem. Isn't that the idea – one very great poem that will contain everything and, oh, that will make all the other poems, the poems she has written, inconsequential, mere trial and error, mere rags? Stars and flowers and birds and trees and angels in the snow and dead children at twilight –

that is not the half of it. You have to get in the obscene racket on Pearl Street and the polished toe of Jarvis Poulter's boot and the plucked-chicken haunch with its blue-black flower. Almeda is a long way now from human sympathies or fears or cozy household considerations. She doesn't think about what could be done for that woman or about keeping Jarvis Poulter's dinner warm and hanging his long underwear on the line. The basin of grape juice has overflowed and is running over her kitchen floor, staining the boards of the floor, and the stain will never come out.

She has to think of so many things at once – Champlain and the naked Indians and the salt deep in the earth, but as well as the salt the money, the money-making intent brewing forever in heads like Jarvis Poulter's. Also the brutal storms of winter and the clumsy and benighted deeds on Pearl Street. The changes of climate are often violent, and if you think about it there is no peace even in the stars. All this can be borne only if it is channelled into a poem, and the word "channelled" is appropriate, because the name of the poem will be – it *is* – "The Meneseteung." The name of the poem is the name of the river. No, in fact it is the river, the Meneseteung, that is the poem – with its deep holes and rapids and blissful pools under the summer trees and its grinding blocks of ice thrown up at the end of winter and its desolating spring floods. Almeda looks deep, deep into the river of her mind and into the tablecloth, and she sees the crocheted roses floating. They look bunchy and foolish, her mother's crocheted roses – they don't look much like real flowers. But their effort, their floating independence, their pleasure in their silly selves do seem to her so admirable. A hopeful sign. *Meneseteung.*

She doesn't leave the room until dusk, when she goes out to the privy again and discovers that she is bleeding, her flow has started. She will have to get a towel, strap it on, bandage herself up. Never before, in health, has she passed a whole day in her nightdress. She doesn't feel any particular anxiety about this. On her way through the kitchen, she walks through the pool of grape juice. She knows that she will have to mop it up, but not yet, and she walks upstairs leaving purple footprints and smelling her escaping blood and the sweat of her body that has sat all day in the closed hot room.

No need for alarm.

For she hasn't thought that crocheted roses could float away or that tombstones could hurry down the street. She doesn't mistake that for reality, and neither does she mistake anything else for reality, and that is how she knows that she is sane.

VI

I dream of you by night,
I visit you by day.
Father, Mother,
Sister, Brother,
Have you no word to say?

April 22, 1903. At her residence, on Tuesday last, between three and four o'clock in the afternoon, there passed away a lady of talent and refinement whose pen, in days gone by, enriched our local literature with a volume of sensitive, eloquent verse. It is a sad misfortune that in later years the mind of this fine person had become somewhat clouded and her behaviour, in consequence, somewhat rash and unusual. Her attention to decorum and to the care and adornment of her person had suffered, to the degree that she had become, in the eyes of those unmindful of her former pride and daintiness, a familiar eccentric, or even, sadly, a figure of fun. But now all such lapses pass from memory and what is recalled is her excellent published verse, her labours in former days in the Sunday school, her dutiful care of her parents, her noble womanly nature, charitable concerns, and unfailing religious faith. Her last illness was of mercifully short duration. She caught cold, after having become thoroughly wet from a ramble in the Pearl Street bog. (It has been said that some urchins chased her into the water, and such is the boldness and cruelty of some of our youth, and their observed persecution of this lady, that the tale cannot be entirely discounted.) The cold developed into pneumonia, and she died, attended at the last by a former neighbour, Mrs. Bert (Annie) Friels, who witnessed her calm and faithful end.

January, 1904. One of the founders of our community, an early maker and shaker of this town, was abruptly removed from our midst on Monday morning last, whilst attending to his correspondence in the office of his company. Mr. Jarvis Poulter possessed a keen and lively commercial spirit, which was instrumental in the creation of not one but several local enterprises, bringing the benefits of industry, productivity, and employment to our town.

So the *Vidette* runs on, copious and assured. Hardly a death goes undescribed, or a life unevaluated.

I looked for Almeda Roth in the graveyard. I found the family stone. There was just one name on it – Roth. Then I noticed two flat stones in the ground, a distance of a few feet – six feet? – from the upright stone. One of these said "Papa," the other "Mama." Farther out from these I found two other flat stones, with the names William and Catherine on them. I had to clear away some overgrowing grass and dirt to see the full name of Catherine. No birth or death dates for anybody, nothing about being dearly beloved. It was a private sort of memorializing, not for the world. There were no roses, either – no sign of a rosebush. But perhaps it was taken out. The grounds keeper doesn't like such things; they are a nuisance to the lawnmower, and if there is nobody left to object he will pull them out.

I thought that Almeda must have been buried somewhere else. When this plot was bought – at the time of the two children's deaths – she would still have been expected to marry, and to lie finally beside her husband. They might not have left room for her here. Then I saw that the stones in the ground fanned out from the upright stone. First the two for the parents, then the two for the children, but these were placed in such a way that there was room for a third, to complete the fan. I paced out from "Catherine" the same number of steps that it took to get from "Catherine" to "William," and at this spot I began pulling grass and scrabbling in the dirt with my bare hands. Soon I felt the stone and knew that I was right. I worked away and got the whole stone clear and I read the name "Meda." There it was with the others, staring at the sky.

I made sure I had got to the edge of the stone. That was all the name there was – Meda. So it was true that she was called by that name in the family. Not just in the poem. Or perhaps she chose her name from the poem, to be written on her stone.

I thought that there wasn't anybody alive in the world but me who would know this, who would make the connection. And I would be the last person to do so. But perhaps this isn't so. People are curious. A few people are. They will be driven to find things out, even trivial things. They will put things together. You see them going around with notebooks, scraping the dirt off gravestones, reading microfilm, just in the hope of seeing this trickle in time, making a connection, rescuing one thing from the rubbish.

And they may get it wrong, after all. I may have got it wrong. I don't know if she ever took laudanum. Many ladies did. I don't know if she ever made grape jelly.

The Children Stay

THIRTY YEARS ago, a family was spending a holiday together on the east coast of Vancouver Island. A young father and mother, their two small daughters, and an older couple, the husband's parents.

What perfect weather. Every morning, every morning it's like this, the first pure sunlight falling through the high branches, burning away the mist over the still water of Georgia Strait. The tide out, a great empty stretch of sand still damp but easy to walk on, like cement in its very last stage of drying. The tide is actually less far out; every morning, the pavilion of sand is shrinking, but it still seems ample enough. The changes in the tide are a matter of great interest to the grandfather, not so much to anyone else.

Pauline, the young mother, doesn't really like the beach as well as she likes the road that runs behind the cottages for a mile or so north till it stops at the bank of the little river that runs into the sea.

If it wasn't for the tide, it would be hard to remember that this is the sea. You look across the water to the mountains on the mainland, the ranges that are the western wall of the continent of North America. These humps and peaks coming clear now through the mist and glimpsed here and there through the trees, by Pauline as she pushes her daughter's stroller along the road, are also of interest to the grandfather. And to his son Brian, who is Pauline's husband. The two men are continually trying to decide which is what. Which of these shapes are actual continental mountains and which are improbable heights of the islands that ride in front of the shore? It's hard to sort things out when the array is so complicated and parts of it shift their distance in the day's changing light.

But there is a map, set up under glass, between the cottages and the beach. You can stand there looking at the map, then looking at what's in front of you, looking back at the map again, until you get things sorted out. The grandfather and Brian do this every day, usually getting into an argument – though you'd think there would not be much room for disagreement with the map right there. Brian chooses to see the map as inexact. But his father will not hear a word of criticism about any aspect of this place, which was his choice for the holiday. The map, like the accommodation and the weather, is perfect.

Brian's mother won't look at the map. She says it boggles her mind. The men laugh at her, they accept that her mind is boggled. Her husband believes that this is because she is a female. Brian believes that it's because she's his mother. Her concern is always about whether anybody is hungry yet, or thirsty, whether the children have their sun hats on and have been rubbed with protective lotion. And what is the strange bite on Caitlin's arm that doesn't look like the bite of a mosquito? She makes her husband wear a floppy cotton hat and thinks that Brian should wear one too – she reminds him of how sick he got from the sun, that summer they went to the Okanagan, when he was a child. Sometimes Brian says to her, "Oh, dry up, Mother." His tone is mostly affectionate, but his father may ask him if that's the way he thinks he can talk to his mother nowadays.

"She doesn't mind," says Brian.

"How do you know?" says his father.

"Oh for Pete's sake," says his mother.

Pauline slides out of bed as soon as she's awake every morning, slides out of reach of Brian's long, sleepily searching arms and legs. What wakes her are the first squeaks and mutters of the baby, Mara, in the children's room, then the creak of the crib as Mara – sixteen months old now, getting to the end of babyhood – pulls herself up to stand hanging on to the railing. She continues her soft amiable talk as Pauline lifts her out – Caitlin, nearly five, shifting about but not waking, in her nearby bed – and as she is carried into the kitchen to be changed, on the floor. Then she is settled into her stroller, with a biscuit and a bottle of apple juice, while Pauline gets into her sundress and sandals, goes to the bathroom, combs out her hair – all as quickly and quietly as possible. They leave the cottage; they head past some other cottages for the bumpy unpaved road that is still mostly in deep morning shadow, the floor of a tunnel under fir and cedar trees.

The grandfather, also an early riser, sees them from the porch of his cottage, and Pauline sees him. But all that is necessary is a wave. He and Pauline never have much to say to each other (though sometimes there's an affinity they feel, in the midst of some long-drawn-out antics of Brian's or some apologetic but insistent fuss made by the grandmother; there's an awareness of not looking at each other, lest their look should reveal a bleakness that would discredit others).

On this holiday Pauline steals time to be by herself – being with Mara is still almost the same thing as being by herself. Early morning walks, the late-morning hour when she washes and hangs out the diapers. She could have had another hour or so in the afternoons, while Mara is napping. But Brian has fixed up a shelter on the beach, and he carries the playpen down every day, so that Mara can nap there and Pauline won't have to absent herself. He says his parents may be offended if she's always sneaking off. He agrees though that she does need some time to go over her lines for the play she's going to be in, back in Victoria, this September.

Pauline is not an actress. This is an amateur production, but she is not even an amateur actress. She didn't try out for the role, though it happened that she had already read the play. *Eurydice* by Jean Anouilh. But then, Pauline has read all sorts of things.

She was asked if she would like to be in this play by a man she met at a barbecue, in June. The people at the barbecue were mostly teachers and their wives or husbands – it was held at the house of the principal of the high school where Brian teaches. The woman who taught French was a widow – she had brought her grown son who was staying for the summer with her and working as a night clerk in a downtown hotel. She told everybody that he had got a job teaching at a college in western Washington State and would be going there in the fall.

Jeffrey Toom was his name. "Without the *B*," he said, as if the staleness of the joke wounded him. It was a different name from his mother's, because she had been widowed twice, and he was the son of her first husband. About the job he said, "No guarantee it'll last, it's a one-year appointment."

What was he going to teach?

"Dram-ah," he said, drawing the word out in a mocking way.

He spoke of his present job disparagingly, as well.

"It's a pretty sordid place," he said. "Maybe you heard – a hooker was killed there last winter. And then we get the usual losers checking in to OD or bump themselves off."

People did not quite know what to make of this way of talking and drifted away from him. Except for Pauline.

"I'm thinking about putting on a play," he said. "Would you like to be in it?" He asked her if she had ever heard of a play called *Eurydice*.

Pauline said, "You mean Anouilh's?" and he was unflatteringly surprised. He immediately said he didn't know if it would ever work out. "I just thought it might be interesting to see if you could do something different here in the land of Noël Coward."

Pauline did not remember when there had been a play by Noël Coward put on in Victoria, though she supposed there had been several. She said, "We saw *The Duchess of Malfi* last winter at the college. And the little theater did *A Resounding Tinkle*, but we didn't see it."

"Yeah. Well," he said, flushing. She had thought he was older than she was, at least as old as Brian (who was thirty, though people were apt to say he didn't act it), but as soon as he started talking to her, in this offhand, dismissive way, never quite meeting her eyes, she suspected that he was younger than he'd like to appear. Now with that flush she was sure of it.

As it turned out, he was a year younger than she was. Twenty-five.

She said that she couldn't be Eurydice; she couldn't act. But Brian came over to see what the conversation was about and said at once that she must try it.

"She just needs a kick in the behind," Brian said to Jeffrey. "She's like a little mule, it's hard to get her started. No, seriously, she's too self-effacing, I tell her that all the time. She's very smart. She's actually a lot smarter than I am."

At that Jeffrey did look directly into Pauline's eyes – impertinently and searchingly – and she was the one who was flushing.

He had chosen her immediately as his Eurydice because of the way she looked. But it was not because she was beautiful. "I'd never put a beautiful girl in that part," he said. "I don't know if I'd ever put a beautiful girl on stage in anything. It's too much. It's distracting."

So what did he mean about the way she looked? He said it

was her hair, which was long and dark and rather bushy (not in style at that time), and her pale skin ("Stay out of the sun this summer") and most of all her eyebrows.

"I never liked them," said Pauline, not quite sincerely. Her eyebrows were level, dark, luxuriant. They dominated her face. Like her hair, they were not in style. But if she had really disliked them, wouldn't she have plucked them?

Jeffrey seemed not to have heard her. "They give you a sulky look and that's disturbing," he said. "Also your jaw's a little heavy and that's sort of Greek. It would be better in a movie where I could get you close up. The routine thing for Eurydice would be a girl who looked ethereal. I don't want ethereal."

As she walked Mara along the road, Pauline did work at the lines. There was a speech at the end that was giving her trouble. She bumped the stroller along and repeated to herself, "'You are terrible, you know, you are terrible like the angels. You think everybody's going forward, as brave and bright as you are – oh, don't look at me, please, darling, don't look at me – perhaps I'm not what you wish I was, but I'm here, and I'm warm, I'm kind, and I love you. I'll give you all the happiness I can. Don't look at me. Don't look. Let me live.'"

She had left something out. "'Perhaps I'm not what you wish I was, but you feel me here, don't you? I'm warm and I'm kind –'"

She had told Jeffrey that she thought the play was beautiful.

He said, "Really?" What she'd said didn't please or surprise him – he seemed to feel it was predictable, superfluous. He would never describe a play in that way. He spoke of it more as a hurdle to be got over. Also a challenge to be flung at various enemies. At the academic snots – as he called them – who had done *The Duchess of Malfi*. And at the social twits – as he called them – in the little theater. He saw himself as an outsider heaving his weight against these people, putting on his play – he called it his – in the teeth of their contempt and opposition. In the beginning Pauline thought that this must be all in his imagination and that it was more likely these people knew nothing about him. Then something would happen that could be, but might not be, a coincidence. Repairs had to be done on the church hall where the play was to be performed, making it unobtainable. There was an unexpected increase in the cost of printing advertising posters. She found herself seeing it his way. If you were going to be around him much, you almost had to see it his way – arguing was dangerous and exhausting.

"Sons of bitches," said Jeffrey between his teeth, but with some satisfaction. "I'm not surprised."

The rehearsals were held upstairs in an old building on Fisgard Street. Sunday afternoon was the only time that everybody could get there, though there were fragmentary rehearsals during the week. The retired harbor pilot who played Monsieur Henri was able to attend every rehearsal, and got to have an irritating familiarity with everybody else's lines. But the hairdresser – who had experience only with Gilbert and Sullivan but now found herself playing Eurydice's mother – could not leave her shop for long at any other time. The bus driver who played her lover had his daily employment as well, and so had the waiter who played Orphée (he was the only one of them who hoped to be a real actor). Pauline had to depend on sometimes undependable high-school babysitters – for the first six weeks of the summer Brian was busy teaching summer school – and Jeffrey himself had to be at his hotel job by eight o'clock in the evenings. But on Sunday afternoons they were all there. While other people swam at Thetis Lake, or thronged Beacon Hill Park to walk under the trees and feed the ducks, or drove far out of town to the Pacific beaches, Jeffrey and his crew labored in the dusty high-ceilinged room on Fisgard Street. The windows were rounded at the top as in some plain and dignified church, and propped open in the heat with whatever objects could be found – ledger books from the 1920s belonging to the hat shop that had once operated downstairs, or pieces of wood left over from the picture frames made by the artist whose canvases were now stacked against one wall and apparently abandoned. The glass was grimy, but outside the sunlight bounced off the sidewalks, the empty gravelled parking lots, the low stuccoed buildings, with what seemed a special Sunday brightness. Hardly anybody moved through these downtown streets. Nothing was open except the occasional hole-in-the-wall coffee shop or fly-specked convenience store.

Pauline was the one who went out at the break to get soft drinks and coffee. She was the one who had the least to say about the play and the way it was going – even though she was the only one who had read it before – because she alone had never done any acting. So it seemed proper for her to volunteer. She enjoyed her short walk in the empty streets – she felt as if she had become an urban person, someone detached and solitary, who lived in the glare of an important dream. Sometimes she thought of Brian at home, working in the garden and keeping an eye on the children. Or perhaps he had taken them to Dallas Road – she recalled a promise – to sail boats on the pond. That life seemed ragged and tedious compared to what went on in the rehearsal room – the hours of effort, the concentration, the sharp exchanges, the sweating and tension. Even the taste of the coffee, its scalding bitterness, and the fact that it was chosen by nearly everybody in preference to a fresher-tasting and maybe more healthful drink out of the cooler seemed satisfying to her. And she liked the look of the shop-windows. This was not one of the dolled-up streets near the harbor – it was a street of shoe- and bicycle-repair shops, discount linen and fabric stores, of clothes and furniture that had been so long in the windows that they looked secondhand even if they weren't. On some windows sheets of golden plastic as frail and crinkled as old cellophane were stretched inside the glass to protect the merchandise from the sun. All these enterprises had been left behind just for this one day, but they had a look of being fixed in time as much as cave paintings or relics under sand.

When she said that she had to go away for the two-week holiday Jeffrey looked thunderstruck, as if he had never imagined that things like holidays could come into her life. Then he turned grim and slightly satirical, as if this was just another blow that he might have expected. Pauline explained that she would miss only the one Sunday – the one in the middle of the two weeks – because she and Brian were driving up the island on a Monday and coming back on a Sunday morning. She promised to get back in time for rehearsal. Privately she wondered how she would do this – it always took so much longer than you expected to pack up and get away. She wondered if she could possibly come back by herself, on the morning bus. That would probably be too much to ask for. She didn't mention it.

She couldn't ask him if it was only the play he was thinking about, only her absence from a rehearsal that caused the thundercloud. At the moment, it very likely was. When he spoke to her at rehearsals there was never any suggestion that he ever spoke to her in any other way. The only difference in his treatment of her was that perhaps he expected less of her, of her acting, than he did of the others. And that would be understandable to anybody. She was the only one chosen out of the blue, for the way she looked – the others had all shown up at the audition he had advertised on the signs put up in cafés and bookstores around town. From her he appeared to want an immobility or awkwardness that he didn't want from the rest of them. Perhaps it was because, in the latter part of the play, she was supposed to be a person who had already died.

Yet she thought they all knew, the rest of the cast all knew, what was going on, in spite of Jeffrey's offhand and abrupt and none too civil ways. They knew that after every one of them had straggled off home, he would walk across the room and bolt the staircase door. (At first Pauline had pretended to leave with the rest and had even got into her car and circled the block, but later such a trick had come to seem insulting, not just to herself and Jeffrey, but to the others whom she was sure would never betray her, bound as they all were under the temporary but potent spell of the play.)

Jeffrey crossed the room and bolted the door. Every time, this was like a new decision, which he had to make. Until it was done, she wouldn't look at him. The sound of the bolt being pushed into place, the ominous or fatalistic sound of the metal hitting metal, gave her a localized shock of capitulation. But she didn't make a move, she waited for him to come back to her with the whole story of the afternoon's labor draining out of his face, the expression of matter-of-fact and customary disappointment cleared away, replaced by the live energy she always found surprising.

"So. Tell us what this play of yours is about," Brian's father said. "Is it one of those ones where they take their clothes off on the stage?"

"Now don't tease her," said Brian's mother.

Brian and Pauline had put the children to bed and walked over to his parents' cottage for an evening drink. The sunset was behind them, behind the forests of Vancouver Island, but the mountains in front of them, all clear now and hard-cut against the sky, shone in its pink light. Some high inland mountains were capped with pink summer snow.

"Nobody takes their clothes off, Dad," said Brian in his booming schoolroom voice. "You know why? Because they haven't got any clothes on in the first place. It's the latest style. They're going to put on a bare-naked *Hamlet* next. Bare-naked *Romeo and Juliet*. Boy, that balcony scene where Romeo is climbing up the trellis and he gets stuck in the rosebushes –"

"Oh, Brian," said his mother.

"The story of Orpheus and Eurydice is that Eurydice died," Pauline said. "And Orpheus goes down to the underworld to try to get her back. And his wish is granted, but only if he promises not to look at her. Not to look back at her. She's walking behind him –"

"Twelve paces," said Brian. "As is only right."

"It's a Greek story, but it's set in modern times," said Pauline. "At least this version is. More or less modern. Orpheus is a musician travelling around with his father – they're both musicians – and Eurydice is an actress. This is in France."

"Translated?" Brian's father said.

"No," said Brian. "But don't worry, it's not in French. It was written in Transylvanian."

"It's so hard to make sense of anything," Brian's mother said with a worried laugh. "It's so hard, with Brian around."

"It's in English," Pauline said.

"And you're what's-her-name?"

She said, "I'm Eurydice."

"He get you back okay?"

"No," she said. "He looks back at me, and then I have to stay dead."

"Oh, an unhappy ending," Brian's mother said.

"You're so gorgeous?" said Brian's father skeptically. "He can't stop himself from looking back?"

"It's not that," said Pauline. But at this point she felt that something had been achieved by her father-in-law, he had done what he meant to do, which was the same thing that he nearly always meant to do, in any conversation she had with him. And that was to break through the structure of some explanation he had asked her for, and she had unwillingly but patiently given, and, with a seemingly negligent kick, knock it into rubble. He had been dangerous to her for a long time in this way, but he wasn't particularly so tonight.

But Brian did not know that. Brian was still figuring out how to come to her rescue.

"Pauline is gorgeous," Brian said.

"Yes indeed," said his mother.

"Maybe if she'd go to the hairdresser," his father said. But Pauline's long hair was such an old objection of his that it had become a family joke. Even Pauline laughed. She said, "I can't afford to till we get the veranda roof fixed." And Brian laughed boisterously, full of relief that she was able to take all this as a joke. It was what he had always told her to do.

"Just kid him back," he said. "It's the only way to handle him."

"Yeah, well, if you'd got yourselves a decent house," said his father. But this like Pauline's hair was such a familiar sore point that it couldn't rouse anybody. Brian and Pauline had bought a handsome house in bad repair on a street in Victoria where old mansions were being turned into ill-used apartment buildings. The house, the street, the messy old Garry oaks, the fact that no basement had been blasted out under the house, were all a horror to Brian's father. Brian usually agreed with him and tried to go him one further. If his father pointed at the house next door all crisscrossed with black fire escapes, and asked what kind of neighbors they had, Brian said, "Really poor people, Dad. Drug addicts." And when his father wanted to know how it was heated, he'd said, "Coal furnace. Hardly any of them left these days, you can get coal really cheap. Of course it's dirty and it kind of stinks."

So what his father said now about a decent house might be some kind of peace signal. Or could be taken so.

Brian was an only son. He was a math teacher. His father was a civil engineer and part owner of a contracting company. If he had hoped that he would have a son who was an engineer and might come into the company, there was never any mention of it. Pauline had asked Brian whether he thought the carping about their house and her hair and the books she read might be a cover for this larger disappointment, but Brian had said, "Nope. In our family we complain about just whatever we want to complain about. We ain't subtle, ma'am."

Pauline still wondered, when she heard his mother talking about how teachers ought to be the most honored people in the world and they did not get half the credit they deserved and that she didn't know how Brian managed it, day after day. Then his father might say, "That's right," or, "I sure wouldn't want to do it, I can tell you that. They couldn't pay me to do it."

"Don't worry Dad," Brian would say. "They wouldn't pay you much."

Brian in his everyday life was a much more dramatic person than Jeffrey. He dominated his classes by keeping up a parade of jokes and antics, extending the role that he had always played, Pauline believed, with his mother and father. He acted dumb, he bounced back from pretended humiliations, he traded insults. He was a bully in a good cause – a chivvying cheerful indestructible bully.

"Your boy has certainly made his mark with us," the principal said to Pauline. "He has not just survived, which is something in itself. He has made his mark."

Your boy.

Brian called his students boneheads. His tone was affectionate, fatalistic. He said that his father was the King of the Philistines, a pure and natural barbarian. And that his mother was a dishrag, good-natured and worn out. But however he dismissed such people, he could not be long without them. He took his students on camping trips. And he could not imagine a summer without this shared holiday. He was mortally afraid, every year, that Pauline would refuse to go along. Or that, having agreed to go, she was going to be miserable, take offense at something his father said, complain about how much time she had to spend with his mother, sulk because there was no way they could do anything by themselves. She might decide to spend all day in their own cottage, reading and pretending to have a sunburn.

All those things had happened, on previous holidays. But this year she was easing up. He told her he could see that, and he was grateful to her.

"I know it's an effort," he said. "It's different for me. They're my parents and I'm used to not taking them seriously."

Pauline came from a family that took things so seriously that her parents had got a divorce. Her mother was now dead. She had a distant, though cordial, relationship with her father and her two much older sisters. She said that they had nothing in common. She knew Brian could not understand how that could be a reason. She saw what comfort it gave him, this year, to see things going so well. She had thought it was laziness or cowardice that kept him from breaking the arrangement, but now she saw that it was something far more positive. He needed to have his wife and his parents and his children bound together like this, he needed to involve Pauline in his life with his parents and to bring his parents to some recognition of her – though the recognition, from his father, would always be muffled and contrary, and from his mother too profuse, too easily come by, to mean much. Also he wanted Pauline to be connected, he wanted the children to be connected, to his own childhood – he wanted these holidays to be linked to holidays of his childhood with their lucky or unlucky weather, car troubles or driving records, boating scares, bee stings, marathon Monopoly games, to all the things that he told his mother he was bored to death hearing about. He wanted pictures from this summer to be taken, and fitted into his mother's album, a continuation of all the other pictures that he groaned at the mention of.

The only time they could talk to each other was in bed, late at night. But they did talk then, more than was usual with them at home, where Brian was so tired that often he fell immediately asleep. And in ordinary daylight it was often hard to talk to him because of his jokes. She could see the joke brightening his eyes (his coloring was very like hers – dark hair and pale skin and gray eyes, but her eyes were cloudy and his were light, like clear water over stones). She could see it pulling at the corners of his mouth, as he foraged among your words to catch a pun or the start of a rhyme – anything that could take the conversation away, into absurdity. His whole body, tall and loosely joined together and still almost as skinny as a teenager's, twitched with comic propensity. Before she married him, Pauline had a friend named Gracie, a rather grumpy-looking girl, subversive about men. Brian had thought her a girl whose spirits needed a boost, and so he made even more than the usual effort. And Gracie said to Pauline, "How can you stand the nonstop show?"

"That's not the real Brian," Pauline had said. "He's different when we're alone." But looking back, she wondered how true that had ever been. Had she said it simply to defend her choice, as you did when you had made up your mind to get married?

So talking in the dark had something to do with the fact that she could not see his face. And that he knew she couldn't see his face.

But even with the window open on the unfamiliar darkness and stillness of the night, he teased a little. He had to speak of Jeffrey as Monsieur le Directeur, which made the play or the fact that it was a French play slightly ridiculous. Or perhaps it was Jeffrey himself, Jeffrey's seriousness about the play, that had to be called in question.

Pauline didn't care. It was such a pleasure and a relief to her to mention Jeffrey's name.

Most of the time she didn't mention him; she circled around that pleasure. She described all the others, instead. The hairdresser and the harbor pilot and the waiter and the old man who claimed to have once acted on the radio. He played Orphée's father and gave Jeffrey the most trouble, because he had the stubbornest notions of his own, about acting.

The middle-aged impresario Monsieur Dulac was played by a twenty-four-year-old travel agent. And Mathias, who was Eurydice's former boyfriend, presumably around her own age, was played by the manager of a shoe store, who was married and a father of children.

Brian wanted to know why Monsieur le Directeur hadn't cast these two the other way round.

"That's the way he does things," Pauline said. "What he sees in us is something only he can see."

For instance, she said, the waiter was a clumsy Orphée.

"He's only nineteen, he's so shy Jeffrey has to keep at him. He tells him not to act like he's making love to his grandmother. He has to tell him what to do. *Keep your arms around her a little longer, stroke her here a little.* I don't know how it's going to work – I just have to trust Jeffrey, that he knows what he's doing."

"'Stroke her here a little'?" said Brian. "Maybe I should come around and keep an eye on these rehearsals."

When she had started to quote Jeffrey Pauline had felt a giving-way in her womb or the bottom of her stomach, a shock that had travelled oddly upwards and hit her vocal cords. She had to cover up this quaking by growling in a way that was supposed to be an imitation (though Jeffrey never growled or ranted or carried on in any theatrical way at all).

"But there's a point about him being so innocent," she said hurriedly. "Being not so physical. Being awkward." And she began to talk about Orphée in the play, not the waiter. Orphée has a problem with love or reality. Orphée will not put up with anything less than perfection. He wants a love that is outside of ordinary life. He wants a perfect Eurydice.

"Eurydice is more realistic. She's carried on with Mathias and with Monsieur Dulac. She's been around her mother and her mother's lover. She knows what people are like. But she loves Orphée. She loves him better in a way than he loves her. She loves him better because she's not such a fool. She loves him like a human person."

"But she's slept with those other guys," Brian said.

"Well with Mr. Dulac she had to, she couldn't get out of it. She didn't want to, but probably after a while she enjoyed it, because after a certain point she couldn't help enjoying it."

So Orphée is at fault, Pauline said decidedly. He looks at Eurydice on purpose, to kill her and get rid of her because she is not perfect. Because of him she has to die a second time.

Brian, on his back and with his eyes wide open (she knew that because of the tone of his voice) said, "But doesn't he die too?"

"Yes. He chooses to."

"So then they're together?"

"Yes. Like Romeo and Juliet. *Orphée is with Eurydice at last.* That's what Monsieur Henri says. That's the last line of the play. That's the end." Pauline rolled over onto her side and touched her cheek to Brian's shoulder – not to start anything but to emphasize what she said next. "It's a beautiful play in one way, but in another it's so silly. And it isn't really like *Romeo and Juliet* because it isn't bad luck or circumstances. It's on purpose. So they don't have to go on with life and get married and have kids and buy an old house and fix it up and –"

"And have affairs," said Brian. "After all, they're French."

Then he said, "Be like my parents."

Pauline laughed. "Do they have affairs? I can imagine."

"Oh sure," said Brian. "I meant their life."

"Logically I can see killing yourself so you won't turn into your parents," Brian said. "I just don't believe anybody would do it."

"Everybody has choices," Pauline said dreamily. "Her mother and his father are both despicable in a way, but Orphée and Eurydice don't have to be like them. They're not corrupt. Just because she's slept with those men doesn't mean she's corrupt. She wasn't in love then. She hadn't met Orphée. There's one speech where he tells her that everything she's done is sticking to her, and it's disgusting. Lies she's told him. The other men. It's all sticking to her forever. And then of course Monsieur

Henri plays up to that. He tells Orphée that he'll be just as bad and that one day he'll walk down the street with Eurydice and he'll look like a man with a dog he's trying to lose."

To her surprise, Brian laughed.

"No," she said. "That's what's stupid. It's not inevitable. It's not inevitable at all."

They went on speculating, and comfortably arguing, in a way that was not usual, but not altogether unfamiliar to them. They had done this before, at long intervals in their married life – talked half the night about God or fear of death or how children should be educated or whether money was important. At last they admitted to being too tired to make sense any longer, and arranged themselves in a comradely position and went to sleep.

Finally a rainy day. Brian and his parents were driving into Campbell River to get groceries, and gin, and to take Brian's father's car to a garage, to see about a problem that had developed on the drive up from Nanaimo. This was a very slight problem, but there was the matter of the new-car warranty's being in effect at present, so Brian's father wanted to get it seen to as soon as possible. Brian had to go along, with his car, just in case his father's car had to be left in the garage. Pauline said that she had to stay home because of Mara's nap.

She persuaded Caitlin to lie down too – allowing her to take her music box to bed with her if she played it very softly. Then Pauline spread the script on the kitchen table and drank coffee and went over the scene in which Orphée says that it's intolerable, at last, to stay in two skins, two envelopes with their own blood and oxygen sealed up in their solitude, and Eurydice tells him to be quiet.

"Don't talk. Don't think. Just let your hand wander, let it be happy on its own."

Your hand is my happiness, says Eurydice. Accept that. Accept your happiness.

Of course he says he cannot.

Caitlin called out frequently to ask what time it was. She turned up the sound of the music box. Pauline hurried to the bedroom door and hissed at her to turn it down, not to wake Mara.

"If you play it like that again I'll take it away from you. Okay?"

But Mara was already rustling around in her crib, and in the next few minutes there were sounds of soft, encouraging conversation from Caitlin, designed to get her sister wide awake. Also of the music being quickly turned up and then down. Then of Mara rattling the crib railing, pulling herself up, throwing her bottle out onto the floor, and starting the bird cries that would grow more and more desolate until they brought her mother.

"I didn't wake her," Caitlin said. "She was awake all by herself. It's not raining anymore. Can we go down to the beach?"

She was right. It wasn't raining. Pauline changed Mara, told Caitlin to get her bathing suit on and find her sand pail. She got into her own bathing suit and put her shorts over it, in case the rest of the family arrived home while she was down there. ("Dad doesn't like the way some women just go right out of their cottages in their bathing suits," Brian's mother had said to her. "I guess he and I just grew up in other times.") She picked up the script to take it along, then laid it down. She was afraid that she would get too absorbed in it and take her eyes off the children for a moment too long.

The thoughts that came to her, of Jeffrey, were not really thoughts at all – they were more like alterations in her body. This could happen when she was sitting on the beach (trying to stay in the half shade of a bush and so preserve her pallor, as Jeffrey had ordered) or when she was wringing out diapers or when she and Brian were visiting his parents. In the middle of Monopoly games, Scrabble games, card games. She went right on talking, listening, working, keeping track of the children, while some memory of her secret life disturbed her like a radiant explosion. Then a warm weight settled, reassurance filling up all her hollows. But it didn't last, this comfort leaked away, and she was like a miser whose windfall has vanished and who is convinced such luck can never strike again. Longing buckled her up and drove her to the discipline of counting days. Sometimes she even cut the days into fractions to figure out more exactly how much time had gone.

She thought of going into Campbell River, making some excuse, so that she could get to a phone booth and call him. The cottages had no phones – the only public phone was in the hall of the lodge. But she did not have the number of the hotel where Jeffrey worked. And besides that, she could never get away to Campbell River in the evening. She was afraid that if she called him at home in the daytime his mother the French teacher might answer. He said his mother hardly ever left the house in the summer. Just once, she had taken the ferry to Vancouver for the day. Jeffrey had phoned Pauline to ask her to come over. Brian was teaching, and Caitlin was at her play group.

Pauline said, "I can't. I have Mara."

Jeffrey said, "Who? Oh. Sorry." Then "Couldn't you bring her along?"

She said no.

"Why not? Couldn't you bring some things for her to play with?"

No, said Pauline. "I couldn't," she said. "I just couldn't." It seemed too dangerous to her, to trundle her baby along on such a guilty expedition. To a house where cleaning fluids would not be bestowed on high shelves, and all pills and cough syrups and cigarettes and buttons put safely out of reach. And even if she escaped poisoning or choking, Mara might be storing up time bombs – memories of a strange house where she was strangely disregarded, of a closed door, noises on the other side of it.

"I just wanted you," Jeffrey said. "I just wanted you in my bed."

She said again, weakly, "No."

Those words of his kept coming back to her. *I wanted you in my bed.* A half-joking urgency in his voice but also a determination, a practicality, as if "in my bed" meant something more, the bed he spoke of taking on larger, less material dimensions.

Had she made a great mistake with that refusal? With that reminder of how fenced in she was, in what anybody would call her real life?

The beach was nearly empty – people had got used to its being a rainy day. The sand was too heavy for Caitlin to make a castle or dig an irrigation system – projects she would only undertake with her father, anyway, because she sensed that his interest in them was wholehearted, and Pauline's was not. She wandered a bit forlornly at the edge of the water. She probably missed the presence of other children, the nameless instant friends and occasional stone-throwing water-kicking enemies, the shrieking and splashing and falling about. A boy a little bigger than she was and apparently all by himself stood knee-deep in the water farther down the beach. If these two could get together it might be all right; the whole beach experience might be retrieved. Pauline couldn't tell whether Caitlin was now making little splashy runs into the water for his benefit or whether he was watching her with interest or scorn.

Mara didn't need company, at least for now. She stumbled towards the water, felt it touch her feet and changed her mind, stopped, looked around, and spotted Pauline. "Paw. Paw," she said, in happy recognition. "Paw" was what she said for "Pauline," instead of "Mother" or "Mommy." Looking around overbalanced her – she sat down half on the sand and half in the water, made a squawk of surprise that turned to an announcement, then by some determined ungraceful maneuvers that involved putting her weight on her hands, she rose to her feet, wavering and triumphant. She had been walking for half a year, but getting around on the sand was still a challenge. Now she came back towards Pauline, making some reasonable, casual remarks in her own language.

"Sand," said Pauline, holding up a clot of it. "Look. Mara. Sand."

Mara corrected her, calling it something else – it sounded like "whap." Her thick diaper under her plastic pants and her terry-cloth playsuit gave her a fat bottom, and that, along with her plump cheeks and shoulders and her sidelong important expression, made her look like a roguish matron.

Pauline became aware of someone calling her name. It had been called two or three times, but because the voice was unfamiliar she had not recognized it. She stood up and waved. It was the woman who worked in the store at the lodge. She was leaning over the balcony and calling, "Mrs. Keating. Mrs. Keating? Telephone, Mrs. Keating."

Pauline hoisted Mara onto her hip and summoned Caitlin. She and the little boy were aware of each other now – they were both picking up stones from the bottom and flinging them out into the water. At first she didn't hear Pauline, or pretended not to.

"Store," called Pauline. "Caitlin. Store." When she was sure Caitlin would follow – it was the word "store" that had done it, the reminder of the tiny store in the lodge where you could buy ice cream and candy and cigarettes and mixer – she began the trek across the sand and up the flight of wooden steps above the sand and the salal bushes. Halfway up she stopped, said, "Mara, you weigh a ton," and shifted the baby to her other hip. Caitlin banged a stick against the railing.

"Can I have a Fudgsicle? Mother? Can I?"

"We'll see."

"Can I please have a Fudgsicle?"

"Wait."

The public phone was beside a bulletin board on the other side of the main hall and across from the door to the dining room. A bingo game had been set up in there, because of the rain.

"Hope he's still hanging on," the woman who worked in the store called out. She was unseen now behind her counter.

Pauline, still holding Mara, picked up the dangling receiver and said breathlessly, "Hello?" She was expecting to hear Brian telling her about some delay in Campbell River or asking her what it was she had wanted him to get at the drugstore. It was just the one thing – calamine lotion – so he had not written it down.

"Pauline," said Jeffrey. "It's me."

Mara was bumping and scrambling against Pauline's side, anxious to get down. Caitlin came along the hail and went into the store, leaving wet sandy footprints. Pauline said, "Just a minute, just a minute." She let Mara slide down and hurried to close the door that led to the steps. She did not remember telling Jeffrey the name of this place, though she had told him roughly where it was. She heard the woman in the store speaking to Caitlin in a sharper voice than she would use to children whose parents were beside them.

"Did you forget to put your feet under the tap?"

"I'm here," said Jeffrey. "I didn't get along well without you. I didn't get along at all."

Mara made for the dining room, as if the male voice calling out "Under the *N* –" was a direct invitation to her.

"Here. Where?" said Pauline.

She read the signs that were tacked up on the bulletin board beside the phone.

NO PERSON UNDER FOURTEEN YEARS OF AGE NOT ACCOMPANIED BY ADULT ALLOWED IN BOATS OR CANOES.

FISHING DERBY.

BAKE AND CRAFT SALE, ST. BARTHOLOMEW'S CHURCH.

YOUR LIFE IS IN YOUR HANDS. PALMS AND CARDS READ. REASONABLE AND ACCURATE. CALL CLAIRE.

"In a motel. In Campbell River."

Pauline knew where she was before she opened her eyes. Nothing surprised her. She had slept but not deeply enough to let go of anything.

She had waited for Brian in the parking area of the lodge, with the children, and had asked him for the keys. She had told him in front of his parents that there was something else she needed, from Campbell River. He asked, What was it? And did she have any money?

"Just something," she said, so he would think that it was tampons or birth control supplies, that she didn't want to mention. "Sure."

"Okay but you'll have to put some gas in," he said.

Later she had to speak to him on the phone. Jeffrey said she had to do it.

"Because he won't take it from me. He'll think I kidnapped you or something. He won't believe it."

But the strangest thing of all the things that day was that Brian did seem, immediately, to believe it. Standing where she had stood not so long before, in the public hallway of the lodge – the bingo game over now but people going past, she could hear them, people on their way out of the dining room after dinner – he said, "Oh. Oh. Oh. Okay" in a voice that would have to be quickly controlled, but that seemed to draw on a supply of fatalism or foreknowledge that went far beyond that necessity.

As if he had known all along, all along, what could happen with her.

"Okay," he said. "What about the car?"

He said something else, something impossible, and hung up, and she came out of the phone booth beside some gas pumps in Campbell River.

"That was quick," Jeffrey said. "Easier than you expected."

Pauline said, "I don't know."

"He may have known it subconsciously. People do know."

She shook her head, to tell him not to say any more, and he said, "Sorry." They walked along the street not touching or talking.

They'd had to go out to find a phone booth because there was no phone in the motel room. Now in the early morning looking around at leisure – the first real leisure or freedom she'd had since she came into that room – Pauline saw that there wasn't much of anything in it. Just a junk dresser, the bed without a headboard, an armless upholstered chair, on the window a venetian blind with a broken slat and curtain of orange plastic that was supposed to look like net and that didn't have to be hemmed, just sliced off at the bottom. There was a noisy air conditioner – Jeffrey had turned it off in the night and left the door open on the chain, since the window was sealed. The door was shut now. He must have got up in the night and shut it.

This was all she had. Her connection with the cottage where Brian lay asleep or not asleep was broken, also her connection with the house that had been an expression of her life with Brian, of the way they wanted to live. She had no furniture anymore. She had cut herself off from all the large solid acquisitions like the washer and dryer and the oak table and the refinished wardrobe and the chandelier that was a copy of the one in a painting by Vermeer. And just as much from those things that were particularly hers – the pressed-glass tumblers that she had been collecting and the prayer rug which was of course not authentic, but beautiful. Especially from those things. Even her books, she might have lost. Even her clothes. The skirt and blouse and sandals she had put on for the trip to Campbell River might well be all she had now to her name. She would never go back to lay claim to anything. If Brian got in touch with her to ask what was to be done with things, she would tell him to do what he liked – throw everything into garbage bags and take it to the dump, if that was what he liked. (In fact she knew that he would probably pack up a trunk, which he did, sending on, scrupulously, not only her winter coat and boots but things like the waist cincher she had worn at her wedding and never since, with the prayer rug draped over the top of everything like a final statement of his generosity, either natural or calculated.)

She believed that she would never again care about what sort of rooms she lived in or what sort of clothes she put on. She would not be looking for that sort of help to give anybody an idea of who she was, what she was like. Not even to give herself an idea. What she had done would be enough, it would be the whole thing.

What she was doing would be what she had heard about and read about. It was what Anna Karenina had done and what Madame Bovary had wanted to do. It was what a teacher at Brian's school had done, with the school secretary. He had run off with her. That was what it was called. Running off with. Taking off with. It was spoken of disparagingly, humorously, enviously. It was adultery taken one step further. The people who did it had almost certainly been having an affair already, committing adultery for quite some time before they became desperate or courageous enough to take this step. Once in a long while a couple might claim their love was unconsummated and technically pure, but these people would be thought of – if anybody believed them – as being not only very serious and high-minded but almost devastatingly foolhardy, almost in a class with those who took a chance and gave up everything to go and work in some poor and dangerous country.

The others, the adulterers, were seen as irresponsible, immature, selfish, or even cruel. Also lucky. They were lucky because the sex they had been having in parked cars or the long grass or in each other's sullied marriage beds or most likely in motels like this one must surely have been splendid. Otherwise they would never have got such a yearning for each other's company at all costs or such a faith that their shared future would be altogether better and different in kind from what they had in the past.

Different in kind. That was what Pauline must believe now – that there was this major difference in lives or in marriages or unions between people. That some of them had a necessity, a fatefulness, about them that others did not have. Of course she would have said the same thing a year ago. People did say that, they seemed to believe that, and to believe that their own cases were all of the first, the special kind, even when anybody could see that they were not and that these people did not know what they were talking about. Pauline would not have known what she was talking about.

It was too warm in the room. Jeffrey's body was too warm. Conviction and contentiousness seemed to radiate from it, even in sleep. His torso was thicker than Brian's; he was pudgier around the waist. More flesh on the bones, yet not so slack to the touch. Not so good-looking in general – she was sure most people would say that. And not so fastidious. Brian in bed smelled of nothing. Jeffrey's skin, every time she'd been with him, had had a baked-in, slightly oily or nutty smell. He didn't wash last night but then, neither did she. There wasn't time. Did he even have a toothbrush with him? She didn't. But she had not known she was staying.

When she met Jeffrey here it was still in the back of her

mind that she had to concoct some colossal lie to serve her when she got home. And she – they – had to hurry. When Jeffrey said to her that he had decided that they must stay together, that she would come with him to Washington State, that they would have to drop the play because things would be too difficult for them in Victoria, she had looked at him just in the blank way you'd look at somebody the moment that an earthquake started. She was ready to tell him all the reasons why this was not possible, she still thought she was going to tell him that, but her life was coming adrift in that moment. To go back would be like tying a sack over her head.

All she said was "Are you sure?"

He said, "Sure." He said sincerely, "I'll never leave you."

That did not seem the sort of thing that he would say. Then she realized he was quoting – maybe ironically – from the play. It was what Orphée says to Eurydice within a few moments of their first meeting in the station buffet.

So her life was falling forwards; she was becoming one of those people who ran away. A woman who shockingly and incomprehensibly gave everything up. For love, observers would say wryly. Meaning, for sex. None of this would happen if it wasn't for sex.

And yet what's the great difference there? It's not such a variable procedure, in spite of what you're told. Skins, motions, contact, results. Pauline isn't a woman from whom it's difficult to get results. Brian got them. Probably anybody would, who wasn't wildly inept or morally disgusting.

But nothing's the same, really. With Brian – especially with Brian, to whom she has dedicated a selfish sort of goodwill, with whom she's lived in married complicity – there can never be this stripping away, the inevitable flight, the feelings she doesn't have to strive for but only to give in to like breathing or dying. That she believes can only come when the skin is on Jeffrey, the motions made by Jeffrey, and the weight that bears down on her has Jeffrey's heart in it, also his habits, thoughts, peculiarities, his ambition and loneliness (that for all she knows may have mostly to do with his youth).

For all she knows. There's a lot she doesn't know. She hardly knows anything about what he likes to eat or what music he likes to listen to or what role his mother plays in his life (no doubt a mysterious but important one, like the role of Brian's parents). One thing she's pretty sure of – whatever preferences or prohibitions he has will be definite.

She slides out from under Jeffrey's hand and from under the top sheet which has a harsh smell of bleach, she slips down to the floor where the bedspread is lying and wraps herself quickly in that rag of greenish-yellow chenille. She doesn't want him to open his eyes and see her from behind and note the droop of her buttocks. He's seen her naked before, but generally in a more forgiving moment.

She rinses her mouth and washes herself, using the bar of soap that is about the size of two thin squares of chocolate and firm as stone. She's hard-used between the legs, swollen and stinking. Urinating takes an effort, and it seems she's constipated. Last night when they went out and got hamburgers she found she could not eat. Presumably she'll learn to do all these things again, they'll resume their natural importance in her life. At the moment it's as if she can't quite spare the attention.

She has some money in her purse. She has to go out and buy a toothbrush, toothpaste, deodorant, shampoo. Also vaginal jelly. Last night they used condoms the first two times but nothing the third time.

She didn't bring her watch and Jeffrey doesn't wear one. There's no clock in the room, of course. She thinks it's early – there's still an early look to the light in spite of the heat. The stores probably won't be open, but there'll be someplace where she can get coffee.

Jeffrey has turned onto his other side. She must have wakened him, just for a moment.

They'll have a bedroom. A kitchen, an address. He'll go to work. She'll go to the Laundromat. Maybe she'll go to work too. Selling things, waiting on tables, tutoring students. She knows French and Latin – do they teach French and Latin in American high schools? Can you get a job if you're not an American? Jeffrey isn't.

She leaves him the key. She'll have to wake him to get back in. There's nothing to write a note with, or on.

It is early. The motel is on the highway at the north end of town, beside the bridge. There's no traffic yet. She scuffs along under the cottonwood trees for quite a while before a vehicle of any kind rumbles over the bridge – though the traffic on it shook their bed regularly late into the night.

Something is coming now. A truck. But not just a truck – there's a large bleak fact coming at her. And it has not arrived out of nowhere – it's been waiting, cruelly nudging at her ever since she woke up, or even all night.

Caitlin and Mara.

Last night on the phone, after speaking in such a flat and controlled and almost agreeable voice – as if he prided himself on not being shocked, not objecting or pleading – Brian cracked open. He said with contempt and fury and no concern for whoever might hear him, "Well then – what about the kids?"

The receiver began to shake against Pauline's ear.

She said, "We'll talk –" but he did not seem to hear her.

"The children," he said, in this same shivering and vindictive voice. Changing the word "kids" to "children" was like slamming a board down on her – a heavy, formal, righteous threat.

"The children stay," Brian said. "Pauline. Did you hear me?"

"No," said Pauline. "Yes. I heard you but –"

"All right. You heard me. Remember. The children stay."

It was all he could do. To make her see what she was doing, what she was ending, and to punish her if she did so. Nobody would blame him. There might be finagling, there might be bargaining, there would certainly be humbling of herself, but there it was like a round cold stone in her gullet, like a cannonball. And it would remain there unless she changed her mind entirely. The children stay.

Their car – hers and Brian's – was still sitting in the motel parking lot. Brian would have to ask his father or his mother to drive him up here today to get it. She had the keys in her purse. There were spare keys – he would surely bring them. She unlocked the car door and threw her keys on the seat and locked the door on the inside and shut it.

Now she couldn't go back. She couldn't get into the car and drive back and say that she'd been insane. If she did that he would forgive her, but he'd never get over it and neither would she. They'd go on, though, as people did.

She walked out of the parking lot, she walked along the sidewalk, into town.

The weight of Mara on her hip, yesterday. The sight of Caitlin's footprints on the floor.

Paw. Paw.

She doesn't need the keys to get back to them, she doesn't need the car. She could beg a ride on the highway. Give in, give in, get back to them any way at all, how can she not do that?

A sack over her head.

A fluid choice, the choice of fantasy, is poured out on the ground and instantly hardens; it has taken its undeniable shape.

This is acute pain. It will become chronic. Chronic means that it will be permanent but perhaps not constant. It may also mean that you won't die of it. You won't get free of it, but you won't die of it. You won't feel it every minute, but you won't spend many days without it. And you'll learn some tricks to dull it or banish it, trying not to end up destroying what you incurred this pain to get. It isn't his fault. He's still an innocent or a savage, who doesn't know there's a pain so durable in the world. Say to yourself, You lose them anyway. They grow up. For a mother there's always waiting this private slightly ridiculous desolation. They'll forget this time, in one way or another they'll disown you. Or hang around till you don't know what to do about them, the way Brian has.

And still, what pain. To carry along and get used to until it's only the past she's grieving for and not any possible present.

Her children have grown up. They don't hate her. For going away or staying away. They don't forgive her, either. Perhaps they wouldn't have forgiven her anyway, but it would have been for something different.

Caitlin remembers a little about the summer at the lodge, Mara nothing. One day Caitlin mentions it to Pauline, calling it "that place Grandma and Grandpa stayed at."

"The place we were at when you went away," she says. "Only we didn't know till later you went away with Orphée."

Pauline says, "It wasn't Orphée."

"It wasn't Orphée? Dad used to say it was. He'd say, 'And then your mother ran away with Orphée.' "

"Then he was joking," says Pauline.

"I always thought it was Orphée. It was somebody else then."

"It was somebody else connected with the play. That I lived with for a while."

"Not Orphée."

"No. Never him."

Afterword

BY JANE URQUHART

One of the many things that Alice Munro teaches us about the state commonly referred to as "falling in love" is that the inner landscape of the fallen lover is a dramatically lit, potentially painful, and sometimes oddly solitary place. It is a territory that one enters precipitously – not necessarily of one's own free will – and one in which the lover, at least in some ways, is forced to wander alone. Though many of us consider falling in love to be a dance conceived for two people, Munro is more interested in the singularity of the experience, in the days and months or years that precede or follow acts of communion, or in the long, inward-looking periods of reflection that are born of a love that is either unrequited, difficult, or impossible.

Consider the first few paragraphs of the story "Bardon Bus." The contemporary, middle-aged, female narrator tells us that for the "madly secretive, tenacious" old maids in her family, the beloved "could be anybody. A soldier killed at the Somme or a farmer down the road with a rough tongued wife," that "the memory of an ambiguous word" or " a hard helpless look" would be enough to cause you to "give yourself up, give yourself over, to the assault which is guaranteed to finish off everything you've been before," enough to bring into being "a lifelong secret, lifelong dream life." How strange to think that a state so often referred to as an awakening can also be a passport into a world of dream, a world of trance. And yet the minute we read these words, we know that Munro is describing something both emotionally and universally true. "My love and my secret," many of the ancient Irish love poems begin, poems that were frequently written or spoken by women. Perhaps it is the word *secret* that is most revealing, for it is only when we have a secret that we are utterly unique, most powerfully ourselves. And a secret – however painful – that is not shared is one of the few things on earth that we can claim as ours alone.

Many of the stories selected for this volume concern a love that is secret in some way or another. "Bardon Bus," "Carried Away," "Mischief," and "The Children Stay" explore relationships that are, on some level, secretive, and that lead, in the psyches of their protagonists, to a pulling away from the world of the ordinary, the world of the everyday. Hence the married Rose in "Mischief," rejected by her likewise married lover before their affair can be consummated, is devastated when he returns her to this everyday world. "The sane and decent things Clifford had said cut no ice with Rose at all. She saw that he had betrayed her. Sanity and decency were never what she had asked of him." And even the elderly and unwell Louisa in "Carried Away," coming across a ghost or apparition of a man she had never officially met, but one with whom she had exchanged love letters during the First World War, sees him as " a traitor, helplessly, a traveller," and feels that "it was anarchy she was up against – a devouring muddle. Sudden holes and impromptu tricks and radiant, vanishing consolations." These holes or tricks could apply equally to her medical condition or to the condition of being in love. And what are the "radiant consolations"? A departure from the dullness of daily routines, or anxieties concerning illness combined with the tremulous development of apartness and, eventually, a vivid inner life on the one hand, or death on the other.

This is not to suggest that Munro in any way trivializes the suffering involved in such situations; anguish is so deftly observed in these stories that not infrequently we find that we are wincing as we read. The ending of "The Children Stay," for example, is almost too painful to read. But, like the old masters in the famous poem by W.H. Auden, "about suffering" she is "never wrong," and understands completely "how it takes place/ While someone else is eating or opening a window or just walking dully along."* The very world that a character abandons to enter a life where she believes that she will "never again care about what sort of rooms she lived in or what sort of clothes she put on" ("The Children Stay") is rendered so palpable by Munro that we wince for all that is abandoned as well. This is, I think, because she is one of those rare writers whose tone strikes a perfect balance between ruthless honesty and empathy. Even in the face of startling revelations of weakness, foolishness, or blatant selfishness, the richness and generosity of the writing make it impossible for the reader to find an enemy anywhere in Munro's fiction.

The beginning of love is almost always a ticket to another world in Munro's stories, another life, the start of a series of vigorous transformations, the end result of which is, in many cases, the return of the self to the self. The very newness of the situation into which a lover is flung suggests that youth is the appropriate time for this to happen. And yet, as Munro shows us over and over again, there is no appropriate time of life for the kind of seismic alterations that love insists on. The "stony-eyed grief" of the elderly lovers who are about to be separated in "The Bear Came Over the Mountain" is as convincing to the reader as is the middle-aged woman's desperation in "Simon's Luck," or that of Lottar in "The Albanian Virgin" calling and

---

* W.H. Auden, "Musée des Beaux-Arts."

calling a word "which means 'leader' or 'master' in the language of the Ghegs," and then seeing his face, which takes "her breath out of her body, as she knew too late."

Sometimes in a Munro story a character will resist these alterations, these transformations, not wanting – either consciously or unconsciously – to be jolted out of the familiar and into a world of dream, conjecture, and longing, or, in some cases, a world of lust and brutality. The nineteenth-century "poetess," for example, in "Meneseteung" immerses herself in the image-laden landscape of her art (as well as in a considerable amount of "nerve medicine") in order to escape the trap of imminent romance, and, perhaps, also to escape the sounds of sex and violence she overhears in the street when she awakens on a night that seems " fiery and hot and full of threats." But it is Rose in "Simon's Luck" who escapes most dramatically and most successfully when, after waiting all weekend for a lover who does not appear, she packs a few belongings into her car and drives the considerable distance between Ontario and Saskatchewan, mile by mile, until "it seemed the world had stopped being a stage where she might meet him, and had gone back to being itself." It is at this point that she realizes that "love removes the world for you, and just as surely when it's going well as when it's going badly," and that

> it might not be the disappointment, the losses, the dissolution, she had been running away from, any more than the opposite of those things; the celebration and shock of love, the dazzling alteration. . . . Either way you were robbed of something – a private balance spring, a little dry kernel of probity. So she thought.

Occasionally the alteration in a character under the influence of love will be an unconscious move towards, rather than away from, inevitable domesticity, but these are usually slower journeys, gentler awakenings, and often allow Munro to examine the serendipity involved in the establishment of certain partnerships. So it is that Enid in "The Love of a Good Woman" develops what could almost be called a disease of devotion to Rupert after a season spent in his home nursing his dying wife. Likewise, in "Hateship, Friendship, Courtship, Loveship, Marriage," Johanna, who is herself a housekeeper by profession, has her own partnered future set in motion by the mischief of two young girls on the one hand and her own domestic skills on the other. As these narratives unfold, we come to realize that one crack in a link in the chain of circumstances – circumstances that can sometimes predate the entry of the individuals involved by several years – could have resulted in an entirely different outcome, or, indeed, in no outcome at all. Edith, one of the mischief-makers, is not particularly pleased by the results of her pranks. When she hears of the birth of Johanna's first child, she thinks: "It was the whole twist of consequence that dismayed her. . . . For where, on the list of things that she planned to achieve in her life, was there any mention of her being responsible for the existence on earth of a person named Omar?"

As would be expected of a writer of Munro's brilliance, there is much more going on in both of these long, multi-layered stories than the eventual establishment of domestic partnerships, just as in other stories in this volume there are many routes to explore, and many lessons to be learned from the author's wisdom. Still, it is the mystery of love and the development of our fully human, multi-faceted natures while under its influence (or while recovering from its assaults) that form the core of this selection. For what is love if not the last splendid, indefinable mystery? As unpredictable and as difficult to dismiss as weather, but unlike weather, completely impossible either to explain scientifically or to find shelter from, it is fiction's greatest subject. How privileged we are, then, to have a writer of Munro's genius to guide us through love's labyrinth, insisting all the while that we keep our eyes wide open to its complicated foliage, its shadows, its piercing blasts of light.

BY ALICE MUNRO

FICTION

Dance of the Happy Shades (1968)
Lives of Girls and Women (1971)
Something I've Been Meaning to Tell You (1974)
Who Do You Think You Are? (1978)
The Moons of Jupiter (1983)
The Progress of Love (1986)
Friend of My Youth (1990)
Open Secrets (1994)
Selected Stories (1996)
The Love of a Good Woman (1998)
Hateship, Friendship, Courtship, Loveship, Marriage (2001)
No Love Lost (2003)
Runaway (2004)
The View from Castle Rock (2006)
Alice Munro's Best (2008)
Too Much Happiness (2009)